Books by Elizabeth Laird published
by Macmillan Children's Books

Crusade

Elizabeth Laird

MACMILLAN CHILDREN'S BOOKS

First published 2007 by Macmillan Children's Books

This edition published 2016 by Macmillan Children's Books
an imprint of Pan Macmillan
20 New Wharf Road, London N1 9RR
Associated companies throughout the world
www.panmacmillan.com

ISBN 978-1-5098-0296-8

1 3 5 7 9 8 6 4 2

A CIP catalogue record for this book is available from
the British Library.

Typeset by Intype Libra Limited
Printed and bound by CPI Group (UK) Ltd, Croydon CR0 4YY

For Rachel and Andrew

THE MAIN CHARACTERS

People of the Holy Land

Salim Ibn Adil, a boy
Adil, his father
Khadijah, his mother
Ali, his sixteen-year-old brother
Zahra, his three-year-old sister

Musa ben Aaron, a doctor from Jerusalem
Leah, his wife
Solomon, a pharmacist

Ismail, a young Mamluk soldier
Arslan Ibn Mehmet, captain of the Mamluk troop

People of Fortis, a castle in England

Adam, son of Gervase, a boy
Tom Bate, his neighbour
Jennet, Tom's seventeen-year-old daughter
Tibby, Jennet's daughter

Lord Guy de Martel, baron of Fortis
Lord Robert, his son
Father Jerome, his chaplain
Master Tappe, kennel master of Fortis

Jacques (pronounced 'Jakes'), a pedlar

Sir Ivo de Chastelfort, a knight of Fortis
Roger Stepesoft ⎫
Treuelove Malter ⎬ Men-at-arms

Joan, a washerwoman

The Animals

Powerful and Faithful, mastiffs
Grimbald and Vigor, warhorses
Kestan, a Mamluk cavalry horse
Suweida, a mule

The Rulers

Sultan Saladin
King Richard of England

A thousand years ago, a storm swept through Europe. Preachers travelled through every land, stirring the people up to leave their farms, cottages and castles and embark on a great crusade to Palestine. They wanted to capture the city of Jerusalem, Christianity's most holy site.

The people who lived in Palestine were mostly Muslim, but there were smaller groups of Jews and Eastern Christians too. They had all lived peacefully alongside each other for centuries, and Jerusalem was a holy city to all of them.

The first Crusaders thought that Muslims and Jews were evil, and deserved to be killed. The people of Palestine feared the Crusaders, because they were so violent, but despised them too for their barbaric, primitive ways. They called all Europeans 'Franks'.

At first the Crusaders were victorious and captured Jerusalem, killing every Muslim and Jew that fell into their hands. They set up a Christian kingdom and ruled for a hundred years. But then a great Muslim prince, the Sultan Saladin, came to power. He drove the Crusaders out of Jerusalem, and took back most of the cities on the coast as well, including the city of Acre.

When this news reached Europe, the call to recapture Jerusalem rang out again in every town and village, and people began once more to flock to the banners of Crusade . . .

CHAPTER ONE

I t was a blistering August day and there was hardly a breath of wind coming in off the dazzling Mediterranean sea, whose waters lapped lazily against the white stone walls of the city of Acre. Several ships were tied up at the quayside, but there were only a few people outside in the hot sun. A couple of men, their bare backs slicked with sweat, were unloading a cargo of wheat on to the baking stones of the quay, and two young boys were diving in and out of the water, shaking the silvery drops off their hair as they came up laughing.

In the great customs house behind the harbour, Salim sat on a bulging bale of cotton, moodily swinging his one good leg. It had been a bad day so far. Adil, his father, had sworn at him twice, once for slipping away from his station at the accounting desk, and once for spilling his pot of ink on the corner of a new bolt of green brocade, which Adil had been counting on selling for a good price. There'd be a beating for that this evening, Salim knew.

The huge square courtyard of the customs house was surrounded on all four sides by two tiers of arched arcades, behind which were the merchants' lock-up stores. There were piles of merchandise everywhere: bundles of silks from Damascus and muslins from Mosul, sacks of wheat from Egypt and incense from Yemen, dried limes from Basra, spices from India, nuts from Aleppo and jars of oil and honey and olives from just about everywhere. Usually, the courtyard was alive with turbaned merchants haggling over prices, camels and donkeys being unloaded, and sailors staggering in through the gate that led directly out to the harbour quays, bowed under heavy loads.

Today, however, everything was quiet. A couple of mules nodded sleepily in the shade of a wall. A few men stood about in the arcades, talking quietly, keeping out of the broiling sun.

Salim kicked at the bale again. He hated it when things were so quiet. For one thing, it was boring. For another, it put his father into a thunderous mood. Adil, unlike everyone else, was wide awake. He was still sitting cross-legged in front of his storeroom, clicking the beads of his abacus back and forth while the worry lines deepened on his forehead.

'Even in the bad old days,' he'd been grumbling all morning, 'when the Franks ruled Acre, and we had to put up with their filth – pigs running everywhere – the stink of wine – the way they never washed – business was never as slow as this.'

The other merchants were used to his complaints. They'd nodded politely, but without much sympathy. Most of them had been trading in Acre only for the past two years, since Saladin had captured the city from the Franks. Adil was one of the few Saracen merchants who had lived in Acre before that time. It had been hard, they knew, living as a Muslim under Crusader rule, and Adil had certainly had much to bear. But in Frankish times the city had been one vast marketplace, with caravans of laden camels pouring through its gates from the far corners of the Muslim east, and ships full of merchandise scudding into the harbour from the fabled cities of Venice and Genoa and every part of the Christian west beyond. The city might have been the dirtiest place on the entire Mediterranean coast, and Adil might have had to put up with endless humiliations at the hands of the European overlords, but everyone knew that trade in those days had offered wonderful possibilities for enrichment. In spite of his constant air of anxiety, Adil had done well for himself.

Salim jumped off his bale and limped out through the sea gate to the harbour. Just outside the customs house, against the wall, were stone benches, covered in rugs. A few officials usually sat here, their ebony inkwells at their sides, writing in huge ledgers lists of the tax due on unloaded goods. No one was here today, not even Salim's older brother Ali, who was usually hanging about with the other merchants' sons by the harbour when there was nothing else to do.

I can slip off home if Ali's not around to stop me, Salim told himself. *I'll tell Mama I've got a headache.*

With luck, his mother would plead for him and stop him from getting a beating. She'd get Selma, the servant girl, to give him honey cakes, and let him go up on to the roof where he could have a quiet game of knucklebones without his little sister, Zahra, interfering.

Shouts from inside the customs house made him hobble back into the courtyard. A caravan of camels was swaying in through the northern landward gate, their drivers, covered with dust and limp with heat, yelling impatiently at them.

The customs house sprang to life at once. Merchants hurried forwards from their shady storerooms. Slaves were kicked awake, and clerks appeared as if from nowhere, ready to get to work.

The camels, groaning like weary old men, sank down to their knees. Usually, the unloading began at once, but today everyone was clustering round the camel drivers, who were waving their arms and talking excitedly.

They'll be in a stupid fuss over something boring, like the prices in Damascus, Salim told himself.

This was his chance. In the commotion, his father and Ali would never notice that he'd gone. He sidled round to the far arcade and slipped out through the gate, then set off, walking as quickly as his short left leg would let him.

The way home led through the covered silk bazaar. The light was dim here, though sunbeams fell at intervals through the round holes pierced in the bazaar's high stone-vaulted roof. Salim was so used to the bazaar that he usually barely noticed the small booths on each side, piled with brightly coloured silks and velvets, or the mass of people, speaking a dozen different languages, who crowded round them. But today things were different. Half the booths were already closed, and the owners of the others were quickly fetching down their displays of cloth and putting up heavy wooden shutters, ready to lock up. The few people hurrying down the narrow walkway between the booths had faces set with purpose.

What's happening? thought Salim.

He turned a corner out of the half-empty covered bazaar into a narrow open street that was packed with people, camels, horses and mules. A man with a handcart piled with household goods was trying to thrust a path for himself through it.

'Let me through, in the name of Allah!' he was shouting, fear in his voice.

Salim shuddered.

The plague! Perhaps it's the plague!

When the plague came, it could strike people at any time, killing them after a few hours of terrible agony. The last outbreak had been in Frankish times. The sickness had sent terror through the city, and hundreds of people had died. He put his hands up over his mouth and nose, afraid of breathing in infection, and hurried on.

There was a mosque on the next corner. It had been a church in Frankish times, but the crosses had been taken down and the pictures of the Prophet Jesus and his saints had been removed. Sacred inscriptions from the Holy Koran now covered the walls instead. Salim hesitated as he passed its open door. His mother was always urging him to pray. Perhaps he should. Perhaps if he did, the plague would pass him by.

The mosque seemed to be unusually full. There was a high pile of slippers by the door, and he could hear the voice of a preacher raised inside.

The doorkeeper appeared, a bunch of heavy keys jangling from the loose belt that gathered in his gown.

'What do you want?' He raised his chin aggressively when he saw Salim hesitating by the door.

'To pray, *ya-sheikh*. The plague's coming, isn't it?'

The old man stared at him.

'The plague? Who told you that?'

'No one, but the bazaar's closing early, and I thought—'

'You thought!' The doorkeeper laughed scornfully. 'Where have you been all afternoon? Haven't you heard? A Frankish army's on its way here. They'll attack tonight or tomorrow. You'd better get on home.'

Salim's heart gave a violent thud and he felt the blood drain from his face. The Franks fought like devils, with wild courage and blind fanaticism, not caring if they died in battle, as long as their side won. And when they'd conquered a city, they'd kill and destroy without mercy, looting everything. The Frankish forces had been cooped up in the northern city of Tyre since Saladin's armies had swept through Palestine. No one had expected them to break out again.

The doorkeeper's eyes had softened at the look on Salim's face.

'It's all right, lad. This city's as strong as a fortress. And our lord Saladin will come rushing to help us, with all his knights.

You'll see. The Franks are nothing compared to him.' He stopped and nodded piously. 'The forces of Islam will not be overcome by the infidel, may Allah curse them.'

Salim frowned.

'You needn't think I'm afraid,' he said stiffly. 'Not of a bunch of Franks, nor of anyone.'

'Are you coming in here to pray, or not?' The man said, unimpressed.

Salim felt obliged to go inside. He kicked off his shoes before entering the small washroom, in what had once been the church's side chapel, to perform his ritual wash. From here, he could hear the preacher's loud, clear voice. He dried himself hurriedly and went to sit at the back of the congregation.

'Muslims of Acre!' the preacher was calling out. 'Will you forget your sacred duty? Will you flee like rats from the path of the infidel? How can you bear to see this sweet city once more overrun by the wickedness of the barbarians? Why do these foreigners come here, to a land that isn't theirs, wave after wave of them, slaughtering us like beasts? I'll tell you. They hate the truth and justice of Islam! They want to insult the Holy Koran and take back the sacred city of Jerusalem in order to defile it! They come to set their crosses up on our mosques, to take our women, and force our children into slavery!'

Salim shivered, in spite of the heat, and plucked at the belt of his tunic.

'Believe me, brothers,' the preacher went on, 'to fight the Franks is not only to defend ourselves, our cities, homes and families. It is a holy act. It is jihad! And who will take up the challenge? The warrior of Islam. Who is this warrior? What is he like? The jihad warrior must be like a lion in courage and a leopard in pride, a bear in strength . . .' His resonant voice was making the hair rise on the nape of Salim's neck, and his fists tightened as he listened. 'He must be a wild boar in attack, and a wolf in the speed of his escape!'

If Salim had been afraid before, he felt the courage of a lion now. He was listening open-mouthed, seeing himself dressed in gleaming new chainmail, a sword in his hand, astride a noble war horse, charging down upon an infidel knight, running him through with his lance, while his father and Ali watched in amazement, cheering him on . . .

The preacher dropped his voice to a lower, thrilling tone.

'All this, my brothers, the jihad warrior must be, but do not forget, never forget, that the greater struggle, the true jihad, is against your own lower self, your baser nature, your cowardice and selfishness. Purify yourselves! Make ready for the trial ahead! Stay in the city, pray for victory and fight! Only then will Allah reward you and save you and your families from perdition.'

The word 'families' jerked Salim back to reality. What was happening in the city outside? What if his father and Ali had already run home and were packing up to leave? What if they'd fled Acre by now and had left him behind?

He shot up and pushed his way to the door. It took him a moment to find his scuffed shoes in the heap outside, but once they were on his feet he was off, moving as fast as he could, working his way through the tortuous maze of alleys to the scarred wooden door set into a high stone wall that led into the small courtyard of his home.

'Mama!' he was calling out before the door had banged shut behind him. 'Baba! Are you there?'

Khadijah, his mother, came unhurriedly out of an inner room, wiping her hands on a cloth, her round face as untroubled as usual. Little Zahra toddled out behind her, lifting her arms to be picked up.

'Is that you, *habibi*? Why are you home so early? Where's your father?'

'Haven't you heard?' He couldn't believe how calm she was. 'A Frankish army's coming! The bazaar's closed up and everyone's running away!'

She gasped and swept Zahra up in her arms, staring at Salim over the little girl's head.

'It's one of your stories, Salim.'

'No!' He was offended. 'It's true! I went to the mosque on the way home. The preacher was calling for jihad. He says nobody ought to leave. We've all got to stay in Acre and fight the Franks.'

'*Ya-haram!* Where's your father? Why did he send you home? Does he want me to start packing?'

He put his head affectingly on one side.

'He didn't send me home, Mama. I've had a headache all day. I came home on my own.'

She was too shocked by his news to show her usual sympathy.

'I can't see to you now. Go on up to the roof. It's cooler there. And all this happening on the very day that dratted Selma goes sick!'

She hurried into the back room of the house where the chests of clothes were kept, and he heard her opening and shutting them, while Zahra began to cry. He went across to the water jars which stood out of the sun under an awning and took a long drink. Then he scrambled up the steep stairs to the flat rooftop where a vine trained over wooden struts made a pleasant shade. There was a good view from here across the huddled, cramped streets of Acre. He screwed up his eyes, looking out for anything unusual and listening for shouts or the clash of arms, but a moment later he heard the street door open and turned to look down into the courtyard. His father had come home.

Salim was about to duck out of sight, when he saw that a stranger had followed his father into the courtyard. Surprised, he stayed a moment too long, and his father looked up and saw him.

'Salim! What are you doing up there? Come down here at once,' he called out.

Nervously, Salim stumbled on the steep stone steps and nearly fell. To his relief, his father was no longer looking at him, but was ushering the stranger hospitably into the long, barrel-vaulted room that ran down one side of the courtyard. He would take him, Salim knew, to the dais at one end, where rugs and comfortable cushions were set out.

'Tell your mother we have company,' Adil said over his shoulder. 'Bring mint tea.'

Salim hurried to the storeroom. Khadijah was on her knees in front of a chest, pulling out clothes and piling them on the floor.

'Baba's home,' Salim said. 'He's got a guest. He wants mint tea.'

She turned an astonished face towards him.

'*Tea*? When the Franks are coming any minute to murder us?'

He shrugged.

'He doesn't seem worried, Mama.'

She sat back on her heels, frowning at him.

'You've been exaggerating again, Salim. Why do I ever listen to you?'

He saw a familiar look in her eyes. She was about to give him a talking to, and would end up by telling him to look after Zahra. Quickly, he slipped out of the room and went to fill a jug from the water jar. Taking a bowl and towel, he carried the water carefully into the big room and went up the few steps to the dais, where his father and the guest had settled themselves cross-legged against the cushions.

'Good.' Adil looked at him with unusual approval, and waved him towards the mysterious stranger. Salim held the bowl under the man's hands with his left hand, and poured water over them with his right, as he'd been taught to do. He passed the stranger the towel, and held the bowl for his father too. Then he stepped back, hoping to be allowed to stay and listen. His father made no sign, so he limped to the door and leaned against the lintel, pretending to look bored and idle.

'Not a great force, you said?' Adil was asking the stranger.

'No. A few hundred knights, if that. And they're not madmen fresh out of Europe, but Franks from up the coast here, who've lived in Palestine for years. It's no more than a show of bravado, if you ask me. The Franks – may God frustrate them! – have been buzzing like angry bees since Saladin took Jerusalem. They're beaten, and they know it.'

Salim saw that Adil had pulled out a string of worry beads from the folds of his gown. He was passing them quickly through his fingers, as he always did when he was anxious.

'It's worrying, though. If the gates of the city have to be shut it'll be another blow to business. Trade's been terrible these past two years. I used to be able to sell an inlaid tray to an ignorant Frank for five dinars. I'm lucky if I can sell a spoon to anyone now.'

His guest raised his huge eyebrows.

'You don't regret that the Crusaders were driven out of Acre?'

Adil looked uncomfortable.

'Of course not, Doctor Musa. But we were used to them. They'd been here for a hundred years, and some of them had become quite civilized. Say what you like, the European trade is most profitable.' He sighed. 'But what worries me more is that the fanatics in Europe are raising a storm over our conquest of Jerusalem. You must have heard the rumours! Huge armies! Thousands of Frankish knights and foot soldiers. Kings, too. Richard of England, may God deliver him to perdition! Philip of France, a devil incarnate. And that red-bearded monster, the Emperor of Germany! They won't rest till they raise their cursed crosses over the holy mosques again.' He was tugging at his thick black beard as he spoke.

A discreet cough from the far side of the courtyard made Salim turn his head. His mother was holding a tray in her hand and nodding at him. He went across to her.

'Who is he? Who's with your father?'

'I don't know. A doctor, I think.'

'Ah.' She looked pleased. 'At last.'

'Why, Mama? Is someone ill?'

'No, of course not. What did you hear? Are we to leave Acre or not?'

'No,' Salim said, feeling embarrassed. 'It's only a raiding party, after all.'

'What did I tell you?' She shot him a triumphant glance. 'Now mind how you go with the tea.'

Salim carried the tray carefully back into the big room and up the dais, walking as smoothly as he could. He hated it when people noticed his limp for the first time. He felt the doctor's eyes on him as he approached, and looked up, setting his face in a repressive frown. But there was only interest in the doctor's eyes, and none of the expected pity or contempt.

'Lame from birth, is he?' The doctor was addressing Adil.

Adil shook his head.

'He was born perfect. A fever struck him when he was about two years old.'

The doctor nodded.

'No other impairment down that side?'

'Some weakness in the left arm. Doctor, is there anything you could—'

'I'm sorry. Such conditions can't be treated. Some strengthening exercises perhaps, a careful diet . . .'

Salim was taking in the stranger's appearance now. He was

a round little man, quite elderly, with long-fingered, delicate hands. His gown was made of fine stuff, but was rumpled round his belt, and his turban seemed about to slip down over one ear. His eyes were penetrating, under their bushy black brows, and Salim had the uncomfortable feeling that they had seen right inside him, and knew everything.

'A clever boy, no doubt,' he said, talking to Adil while looking at Salim. 'He'll live on his wits. What could be better?'

Salim scowled. He resented being talked about as if he wasn't there.

Adil poured out a glass of mint tea and handed it to his guest.

'Live on his wits? We all have to do that nowadays. And though I'm his father, I must say that Salim has more wits than most. Quick as a bagful of monkeys, he is.'

Salim had never heard praise from his father before. His mouth dropped open with astonishment. Then he shut it again, and tried to look intelligent.

'Oh yes,' Adil went on, sipping his tea and looking at his visitor. 'The boy's gifted. Especially with language. He reads and writes like a scholar. He even speaks Frankish!'

Salim felt a blush of embarrassment surge up into his face. He had learned to speak Norman French from the Frankish merchants' sons, who had hung about the customs house in the days when the Crusaders had ruled Acre. They'd teased and tormented him, but accepted him in a rough way. There had been no one else to play with, anyway. In the two years since they'd gone, he'd almost forgotten their sharp, crude language, so different from the fluid, gutteral Arabic of his parents. Speaking French was a skill he was ashamed of and he couldn't understand why his father was boasting of it.

But the doctor's eyebrows had lifted with interest.

'Ha! Unusual! You really speak Frankish?' he said, addressing Salim for the first time.

'Try him,' Adil said eagerly. 'Say something, Salim.'

Salim's mind went blank. He licked his lips, anxious not to look a fool.

'Um – *Good day to you, sir*,' he managed at last, in halting Norman French. '*The weather is hot.*'

'Yes, yes, and? What does it mean?' Adil said impatiently.

Salim translated. The skin round Dr Musa's dark eyes crinkled into fine lines as he began to laugh again.

'Ah, the Franks! The Franks! Always talking about the weather. Not surprising, I suppose. Think what cold wet lands they come from. Cruel, fanatical people. The humours of their blood make them hard and merciless.'

Adil coughed delicately.

'I hear that your people have suffered again? In the land of England?'

Dr Musa shook his head, as if trying to clear it of an unpleasant vision.

'Yes. Hundreds massacred, in many cities. They hate us Jews. What God-forsaken people they are. If only I was young and strong, I'd . . . But what can I do? A poor old doctor. And I tell you this, Adil, they'd treat you Muslims the same if you dared set foot in their cursed lands. You're quite right to be scared of a new invasion from the west. Richard of England is terrifying. Terrifying! Tall as a tree! Strong as a lion too. And cunning – he'd trick his way out of hell. If they come, Acre will be their first target. They'll have to take this city before they can go to Jerusalem. May the Lord be our refuge if they succeed.'

Dr Musa and Salim's father sat talking for a long time while the sun faded from the wall of the courtyard and the leaves of the vine on the roof were rattling in the evening breeze. Salim stayed where he was, in the doorway, pretending to whittle a piece of wood with his pocket knife, trying to listen, but the men had dropped their voices and he couldn't hear what they were saying. Though the doctor was so short, and so rumpled in his appearance, there was something impressive about him, something different from the merchants and money traders his father usually entertained.

At last the doctor made a move to go, pulling his flimsy cloak carelessly over his shoulders and shoving his turban back in place. Salim scrambled to his feet as the two men emerged into the courtyard. Just then, the street door opened with a crash and Salim's older brother, Ali, burst in.

'Ali!' Adil called out sharply. 'Stop charging about like that. Can't you see we have a guest?'

Ali made himself slow to a walk and went across to his father.

'*Salaam alaykum*,' he said, bowing to the doctor.

'A firebrand!' Dr Musa's eyebrows had risen. 'A young man of passion, Adil.'

'You don't have to tell me,' Adil said, shaking his head disapprovingly.

Salim could see that Ali was burning up with impatience, absolutely dying to speak, but didn't dare until he'd received permission.

'Two fine boys. God has blessed you,' Dr Musa said.

Salim felt a small glow of pleasure. It wasn't often that praise came his way. It was usually reserved for Ali.

'Your sons, I'm sure, are better than these worthless rogues,' Adil responded politely.

Dr Musa shook his head.

'The Almighty didn't see fit to make my marriage fruitful. I shall die childless, unless he takes pity on us in our old age. Who knows? Think of Abraham and Sarah.'

Ali, who had been bursting to speak, could keep silent no longer.

'Father, excuse me,' he burst out. 'I must tell you. The

Franks are moving south fast. And it's not just a small raiding party, like they were all saying this morning. There are thousands of them! The Sultan Saladin has sent a messenger. I saw him. Father, you should have seen his horse! Black, and the biggest, most beautiful—'

'Never mind his horse!' Adil had stepped backwards, shocked. 'What did this messenger say?'

'He's ordered the city to prepare. We've got to get in as much food as possible before the gates are closed, and sharpen our swords and everything. There's going to be a siege!'

The preacher was right, Salim thought, with a lurch of his stomach. *Mother should have listened to me.*

'Sharpen our what?' Adil was saying distractedly. 'Swords? What swords? What would I do with a sword?'

'Everyone's leaving who can,' Ali was running eagerly on. 'But we're going to stay, aren't we, Father? I spoke to one of the garrison sergeants. They're handing out weapons already. I told him you didn't have any. Not even a dagger. The sergeant promised me a sword, one of the finest, if I join them.'

Adil was struggling to keep up.

'A siege? Are you sure?'

'Yes! Certain! Everyone's running to buy food.'

Salim's skin pricked with excitement and fear. He was watching his father's face, and saw with alarm that Adil was chewing his lower lip with anxiety.

'How far away are the Franks? How long have we got before they close the city gates?'

'Several days' march, I think. And there are ships moving alongside them up the coast.'

Adil smacked his hands together in distress.

'Ships! They'll close the harbour. It'll be ruinous!'

'The Sultan's sending reinforcements, Father. The messenger said so. They'll be here in a week. I don't know when they'll shut the gates though.'

Salim couldn't hold back any longer. His heart was pounding.

'I'll join the garrison too, Baba. Please let me. I can shoot arrows really well, I'm sure I can, and you know how good I am at throwing stones.'

Ali turned on him.

'Shut up, you fool. Who do you think you are? They don't want kids, especially cripples like you.'

'Kid yourself,' Salim shot back at him. 'Just because you're three years older than me . . .'

Adil, ignoring his sons, had jumped to his feet.

'A week till the Sultan gets here!' He was talking mainly to himself. 'And an enemy fleet to blockade the harbour! We must leave. At least get Khadijah and Zahra away. But my galley! It's at sea now, not due back till next week. I have to be here to unload it. I'll lose a fortune if it falls into the wrong hands. I can't possibly leave Acre now.'

Dr Musa had stood up too.

'Is the Sultan's messenger still here?' he asked Ali. 'Is he staying in the city?'

'I'm sorry, sir. I don't know. He had a troop of Mamluk soldiers with him. They're amazing! They've got so many weapons. And their saddles! You should just see them. They're . . .'

He stopped, as if lost for words.

Salim crept forwards, fascinated, wanting Ali to go on. He had never seen Mamluk troops. They were the best, the fastest and the bravest of all the Turks.

Dr Musa was gathering his gown up, ready to hurry away.

'I must go,' he said to Adil. 'Thank God my wife is in Jerusalem with her family. She'll be safe there for the time being. I'll take what I can carry on my old mule, and get off on the road tomorrow. Eh, my poor old bones! Racketing round the country, an old man like me, soldiers running everywhere . . .'

'You must go, of course. No! Wait, please, a moment.' Adil put out a hand to stop him. 'There's something I must ask you. I hadn't intended – in such a rush – without proper preparation – but this changes everything.'

Dr Musa was already at the street door, but he turned politely.

'You'll be surprised, perhaps, by this request.' Adil was looking harassed. 'It's – well, it's about Salim.'

Salim started when he heard his name, and looked over his shoulder, almost as if he expected another Salim to be standing behind him.

'You've seen the boy, doctor,' Adil went on. 'I've been wondering for months now what to do for the best. He's not suited to my business. Besides, Ali will take over from me, when the time comes, and no business does well with two masters.'

Salim, stunned, was looking from his father to Dr Musa and back again, filled with a growing dread.

'I'll come to the point,' Adil said quickly. 'The long and the short of it is, my dear sir, that I've been wondering if you would take Salim on as your servant apprentice. Train him in the arts of medicine.' Salim took a step backwards, his mouth falling open in horror. Ali gave a snort of derisive laughter, quickly suppressed. 'He's quick,' Adil went on. 'You've seen that yourself. His lameness would be no bar to success in your profession. In trade – you know how people are. So superstitious where money is involved! They see ill luck everywhere. A merchant with a limp – well . . .'

He stopped. Salim screwed his eyes tight shut, blocking out his father's supplicating look and the astonishment on Dr Musa's face.

No! he was screaming silently to himself. *No!*

'Are you sure about this?' Dr Musa said doubtfully.

'Wouldn't you rather apprentice him to a doctor of your own faith?'

Adil shook his head.

'You're the best, Dr Musa. Your reputation is supreme. You'd give my boy a wonderful start in life.'

'I don't know.' Dr Musa's voice was so doubtful that Salim opened his eyes again in hope. 'I'll have to think about it. An apprentice! What an idea! Obedience, of course – I'd insist on obedience. And hard work. How strong is he? Could he manage my mule? She's a devil, I tell you.'

'The idiot couldn't manage a kitten,' Ali muttered under his breath.

For once, Salim felt grateful for his brother's ill-natured scorn. But Adil shot Ali a furious look to silence him.

'He's much tougher than he looks, doctor. And growing stronger all the time. You won't be leaving Acre tonight? It's too late, surely. It'll be dark in half an hour. I'll come to your house first thing in the morning, and you can give me your answer then. Just consider it, think it over, that's all I ask.'

Dr Musa was already down the steps, and halfway across the courtyard towards the door.

'I will, *ya*-Adil,' he called back over his shoulder. 'Come to me in the morning, and bring the boy with you. An apprentice! It's quite a thought.'

Salim tossed and turned on his sleeping mat throughout the long night. He had been away from home only once before. Two years ago, Saladin had reclaimed the city of Acre from the Franks, and raised the banners of Islam over its domes and turrets. Just before the battle, Adil had quietly evacuated his family, but they had stayed away for only a few short weeks. The idea of going away for a long time, perhaps forever, was impossible. Salim couldn't take it in. Twice he was woken from a nightmare by a nameless terror, and had to stifle a yell of fear in case he roused Ali.

Adil woke him from an uneasy sleep just as the approach of dawn was tinging the black sky with grey. At once Salim was wide awake, his heart thudding uncomfortably.

'Baba, please, I want to stay at home. Don't send me away,' he pleaded.

Adil frowned.

'Stop that, Salim. I've made up my mind. This is a good chance for you. It's for the best. There's no use whining to your mother, either. If you disobey . . .'

He left the threat open.

Salim struggled after him into the courtyard where Khadijah was pouring water from a large jar into a small pot. Her eyes were red, and her hands were trembling. She tipped some water over his head and smoothed his hair down, then pulled him into a fierce hug.

'Always remember your manners,' she said in a thick voice. 'Don't follow the ways of unbelievers. And never drink too much cold water on an empty stomach.'

He pulled away and looked up at her face, trying to make out her expression in the dim light.

'You don't need to say goodbye, Mama. We're only going to see him. He won't want me. I know he won't. I'll be back in a little while.'

She turned away, putting the corner of her headdress up to wipe her eyes, then picked up a bundle lying by the door and put it into his arms.

'Your other tunic, *habibi*. I washed it last night. A cloak for when it gets cold. And there are some honey cakes. Your favourite.'

He stared at her, anger pulsing through him.

'You're sending me away! You want to get rid of me!'

Ali stumbled outside, yawning.

'Of course she does. We all do. Specially me.' But there was no sting in his voice for once.

Salim stepped backwards away from them all.

'You can't do this, Baba. I don't know Dr Musa. I don't know anything about being a doctor. I want to stay at home and fight the Franks. You've got to let me!'

Adil had already drawn back the heavy bolts and opened the street door. He lashed out suddenly with his hand and caught Salim a stinging blow on the side of his head.

'You think I've got all day? Come on.'

Salim had never disobeyed his father and he couldn't now. He clutched the bundle to his chest and began to limp after him. Before he had gone more than a few paces he felt Ali's hand on his arm. He flinched, expecting a slap or a pinch, but Ali put a rough hand round his shoulders and squeezed them.

'*Rahmat Allah aleik*, little brother,' he said. 'God bless you. Admit it, you'd have been a useless merchant.'

The streets of Acre were unusually crowded at such an early hour. People were hurrying grim-faced towards the food bazaar, and some were already returning, driving donkeys laden with sacks of corn and jars of oil.

'The prices will be out of reach by midday,' Adil muttered. 'Come on, Salim. Don't dawdle like that.'

That stupid doctor won't take me. He won't want me. We'll be home again soon, Salim kept saying to himself.

Dr Musa's home was on the far side of the city, in the Jewish quarter. The narrow streets were so packed that Adil and Salim could barely cut their way through. People were throwing bales and bundles out of the windows, loading pots and pans chaotically into carts, tying chests to the backs of protesting mules and screeching to children to get out of the way.

Adil turned out of the main thoroughfare into a dead end.

'This is the place, I'm sure of it,' he said uncertainly.

A lattice window above rattled open and Dr Musa's bare head poked out.

'Is that you, *ya*-Adil? I'm coming down.'

A moment later, Salim heard the bolts on the street door squeak back and they were inside a cool narrow passageway.

'This comes at a fortunate time,' Dr Musa said, running a hand through his thick curly hair. 'My rascal of a servant came to me last night. Pleaded with me to let him go. His wife – sick in Haifa. What could I say? I was in two minds about the boy, but that's settled it. I'll take him. Am I insane? Of course I am! Anyway, it'll have to be an informal arrangement till things settle down. I'm not committing myself to keeping him if he doesn't suit me. If there's laziness or bad behaviour – but I'm sure you've trained him too well for that.'

Salim's heart plummeted. He took a step back, and had to stop himself crying out in protest. Then he saw with disgust that his father was almost cringing with gratitude in front of the doctor, and felt a wave of shame and anger.

'The first test comes today.' Dr Musa looked harassed and spoke briskly. 'I'm leaving now, for Damascus. We'll be walking all day. You can walk far and fast, Salim, on that leg?'

No, Salim wanted to say. *I can't walk far at all. I'm not used to it.*

'He'll be fine.' Adil was groping inside his cloak. 'He's much stronger than he looks. He's been spoiled by his mother. Toughening up will do him good. Don't let him fool you with his play-acting. Don't stand any of his nonsense!' He took out a leather pouch and put it in the doctor's hand. 'We haven't discussed the terms of the apprenticeship, doctor, but there are ten gold pieces in there.'

'Good. That'll do.' Dr Musa pocketed the money. 'I would ask you to seal the matter with a sherbet, but I must be off this morning. The long road to Jerusalem! Think of it. At my age! Say goodbye to your father, boy.'

Salim, looking up through eyes blurred with tears, heard his father's impatient words of blessing and felt his hand rest briefly on his shoulder. He wanted to protest, to dig his heels in and refuse to budge, but he knew it would do no good. Questions raged through him. Would his family be staying in Acre, braving the Frankish army? And if they fled, where would they go? How would he ever find them again? How long was he supposed to stay with this stupid doctor anyway?

But Adil had already turned and was hurrying away.

'Goodbye, Baba,' Salim called out miserably after him.

Far to the west of Acre, in a fertile valley in the centre of England, a village lies under the hazy August sun. A couple of miles away, the huge grey castle of Fortis rears like a mailed fist above the surrounding woods and fields, where men and women work in bonded servitude to the lord of Fortis, Baron Guy de Martel.

CHAPTER TWO

There was no coffin for the woman's body, not even a linen shroud. She had simply been wrapped in her ragged woollen cloak and laid on the bier, which two men were carrying down the rough lane towards the church in the valley below.

The man in front slipped on a loose stone and stumbled, but he bit back his curse out of respect for the dead woman, and to save the ears of the priest who walked in front. The only other member of the little procession was a boy, tall for his age and big-boned, but thin.

New life was bursting out of the banks on either side of the lane. Bumblebees fussed in the hawthorn blossom and cowslips and violets jostled for space in the lush grass.

The boy didn't hear their incessant buzzing. He was thinking only of his mother, who had coughed out her last breath the night before as she lay on the pile of straw in a corner of their hut. He had held on to her arms, shaking them and calling out, 'Don't go, Ma! Don't!' but she had died anyway.

He kept his eyes fixed on the back of her head. The cloak had come loose with the jolting of the bier, and a strand of her dark hair had escaped. It fluttered in the breeze, and looked so alive that his heart leaped for an ecstatic moment.

She's going to sit up! She's going to say something! he thought.

But then her head lolled sickeningly to the side, and his hope died.

They were only a few paces away now from the huddle of thatched cottages in the centre of the village.

'Tom!' the boy called out to the man in front. 'Stop a minute. Her cloak's coming off.'

He couldn't bear the shame of the villagers seeing his mother's gaunt dead face.

The men grunted, but stopped and lowered the bier from their shoulders. The boy tucked the old blue cloak more firmly round the body. He shivered at the feel of her coldness, in spite of the warmth of the bright morning.

'That's all right, son. She's all right now,' Tom Bate said with awkward sympathy.

The priest turned at the sound of his voice, and frowned, his bloodshot eyes narrowed with disapproval.

'All right? All *right*? Dying unconfessed? Without a priest? A soul in mortal peril!' He stabbed a dirty fat forefinger at the boy. 'You'll have to perform a lifetime's penance. God only knows how many masses can save her soul from the fiery torments of hell.'

The boy's black brows twitched together.

'I came for you, Father. I ran all the way, and begged you. And you wouldn't come to hear her confession.'

Tom Bate and the other bier carrier sucked in their breath and looked accusingly at the priest, who shifted his eyes uncomfortably, then turned his back on them and walked on unsteadily down the lane.

Another few steps took them to the stone cross that stood in the centre of the village. No one was about, except for a small girl who was minding a flock of geese by the pond. The little procession was about to turn up the path that led to the church, when a clatter of hooves and jingle of harness brought them once more to a halt.

Two horsemen were trotting down the rough track from the castle of Fortis, whose mighty walls rose up on the great grass mound a mile or two from the village.

'It's Lord Guy. Lord Guy!' the bier carriers muttered. They lowered the bier to the ground again, and stood respectfully, waiting for the baron to go past.

Lord Guy de Martel, a heavy, florid man, sat easily on his horse, a hooded hawk on his wrist. His falconer, in the plainer, workaday clothes of a servant, rode on a smaller horse beside him, the lures for the bird slung across his saddle.

Lord Guy's eyes swept indifferently across the little funeral procession, and he seemed about to trot on, but, whether from boredom or curiosity, he reined his horse in and nodded at the priest.

'Who's died?'

The boy, though he'd often seen Lord Guy in the distance, had never heard him speak before, and he could follow his aristocratic Norman French only with difficulty.

'Strangia, my lord,' the priest answered, a smile of sickly humility on his round face. 'Gervase's woman.'

A sudden movement of Lord Guy's knee made the horse trample restlessly, and the baron's attention was distracted as he tried to control him.

'What did she die of? There's no plague in the village, I hope?'

'No, my lord. She had some kind of a fever. And a cough.'

Lord Guy's eyes had settled on the boy.

'Who's this?'

'Strangia's son. Adam.'

The boy shifted from one foot to the other, uncomfortable under the gaze of the baron's hot blue eyes.

'What age?'

The priest dug Adam sharply in the ribs.

'Answer Lord Guy,' he hissed.

'Fourteen last month,' Adam mumbled. His heart was pounding. Attracting the attention of Lord Guy was likely to be the start of trouble, as anyone in the village could tell.

'Is the boy destitute? Are there relatives?'

Tom Bate shot a sympathetic look at Adam.

'No, my lord,' he said. 'Strangia died poor. There was only her little croft, and the hovel on it. Not enough to feed a rat after Gervase died.'

Lord Guy's blue eyes were still fixed on Adam's face. On his own right cheek a patch of red roughened skin was flaring uncomfortably.

'Bury your mother,' he said, 'then come up to the castle. I suppose I need a dog boy in the kennels.' He turned to the falconer. 'You'll inform the kennel master.'

'Aye, my lord,' the falconer said.

A moment later, the two horses had clattered on.

'Think of that!' Tom Bate gave Adam a hearty clap on the shoulder. 'Dog boy! Keep out of trouble, young Adam, and do as you're told, and you'll rise to kennel master yourself, or even falconer, before you're much older.'

Panic was rising in Adam's chest, threatening to stifle him.

'When have I got to go?' he asked no one in particular.

'Go?' Tom said. 'You heard Lord Guy. When you've buried your ma. Today, at once, before he puts you out of his mind.'

Adam bit his lip, trying to control the tears that pricked his eyes. He'd had no idea what he would do when his mother was safe in the churchyard. He'd only vaguely assumed that he would go home, to the hut that Tom had called a hovel, and see if some little part of her spirit might still be there in the blanket which she'd wrapped round him on cold nights, or in the iron pot in which she had cooked his food, or by the chipped wooden spade that still stood beside the door, with which she'd feebly tried to turn the heavy soil two short weeks ago.

His loss was suddenly unbearable.

The little procession had set off for the last time and was turning into the gate of the churchyard. Adam gave up trying to suppress his tears, and as they reached the freshly dug grave in the corner by the yew tree, they streamed freely down his cheeks.

The short ceremony was over fifteen minutes later. The priest had mumbled the last Latin phrase, and clods of earth were already raining down into the grave from the sexton's shovel.

Adam watched till the hole had been quite filled in, then he ran across to the edge of the graveyard and was sick behind a tree.

When he'd finished, and had wiped his face and hands on a clump of torn-up grass, the priest and the second bier carrier had gone, but Tom Bate was still there, rubbing his huge hands together as if he didn't know what to say.

He came over and put an awkward arm round Adam's shoulders.

'It's for the best. She's been suffering for months. Last time I saw her – last week it must have been – I thought the breeze would blow her away, she was so thin. Now she's in Paradise, sitting with the Virgin.'

Adam shrugged his arm away.

'Father Gilbert says she'll have gone to hell, because she never made her last confession.'

'Him?' Tom Bate spat. 'Lazy old sot! He's drunk half the time – what does he know? Didn't she confess to you?'

'I saw her lips moving. I knelt down close, but I couldn't hear what she was saying.'

'But she was confessing. You can be sure she was. And you said a prayer?'

'A paternoster. Twice.'

'There you are then. She died confessed.'

But there was a slight frown on his forehead, and his eyes didn't meet Adam's.

'Masses for her soul, Father Gilbert said.' Adam's face was screwed up with worry. 'How can I pay for them? I've got no money. Burning in hell, he said. For ever and ever. She mustn't! She can't! What'll I do?'

'There is a thing,' Tom said uncertainly. 'I was in Ashton at the fair last week. There was a man. He was just a pedlar, really, but there was something about him. He had a little bottle of special dust, dust from the Holy Land, from Jerusalem. Trodden by the feet of Our Lord. If you sprinkle it on the grave of your loved ones, he said, their souls will go straight to Paradise.'

Adam drew a deep breath.

'He was a cheat, most likely.'

'I don't think so, because I asked a monk. He said it was true. The dust of Jerusalem works all right. Straight to heaven the soul goes, so he said.'

'He was selling it then, this pedlar? The dust?'

'Yes. A penny for the bottle.'

Adam's hands were clenching and unclenching.

'A penny. I've got a penny. That's all I've got. Are you going back to Ashton, Tom? Will you buy it for me?'

'Nay, lad. He won't be there now. Moving around all the time, pedlars are. But he'll be here any day now. This afternoon even, I shouldn't be surprised. There's good business for him at Fortis, up at the castle and here in the village.'

Adam looked up at Tom, his eyes pleading.

'And you think I'll be able to rescue her from hell, with the dust of Jerusalem? You're not teasing me, Tom?'

'I wouldn't do that, Adam. I know your ma had sinned, but . . .'

Adam's thin face closed.

'What do you mean? She never sinned. She was good, all the time.'

'Yes, yes,' Tom Bate said hastily, looking away. 'I only meant – we're all sinners, aren't we? No point in worrying about what's behind you. You've got to think of the future. You'd better fetch what's yours from the cottage, and get on up to the castle. What a chance, eh? Dog boy! Look out for my Jennet. Laundry maid she is now, to Lady Ysabel.'

He couldn't keep the pride out of his voice.

'I know.'

Adam's spirits lifted a little. He'd always liked Jennet Bate. They'd grown up almost alongside each other on neighbouring crofts. Jennet was five years older than Adam, and she'd carried him round on her hip when he could barely walk. Later, he'd gone out with her to mind the sheep. She'd looked after him in a rough and ready way and been patient with him most of the time, except once, when he'd shut her hand accidentally in a door, and she'd pushed him into the nettles by way of a thank you. When her mother had died, he'd picked her a bunch of dandelions in a fruitless attempt to cheer her up. At least he'd have one friend up at the castle.

A thought struck him as he walked up the lane behind Tom Bate.

'The cottage and the croft. Am I the holder of them now?' he asked.

'No, Adam. Your mother was a tenant for life. It was all settled after Gervase died. The little bit of land and everything on it goes back to Lord Guy.'

'Not Mother's hens?'

'Strangia's hens? Who's to know about them?'

'I'll give them to you then, Tom. And her stool. And the cooking pot and spade.'

Tom turned round. A slow smile crossed his face.

'Kindly meant, Adam, and kindly received. I'll look after them for you. If you ever come back, and take a new lease on the croft, your hens will have chicked themselves into a whole flock!'

Less than an hour later, Adam was trudging down the hill again. He'd run back home, picked up his blanket and spare jerkin, and searched every corner of the bare hut in case he'd missed a coin or anything that might be of value. There was no sense of his mother there any more, just an awful, silent emptiness. He was glad in the end to shut the door behind him, whistle one last time to the few hens by way of goodbye, and set out for Fortis castle.

The village cross had been all but deserted that morning, but a sizeable crowd had gathered now. They were mostly women, pressing eagerly round a tall, thin man in tattered clothing, who was displaying wares for sale from a box slung from his neck on a leather strap.

'Ribbons, my sweethearts! Luvverly, luvverly colours! Of the rainbow!' he was singing out cheerfully. 'Giving them away to you since you're all so beautiful! Cheap today, they are, because it's my birthday.'

One of the women burst out laughing.

'Don't give us that, Jacques! That's what you was saying Wednesday last, when I saw you up to your tricks at Ashton fair!'

'That was my bath day, mistress,' the pedlar said, winking at the other women. 'Now then, a jewel for your finger, a knife for your pocket, a comb for your hair . . .' He caught sight of Adam, who was trying to elbow his way through the crowd of women. 'Here's a young man wants something special, I can tell. What is it, son? A token for your lady love? A—'

'The dust of Jerusalem!' Adam burst out. 'Are you the man who was selling it in Ashton? I need it for my mother's grave.'

The women had parted to let Adam through, and were murmuring sympathetically.

'Strangia's poor lad. Alone in the world. It'll be hard for him now. Fine boy, ain't he?'

A change had come over the pedlar. His merry manner had dropped away, and he was looking at Adam searchingly, his bottom lip caught in his teeth, as if he was uncertain of something. He seemed to come to a decision, and began to ferret around inside his tunic. His brown eyes, bright as garnets in the wrinkled, weather-beaten leather of his face, were fixed on Adam.

'Your mother's grave, eh? Died a while ago did she?'

'Buried her this morning, the poor child did,' one of the women cried out, while the others nodded and clucked sympathetically.

The pedlar pulled a small leather pouch out of some hidden cavity. He untied the string round the pouch's neck and withdrew, with seeming reluctance, a little glass bottle. He held it up reverently, and his voice dropped to a deep, solemn tone.

'My last. My very last bottle,' he said, gravely shaking his head. 'I always meant to keep it by me just in case, by the will of Our Saviour, I myself was to die far away from a priest. For, as this intelligent young man seems to know, there is, in this simple little bottle, the dust – the *very* dust – of the Holy City of Jerusalem, on which our dear Lord and his pure mother passed to and fro, blessing the very ground – *this* ground – on which they trod.' He shook the bottle gently in front of the now silent, rapt audience. 'He trod it with his sacred feet.'

Hands reached out to touch the bottle. A murmur swelled and died again. Adam fumbled desperately inside his pocket and brought out a coin.

'My last penny,' he said hoarsely. 'It's all I have.'

The pedlar ignored him.

'A sprinkling of this precious – this *priceless* – dust, on the grave of your loved one will send his – or her – soul straight from hell, within the hour, to the rapture of Paradise. Into the very arms of Jesus.'

The crowd was impressed.

'A penny!' Adam pleaded. 'Give it to me.'

Slowly, as if regretfully, the pedlar took the penny and held the bottle out to Adam, who grabbed it and pushed his way back through the crowd of women.

A few minutes later, he was in the graveyard. He knelt by the low mound of soil which marked where Strangia lay, pulled out the stopper, and poured the dry dust from one end of the grave to the other.

'You'll be all right now, Ma,' he told the earth. 'This is the holy dust of Jerusalem. You'll be in heaven soon. Pray for me there, Ma, to the Virgin.'

After a few minutes, he stood up, brushed the loose soil from his knees, and with a lighter heart, set off towards the castle.

The sun was already high in the sky when Adam started along the dusty track that led to Fortis castle. In all his life he'd never set foot inside the towering grey walls. He'd only ever stood at the forbidding gateway, peering into the wide bailey, the open space that surrounded the castle tower itself, which rose, high and formidable, on the great central mound, protecting and threatening at once the countryside all around.

He paused for a moment at the low wooden bridge over the stream, and turned for a last look at the village. His palms were sweaty with nervousness.

I hope I see Jennet soon, he thought.

From the corner of his eye, he caught a movement a little

way downstream. Someone was down among the willow trees there.

He thought it might be Hob, the shepherd. The old man had been kind to him in the past, and had helped Strangia once or twice. He wanted to tell him of his good luck before he went on.

He stepped back off the bridge and went round behind the willows, his feet making no sound in the grass. From here he could clearly see the sandy bank of the stream, and the thin, scrawny man who was squatting on the dry sand, scooping handfuls of it into little glass bottles, exactly like the one Adam had bought an hour ago and emptied on his mother's grave. It was Jacques the pedlar.

It was a moment before Adam took in what he was seeing. Then he felt rather than heard the howl of rage that burst from him, and he leaped forwards.

'You cheat! You swindler! I'll kill you!'

The force of his assault sent Jacques flying. He lay on his back, holding his hands up in a feeble attempt to protect himself.

'No, no! You're wrong! You're making a mistake! Don't hurt me! God's bones, boy, you're killing me! Listen – wait till I tell you. Ow! Stop it!'

Adam had landed a satisfying kick against Jacques's thin ribs. He drew his foot back to kick him again, but there was something so weak and abject about the man lying in the dust in front of him, so helpless and ridiculous, that he couldn't bear to touch him a second time. Instead he swung round and lashed out at the stump of the nearest willow, bruising his toes.

Jacques had rapidly crawled out of reach and was now sitting, panting, on his haunches, eyeing Adam like a wary cat.

'You have seen!' he whined. 'You knows! I am a cheat. A swindler. Worse than that. A liar! A rogue! But—' he held up one trembling hand as if to stop Adam interrupting 'but it went to my heart to do you wrong. Straight there. It pierced me.'

He thumped himself on his chest in penitence, but his eyes were crafty and unblinking.

'You – you . . .' began Adam, lunging forwards.

Jacques scrabbled backwards. He was still crouching down, his arm held up defensively, as he looked up at Adam with feigned innocence.

'To be honest (though I grant you, I have no right to use the word), to be *sincere*, I saw that you was in grief. Fresh grief. For a loved one. But what was I to do? My audience was watching me. Everyone knows Jacques! My clients! My patrons! And the dust of Jerusalem – my most famous item.' He was holding Adam's eyes, as if trying to mesmerize him. 'Ah, if only I'd stuck to ribbons and buttons! If only I hadn't branched out into the sphere of the divine! But, my dear young man, my dear young *mourner*, tell me just one thing, before you beats the living daylights out of me – as I can see you are itching to do – let me ask you one thing.'

Adam sprang forwards again, but Jacques was too quick for him. He was up on his feet already and behind the protecting trunk of a willow tree.

'Let me ask you.' Jacques's voice was soothing. 'Did the dust I sold you ease your pain? As you spilled it on to the place where – your mother, was it not – rests in peace, did you not feel something? A sense of certainty? An assurance that her soul was released from its suffering?'

Adam saw suddenly the fresh earth of Strangia's grave and the dust floating down on to it, and he remembered the relief that had flooded him as he sensed that her soul was flying to Paradise.

'And who are we to know?' Jacques had dropped his voice to a deep, thrilling, reverent tone. 'Can we not opine that your true faith in God and his Blessed Mother, and the sacrifice of your last coin, did not, by a miracle, transform the sand of, I admit it, this humble stream, into the very dust of Jerusalem? Just as, at the touch of the priest, the bread and wine of communion becomes the very body and blood of our dear Lord?'

In spite of himself, Adam hesitated. Perhaps – could it be? – No! He wouldn't fall for this man's cheating again.

'I'll tell everyone,' he said, but his voice came out wrong. It was trembling instead of gruff. 'Lord Guy will have your tongue cut out. Or your ears cut off, anyway.'

To his surprise, Jacques laughed and pulled off his cap.

'Too late, my boy. They were cut off years ago.'

Adam looked with horror at the mangled lumps of scarred gristle which were all that remained of the pedlar's ears. He took a step backwards.

'Give me back my penny,' he growled.

Jacques seemed to sense that there was no more to fear from Adam. Moving cautiously, he stood up, then bent again to brush the dust from his knees.

He felt inside his jerkin, and tossed over a coin.

'Fair's fair. No harm done. Quits, ain't we?'

Adam caught the penny and turned away.

'Just one last word, my young friend.' Jacques's voice was no longer wheedling but silky with menace. 'You tell anyone what you seen, you rat on me, and I'll curse you. I can make a man blind. Blind. I can turn a man mad. You're warned.'

Adam was already scrambling back on to the bridge.

'You think I believe that?' he shouted back. 'You won't trick me again.'

But he shuddered as he spoke, and knew that Jacques had seen his fear.

I tried to help you, Ma, he whispered to himself. *I won't give up. I'll get the real dust of Jerusalem for you somehow. Just wait,*

Ma. You won't have to suffer in purgatory for long. I'll walk all the way to Jerusalem myself, if I have to.

The pedlar's mocking laughter followed him as he hurried away.

CHAPTER THREE

I t was mid-morning by the time Dr Musa and Salim left Acre. Salim had stood, stiff with rage and misery, uselessly watching as the doctor fussed over his bottles and jars of medicine, wrapping his surgical instruments into cloths and packing everything into a heavy wooden chest.

'That rogue of a servant!' he was muttering. 'The knave! To lie to me! I've been his honest master for ten years. His wife is ill, he says. In Haifa! When I know perfectly well that she died in Aleppo three years ago.' He turned suddenly to Salim. 'Well, boy? Did I deserve such treatment? Did I?'

'I – I don't know,' Salim stammered.

He couldn't believe what was happening to him. This time yesterday he'd been idling away the morning in the customs house as usual, knowing that he'd eat his mother's cooked supper that evening and sleep on his own mat at night. Today he was suddenly cast out into the world, the servant of a strange master, who wasn't even a Muslim.

If the Franks catch us they'll probably murder us both straight away. They hate Jews even more than they hate us Muslims. Father will be sorry then, he told himself with sour satisfaction.

At last, Dr Musa led Suweida, the mule, out of her stall,

and told Salim to lift the chest on to her back and hold her still while he tied it on. The chest was heavy, and Salim had to strain to lift it. He was straightening his back when he heard a shout from behind.

It's Ali! he thought joyfully. *He's come to take me home!*

He turned excitedly, only to see another young man, a stranger, who was calling to a friend.

The mule was startled by his sudden movement and trampled backwards. The heavy chest slipped in Salim's arms, and he caught hold of it just in time before it crashed to the ground.

'What do you think you're doing?' shouted Dr Musa furiously. 'Do you want to smash all the bottles?'

He came up to Salim with his hands raised. Salim cowered, expecting a blow, but the doctor was only reaching for the chest. He took the weight of it from Salim's straining arms and held it on the mule's back.

'Pick that up,' he said impatiently, nodding at the leather strap lying on the ground. 'And hurry up, before this mother of iniquity bolts.'

There were streams of people pouring out through the high eastern gate of Acre. The lucky few had tied their possessions to the backs of mules or donkeys, but most were on foot, staggering under huge bundles tied up in cloths, the women with babies in their arms and children clinging to their skirts.

Salim felt a shudder of finality as they walked out through the great stone portal of Acre into the flat coastal plain outside the city walls. He turned and looked back longingly into the narrow, familiar city streets behind.

'Keep up!' barked Dr Musa, who was leading Suweida by the bridle. 'You can walk faster than that, can't you?'

Salim could walk well enough, but the doctor's question had given him an idea.

I'll fake it, he thought. *I'll go slowly. And I'll say I've got a headache. He's a doctor. He'll take me seriously. He'll think I'm too weak and send me home.*

He put on the suffering expression that had always roused his mother's sympathy and exaggerated his limp, putting one hand on his hip to increase the effect. Dr Musa burst out laughing.

'A play-actor as well as a linguist! You don't fool me, young man. A good thing your father warned me. I know you can walk perfectly well.' Salim blushed with embarrassment, and resumed his usual gait. 'You want me to punish you?' the doctor went on. 'You don't know what I can do! You see this arm?' He rolled back the sleeve of his gown and flexed his short muscular forearm. 'Beware! My strength is mighty and my vengeance terrible! You'll see! You'll see!'

Salim bit his lip and quickened his pace, till he was walking beside the doctor.

'Your father, is he planning to leave Acre?' Dr Musa said suddenly, after a short silence.

'I don't know,' Salim said sulkily. The doctor's forehead creased in a frown at his disrespectful tone. 'I don't think so, *ya-hakim*,' Salim said hastily, trying to sound more polite. 'He's waiting for a shipment to arrive. He has a galley at sea. It's due to dock any day now.'

Dr Musa shook his head.

'An obstinate man, Adil. Obstinate! He'll take his chances, I suppose. He stuck it out under the Franks before.'

'You don't think – surely the infidels won't take the city?' Salim tried unsuccessfully to keep a tremor out of his voice. He'd been so angry with his parents for sending him away that he hadn't given a thought to the danger they might be in.

'You think I'm a soothsayer?' the doctor snapped. He waved his arms, shaking Suweida's bridle so that she tossed her head in alarm. He shot a sideways glance at Salim. 'Turn around, you foolish boy. Look at the walls of Acre. Who is going to batter his way through those? Have faith. Say your prayers as your father taught you.'

Although it was still quite early in the morning, the August sun was strong, and after a couple of hours of walking Salim was hot, thirsty and footsore. The straggle of refugees had thinned out now, some striking off on small paths towards the farms that ran along the low hills to the east of the city, while others had hurried on ahead. The doctor, leading Suweida, plodded on in silence, with the quiet rhythm of a man used to travelling long distances on foot.

As he limped alongside, wild, angry plans chased through Salim's mind. He'd wait till the doctor had stopped for a rest, as he surely would soon, and nodded off, like old men always did, then he'd slip away and hobble back home. He'd tell his parents that the doctor had changed his mind, or been captured by the Franks, or – or fallen prey to robbers. Even if Baba didn't believe him, Mama would, and she'd stop his punishment from being too severe. As for the danger from the Franks, the doctor was right. You only had to look at the massive stone wall that encircled the city, with its formidable battlements, corner towers and the great ditch beneath, to know that the Franks would never be able to take Acre back. The Sultan Saladin would send an army, and crush the stupid Crusaders like ants under his feet. Baba had been right not to panic, and to stay at home.

Salim was so busy imagining the delicious meal that Mama would cook for him when he made it back home – the chicken stewed in lemons, the rice studded with raisins and nuts, the skewers of roasted lamb – that he had stopped looking down at the rough, stone-strewn path. He gave a sudden shout of pain as his foot, unprotected by its open sandal, crunched against a sharp stone, tearing off half his big toenail. Ripples of agony shot up his leg, and he crouched down to look at the damage.

The doctor, walking on steadily, looked back in annoyance.

'I told you. No play-acting. You want a beating? You want a fight with me? Try me, my young friend. Try me. You'll soon learn.'

Salim, gulping back his tears, stood up and hobbled on, trying to catch up. Every step was excruciating now. To spare his right foot, he tried to rely more on his shorter left leg. Usually, he walked only on the ball of the left foot, which was unused to bearing his full weight. Within a few minutes, he felt cramps spreading up his calf, and had to rely once more on the right foot. For a half a mile he struggled on, biting his lip to stop himself crying, while the doctor grumbled to himself.

'How is it that I am so unfortunate! Forced to take to the road again, at my age, my servant a deserter, a mule that's a daughter of Satan and a fool of a boy who thinks he can trick me. Me! Musa ben Aaron! Why, O Lord, have you brought these troubles down upon my head?'

Just when Salim had decided that he could take no more pain, Suweida suddenly came to life and swerved off the road, almost dragging the doctor behind her. She broke into a trot as she neared a clump of trees. Under their dense, dark shade was a wall with an arched niche in it, and a set of steps below, leading down into the ground, showed that it was a well. Several women were sitting on the stone wall, their water jugs in their hands, but as they saw men approaching they reluctantly stood up, heaved their jars on to their shoulders and moved away.

It was the smell of water that had excited Suweida. She broke into a clumsy canter as she neared the water trough, where a few centimetres of water lined the bottom.

'Quick, boy! The chest! Untie the chest, before she takes it into her evil head to roll!' shouted Dr Musa.

His fingers trembling with exhaustion, Salim tried to obey, untying the tightly drawn knots on one side of Suweida, while Dr Musa worked on the other. He lowered the chest carefully to the ground. Dr Musa was already working the pulley to draw more water up to the trough, and Suweida was drinking steadily, her black tail flicking contentedly over her rump.

'There. Enjoy yourself, you imp of wickedness!' Dr Musa was saying fiercely, but Salim noticed with surprise that he was gently fondling the bristly mane that stood up all along her neck.

Unable to stand a moment longer, Salim sank down on to the end of the stone trough and dropped his head into his hands, not caring if he was to suffer one of the fearsome punishments Dr Musa had promised. His head was genuinely aching now, from the heat and the thirst. He was bitterly regretting that he'd tried to fool the doctor earlier. There would be no use complaining from now on. He wouldn't be believed.

He became aware of the doctor's two sandalled feet on the ground just in front of him, and put his hands up to cover his head, afraid of a blow. But to his surprise, the doctor took his sore foot in one gentle hand, and bent to examine it.

'When did you do this?' He sounded surprised.

'Half a mile back. I hit it on a stone.'

'Hm. Well, well. Half a mile, you say. How did you walk?'

'I tried to use my left leg, but I had the cramps in it so I had to walk on the sore foot anyway.'

'Ah. I see. Some fortitude. Yes, very good.'

Dr Musa straightened up and went to open the chest. He rummaged for a moment, selected a few items, filled a little bowl of water from the trough and sat down on the low wall beside Salim.

'First lesson in doctoring,' he barked, pushing back his turban, which was threatening to slip down over his eyes. 'Wash. Remove dead matter and foreign bodies. Salve. Bandage.'

Salim watched gratefully, trying not to wince, as the doctor washed the toe, cut off the hanging nail, put ointment on it and tied a bandage deftly in place. When the job was done the toe felt much less raw. He wriggled it experimentally.

'Thank you, *ustadh*.' He didn't realize until he'd spoken that he'd called the doctor 'master' for the first time.

Dr Musa had now seized his left leg and was probing the calf with his strong fingers, working away at the cramped muscles, easing and releasing them. He finished with a painless cuff across Salim's shoulders.

'The saddlebags!' he growled. 'Fetch them down.'

The two striped saddlebags were quite easy to lift off. Salim slung them over his shoulder and carried them across to the doctor, who was standing at the edge of the clump of trees, looking back along the dazzlingly bright ribbon of road towards the creamy white walls of Acre, now far in the distance.

'Open them, boy. Where are your wits?' he said, without turning round. 'Spread out the mat. Unwrap the food. There are beakers. Fill them from the well.'

Salim did as he was told. He could walk without too much discomfort now.

He shook out the thin mat that was rolled up and tied above the saddlebag, and laid it on the ground. The action reminded him that it must surely be past the time for the midday prayer.

Two beakers had fallen out of the mat. He picked them up, went back to the well and felt his way down the steps into the blissfully cool, dim stone interior, where a pool of limpid water smelt delicious. Quickly he filled and drank to the bottom of one beaker, then filled them both again and carried them carefully back to the doctor, who had already unwrapped a bundle of food and was laying out dates, olives and flat bread on the mat.

'Excuse me for my prayers, *ustadh*,' Salim said, fearing another outburst. He wasn't used to Jews and didn't know how the doctor would react. The Franks, he remembered well, used to laugh at the Muslims for praying in the way they did.

Cross yourself when you pray to God, you ignorant savage, the Frankish boys had shouted at Salim. *Where's your respect?*

But Dr Musa simply waved Salim towards the trough to perform his ritual washing. He himself had covered his head with a shawl, strapped little boxes to his forehead and arm and seemed to be saying a prayer of his own.

Salim looked round for a good place to pray. He had no prayer rug, so he carefully cleared a spear's-length patch of ground. Then he squinted up at the sun to check which way he should face and, hoping that he had judged the position of Mecca correctly, he knelt down and murmured the familiar words.

The dates, when he finally sat down to eat, were sweet and delicious, and the bread, though not quite like his mother's, was good. The thought of Khadijah's bread reminded him of the honey cakes, still wrapped in his bundle inside the other saddlebag. He'd been holding them in his mind as a talisman, a last link with home. He'd been hoping to keep them to himself, and eat them slowly, one by one, when he was out of sight of the doctor. But he remembered how the doctor had caught him out for play-acting. It would be better to share them than to risk any more misunderstandings.

'My mother gave me some honey cakes, *ustadh*,' he said unwillingly.

'Very good, very good. Eat them yourself,' said the doctor. He had scrambled to his feet, almost tripping over the hem of his long robe, and was staring out along the road to the north.

'Pack up, quick! Fetch Suweida!' he cried.

Salim had crammed a cake into his mouth. He tried to speak but choked on the crumbs.

'Devil take your cakes!' the doctor exploded. 'Look, over there!'

Salim spun round. A cloud of thick white dust was rolling down the road towards Acre. Inside it he could make out the glint of sunlight on metal helmets, while above it floated banners attached to lances, which were held in the fists of mail-clad men, riding enormous horses.

'The Frankish army!' he whispered, his belly turning to water.

He stood frozen with fright, but a prod from Dr Musa sent him scurrying across to where Suweida was nibbling peacefully at a patch of grass.

Dr Musa had already swept everything up from the picnic into the saddlebag, and was running at a lumbering trot towards the precious medicine chest. Salim snatched up the bags and flung them across Suweida's back. Between them, he and the doctor lifted the heavy chest and tied it on.

'We could hide in the well,' Salim whispered, though the Frankish army was still much too far away to hear.

'Where are your wits, child? They'll stop here to drink and water their horses. This place will be buzzing like a beehive as soon as the horses smell the water. Quick. Follow me.'

Dr Musa was already out of the trees and jogging towards a nearby farmstead on the side of the hill above the road. It was surrounded by mud-covered stone walls, along the top of which grew a ragged mass of prickly pear cactus. One end of his badly tied turban had come undone, and as it unravelled the long piece of cloth sailed out behind him like a streamer. Suweida, who seemed to sense her master's anxiety, was trotting briskly beside him, and Salim had to work hard to keep up. A few minutes later, all three were hidden from the road and the well by the farmstead's outer wall.

They found themselves in an empty courtyard. Two or three low stone rooms stood at the far end, but there were no signs of the farm's owners. No vegetables were laid out to dry in the sun. No chickens scratched in the dust. No bundles of cotton lay about, waiting to be spun.

The doctor was chewing at his lower lip, looking round anxiously.

'Not good,' he said at last. 'We're not safe here. Armies are all thieves. They'll come up here when they've drunk the water, looking for food. The farmer knew what was coming. He had the sense to flee. Come on, boy. We'll go further up the hill.'

He took hold of Suweida's bridle and was about to lead her out of the courtyard when shouts, the clash of metal and the neighing of horses sounded, horribly close.

'Too late!' muttered the doctor.

Salim was working at a loose stone in the wall with his fingers, poking out some mud. He made a little hole, looked through it and gasped with fright. The doctor was right. The Franks were flocking off the road towards the well. They were only a few hundred metres below the farmstead.

The foot soldiers, in their heavy padded jerkins, were almost fighting to get at the water, tearing off their round, basin-like metal helmets and plunging them into the trough, pouring water over their sweating faces, scarlet with heat, then drinking deeply with their heads thrown back. Their commanders were beating at them with the flats of their swords.

'Rabble! Scum!' they were shouting. 'Get away from the water! Are you not ashamed to drink before your betters?'

The doctor was at Salim's shoulder, looking through a hole of his own.

'Can you understand them? What are they saying?' he asked.

'They're insulting each other,' he said. 'They say the lords must drink first.'

A group of knights on huge horses had trotted up now. They were lifting the massive helmets from their heads.

'A bigger force than I had thought. Not good, not good,' the doctor was muttering.

But Salim had seen something that was turning his knees to jelly. Two foot soldiers had spotted the little farm. They were pointing it out to the others. Five or six of them had already broken out from under the trees and were running up the little hill towards the hiding place.

'They're coming! They're coming up here! We haven't even got a sword or – or a bow,' he said, breathless with panic. 'They'll kill us!'

He bent down to pick up a couple of stones. He'd throw them if he got the chance.

'Put them down!' Dr Musa said sharply. 'What use are stones against chainmail? We have much better weapons.'

'What? Where?' Salim was searching the doctor wildly with his eyes, expecting him to pull out a dagger or a scimitar from inside his robe.

'Words, Salim! Words! And knowledge. The greatest weapons of all. Now come here and stand beside me. You will speak to them in Frankish. I will tell you what to say.'

The first of the Frankish soldiers was no more than a stone's throw away now. Through the hole in the wall, Salim could see his coarse, matted blond hair, the stubble on his chin and the sunburned skin peeling from his nose. Without knowing what he was doing, he put his hand into the doctor's and squeezed it tight, then stood, expecting to be killed, his heart thudding inside his chest like the beat of a war drum.

The next thing he heard was a whoosh, as faint as a sigh,

from overhead, then another, and another. He looked through the hole again. The Frank had staggered backwards, holding his hand to his neck, from which a long feathered arrow was sticking. The second Frank faltered too, swayed for a moment, then fell on his face, an arrow embedded in the base of his skull. The other men were already scrambling with desperate haste back towards the well and the road.

'Ambush! Ambush!' they were screaming.

Within a few minutes, the chaos at the well was over. The last of the Franks had run quickly back to the road and their long orderly columns had re-formed. The knights, roasting in their chainmail and box-like metal helmets, rode in the centre. On each side of them marched lines of leather-clad foot soldiers, their brightly painted shields in their left hands held up to protect their heads, their right hands clutching pikes and swords, their backs straining under their heavy packs.

Salim and Dr Musa were no longer looking at them. They had turned to watch a troop of cavalry who were riding down to them on stocky, agile little horses from a covering of trees on the hillside above.

CHAPTER FOUR

I t was late afternoon when Adam's reluctant feet finally took him through the gate tower of Castle Fortis. In its shadow, two men-at-arms were squatting in the dust, throwing dice.

'Hey, you!' one of them called out. 'Where do you think you're going?'

'Lord Guy told me – I'm the new dog boy,' Adam said, frowning to hide his nervousness.

'Stables and kennels over there.' The second man jerked his head in the direction of a row of thatched lean-to sheds, built against the inside of the wall.

Adam set off across the rough patch of ground between the gatehouse and the stables. He had never been more than a little way into the bailey before, and had often wondered what it would be like inside the massive walls.

His ears, used to the quietness of the isolated croft, were assaulted by strange jarring noises. The clash of a hammer on metal came from a small forge. Someone was sawing timber in a shed nearby. Wagon wheels rumbled on stones as a load of barrels came in through the gatehouse. People were calling out to each other. Dogs were barking. A rooster on a dung heap was crowing at the top of his voice.

A shriek rang out, and from a small shack near the wall ran a girl. Dark brown curls were escaping from beneath her white cap, and she was holding up the front of her full russet-coloured skirt to prevent herself from tripping. A boot flung after her narrowly missed her, and she veered to the right, almost crashing into Adam. She pulled herself up and grabbed his arms.

'Adam!' She'd been scowling but her face had softened. 'I only just heard this morning about your ma. I'm really sorry. I wanted to come to the burying but that old cat Margery wouldn't let me. Your ma was always lovely to me. I knew she was sick, but still . . . Are you all right, Adam? You must be feeling so bad. What are you doing here?'

She stopped talking at last and let go of him. Adam had been staring at her, hardly hearing a word she was saying. He could barely recognize Jennet Bate, the girl he'd grown up with, in this bold young woman. Although the Jennet he'd known had been cheerful and noisy with the people she knew, she'd been quiet and shy when anyone else was around, turning scarlet if a stranger came near and hardly daring to lift her eyes. This Jennet was forceful and confident, her cheeks flushed with excitement rather than embarrassment, and her brown eyes alive with energy in spite of the sympathy now clouding them. She'd been a girl when he'd seen her last, a year ago. Now she was a woman.

Adam was oddly disappointed. The Jennet he'd relied on had gone, and someone else had taken her place. The knot of misery in his stomach tightened, but he tried to smile at her.

'Lord Guy came past when we – when we were carrying her to the churchyard. He told me to come up here. Said he needed a dog boy.'

'That's great, Adam! Master Tappe, he's the kennel master.

He's so old and doddery he lets the dogs run everywhere. Paw marks all over my lady's shifts. Mean old sour-face he is too. Not as bad as Margery, my mistress. She's the laundress. I'm her helper, but Lord Guy's son, Master Robert, he stopped to chat to me the other day, just as if I'd been a lady. Said if I'm good I might go on to be Lady Ysabel's maid one of these days. Can't be too soon for me. That Margery, she loses her temper with every little thing. Threw her boots at me just now. She misses, though, every time.'

'Aren't you scared?' Adam said, impressed.

Jennet shrugged.

'Me? Of old Margery? Course not. It'd take more than *her*. But look at me, going on. Tell me about your ma. What was it like? Did she suffer? I loved her too, I really did. I cried like a waterspout when I heard.'

'It was awful,' began Adam. 'She—'

'Jennet, you little slut! Where are you? *Jennet!*' came an enraged shout from the laundry shed.

'I'd better go,' Jennet said hastily.

She leaned over and kissed Adam's cheek.

'That's for losing your ma, Adam, and because I'm so glad you're here. Tell me all about it soon, eh?'

She turned.

'Jennet!'

'What?'

He didn't know what to say, only that he didn't want to be left alone.

'When am I going to see you?'

'Everyone eats together in the great hall. I'll see you there.'

He watched till her bright skirt had whisked itself inside the laundry shed, then walked reluctantly over to the stables.

No one was there, and only one horse was looking out of the row of stalls. Adam went up to look at it. Its long nose was velvety smooth, and it eyed Adam nervously, laying back its ears and trampling backwards in the stall.

A deep bark just behind him made Adam whirl round, and he stepped back hastily as a huge mastiff leaped at him, threatening to knock him to the ground. It halted in mid-air as the wizened old man holding its lead yanked it backwards. Half choked, the great dog dropped obediently to the ground.

The old man laughed unpleasantly.

'Thought you was a goner, didn't you?' he wheezed. 'So you would have been, without I'd pulled him off. Can tear a man's throat out if he's a mind. Now who are you, and what d'you think you're doing, so close to my lady Ysabel's palfrey?'

Adam, keeping a wary eye on the dog, moved hastily away from the horse.

'Lord Guy said I was to come. Said he needed a dog boy.'

The man stared at him, the eyes in his gnarled face bright and unwinking.

'Said that, did he? Now what would I be needing with a dog boy?'

Adam looked at his feet, not knowing what to say.

'Have you got a name, boy?'

'Yes. It's Adam, son of Gervase.'

'Gervase, eh? I remember him, worse luck. A wastrel if ever there was one. What happened to your ma? Handsome piece, Strangia.'

'She died. Yesterday.'

Adam felt a prickling in his eyes, and blinked fiercely.

The kennel master tutted but without much sympathy. He bent down to remove the leash from the mastiff's collar. The dog advanced on Adam, his teeth bared.

Adam had only ever known the mangy mongrels in the village before. They'd scuffled over scraps on the midden and barked half the night at prowling foxes, but they'd been quite easy to control, with a sharp word or the wave of a stick. This ferocious animal was of a very different kind.

He wanted to back away but he knew he must stand his ground. He squared his shoulders and frowned at the dog. The mastiff dropped his head, then walked up to Adam on stiff legs and sniffed at his cracked shoes. Adam felt the toes curl inside them, but he forced himself to speak, though he hardly knew what he was saying.

'Good boy. Good dog.'

The dog was walking round behind him. The soft growl in its throat had gone. It lost interest in Adam all of a sudden, went across to the door of the kennel, flopped down and yawned.

'His name's Powerful,' Tappe said, sounding almost disappointed. 'Powerful he is too. Keepin' him out of fights, that'll show what you're made of – if there's more to you than there looks.' He held out the leash. 'Go and fix this back on his collar.'

Adam took the leash and advanced on Powerful, trying to look confident. He bent down and touched the mastiff's studded collar. Powerful growled and snapped at his hand, but without conviction. Fumbling, Adam tied the leash to the collar.

Powerful stood up, his legs stiff, his ears pricked, and gave a deep throated bark. A chorus of baying came from kennels behind Adam, and higher, answering barks from two sleek greyhounds which were bounding towards the kennels from the gatehouse, followed by a jostling, joyful pack of hounds and spaniels, as well as a skinny young man.

'Mirre and Ostine,' said Tappe unwillingly, pointing to the greyhounds. 'My lord's best hunting levriers. One scratch on their hides and you're for it, boy. Don't forget.'

A moment later they were in the centre of a whirlpool of dogs.

'Who's this, Master Tappe?' the young man said, staring at Adam.

'Says his name's Adam. New dog boy,' Master Tappe said with a sniff.

By the end of the next hour, Adam had learned only half the names of the dozens of dogs that lived in the kennels. Spaniels, foxhounds, boarhounds, lymers and brachets each had their separate pens, with their own water and feeding bowls. Adam had opened his eyes wide when he'd first gone inside the kennel. It was larger and more luxurious by far than the hut where he'd grown up. There was an upper and lower floor of pens, and all was made of smooth oak. It smelled cleaner and fresher than any cottage he'd ever entered.

Tappe and the other man went silently about their work, filling water bowls and mixing the dogs' food in a huge iron kettle. Adam watched closely, moving in to help when he could. He got a kick from Master Tappe for getting in the way, but the younger man, whose name seemed to be Snig, showed him how to check the spaniels' coats for burrs, and even smiled at him once or twice, through a mouthful of broken teeth.

'New dog boy, he'll be sleeping in here then, will he, Master Tappe?' he called out to the kennel master.

Tappe grunted assent.

'That's me out of here then,' Snig said delightedly. 'I'll be bedding down in the great hall with everyone else like a Christian.'

Adam looked round, wondering where he was supposed to sleep.

'Over there's best,' Snig said, pointing with his chin. 'That's my pile of straw. You can have it if you can stand the fleas. 'Taint bad there. No draughts.'

'What do I have to do in the night?' Adam asked.

'Nothing much. Stop 'em fighting. Come over and fetch

Master Tappe if one of 'em goes sick. Check on the fire in the winter, in case it sets the straw alight. It's all right in here. Warm and all.'

A bell jangled out across the bailey from beside the massive studded main door of the keep.

'Supper,' Snig said with satisfaction. 'I'm starved. We've run these hounds more 'n twenty mile today.'

Adam suddenly realized that he was famished too. He'd eaten nothing all day, except for a handful of newly unbudded beech leaves.

Master Tappe, Snig and the other man were already leaving the kennels. Adam began to follow.

'Not you,' growled the kennel master. 'Dogs ain't settled yet. And Braceleur's paw looks sore. Needs inspectin'. Thorn in it, probably.'

He took a few paces then said over his shoulder, 'Not a scratch on their hides, mind, or I'll have you whipped.'

Adam leaned against the doorpost of the kennel's entrance. He felt weak with hunger and slid down to sit on the ground. The castle bailey, which had been so noisy and crowded a few minutes earlier, was suddenly empty and quiet. Everyone had gone in to supper, except for a pair of sentries, still playing dice by the gate.

Adam felt a sob build up in his chest. He swallowed it down, but couldn't stop the next one from rising, and then he gave in and allowed himself to cry in earnest, sitting with his arms round his knees and his forehead resting on them.

I'll have to stick it out here, he told himself, trying to cheer up. *That Snig, he might be all right. And there's Jennet.*

He felt a sudden movement beside him and started as something cold and wet butted against his wrist. Powerful had padded silently across to him and was standing at his shoulder. The dog was so huge that his face was on a level with Adam's.

Adam put out a tentative hand and touched the mastiff's neck. Powerful gave a yelp that turned into a low growl, but it was a sound of pain rather than anger.

Adam moved up to a crouching position and held out his hand.

'Here, boy. Here, Powerful.'

The dog edged up to him and again dropped his head, wriggling his neck uncomfortably.

'There's something there. Under the collar, is it?'

Gently, Adam felt for the buckle on the heavy studded collar and undid it. He could see the problem now. A splinter of wood had somehow been caught under the collar and was entangled in a mass of hair. Crooning softly to calm the dog, Adam eased the splinter out and smoothed the hair down, then buckled the collar back on again.

He sat back in his old position by the doorpost. Powerful lifted his head, shook it, gave a mighty snuffling sigh and lay down beside Adam, who placed a hand on his head and began idly to massage his ears.

He was almost asleep, worn out by hunger and exhaustion, when he heard voices. He opened his eyes. The castle door was open, and the bailey was filling up with people again. Master Tappe and Snig and were already only a few yards away.

Adam scrambled to his feet, afraid he'd done something wrong. Master Tappe was looking at him curiously.

'Mighty friendly with Powerful all of a sudden, ain't you? That dog don't take easy to strangers.'

'He – he had a splinter under his collar. I took it out for him,' stammered Adam.

Snig was staring at him uneasily.

'No one gets near that dog. I been working in this kennel for years. He never lets me touch him. Here, you ain't done a spell, have you? You ain't got magic or nothing like that?'

'Pah!' Master Tappe spat on the ground. 'Magic! Boy's got a way with dogs, that's all, which is more than can be said for you, Snig, kennel lad though you be all your life.' He shot out a sudden hand and landed a stinging slap on Adam's cheek. 'That's for getting above yourself. You'll know your place or I'll make sure you're sent back to the hovel you came from. Now get along to the kitchen for some supper and tell them I sent you.'

Half an hour later, the world seemed a better place to Adam. Squatting in a corner of Fortis's cavernous kitchen, out of the way of the cooks and scullions, he had been given a bowl and spoon. Into the bowl had been flung a thick wedge of bread and a dollop of rich and satisfying pea soup, with a layer of minced meat slathered on top. Adam had eaten meat no more than once or twice a year throughout his life and the lavishness of the meal astonished him. To cap it all, when he had looked up at last from his empty bowl, a girl had laughed and tossed him a venison bone. A little meat and gristle was still clinging to the knuckle, and Adam had gnawed at it until the bone was white and shiny. He had never eaten venison before. He thought it was delicious.

It was only when he'd finished with the bone that he realized someone else had been watching him. Jacques the pedlar was sitting on a stool, leaning his back against the wall, his long legs stuck out in front of him. He looked as relaxed and at home as if he was Lord Guy himself.

Adam frowned. Slowly, Jacques raised his left hand and pointed the index and little finger at Adam. It wasn't a sign that Adam recognized, but the menace in it was unmistakable.

I can make a man blind. I can turn a man mad, Jacques had said.

In spite of himself, Adam shivered. Jacques lowered his

hand, grinned and gave Adam a broad wink. Adam stood up and hurried out of the kitchen.

That night, in spite of the strangeness of the place, Adam slept more deeply than he had for months. Shut in their pens all round him, the dogs restless, sometimes whining as they dreamed, or growling at a marauding rat, but their snufflings were almost comforting to Adam, who had been used for a long time to listen to Strangia's rasping breathing and choking coughs, fearing, whenever she fell silent, that she had slipped away.

The only dog unpenned was Powerful. Attached by a long chain to the kennel doorpost, he lay at first outside the door, across the threshhold, but some time in the night he nosed the latch up and pushed the door open, and when Adam woke at first light he found the huge dog curled up beside him.

Powerful's instant devotion to him had gained Adam Master Tappe's guarded approval. It was clear too that the other dogs took their cue from Powerful, who was obviously the king of this canine world. Snig struggled to keep the boisterous, quarrelsome brachet hounds in order, and was even nipped painfully by Fillette, Lady Ysabel's tiny lapdog, who was brought by a maid every morning to the kennels for a pampered grooming.

There was a routine to the morning work, but Adam found it confusing and hard to understand. Master Tappe, short on words, pointed to what had to be done, but offered few explanations, and Snig, jealous of Adam's success with Powerful, had plunged into a sulk.

The sun was nearing its height when from a distance, some way outside the castle walls, came the sound of a horn. An eerie quiet fell inside the bailey. For a moment, no one moved, then everything came to life. The blacksmith emerged from his forge, his hammer still in his hand. At high windows in the keep women's faces appeared. Kitchen maids ran out to the entrance of their yard, wiping their hands on their aprons. Men-at-arms poured out of the keep, clapping on their helmets and hoisting quivers of arrows on to their shoulders, running across the open spaces and pounding up the stairs to the ramparts. Lord Guy appeared at the doorway to the keep, with a black-robed priest at his side.

The commotion had set the dogs barking and for a few moments there was chaos in the kennels. Then shouts from the ramparts seemed to calm things down.

'What's happening?' Adam dared ask Snig.

'Don't know much, do you?' Snig said, his sulk over now that he knew something Adam didn't. 'Could have been an attack, couldn't it? Can't you hear them shouts? King's messenger, that's who it is. He comes from time to time. There'll be a feast tonight. Music. Plenty of meat. You'll see.'

Grooms had sprung to action in the nearby stable and were now leading out a pair of elegant palfreys, flinging brightly patterned caparisons over their backs and buckling on saddles. Lord Guy had taken from a servant's hand a magnificent fur-trimmed cloak. He was fastening it with a gold pin. Lord Robert, his fifteen-year-old son, was at his heels, his face flushed with excitement. A moment later, they had both mounted their horses and were trotting out through the gate-house, followed by half a dozen knights.

Adam was standing to watch, a broom in his hand, when a smack on the head nearly knocked him flying.

'Get back to work, you,' grunted Master Tappe. 'King's messenger, he ain't nothin' to the likes of you.'

By chance, out of nearly everyone in the castle, Adam was one of the first to see the arrival of the king's messenger. Master Tappe had sent him to fetch a bale of straw from the heap beyond the gatehouse, and he was returning with it in his arms when the procession swept in through the gate.

He had to stand back to avoid being trampled by the dozen or so horses and the troop of armed men running behind them. Sunlight sparked off the horses' polished tack and the soldiers' helmets, and glowed on the scarlet and blue of their surcoats.

From all round the bailey, the castle's inhabitants were running forward to watch the King's men come in. Women from the kitchens, laundry and still rooms, men from the smithy, stables and guard room pressed up to the gate, threatening to block the way.

Lord Guy's cheek and neck flared angrily.

'Get back!' he roared. 'Get to your work!'

Reluctantly, he was obeyed.

The horses cantered on up to the door of the keep, the royal men-at-arms walking more leisurely after them.

In the scrum, the straw bale Adam had been holding had been accidentally knocked out of his arms. He bent down to pick it up and felt a claw-like hand close about his arm.

'Blind,' Jacques was whispering with malevolent force. 'Stone blind. Both eyes. *You'll* know.'

Adam stood up, his blood chilling, and tried to shake Jacques off.

'Leave me alone,' he said gruffly. 'What have I ever done to you?'

But Jacques was no longer interested in Adam. He had let him go and was staring at someone behind him. Adam swung round and saw that Lord Robert, a tall, pale boy with a long pinched face and close-set blue eyes, had dismounted from his horse and was hurrying towards them on foot.

Jacques glided forwards, every bone in his body melting in an oily rapture of fawning.

'The noble young lord!' he crooned. 'Lord Robert himself!

Ah, sir, I received your message. Yes indeed! Your servant was discreet. Oh, definitely! But I know what your heart longs for, and I have it! By a lucky chance, here, on my person, is the precious dust which every man – emperor, rogue or simple pedlar – most desires.'

Adam had stepped quietly behind a pile of casks, not wishing to draw attention to himself by moving off too quickly. Now half hidden, he bent over his bale and pretended to retie the straw twist that bound it together. Peering round the highest cask, he saw Jacques draw one of his leather pouches out from inside his jerkin.

Lord Robert held out an eager hand, opened the pouch and took out a little glass bottle.

'Is that it? It's nothing by dust! You're a cheat. I'll have you whipped.'

Jacques writhed like a supplicating cat.

'Dust it looks like, master, and dust it is. But where from? *That* is the question. And I will answer it. From the birthplace of Venus, the goddess of love! And how do I know? Because this precious – this *priceless* – stock was sold to me, not one week since, for my whole life's savings, by a merchant from Athens, who had it off a maiden reared in the goddess's grotto, what they call the navel of Venus. Strike me dead if I lie. It's God's own truth.'

Lord Robert was staring at him in disgust.

'What do you take me for? A complete fool?' He turned, as if he was about to call the guards.

Jacques started back. He looked shocked.

'*You*, sir? A *fool*? The only son of Lord Guy? The finest young nobleman in the country? That time you rode in the tournament, over Chester way, when you unhorsed Sir Giles de Chastel. They're talking of it still. Your looks, your courage—'

'That's enough, you clown,' Lord Robert interrupted, but Adam could tell he was pleased.

Jacques held out his hand for the pouch.

'You must forgive a poor pedlar, sir. How could I have thought that a young man like yourself would need the assistance even of the goddess of love? Let me sell it to some lesser mortal, less god-like than yourself!'

Lord Robert held the pouch away from him.

'Wait.' He was looking inside it again. 'What's this stuff supposed to do for a man, anyway?'

Jacques leaned towards him and whispered in his ear.

Adam, daring to look up, saw an eager, greedy look come into Lord Robert's eyes.

'I'll give you sixpence for it,' he said, trying to sound careless.

'Sixpence!' Jacques squealed. 'But master! My life's savings! A gold piece, at least!'

Lord Robert had already pocketed the pouch of dust, taken a coin from his pocket and spun it in the air. It landed wide and rolled to rest at Adam's feet. Lord Robert was about to stride off, but as he turned he caught sight of Adam, who had dropped his eyes a second too late.

'You dare to look at me?' he shouted, his fair face flushing. 'Come here!'

Reluctantly, Adam went forward. The next thing he knew, a fist had crashed into his chin and he was sprawling on the ground.

'Insolence!' Lord Robert hissed. 'God's breath, but you stink!'

He kicked savagely at Adam's ribs, then hurried off towards the keep.

Jacques, scrabbling in the dust, found his coin and held it up mockingly in front of Adam's face.

'Know your betters, my dear young friend. Study them.

Find out their weaknesses. Take my advice. It's worth more than a gold piece. You'll see.'

By the end of the next day, it seemed to Adam as if he'd been condemned to live in Fortis Castle forever, and the years unrolled ahead like a life sentence of trouble. Still smarting from his bruises, he felt as if he'd made enemies of everyone. Master Tappe, far from being pleased at his success with the dogs, seemed to resent it. He gave Adam the hardest tasks, kicking him awake before dawn to take the spaniels out with the bird catchers in pursuit of ducks in the marsh by the river, so that he returned chilled, soaked to the skin and too late for the morning meal. Then he was set to work at once on preparing the dogs' hot mash. Snig had taken his cue from Master Tappe and was not inclined to be friendly.

A couple of times Adam had seen Jennet's russet skirt in the distance and had heard her laughing with one of the grooms.

I thought I'd be able to count on her, he thought bitterly. *Stupid, that's me.*

At least Jacques seemed to have gone. Having won too many pennies off the men-at-arms, he'd been accused of loading the dice, and had taken himself and his pack off at a dancing run, pursued by a hail of stones.

What he said, about making me go blind if I told anyone, that was all lies, like the rest of him, Adam told himself, but he couldn't forget the menace in Jacques's voice and eyes.

The castle itself was in a ferment of preparation for the feast in honour of the King's messenger, who had been closeted in the keep all day with Lord Guy. Hunters had gone out early and returned with a couple of deer carcasses loaded on a cart, their tongues lolling out of their dead mouths. The warren had been plundered for rabbits, the coops for chickens and eggs, and the vegetable gardens ransacked. Even as far away as the kennels irritable shouts could be heard from the kitchens, where the overwrought cooks were racing against time.

Adam's thoughts strayed again and again to his mother, to that long tress of dark hair escaping from the shroud and blowing in the wind, like a soul trying to free itself from the grip of death. He was tortured by the thought that she might be burning in hell, in everlasting torment, because he'd been unable to persuade the drunken priest to come to her deathbed and grant her absolution.

What if the dust of Jerusalem does work? he kept asking himself. *The real stuff? I'd do anything to get it. I'd kill for it.*

The bell summoning everyone to dinner clanged out at last across the bailey.

Adam took no notice, but went on combing the burrs out of the silky ears of the spaniel he held between his knees.

'Stop that,' Master Tappe snarled at him. 'You heard the bell. Wash your filthy face, get that muck off your hands and get over to the keep. Do you want to miss your dinner?'

Surprised, Adam put the comb back on the shelf and ran off, smoothing his unruly black hair as he went.

The great hall of Castle Fortis was already full of people. A sumptuous display of flagons and dishes was laid out on the cloth-covered table set on a dais that ran along the far end of the hall. Bare wooden trestles ran away from it down the length of the hall, and the many castle inhabitants were already crowding up to them to take their seats on the benches. Adam was about to sit down when someone yanked his arm.

'Who do you think you are? Not here. It's down the bottom, with the likes of you.'

Embarrassed, he moved in the direction of the man's pointing finger and found a place at the farthest end from the dais, between a mumbling old woman and a greasy boy who stank of pigs.

The sudden braying of a trumpet startled him so much that he nearly shot up off the bench. He looked round. Luckily, no one seemed to have noticed. They were all scrambling to their feet and watching the door behind the dais.

A hush had fallen on the crowded hall. The door opened. Lord Guy walked through it with the King's messenger at his side. He was followed by Lord Robert, resplendent in a scarlet tunic belted with a silver girdle. A tall pale woman and two little girls came next, and last of all came the gaunt black-robed priest Adam had glimpsed before.

'You're new, ain't you?' the pig boy whispered with a snuffle into Adam's ear. 'Father Jerome, that is. Eyes in the back of 'is 'ead. You want to watch out for 'im.'

Adam studied the priest. He'd never seen anyone with such a penetrating gaze. The man was scanning the hall with glittering eyes, like a hawk seeking prey, turning his long lean face as he did so to show his magnificent beak of a nose.

The nobles sat down in the high-backed chairs behind the dais. Father Jerome cleared his throat and in a harsh voice intoned a Latin prayer. There was a muffled scraping of wood on the rush-strewn stone floor when he finished, as everyone sat down and pulled the benches up to the tables.

Adam's experience of life had led him to expect very little for himself, so he didn't share the pig boy's greedy interest in the platters of food passing by, carried high by a procession of pages to the nobles at the top table. He barely glanced at the haunches of roast meat, the tureens of steaming stews, the raised pies, mounds of vegetables and loaves of fine white bread. He was too busy looking round at the people, trying to work out who was who, and if there might be anyone in this noisy crowd who might turn out to be a friend. It took him a while to pick out Jennet, but saw her at last on the bottom end of another table. She had her back to him, but he could see she was constantly glancing up to the top table where Lord Robert stood, like a proper squire, behind his father's chair.

'Don't think any of that stuff's for us,' the pig boy was grumbling beside him. 'The leftovers. That's all we'll get.'

The lowest end of the hall was served last, and though the tureen full of vegetable stew with a few pieces of meat floating on the top was almost cold, it was good enough for Adam.

Beside him, the pig boy was tearing at a bone, the juice from the meat running down his chin to splatter his already filthy clothes.

'Nice bit o' pork,' he said through a full mouth. 'Must be one of my own piglets what I slaughtered this morning. I knew they'd be a tasty lot.' He had picked his bone clean, held it up and stared at it. 'I bet you that's the mark of my knife, there, where I stuck it into 'im.'

Adam stared at him with distaste.

'You like killing things then, do you?'

The pig boy grinned.

'Course I do. You should hear 'em squeal! Like babies. And when the blood runs they struggle. That's the best part of it for me.' He began to gnaw at the lump of gristle at the end of the bone. 'Talking of killin', did you hear about the Jews? In York? Hundreds of 'em. Rounded up, stuck with knives, killed dead good and proper.'

'What? Who?' Adam was bewildered. 'People killed?'

'Don't know much, do yer? Not people. Jews! Them as killed Christ our Lord! Good riddance, that's what I say. Wish I'd been there to see.'

'They killed Christ? But that was years ago. They're long dead. They must be.'

'Not *those* Jews. That was their grand-daddies. But they're all the same, ain't they? Kill a Christian for the fun of it. They deserve what they got.'

'What had they done?'

'Done? Wicked evil, that's what they done. Don't want 'em in England, do we? Good Christians we are, ain't we?'

He gave a self-righteous sniff, threw the bone over his shoulder and wiped his fingers across his tunic.

Adam ate on, thinking about what he'd just heard. He knew little about the world outside the valley where he'd been born. Castle Fortis at one end of it and the town of Ashton at the other, with the woods on the hilly crests above, had always been the boundaries of his small world. He'd heard of cities and even countries beyond, of other people, who spoke in different languages. He'd even heard of people called Jews, from the ramblings of Father Gilbert, who had sometimes been bothered to mumble a sermon at the Sunday mass.

Christ was a Jew, wasn't he? he asked himself. *And Our Lady? Or weren't they?* He decided to keep his mouth shut and his ears open in future. He didn't want to show himself up like an ignorant fool.

When they had almost finished eating, the music started. It surprised Adam so much that he sat for a full half-minute with his spoon suspended in the air. Apart from the dirge-like chanting of the mass in church, the ragged chorus of singing that followed the annual saint's day procession in the village, and a hurdy-gurdy in the market in Ashton, the only music Adam had ever heard had been his mother's occasional singing. The sound of the flute, viol and tambourine, coming from the corner of the hall, was so glorious that the hairs rose on his arms and back.

When the music paused, he let out a long sigh. He looked up. Most people, except the nobles on the top table, had fallen silent to listen and were murmuring in appreciation. Then he saw, with a shock, that Lady Ysabel, Lord Guy's pale, rigid wife, was staring at him. He turned round to look over his shoulder, sure that her attention must be fixed on something behind him, but there was nothing and no one there. Her lips, thin as her son Robert's, were pressed together, and her blue eyes were expressionless. Adam uneasily dropped his own, but before he did so, he saw her touch Lord Guy's arm and whisper in his ear, her mouth set in a hard line of disapproval.

When he dared to look up again, Lady Ysabel had looked away, but now it was Lord Guy who was staring at him. The hall was warm and the wine had been flowing freely. The baron's face, with its patch of raw red skin, was scarlet all over. He was fingering a jewelled goblet with one hand, and with the other was restlessly stroking the gold chain round his neck.

I must have done something, thought Adam, panic stricken. *I should have stayed with the dogs.*

He wanted to get up and creep away, but before he could move, Father Jerome rose to his feet and held up a hand. The musicians stopped playing. The falcon, which had been sitting on the back of Lord Guy's chair, jumped down on to his shoulder, and Lord Guy's eyes moved away from Adam as he picked out a piece of meat from the mangled joint in front of him and fed it to the bird. Adam let out a sigh of relief.

Everyone stood as Father Jerome, in a precise, resonant voice, intoned the end-of-dinner grace. The grander members of the household, the chamberlain and steward, along with a group of knights who had been sitting nearest the top table, clustered together to talk, while the humbler people, the grooms, carpenters, huntsmen, gardeners, general servants and ordinary men-at-arms, stood back against the walls to wait respectfully while their betters left the hall. But Lord Guy, rising unsteadily to his feet, called out, 'Silence in the hall! Sir Ranulf, the King's messenger, will address you.'

Adam had barely looked at the King's messenger. Now, as the man stood up, he saw that he was tall and lean and perfectly sober, unlike his host.

'People of Fortis,' he began, 'today your noble lord, Baron

Guy de Martel, Lord of Ashton, Sieur of Martingale, has performed a solemn vow. In answer to the summons of Richard, who is, by the grace of God, King of England, he has taken up the cross of Christ. He has sworn a sacred oath that he will lead a band of faithful men to Jerusalem—' a gasp from the two hundred people in the hall interrupted him. He paused for a moment, then continued, '– to wrest the holy places from the evil monster, Saladin, who even now, with his Saracen hordes, is desecrating the sepulchre of Our Saviour, causing Our Lady to weep bitter tears of sorrow. The question is, will he go alone, or . . .'

Something had caught in his throat and he began to cough. He took a sip from his goblet of wine and was about to continue when Father Jerome touched his arm and pointed behind him. The King's messenger looked round and saw another man, a monk, enter the hall from the door behind the dais. He nodded and sat down.

The word 'Jerusalem' had sent a thrill through Adam. He longed for the King's messenger to say more.

Astonished murmurs had broken out all round the hall but they died down as the monk strode to the front of the dais. His eyes burned in his thin face. He held out his arms and waited until not a sound could be heard in the hall, then waited a moment longer while the tension rose.

'Christian souls!' he cried, his voice rich with emotion. 'Praise God for the example of your master, the noble Lord Guy! Do you know what a great thing he has done? Do you understand what great things he will do? He will brave the peril of the seas, but this will be nothing to him, for the cross of Christ will protect him. He will journey through far countries, over mountains and deserts, but these will not trouble him, for Christ will go on before to show the way. Storms will not harm him, robbers will not dare approach him—' Adam's eyes flickered for a moment to Lord Guy's face. He wore a tremendous scowl and was taking another deep draught from his goblet. Beside him, Lady Ysabel was paler even than before, and she was biting her lower lip. But the monk's thrilling voice drew Adam back again.

'Men of Fortis, will you let your lord go alone? Will you wait for him alone to reap eternal glory and the favour of our Blessed Lady? But, you say, Lord Guy is our lord. If he commands us, we must obey. If he tells us to follow him, we will. And I say to you, that is not the way of the Crusader! Brothers, no unwilling soul must take up the cross! Only those who yearn for glory will be acceptable to Christ! Now who among you is man enough to follow where your liege lord leads?'

The four knights standing near the dais, acting as one man, surged forwards and knelt in front of the monk. One by one, half the men-at-arms, led by their sergeant, stepped up behind them.

'And you! You! You!' the monk went on, lifting a finger to point, one after the other, at the men of the lesser orders who, with lowered eyes, were shuffling their feet uneasily at the far end of the hall, 'Who among you will follow Christ's call?'

Something was stirring in Adam's chest, a deep wave of feeling, but shyness held him back.

The monk dropped his voice a tone.

'I will not hide from you, my brothers, the difficulties of the Crusader way. The hardness of the road, the weariness and pains of battle, the determination of a wicked, infidel enemy. Only the pure, only the brave, only the just and true will reach their journey's end. But all of you, every one, however lowly you feel yourselves to be, every man has within him that seed of greatness! All, all I say, can become true soldiers of Christ!'

The shufflings had stopped. The monk held everyone in thrall. Only a woman could be heard, muttering discontentedly. Her neighbours frowned her to silence.

'I heard someone say,' the monk went on, '"The Saracen

has never harmed me! Why should I take up the cross to fight him?" But he *has* harmed you, oh my brothers. Do you not feel Our Lady's tears as the enemy tramples on the grave of her precious son? Do you not hear the True Cross, the very wood on which our dear Lord died, calling to you? That most precious of all the relics, which the devil Saladin has stolen and now holds in his sacrilegious hands! Do you not feel in your hearts the groans of Christ as he longs to be delivered?'

An answering groan came from a hundred throats.

'And what will you gain, I hear you ask, from making so great a sacrifice? You will not come home laden with riches or the spoils of war. You may come home with nothing more than honourable wounds. But I tell you this. You will have something far, far finer! For every man who takes up his cross to fight the infidel ensures the salvation of his soul! No hell, no purgatory for him. The pope himself has promised it. And those who die in battle will be holy martyrs, and their souls will fly straight to Paradise on the wings of angels. Their loved ones, too, will be spared the pains of purgatory.'

Ma! Adam nearly called out loud. His sharp intake of breath made those beside him nudge him to be quiet.

All around him, people were staring at the monk with shining eyes.

'Will you hesitate, dear brothers? Will you turn aside from the call of Jesus? Or will you follow the path to glory? Why, why do you wait? Step forwards! Come to me! Take up the cross! Take up the cross!'

Before he knew what he was doing, Adam had broken away from the wall and was stumbling towards the dais. He didn't hear Jennet's anxious voice call out, 'Adam! No!' Others were rushing forwards too: the carpenter's boy, two of the grooms, dozens of men he didn't recognize, even an old house servant hobbling up on arthritic knees.

'The cross! Take up the cross!' the monk was chanting.

Adam was trembling with an excitement deeper than any he had ever known. He reached the dais and knelt down behind the others, but his head was reeling, and he was afraid he would faint. He leaned forward to take his weight on his arms. Beside him, someone was babbling uncontrollably.

The faintness passed. Adam lifted his head. Lord Guy was standing to one side, beside Father Jerome, frowning at his ecstatic household through bloodshot eyes. Father Jerome himself watched eagerly, his hands gripping the high-carved back of one of the dais chairs. Lady Ysabel and her daughters had disappeared, but Lord Robert was talking to the King's messenger, who was running a calculating eye over the numbers coming forward.

At a signal, a page approached the monk. He carried a pile of crosses cut from cloth. The monk leaned forward to place one on each man's shoulder. As his hand brushed Adam's cheek, he felt a shudder go through him, as if he had been touched by fire. He picked the cross off his shoulder, and without knowing what he was doing held it to his lips.

'You have chosen the true way!' the monk called out, in a great voice that resonated beyond the hall. 'Soldiers of Christ, follow your liege lord, your king and your Saviour. I proclaim that you are now Crusaders, and that from here on, while you bear with pride the cross of Christ, no man will dare to lay a finger on you, for Christ himself has written your name in his great book!'

Adam breathed in gulps of fresh air as he tumbled down the rough stone steps of the keep into the bailey. He felt as if he was living in a dream.

What have I done? he thought. He put up a hand to finger the cross which he had replaced on his shoulder. *Jerusalem! I'll go there! I really will!*

All around the bailey, knots of people were talking in

enthralled huddles. Someone was sobbing. Adam began, with steps that felt light as air, to cross the rough ground towards the kennels.

When do we go? he was asking himself. *Tomorrow?*

The thought of leaving the valley, for the first time in his life, was so amazing that he stopped, breathless, as if he'd been struck in the chest.

He was about to walk on when someone grabbed his sleeve.

'Adam!' Jennet sounded as if she had been crying. 'This can't be happening! Half the men going away! How are we going to do without you all? Who'll bring in the harvest? Who'll fight if the castle's attacked? For God's sake, Adam!'

He wanted to say, *Yes, for the sake of God, that's why we're going*, but he wasn't used to making pious speeches.

'It's for Ma,' he said at last. 'I've got to save her from purgatory. She died unconfessed, Jenny.'

'Oh. Oh, I see.' She sniffed ferociously, swallowing her tears. 'Well, that's reason enough, I give you that. I'd go for that, to save my ma.' Her mood turned in an instant and she flung out her arms. 'You're so lucky!' she cried passionately. 'I wish I was a man! I'd give anything to come with you. Think of it, Adam, all them things you hear people go on about. You'll see the sea! Sea monsters! Miracle things in foreign countries – people with two heads, and animals as tall as trees. And cities! I'm so jealous I could kill you.'

He laughed delightedly. This was the Jennet he'd always known, his passionate, boisterous older sister.

'Go on then,' he said, catching her mood. 'Come with us.'

She hit him across the arm, nearly dislodging the cross on his shoulder.

'Don't be so mean. You know I can't. Women don't go on crusades. Not girls like me, anyway. Ladies, maybe.'

'Is Lady Ysabel going then?'

'I wish she was. I hate her, sour old cat. She'll be keeping us all hopping here, making everyone miserable.'

'No, but Jenny, you might be able to come,' he said earnestly. 'Who's going to wash Lord Guy's linen? They've got to have someone. None of the men will do it. It's women's work.'

She stared at him. In the failing light he could see that her mouth was open and her eyes were dancing. Then her face closed again.

'Thanks for trying, Adam, but it won't happen. Come over to the laundry tomorrow. I'll sew your cross on to your tunic for you. Did you see who else went forwards? That sergeant, he's a one. I saw him—'

A shuddering scream from behind made them both spin round. A man was standing with his head flung back and his mouth gaping open, jabbing a finger at the sky.

'Look! A sign! A miracle! The cross of Christ!'

Everyone's face was now turned upwards. The sun, setting behind bands of purple cloud, was shooting orange and scarlet rays across the sky.

'I see it!' people were shouting. 'There! Yes, it's the cross!'

Adam could see nothing more than a pattern of rays and clouds, changing with each passing moment, but all around him people were falling to their knees, staring up at the sky and praying.

I can't see it, he thought, frantically searching the sky. *I'm the only one who can't see it!*

He shut his eyes. The pattern of rays and clouds printed a cross-like shape inside his eyelids. He felt a surge of relief.

Is that a miracle? he wondered. He opened his eyes to tell Jennet, but she had gone, and when he shut them again, the pattern had faded away.

Another thought came to him, making him smile.

The real miracle, he told himself, *is that a few hours ago I longed to go to Jerusalem, but thought I never would, and now I'm on my way.*

In the weeks that followed the visit of the King's messenger, the castle was in turmoil. The forge worked day and night, turning out spearheads and pikes and sharpening swords for the knights. The fletcher was red-eyed with the strain of making thousands of arrows. Fights constantly broke out between those who had been given leave to join the Crusade and those who were ordered to stay.

Lord Guy had taken no notice of his people's response to the monk's call to take up arms for Christ. Ignoring the pleas both of those who had volunteered, as well as those who had hung back, he simply picked the men he wanted, choosing the fittest, the best fighters and the most useful craftsmen, but leaving a skeleton staff fit enough to run Fortis in his absence.

'Crusader? Lord Guy?' Snig said, as he leaned against the kennel doorpost. 'He wants to go out there as much as I wants to take a runnin' jump off the top of the gatehouse. Taxes, that's what it's about. If he goes, he doesn't pay. If he stays, he does.'

'No. He's going for Our Lady, like we all are,' Adam said self-righteously, the warmth of zeal still burning bright within him.

Snig crossed himself quickly, fearful of having blasphemed.

'Oh aye, of course. He wants to save himself from the eternal fires same as the next man. And Lord knows, he's got more sins to forgive than most.' He sniffed, the phlegm rattling in his leaking nose. 'You'll be on the high road to Paradise an' all,' he said, half enviously. 'Still, why you wants to go roarin' off to get yourself sliced in half by a murdering Saracen, or boiled in oil, or stuck full of arrows, when there's a nice cosy place for you in these kennels, I'll never know.'

Adam didn't answer. He'd been as much surprised as elated

when Lord Guy had sent for him and told him that he'd been picked as one of the elite band to join the Fortis party of Crusaders.

'Six dogs I'm taking,' the baron had said, running a cold eye over Adam. 'Your responsibility. And you'll report to the tiltyard every morning from now on for archery practice.'

The hours in the tiltyard had, in fact, been a welcome reprieve from the kennels. Master Tappe, who hadn't wanted Adam in the first place, seemed enraged that he was now being taken away, and took it out on him at every opportunity. Adam had thought at first that Hugo de Pomfret, the sergeant-at-arms, would be an even worse taskmaster, but he'd come to respect the tough old soldier, whose bellow was worse than his bite. He'd started to enjoy the military training, learning to thrust with a spear, chop with a pike and shoot arrow after arrow with increasing speed.

He sometimes wondered how it would feel when his blade or his arrow tip was aimed at human flesh.

'They'll only be Saracens,' he told himself sternly. 'I'll be killing them for the glory of God. And for Ma. The more the better, I suppose.'

But he preferred not to think of it if he could.

He was coming out of the kitchen one afternoon with a sack of bones for the dogs when he heard a girl's voice, raised in laughing protest. He looked round. Directly outside the kitchen door was a yard surrounded by a wall. There was a small vegetable and herb plot here, and a jumble of sheds and outbuildings. A cart, upended with the shafts in the air, stood in front of one of these, and as Adam walked across the yard he heard the girl's voice again, coming from the shed behind.

Jenny? he thought. *It sounded like her.*

He ran round behind the cart and stopped, appalled. Jennet had been pushed against a pile of bulging sacks and, pinning her down, with his back to Adam, was a tall young man. Before he'd had time to take in the richness of the boy's green cloth tunic or the fineness of his red leather shoes, Adam was racing up to him, shouting, 'Get off her! Stop!'

He was about to grab the boy by the shoulder, spin him round and punch him, when Jennet shrieked.

'Adam! No! Don't!'

The terror in her voice was so real that it stopped Adam in mid-air. The boy had spun round and Adam had only a moment to recognize Lord Robert when his eyes were caught and held by the slim, wicked knife the young nobleman had whipped out from his belt.

'You dare to *touch* me? Who are you?'

His heart beating fast with fear, Adam dropped his head in a gesture of automatic humility and stepped back.

'It's Adam, my lord. He's almost – like my little brother,' Jennet was babbling. 'He's the new dog boy.' She stood up and bobbed a curtsy. He ignored her.

'You know what happens if you strike me?' The needle-sharp point of his dagger was an inch from Adam's nose. 'Which would you prefer? A hot iron to brand your forehead? Or a hand cut off, perhaps? Though the choice would be mine, not yours.'

The dagger moved sideways, drawing a line from Adam's nose across his cheek to his ear. Adam felt beads of blood trickle down towards his neck.

'Your *brother* must watch himself, little laundry maid,' the boy went on. 'Make no mistake – I shall be watching him.'

He swaggered off across the kitchen yard.

'You must be mad,' Jennet was trembling. 'Didn't you know who he was? If you'd hit him, Adam . . .'

Adam's fear was turning to anger. He took hold of Jennet's arm and shook it.

'What did he want? What did he do to you?'

He'd expected Jennet to look upset, but she stared back at him angrily.

'He likes me,' she said. 'He's always looking at me. He's never got me alone before. He was going to kiss me, I think, when you came along.'

She sounded almost disappointed.

'Jenny!' Adam was shocked. 'You mustn't let him! He'll ruin you!'

'Oh Adam!' She pulled a kerchief out from her sleeve and reached up to wipe the blood from his cheek. He flinched away from her. 'You're still a kid. You don't understand. It's not the village here. If Lord Robert likes me, I'll go up in the world. I might even get to be a lady's maid. Don't look at me like that. I'm not going to wash clothes for the rest of my life and end up like old Margery. Look at my hands!'

He glanced down at the raw red fingers she had thrust in front of him.

'Jenny! You mustn't! It's a mortal sin! Your pa . . .' he began.

A pink flush of annoyance was rising in her plump cheeks.

'You've no right, Adam. You of all people!'

He frowned, puzzled, but before he could ask her any more a furious screech came from the other side of the wall.

'Jennet! Where is that dratted girl?'

Jennet made a face.

'Margery. I've got to go.' She leaned forward again and this time managed to dab at the already drying blood. 'It's only a scratch. It won't even leave a scar. You know what, Adam? You think too much. You've got to start enjoying life a bit more, like me.'

With a whisk of her skirt, she was gone.

On the few occasions when Adam saw Jennet after that she turned a huffy shoulder. But when the time came to leave, and the wagons were being loaded with every kind of provision, she sought him out.

'Have you come to say goodbye, Jenny?' he said gruffly. 'I'll miss you.'

'You won't miss me at all, Adam,' she told him, her eyes dancing.

He stared at her suspiciously.

'You're up to something!'

'Who? Me?' Her eyes were wide and innocent. Then she'd darted off to disappear with a flounce into the wash house.

The barley was inches high in the strip fields by the stream when the Crusaders of Fortis lined up in the castle bailey for a final inspection before the departure. Adam's heart was pounding with excitement. The bailey, huge as it was, seemed to be packed with people. Ten knights, each one with his squire, groom and servants, had rallied to Lord Guy's banner. They had donned their finest surcoats for the send-off and were riding one of their string of massive warhorses. The sun glinted on their chainmail and on their pointed helmets. The breeze was catching the banners that floated from their spears, each of which held the de Martel device: a sable hammer embroidered on a field of argent. Black on white. Strong. Unmistakable. Adam glowed at the sight of them. The black hammer was his sign now. He'd soon be fighting under that flag. He was a de Martel man, and proud of it.

People of all kinds were milling around the mounted knights, men-at-arms, grooms, servants, weeping women and excited children. The noise was affecting the dogs that Adam was holding on six long leashes.

'Steady, Mirre. Quiet, Ostine,' he growled at the two nervous, whippet-thin levriers, which Lord Guy had personally chosen to accompany him, hoping for some good days of hunting along the way. The four floppy-eared lymers, with their droopy jowls and mournful eyes, seemed less affected by the excitement.

'You'll be off then in a minute,' a gruff voice said behind him, and Adam turned to face Master Tappe. The old man wasn't quite smiling, but there was a warmer look in his eye than Adam had seen before. The six dogs crowded up to him, fawning at his feet.

'Don't forget. Rub the levriers down well after each run and check the lymers' ears for ticks.'

Adam nodded without speaking. He knew there were things he should ask the kennel master before it was too late, but his mind had gone blank.

Then, to his amazement, Master Tappe reached inside his coat, pulled out a wriggling mass of tawny fur and tucked it inside Adam's jerkin .

'Runt of Powerful's new litter,' he said gruffly. 'I was about to drown the little loser, but you might as well take 'im. If he dies, he dies. If he lives, a mastiff's a useful dog in dangerous parts. Faithful. Vicious in a fight.' He stopped and cleared his throat. 'When you get to Jerusalem, pray for me. For the salvation of my soul. And if you don't bring back these dogs in one piece, I'll beat the nonsense out of you, once and for all. Our Lady bless you, and the dogs. Mirre in particular.'

And with a last pat on his favourite levrier's head, he pushed his way through the crowd, back to the kennel.

A trumpet sounded, wild and strident. A cheer went up from the departing men. With a clatter of hooves the caval-cade began to pass out under the gate tower, led by Lord Guy on Vigor, his huge black warhorse. Lord Robert rode at his side.

Adam looked round anxiously, scanning the windows of the keep. From each one a woman was waving, her white coif fluttering against the grey stone walls.

Jenny! Where is she? Why didn't she say goodbye? he thought.

The loaded wagons were creaking slowly into motion, their sides clanking with cooking pots and spare helmets. As

84

one of them passed, Adam caught sight of a familiar russet skirt poking out from beneath the linen cover. As he watched, it twitched quickly out of sight.

Jenny, you devil! he thought, his face breaking open in a grin.

Knowing that she would be with him on the great adventure filled him with happiness. He squared his shoulders, lifted his head and, his eyes fixed on the floating banners in front, marched out through the castle gate along the road to Jerusalem.

CHAPTER FIVE

S alim watched uncertainly as the little troop rode
towards the entrance of the farmstead. There were no
more than a dozen men. They wore brigandines –
scarlet padded jackets studded with brass nails – over suits of
chainmail, and plumes that nodded above their tall conical
helmets. Each man carried an armoury of weapons: a bow and
quivers of arrows, a sword and a lance, and a shield at his
elbow. They rode with perfect grace, every soldier at one with
his horse, as if the man and the animal were a single creature.

When they came close enough for Salim to see their pale,
high cheek-boned faces he took in a deep breath.

'Mamluks,' he whispered, struck with awe. These, he knew,
were the best, the toughest and most brilliant soldiers of
Islam. Snatched as boys from the Turkish steppes of Southern
Russia, lost forever to their families and trained with legend-
ary ruthlessness, they served their sultan with unshakeable
loyalty and followed Islam with absolute devotion.

The Mamluks had reined in their horses and were watching the Crusader army on the road below through narrowed
eyes. There were far too few of them to mount a more serious
attack on the long, heavily armoured column, but the

Mamluks looked satisfied, pleased that at least they had prevented the Crusaders from quenching their thirst.

Salim could see that they were about to wheel round and gallop back up the hill without noticing him and the doctor, who were standing quietly just inside the farmstead's courtyard. He was disappointed. He would have liked to get a closer look at their gear and their wonderful horses. But Suweida, made nervous by the nearness of so many strangers, was tossing her head. The Mamluk captain heard her harness jingle and turned round. His sharp black brows snapped together.

'Here!' he called out with an imperious beckon.

Dr Musa muttered under his breath and went forward unwillingly. Salim followed him and stood by the captain's stirrup, trying to look unconcerned and to hide his admiration for the man's gleaming gilded shield, the rippling chainmail that hung from his helmet and the scarlet tassels dangling from the horse's chest and neck.

'Who are you? What are you?' the captain asked Dr Musa harshly. He spoke Arabic with a Turkish accent.

'My name is Musa ben Aaron. I'm a doctor,' Dr Musa said warily.

'What are you doing, hiding here?'

'I am on my way to Jerusalem. We left Acre this morning, fearing a siege. We were at the well up there, just now, and took refuge here when the Franks passed.'

'And the boy?'

'My apprentice.'

The captain was frowning, chewing his bearded lower lip as he stared at the doctor. Salim's confidence waned. Something appeared to be wrong.

'You're a Christian,' the captain said with sudden harshness. 'You're spying for the Crusaders.'

'I'm a Jew,' Dr Musa said calmly. 'My boy here is Muslim. His father is a respected merchant of Acre.'

'Your name?' the captain rapped out, looking at Salim for the first time.

'Salim Ibn Adil,' Salim said, clearing his throat and standing as tall as he could.

'The chest,' the captain said, pointing to Suweida. 'What's inside it?'

'Medicines. Surgical instruments.' Dr Musa moved back towards the mule. 'If your honour wishes me to open it . . .'

'No, no.' The captain turned to the man at his side, and they spoke rapidly in a language that Salim didn't understand. He was nervous now. There was no friendliness in the captain's manner, and none of his men were smiling. He stepped a little closer to the doctor and glanced up at him.

Dignity wasn't a word Salim would have used to describe Dr Musa, with his short round body, untidy clothes and unravelling turban, but there was an unruffled assurance in his manner that was at last impressing the captain.

'Allow me to introduce myself, *ya-hakim*,' he said, in a politer tone. 'I'm Arslan Ibn Mehmet, captain of this Mamluk troop. You'll have to come with us. Orders are to recruit all appropriate personnel. You're needed with the army.'

Dr Musa's brows rose with almost comical horror.

'Impossible, captain. I'm expected in Jerusalem. I can't possibly—'

'By the Sultan's orders, peace be upon him,' the captain interrupted. 'He is preparing an army to attack these Frankish infidels. He'll hang their leaders from the walls of Acre and give their blood to the dogs to drink.' He showed his teeth in a grin as he spoke.

Salim thrilled at his words, but Dr Musa's calm had deserted him.

'What have I done, O Lord, to deserve this?' he wailed,

raising his arms in a despairing gesture. 'If only I'd left Acre last week, I would have been in Jerusalem by now, quietly tending my herb garden and my patients. Listen, captain, I'm a man of peace. A doctor, not an army surgeon. Running about with soldiers, pulling arrows out of flesh, stitching up sword wounds – at my age! Look at me! Have a little consideration, I beg you. Pretend we never met. Go on your way, and I'll go on mine.'

'If we hadn't met, my friend, you would by now be stuck on the end of a Crusader sword,' the captain answered drily.

'But I have no horse!' Dr Musa said desperately, 'and my boy here is lame. We could never keep up with you.'

'We'll mount you,' the captain said, clicking his fingers.

Salim, looking round, saw that two of the soldiers were trotting up, each with a riderless chestnut horse held on a leading rein. The doctor's shoulders seemed to sag as he accepted the inevitable. A soldier dismounted and cupped his hands by the horse's stirrup. Dr Musa put his foot into it and was thrown up on to the horse's back, landing with a scramble in the saddle. Then Salim felt rough hands seize him, and found himself astride the second horse. He clutched nervously at the reins. He had ridden countless donkeys, mules and packhorses before, but this mare had all the fire and steel of her Arabian ancestry. His heart thumped as he tried to control her fretful prancing.

Whatever happens – whatever *happens*, he told himself ferociously, *I won't fall off. I won't!*

A moment later, the troop had wheeled round and was cantering up the slope, with Suweida, held on a leading rein, bumping along in the rear with the other pack animals. Below, further up the road, the cloud of dust billowed on, as the wagons of the Frankish baggage train lumbered after the fighting men towards the walls of Acre.

For the next half-hour, Salim bumped painfully along,

clutching ignominiously at the saddle, and even to the horse's mane when he seemed about to lose his balance completely. Once or twice he had slipped sideways and was sure he would fall, but both times he had managed to right himself in the nick of time, and had looked round furtively, hoping that no one had noticed.

Gradually he settled into the ride. The track which the little troop was following was no more than a rough trail, meandering along the hillside, curving round old trees and running below the walls of the occasional sheepfold and the more frequent stone embankments that shored up terraces of olive trees. The ground was so rough that it was impossible for the horses to move at more than a walking pace most of the time, but whenever it levelled out, the captain led at a fast trot or even a canter. Salim learned to look ahead and watch so that he was ready when his horse suddenly took off. He found after a while that he was moving more easily, riding smoothly and with increasing confidence. For once he didn't have to struggle to keep up with anyone else. The horse made sure of that. No one could see his limp. No one could mock or threaten or pity him.

If the boys in Acre could see me now, he kept saying triumphantly to himself, *riding with the Mamluks!*

He imagined himself galloping with glory up to the walls of Acre, wearing a Mamluk coat of mail and with a Mamluk sword in his hand. He'd charge with them into the sweating, red-faced ranks of infidel Crusaders under the banner of the great Sultan Saladin, the cry of *Allahu akbar!* on his lips. He'd scatter the enemy with the sheer force of his courage and the might of his razor-sharp sword, under the very eyes of his brother, Ali, who would be staring down at him helplessly from the city wall. Together, he and the Mamluks would drive the invaders away, back to the cold, misty, barbaric lands of the north where they belonged.

His dreams were interrupted by irritated shouts from the back of the column. He turned to see that Suweida had dug her hooves into the ground and was refusing to budge, in spite of the violent tugs on her bridle by one soldier and whacks on the rump by another.

'*Ustadh!*' Salim called out nervously, addressing the back of the doctor, who was jolting about uncomfortably on the back of the horse in front of him. 'Suweida won't go on.'

Dr Musa reined in his horse and turned. He took one look at the mule, and the medicine chest that had slipped down from the top of her back and was hanging at an angle from her side, and a thunderous frown settled on his forehead.

'My chest!' he roared. 'Salim! Get down off that nag. Come and help!'

He had already handed his reins to the nearest soldier, had clambered awkwardly out of the saddle and was running back to Suweida. Salim, reduced suddenly from glorious warrior to humble servant, reluctantly slid off his horse and followed him.

'Shake your load off, would you, you daughter of Beelzebub?' the doctor was saying as he untied the straps round the mule's chest.

Salim reached him in time to take one end of the chest and lower it carefully to the ground.

'What is this? Why are you doing this?'

The captain had ridden back to find out what was holding up the troop.

'My chest! My medicines! Everything about to smash to the ground!' Dr Musa said indignantly. 'And all these two idiots of yours could do was beat the beast. They would have let it fall!'

Salim drew in his breath at the doctor's audacity. The captain, with magnificent haughtiness, stared down at him for a moment, then nodded curtly to the two soldiers and addressed them briefly in Turkish.

'They'll stay with you, *ya-hakim*,' he said at last. 'You'll follow on when you're ready. Our camp's only a mile away, beyond the next village.'

He rode back to the front of the column, barked a command and the troop trotted off, leaving the doctor, Salim and the two soldiers surrounding the obstinate Suweida.

'You vile animal!' the doctor was expostulating as he lifted the saddlebags from Suweida's back to adjust her girth. 'You . . .' He stopped as he saw the ugly sore where the bumping chest had rubbed the mule's back red and sore. He smacked a hand to his forehead.

'Call yourself a doctor!' he groaned. 'To tie your load so badly!'

He fished a handful of nuts from a hidden pocket inside his gown and fed them to the mule, then picked up the saddlebags and flung them into Salim's buckling arms. 'You and I will ride your horse together. These men –' he waved at the two soldiers, who were watching their troop disappear into the distance – 'will atone for their foolishness by loading the chest on to the horse (a demon if ever there was one) it has been my ill fate to ride.'

Sheepishly, the soldiers obeyed. A few minutes later, the chest and the saddlebags were securely tied to the back of the doctor's horse, and he and Salim were uncomfortably sharing Salim's. They set off again, with one soldier in front and the other, in the rear, leading the now obedient Suweida.

Salim bit his lip with embarrassment as he saw where the Mamluks had halted: on a field of wheat stubble above a small village of square stone houses. He had hoped to ride into their camp confidently, showing off his new prowess as a horseman. Instead here he was, bumping along ridiculously behind the doctor, his feet, lacking stirrups, dangling stupidly on each side of the horse's belly.

He need not have worried. No one was taking any notice of the doctor's little procession. Only one tent, for the captain, had been pitched, and the two servants were unloading cooking pots and vessels from one of the packhorses. The soldiers' horses had already been unsaddled and tethered, and the men had removed their padded jackets, chainmail tunics and helmets and were now dressed in loose wrap-around robes, their hair flowing free. They were standing in a group on a promontory, staring down across the narrow plain towards the walls of Acre and the sea beyond. As he looked in the same direction, Salim realized that the captain had led them on a roundabout route. They'd ridden back towards the city, on a path parallel to the road which ran along the hillside. Acre lay below them, no more than three or four miles away.

They were too far away to see the Frankish army, but there was no mistaking the hundreds of little coils of smoke rising into the air from below the city walls. The Franks must have made camp there. They would be lighting their cooking fires. Salim's heart missed a beat. Knowing that the enemy was there, so close to the city, was filling him with dread. Would they – could they – take Acre? Everyone had seemed confident that there were too few of them, and that the walls could withstand anything. But now he saw in his mind's eye the frightening faces of the blond, matted-haired warriors as they'd rushed at the farmstead. What would happen to Mama, Baba, Ali and Zahra if they succeeded, against all odds, in storming the city? Why hadn't he really thought about it before?

Now he could see something else, something that made him gasp with fright. The sun, setting across the distant golden sea, was catching the sails of dozens of square-sailed ships, Frankish ships, which were gliding with horrible deliberation towards Acre's open harbour.

It was late afternoon by now and the shadows were lengthening. Suweida, loosely tethered under the shade of a huge fig tree, was lipping over the pile of dry yellow grass that Salim had foraged for her, and the doctor was packing away the soothing balm with which he had treated her sore. The soldiers were busy about their camp duties, feeding their horses, collecting firewood and fetching water from the village well nearby, while their two servants were lighting the cooking fire and bringing out their dry stores.

Salim realized that he was extremely hungry and thirsty. He'd had no breakfast, and had eaten only a few mouthfuls of the doctor's lunchtime food before the arrival of the Franks at the well had made them sweep it all away. He was about to pluck up the courage to ask the doctor about the arrangements for supper when an odd little procession entered the camp, climbing up from the village below.

First came an old man, dragging a reluctant goat on a twisted straw rope. Two younger men followed, each holding a pair of flapping chickens by the feet. Behind them came a row of boys, one with a bowl full of eggs, another with a dish of figs and a third with bundles of fresh green vegetables. Last of all came a little girl, staggering under a tray piled high with flat bread.

The captain went forward to meet them.

'*Ahlan wa sahlan*,' the old man with the goat said. 'You are welcome,' but Salim saw that he wasn't smiling.

'Welcome? I doubt it,' the doctor muttered. 'Soldiers never are. Wise, though, to bring provisions before they've been commandeered.'

'Will we eat with them? With the soldiers, I mean?' Salim said, hungrily eyeing the figs.

'You think they'll starve us? Of course we'll eat with them,' said the doctor. He shot Salim a searching look. 'Your toe. It throbs? It feels hot?'

'No, *ustadh*.' In the excitement of the afternoon, Salim had almost forgotten his sore toe.

'Good. There's no infection then. Now spread out my mat. That limb of Lucifer I was forced to ride this afternoon has shaken my old bones to pieces. If I don't rest soon I shall be gathered to my forefathers well before my time. And fetch me some water. Do you want me to die of thirst?'

It took several visits to the well and many beakers of water before both Salim's and Dr Musa's thirst had been quenched. At last, the doctor took a scroll out of the saddlebag, opened it and waved Salim away; then he sat studying it, his lips moving, rocking backwards and forwards as he read.

Salim squatted down near Suweida, his back against the rough grey trunk of the fig tree, unsure what to do. More than anything else he wanted to go and look at the horses, to study and compare them. He wanted to examine the Mamluks' weapons, too, feel their weight and try out one of the bows with some arrows, but he felt too shy to move far away from Suweida and the doctor.

The villagers had gone now and the fire was blazing brightly. The goat, with a final protesting bleat, had had its throat cut and was being expertly butchered. The chickens, their necks severed, were already plucked. Pots were being set on to boil, and the heavenly smell of frying onions was making Salim's mouth water.

The smell summoned up Mama and the old house in Acre. Homesickness hit him like a blow. He had to bend his head to hide a rush of tears, and wiped a savage fist across his eyes.

One of the Mamluk soldiers passed nearby and noticed him. His beard was still sparse and Salim guessed he was not much older than Ali, eighteen or nineteen perhaps.

'Hey, little brother,' he called out. 'Are you all right?

What's the matter?' He spoke Arabic with a heavy Turkish accent.

Salim scrambled to his feet.

'I'm fine, sir,' he said, desperately hoping his watery eyes hadn't been noticed.

The soldier sauntered up to him.

'What's your name?'

'Salim. Salim Ibn Adil.'

The soldier nodded.

'I'm Ismail. Are you hungry?'

Salim nodded eagerly.

'That's good. Nice food tonight. Fresh meat. Your old man, does he eat with us?'

'Yes.'

Ismail nodded again. His eyes, barely interested, swept Salim from head to foot.

'What happened to your leg? Why's it short? Did you break it?'

Salim's jaw tightened. He hated it when people noticed his leg for the first time. With the boys in Acre it was usually the beginning of taunts and teasing.

'No. A sickness. When I was little.'

'Ah.' Ismail put up a lazy hand, plucked a fig from the tree and bit into it. 'You've never ridden before, have you? I was watching you. Like a sack of old wheat, you were. Bump, bump, bump!'

He laughed. Salim did too. He felt himself relax.

'I've only ridden on old packhorses and donkeys,' he said. 'I – I want to learn to ride properly, like you.'

He'd said the wrong thing. Ismail jerked his chin up scornfully.

'How old are you?'

'Thirteen.'

'You're too old. To ride well, you have to start young.

You'll never learn to ride like a Mamluk now.' He gestured contemptuously towards Dr Musa. 'Look at your boss. He's useless. I bet he never even rode a donkey when he was a kid.'

Salim felt an unexpected wave of loyalty.

'He doesn't need to ride a fast horse usually. He's a good doctor. That's all that matters.'

'Mamluks never need doctors,' Ismail said boastfully. 'Toughest troops in the world, we are.'

He flexed his magnificent shoulders. Salim stared at him enviously.

'Can I – would you show me your weapons?' he said in a rush. 'Your bow and arrows and everything?'

'No.' Ismail was clearly bored. 'They're too heavy for you, anyway. Only a Mamluk could handle them.' He walked away.

Disappointed, Salim watched him go. He was about to sink down again with his back against the tree when a thin, high voice from the village below sounded the call to evening prayer. The soldiers were already making their way down to the well to perform their ritual wash. Shyly, Salim followed them, and when they had returned and spread out their prayer mats, he took his place beside them, kneeling and rising with them.

We're equal, at any rate, before Allah, he told himself comfortingly.

Darkness had fallen by the time the longed-for meal was over. It was the best, Salim thought, that he had ever eaten. The cooking was nowhere near as good as Mama's, but the sharpness of his hunger had made everything taste delicious, and the thrill of sitting round the fire, out on the hillside, at night, with Mamluks, was so great that Salim would have eaten anything with enjoyment.

He could never have known, he would never have guessed, only this morning, when he'd been so angry with his father, and felt so betrayed by Mama, that he would be ending the day like this. Now that his hunger was satisfied, his homesickness had gone. His head was swimming with new sensations. He sniffed up eagerly the smell of the horses and the sweet smoke of the figwood fire. His ears had always been used to the din of the city: the clattering of hooves on stone pavements, the clash of the metal workers' hammers, the shouts and quarrels and laughs from thousands of close-packed people. There were quite different sounds here: men talking quietly in a foreign language, the crackle of the burning twigs, someone singing in the village below, the bleating of a sheep, the soft sighing of the evening breeze in the leaves overhead.

Suddenly he was so tired that he could barely keep his eyes open. The doctor tapped him smartly on the shoulder.

'So I'm the servant now, am I? And you're the master? You plan to sit there all night, enjoying yourself? If we must sleep under the stars, let's at least prepare for the chills of the small hours, like civilized beings. There are blankets in the saddlebag. Lay them out, then come and sleep. And I'm warning you, my boy, that if you snore, the fires of my vengeance will be called down upon your head in a punishment so terrible . . .'

He broke off with a gigantic yawn.

Salim, rising groggily to his feet, smiled at him sleepily. The doctor's threats, he now realized, were empty. He couldn't understand why he'd been so afraid of him a mere twelve hours before.

The camp was astir before the sun had risen over the eastern hills. Salim woke with a start, roused by the muezzin in the village below, who was singing out the dawn call to prayer. Exhausted, he'd slept like the dead, hardly stirring all night, in spite of the strangeness of being out in the open, surrounded by people he didn't know. He lay still for a long minute, wondering where he was, then the whickering sound of a horse blowing down its soft nostrils brought the events of yesterday flooding back.

A heavy dew had fallen in the night, and the blanket he'd wrapped himself in was damp, but his goat-hair cloak, which he'd rolled up to use as a pillow, was dry. He got to his feet, suppressing a groan of pain. Every muscle in his body was stiff and aching from yesterday's ride.

He groped his way sleepily to the well to wash, following the sounds the soldiers made. By the time the prayers were over, the first faint greyness was showing in the sky.

A hollow feeling had been growing in the pit of Salim's stomach as he prayed, and as soon as the prayers were over he went to find Dr Musa. The doctor was standing by Suweida, rubbing her nose and talking softly into her ears.

'After all these years!' Salim heard him murmur. 'To permit a sore like that to burst out on your back! If you give me a kick, my girl, right here and now, I won't blame you. Not at all. Not at all!'

He turned when he heard Salim approach and assumed a scowl of the utmost severity.

'I've been telling her, this child of perdition – not one more attempt to throw off the chest! Not one! Or she'll be sent to the knacker's. Oh, certainly.'

Salim could hardly wait for him to finish speaking.

'Please, *sidi* Musa,' he said, unaware that he was using the affectionate term for an elderly relative, 'do you think the Franks will attack Acre today? And if they do, what if they take it?'

'They will be repulsed!' the doctor thundered. 'Thrown back from the walls! The city will hold them off! Can you doubt it? Sultan Saladin will swoop upon them, like a wolf from the mountains, as soon as he has gathered his army together. He'll send them, bag and baggage, back to their freezing forests. Not a doubt will I permit, do you hear me?

Not a moment of worry! Confidence in victory, that's the way. Now do I have to fetch my own washing water from the well? Is that how it's to be from now on?'

'Sorry, I'm sorry,' Salim said, comforted. He hobbled off to the well as fast as he could.

By the time the sun was over the horizon, the troop had led out their horses, rolled their belongings into neat packs and tied them behind the horses' saddles. To Salim's relief, the medicine chest had been roped on to one of the packhorses, along with the captain's tent and the cooking vessels. The doctor, calling on heaven for pity, had been thrown up into the saddle of the quietest horse the captain could provide, while Salim was thrilled to see that Ismail was bringing up for him the same high-stepping, long-maned mare he'd ridden yesterday.

'So you want to ride like a Mamluk, do you, little brother?' Ismail said, smiling, but his mockery was without a sting. He stood back to let Salim scramble unaided into the saddle, then adjusted the left stirrup so that it fitted his shorter leg more comfortably.

'Just watch us,' he said complacently. 'You might learn something. No more sacks of wheat today, huh?'

Salim didn't answer. In spite of his stiffness, he was already back in his dream of glory. As the troop filed down from the night's campsite, the horses picking their way along the stony path towards the plain below, he was, in his own eyes, a fearsome Mamluk. Instead of the little brown skullcap on his head, he wore a plumed helmet wrapped round with a silken turban, and instead of his old dun-coloured hooded robe, he was clad in a scarlet studded brigandine over a coat of the finest mail. He watched every movement of Ismail, who was riding directly in front of him, noticing carefully how he rose and fell with each movement of the horse, how straight his back was, and how easily he balanced the long lance in his hand.

They stopped, before the sun had reached its full height, by a spring set in a grove of trees beside a broad, flat, dry river bed. They were no more than two miles from the walls of Acre and the tents of the Crusaders.

Salim dismounted, reluctant to be earthbound and on his own feet again. Dr Musa, grumbling noisily, had already gone off to harangue the captain. Salim could make out no more than a few words.

'Outrageous . . . a pretext . . . Jerusalem . . . man of peace . . . be on our way . . .'

Captain Arslan was listening impassively, and answered in a few words. Salim couldn't hear what he said, but he saw Dr Musa turn round, raising his arms to heaven in exasperated resignation. Salim couldn't help smiling. They'd be staying with the Mamluks, then. The adventure would go on.

Food was produced and eaten. The horses were watered and led to rest in the shade. The men sat about quietly, huddled over a complicated game. The doctor, having removed the dressing, looked at Salim's toe, pronounced that it was healing and needed no further treatment, then retired to a quiet spot and lay down to doze.

As the shadows began to lengthen, there was a sudden stir.

'Are we staying here tonight? Are we moving on again?' Salim asked the doctor.

'You think I'm a mind-reader?' the doctor answered crossly. 'If you wish to inform yourself on military movements, enquire of the captain. I'm just a useless old man, without even enough sense to achieve a perfectly simple journey from Acre to Jerusalem without being kidnapped. Taken hostage!'

He was still shaking his head as Salim slipped away.

'Are we going on somewhere else now?' he dared to ask

Ismail, who was saddling up his horse and leading it out from under the trees.

'No, no!' Ismail grinned, showing his strong white teeth. 'It's Mamluk training time. Now you'll see something you won't forget!'

Only six of the soldiers, the younger ones, on foot but leading their horses, had followed Ismail out on to the dry river bed, where there was a broad stretch of smooth dry sand. Captain Arslan, mounted, had ridden after them. He halted his horse in a commanding position above them on the bank and shouted out an order. Salim followed and stood behind him, trying not to be seen as he watched.

One soldier, gripping his lance tightly, walked some way from his horse, then, having stood on tiptoe for a moment, measuring the distance through narrowed eyes, he balanced his lance on his right shoulder, sprinted forwards, planted the tip of the lance into the ground and pole-vaulted himself up into the air, landing smoothly astride the saddle of his horse. He raised the lance in a victory salute, while his horse pranced beneath him, sending the tassels of his bridle flying. A cheer of nervous congratulation went up from the other five soldiers. Salim, stunned by this feat, crept forward till he was at the very edge of the bank, as near as he could get. He saw that Ismail was clutching his lance in nervous hands, biting his lip with anxiety.

The captain shouted again. A second soldier ran forward, but lost his nerve at the last moment and dropped his lance, which fell against the horse's rump, making it bolt up the river bed in fright, its master in pursuit.

Salim watched, his heart in his mouth, as one after another, the soldiers attempted the manoeuvre. The older ones had come out to the bank to judge the young ones' efforts and were chatting among themselves, laughing at the failures and shouting encouragement when any of them succeeded. At last it was Ismail's turn. Salim tensed, willing him to do well, and watched with helpless sympathy as again and again he failed, placing his lance tip wrongly, taking off too soon, or startling the horse so that it moved away at the last moment, while Captain Arslan's shouted instructions grew more impatient.

Salim heard a disapproving cough and turned to see the doctor standing behind him.

'Dangerous folly,' he was muttering. 'Sheer bravado. If the Lord had wished us to fly . . .'

Ismail was trying again. His lance gripped in a ferociously clenched fist, he ran forward and gathered himself for the leap, tilting his lance down to the ground as he neared his horse. But once again he had misjudged the distance. Propelled by the lance, he flew up into the air, but instead of landing on his horse's saddle, he came down with a thump on the animal's rump. The horse reared up, hiding Ismail from Salim's view. Salim's blood ran cold as he heard a terrible scream. The horse trotted away. Salim could see Ismail now. He was lying on the ground, impaled through the shoulder by his lance. Blood was spreading out across the sand in a thick dark pool.

Salim stood still, frozen with horror. A groan broke from the doctor.

'Suicidal! What foolishness!'

Captain Arslan had heard him. He frowned haughtily down at the doctor.

'Folly? You call the arts of manhood folly? It was his job to learn and to succeed. He is a Mamluk. It's your job, old man, to heal him.'

He wheeled his horse and trotted back to the trees, though his hand on the bridle was trembling.

Salim was already running across to where Ismail lay, surrounded by a ring of shocked, silent soldiers. He wormed his way through them and caught his breath at the sight of Ismail's face. It was deathly pale, and his eyes were closed.

He's dying, Salim thought. *He can't live.*

The doctor arrived, out of breath from running.

'Fetch the chest,' he panted to Salim. 'No, wait.' He pointed to a soldier. 'You'll do it faster. You, boy, get me olives.'

Salim stared, unsure if he'd heard correctly.

'Olives?'

'Are you deaf? Olives. And fire. Hot embers on a tray. Don't stand there. Run! A man's life depends on it.'

It seemed to Salim, frantically rushing about the camp under the trees, that he was taking forever to fulfil the doctor's commands. Luckily the servants had already lit a fire and were able to produce a jar of olives quickly from their stores. No more than a few minutes had passed before he was back by the huddled group on the river bed, holding out the olives and the tray of hot embers to the doctor, who was rummaging in the open medicine chest. The entire troop had gathered round, and even the captain, feigning a stoical indifference, was hovering nearby.

'Stand back!' Dr Musa called out irritably. 'Captain Arslan, take everyone away. No – leave two men here. Salim, the olives. Pick out half a dozen of different sizes and put them on the embers. They must be hot. Scalding! Quick!'

With trembling fingers, Salim was fishing olives out of the jar and dropping them on the glowing embers.

The doctor had cut through Ismail's red brigandine, now stained dark with blood. He was arranging on a cloth tongs, swabs and a scalpel. Salim could see that the lance was embedded inches deep just under Ismail's collarbone. It was sticking up vertically, as high as a man.

'Hold him down, boy. If he comes round, he mustn't move. He must be quite still and steady,' the doctor said.

Salim put his arm over Ismail's chest and lay across him, oblivious of the blood staining his own tunic. The doctor grasped the lance, and with one swift movement, wrenched it out and flung it away. The grating sound it made as it slid over Ismail's collarbone made Salim shudder and his stomach heaved.

Dr Musa had dropped to his knees and was looking into the wound. Blood gushed out.

'As I thought. A major vein. The olives. Hold them out.'

Salim sat back and held out the tray. It was so hot that it was burning his fingers, but he ignored the pain. The doctor chose an olive, picked it up with the tongs and thrust it into the wound. It sizzled as it touched the wet blood. He held it in place with his right hand, while with his left he lifted Ismail's limp arm to feel his pulse.

'Is he going to die?' Salim couldn't help asking.

The doctor didn't answer.

'Water!' he said, looking up at last. 'Quick!'

One of the two soldiers was sprinting away before Salim had time to move. He came back seconds later with a brimming flagon in his arms.

'Swabs,' the doctor barked at Salim. 'Wet them. Wash the blood away. I can't see what I'm doing with all this mess.'

Gently, Salim dabbed at Ismail's gore-covered skin, ineffectually at first, then with increasing boldness.

'Good. Enough,' the doctor said at last.

It was clear that the bleeding had stopped. The doctor sighed with satisfaction.

'An old method, tried and trusted,' he said. 'There's a cut artery in there. Leave it, and the patient will quickly bleed to death.'

'Is there magic in olives then?' Salim asked reverently. He was squatting as close to Ismail as he could, watching the doctor's every move.

'Magic? Pah!' scoffed the doctor. With infinite care he had eased the olive up and out of the wound, and was now picking out threads from the torn brigandine caught in the flesh. 'It's a clean thing, an olive, and the oil in it makes it keep its heat. It's the heat that works to seal the blood vessel.'

'Can we move him into the shade now, doctor?' one of the soldiers asked respectfully.

'Move him? No! You want to start the bleeding again? Make a shade over him. Bring something to put under his head. A sheet too, to keep the flies off the wound. He stays here for the next few hours till I can be sure the bleeding has stopped.'

'Will you bandage the wound now?' Salim asked.

'And trap infection inside? No. The humours will have been unbalanced. Black bile may need to come out. In the meantime, we'll wait and see.'

'Are you sure . . . isn't he dead already?' Salim whispered in a quavering voice. 'He's so pale!'

'Look at his chest, boy! It's rising and falling with his breath. A fine young man. Strong. A fool, but brave. If there is no fever, and infection doesn't take hold, he may pull through.'

Salim, anxiously watching Ismail's deathly pale face, thought he saw the eyeballs flicker beneath the heavy lids, and then was sure of it, as a moment later Ismail's eyes fluttered open and a moan escaped his lips.

'*Allahu akbar!*' Salim whispered fervently. 'He's alive!'

The next two days were spent in anxious watching beside the makeshift pallet bed on which Ismail lay, under an awning set up between two trees. Dr Musa showed Salim how to check his pulse and examine his urine.

'And don't think, my boy, that you'll be any kind of expert

soon. Years of study under the finest doctors in Baghdad I went through, and a correct diagnosis is still hard to make.'

He allowed Salim to bathe the wound daily and apply healing poultices. For the rest, he said, a light diet of chicken soup, fresh vegetables and plenty of eggs, milk and sugar water were needed, and the result would be according to the divine will.

'Lucky for you we're not on the march,' Captain Arslan grumbled, but he gave the necessary orders and sent his men out to acquire what was needed from nearby farms.

There was a different feeling among the troop now. Before the accident the men, though polite, had treated Dr Musa with indifference, and had ignored Salim. But the doctor's astonishing skill in saving Ismail's life had impressed them all deeply. They addressed him with awed respect and willingly performed any small service he asked for. Some of this new attitude rubbed off on to Salim too. He was losing his shyness and held his head high as he limped about the camp, fetching things for the doctor, or returning to squat beside Ismail and fan him with a bunch of fig leaves.

'It's not so bad being a doctor after all, then?' Dr Musa asked him shrewdly on the third afternoon, after Ismail, sitting up for the first time, had drunk an entire bowl full of chicken soup and asked for more. 'I don't seem to remember that you were very pleased with the idea at first. Wanted to be a knight, I suppose, and stick lances into other poor young men.'

Salim shook his head, but he felt confused inside. He did still want to be a knight, of course, but the doctor was right. The craft of medicine had power, the power over life and death. It won respect too. He knew in his heart that he would never be a knight, never ride gloriously into battle on a noble warhorse, plumes streaming out from behind his helmet. But he could – he *would* – become a doctor, and one day he'd see in men's eyes the admiration he'd seen in the Mamluks' when Dr Musa had saved Ismail's life.

He was watching with interest as Dr Musa ground together the ingredients to make a salve for Ismail's wound when a soldier, sent out to scout by Captain Arslan, came pounding into the camp on his sweating horse.

'The Franks have attacked Acre!' he panted.

Salim gasped with fright. He barely heard the man go on to say, 'They were beaten off. The city stands firm.' He only knew that all was well by the smiles on the faces around him, and his own face split open in a grin of joy.

'What did I tell you?' Dr Musa said, rubbing his hands. 'The crisis is over. No problem. We can resume our journey to Jerusalem, and—'

'The Franks have retreated?' the captain interrupted, frowning at the messenger.

'No. They're preparing for a siege. And more Frankish ships are arriving all the time.'

'Frankish ships? From where?'

'From further up the coast. From Tyre.'

The captain spat scornfully.

'Not much to fear from them. Saladin, peace be upon him, has already beaten them in battle. They're old enemies. We know them. When Saladin arrives he'll sweep them into the sea. No, it's not them I fear.'

'Then who? Who?' the doctor burst out.

The captain was rubbing his cheek.

'Richard of England, Philip of France and the Emperor of Germany. You must have heard. The Crusaders are assembling fresh armies. They're on their way now, to Palestine, and when they arrive . . .'

'On their way? Assembling armies?' the doctor said impatiently. 'It will take them years to get here!'

'A year. Maybe two,' said the captain. 'But the siege of Acre may well last that long. And when they come—'

'I'll be in Jerusalem, may the Lord's name be praised,' the doctor said fervently.

'No no, doctor.' The captain smiled apologetically. 'You'll be with Saladin's army, as he commanded. We're leaving tomorrow to meet him.'

CHAPTER SIX

T he first two weeks of the great journey to the Holy Land were the hardest Adam had ever known. The thrill of leaving the valley and venturing into lands unknown lasted no more than a day. By the end of a week he was swaying on his feet with exhaustion, the leather of his shoes had worn through, and his feet were sore and bleeding.

He had the fine weather to thank for his problems. The huge Fortis cavalcade, with more than two hundred people and many more horses, would set off every morning just after dawn. It could only move at the pace of the baggage wagons, and as these were heavy and went slowly, and were often held up by tricky streams to ford, or broken wheels, or rough, steep hillsides, it was impossible to cover more than fifteen miles a day.

For Adam, used to walking long distances, fifteen miles would have been nothing, but he was obliged to keep up with Lord Guy, Lord Robert and the ten knights, who trotted ahead on their smart palfreys. With their passion for hunting, the slightest sign of game would have them calling for the dog boy and the dogs, and Adam would have to run after the horses, covering many more miles at a furious pace, returning at last to the monastery or castle where the Crusader band had halted for the night, only to have to spend hours preparing the dogs' food and checking them over for injuries. Whenever he was offered food, he wolfed it down, and as soon as his duties were over he lay down where he happened to be and sank at once into a profound sleep.

Fortunately, when he was nearly at the end of his strength, the weather broke. Instead of scrambling through endless forests, diving in and out of streams and trampling down the crops of scowling villagers in pursuit of a hare or a wild boar, the gentry rode silently under the dripping trees, their horses splashed to their bellies with mud, worrying about rust attacking their suits of chainmail and the weapons in the baggage train.

Adam didn't mind the rain. He was used to being out in all weathers. He was simply relieved that he could now walk with the rest of the convoy, and stop when they did.

Perhaps because he'd been forced to keep up with the mounted nobility, Adam hadn't been absorbed into any of the groups which had formed along the way. The men-at-arms, of course, under Hugo de Pomfret, their sergeant, were trained soldiers and marched together, but the mass of squires, servants, grooms, wagon drivers and general hangers-on had quickly sorted themselves into little 'families', who ate together and slept close to each other at night. Adam hadn't been invited to join any of them.

Until the weather changed he had hardly caught sight of Jennet, but as soon as the rain began he sought her out. She was splashing along cheerfully, holding her skirt up to keep it out of the mud, her dark curls lying flat against her glowing cheeks. She was clearly in the best of spirits, answering the soldiers back when they called out teasingly to her.

'Adam!' she cried, her face lighting up when she saw him. 'Where have you been? I never see you.'

'Running after the dogs in the hunt.' He grinned back at her, relieved to see a friendly smile for once. 'Wished I was a dog myself. I needed two extra legs these past two weeks.'

She looked down at the six dogs who were padding quietly beside him.

'They look tired too.'

'They are, poor beasts. But Jenny, how did you get away? I thought they'd never let you come. There aren't any other women.'

'That's what you think! There are six of us at least. Most of them are old grandmas. They ride in the wagons most of the time. There's Susan – she's come to keep an eye on her husband, and Joan's son ran off to France years ago. She thinks she's going to find him. Fat chance. And—'

'Yes, but how did you get round old Margery?'

'Get round her? I didn't bother. I just hid in a wagon and came.'

'I saw your skirt. I knew it was you. Wasn't there a fuss when they found you?'

'A bit. Father Jerome went mad. He said all the usual – about Crusaders and purity and women being the work of the devil. But Lord Robert spoke up for me. It was him told me to come, anyway. He just said to everyone he needed a washer-woman and told them to lay off. He's a real noble, Lord Robert is. He gets his own way. He looks after me. What are you making that face for, Adam? You said yourself I ought to try and come.'

'Not like this,' he said, trying to look into her face, which she had turned away. 'Not as Lord Robert's . . .'

She tossed her head.

'Much you know about it. I ain't never been so happy in my life. It's only a little bit wrong. Father Jerome himself says we got to obey our lords. I'll confess and be forgiven one day. All our sins will be forgiven anyway, when we reach Jerusalem.'

He looked down, confused.

'But what if you die now, unconfessed, like Ma?'

She turned and scowled at him, the rain running down her face.

'Quite finished, have you, mister dog boy? Do you want to stay friends with me? If so, then shut your gob and keep it shut.'

They walked on in silence for an angry half-hour. Then Jennet gave a sudden scream.

'Adam! There's something moving! In your bag. Something's in there and it's *alive*!'

Adam put his hand into the cloth bag which he carried slung over his shoulder and pulled out a wriggling bundle of sand-coloured fur.

'By the Virgin!' Jennet burst out laughing. 'It scared me stiff! And it's only a puppy!'

'He's a mastiff,' Adam said, relieved that the tension was over. He was gently pulling at the little dog's ears. It turned in his arms and snapped at his fingers with sharp teeth. 'You ought to see his dad. He'd scare off an army. This one's going to be the same. And you know what, Jenny? He's mine. My very own. Master Tappe gave him to me. I've called him Faithful, because that's what he's going to be. Faithful to me.' His voice was gruff with pride.

She looked briefly at the puppy, but something ahead caught her attention.

'There it is. That must be Belfort Castle. It's where we're sleeping tonight. There's only one more day's march after that until we reach the sea.'

Adam's first sight of the sea filled him with sick horror. The largest expanse of water he'd ever seen had been the duck pond in the village at home. The heaving, grey, cold mass of the English Channel, stretching endlessly to the bare horizon, terrified him.

The Fortis Crusaders, already travel-worn, stood silently on the beach, their faces ashen with fear.

'There's giant animals in there, so I've heard,' a man near Adam said. 'You have to keep 'em sweet, sing to 'em and suchlike, or they sucks you down into the deep.'

'Look there! Look!' Adam shouted. Heads swivelled in the direction where he was pointing. A ship had appeared. It was sailing close into the coast, making for the harbour beyond the headland.

'Is that people on it?' someone said disbelievingly. 'Must be mad fools. Must be insane, to go on a thing like that.'

'No madder than what we'll be,' another said. 'How else do you think we're going to cross to France?'

The wind had veered and the ship lurched as the sails filled.

'God help me! I can't! God forgive me!' a young man sobbed. 'I'm going home!'

He was backing away from the sea as if afraid that the waves would curl up the beach and lash out to capture him, and now he turned to run away. The old man next to him caught him by the arm.

'Stop that, Dickon! You took the cross, didn't you? You made a vow. If you drown you'll go straight to Paradise. Break your vow and hell's waiting for you.'

The young man pulled himself free. He didn't run, but stood shivering, moaning to himself.

He took the cross. I took the cross, Adam said to himself, trying to make himself feel again the glory of that ecstatic night at Fortis, but the glow had faded.

Someone further along the beach began to sing 'Wonderful Jerusalem' in a quavering voice. Others picked up the familiar tune and moved closer together for solidarity.

Above the song another voice could be heard, sharp and

persuasive. Adam drew in his breath. It couldn't be, surely – not here, not so far from Fortis?

He could see now that a huddle of people had collected round a tall, thin man with a close cap on his head, who was holding up a bundle of cords with a pierced cockle shell hanging from each one.

'The shell of St James!' Jacques was shouting. 'These charms, blessed by no less a personage than the Bishop of Lincoln himself, will save you, my dear fellow pilgrims, from drowning, from the monsters of the deep and the magic of the mer-people. Oh yes, you, sir, and you, my young friend, even you, old man, you may rest assured of the wonderful, of the *miraculous* strength, of these marvellous objects, which will protect you from all the perils and dangers of the ocean.'

He'd leaped on to a large boulder now. Over the heads of the crowd he had caught sight of Adam. One of his eyelids fluttered down and up again in a wink so menacing that Adam took a step backwards, even though he was standing far away.

People were already pulling their purses out, and a few minutes later, Jacques's hands were empty, his pockets were full and he had disappeared.

Jennet came flying down the beach towards Adam.

'I got you one, Adam, a charm,' she said, flinging the loop of leather cord with its pendant shell round Adam's neck.

He wanted to take the thing off and fling it away, but didn't like to hurt her feelings.

'Why haven't you got one, Jenny? Didn't you get one for yourself?'

'No more money,' she said, looking wistfully after Jacques.

Adam was touched. He took the shell off and hung it round her own neck.

'You have it. You'll need it more than me.'

'Why?'

'I've got Faithful, haven't I? Sea monsters wouldn't dare to tackle him.'

She laughed and bent down to stroke the puppy, who was now busy investigating a dead crab nearby. Faithful bared his teeth and growled, but let her pet him.

It was late June before the Fortis party was able to embark for France. A week passed before the ships could be hired, and then, when the dreaded sea crossing was about to begin, the wind changed and strengthened, throwing mountainous waves against the harbour wall.

In the end, the voyage wasn't as bad as Adam had feared. His eyes had opened wide with amazement when part of the wall of the ship had swung open, and he saw how easily the wagons rolled inside, and how the horses could be stalled as if they were in their stable at home. The ships' timbers were reassuringly solid, and the sailors, whose Cornish language Adam couldn't understand, seemed to fear nothing as they raised the sails, pushed off from the land and pulled on mysterious ropes at the captain's shouted command. He took comfort too from the dogs, who trotted on to the ship with no fear and settled themselves comfortably in the sheltered corner Adam found for them.

Jennet had been travelling in one of the other ships with the nobility, and Adam was shocked to see, when he met her on the French quayside after the two-day voyage, how pale and ill she looked.

'I haven't stopped being sick since I set foot on that thing,' she said, looking back at the ship with loathing. 'I thought I was going to die.'

Travelling through France was easier for Adam than the journey across England had been. There was no hunting now. Lord Guy, Lord Robert and the knights had set off at a fast pace as soon as they'd gone ashore, leaving the sergeant, Hugo de Pomfret, to lead the Fortis expedition.

'They've gone to meet King Richard,' Jennet said, her voice reverent at the thought of the King. 'He's here already. Lord Guy's scared we'll miss him.'

She'd lost her vitality since Lord Robert had gone. The sea sickness seemed to have lingered. She complained all the time of a queasy stomach, and looked pale and tense. As before, they were covering fifteen miles a day, and sometimes, as the afternoon wore on, Adam had to help her along, carrying her bag and letting her lean on his arm.

Faithful was growing day by day. His pale coat was no longer so soft, but was increasingly rough to the touch, and the pouchy darker skin around his face was already hanging in loose folds round his massive jaws. He was able to walk with the other dogs now and no longer needed to be carried. He was as good as his name too, trotting always at Adam's heels, baring his teeth at anyone who came too close.

He had increased Adam's popularity. The English travellers, nervous of being in a strange country, where even the houses looked different, told each other fearsome stories of robbers who would murder stragglers for the few groats in their pockets, and companies of bandits who would fall on whole encampments at night. Adam was never without an invitation now to bed down with a group of others and share the contents of their pot. Everyone wanted to have the dogs nearby, especially the mastiff, to bark if danger threatened and scare off attackers.

To his surprise, Adam found that he was enjoying himself. The atmosphere was cheerful, even carnival-like. The weather was perfect, balmy but not too hot, the day's march was always easy, along straight roads, and best of all the absence of Lord Guy and the knights had made everyone almost light-headed with a sense of freedom. Few of the travellers had ever in their lives had a rest from the hard toil of serfdom, and no one had been far from home before. They told each other long, rambling stories, sang endless songs, and basked in self-congratulation at their courage and self-sacrifice in going to wrest the True Cross from infidel hands and take back for Christ the city of Jerusalem. Only the thought of the battles to come, and the evil powers of their devilish foes, could dampen their spirits. At night, they would sit around their fires, scaring each other with tales of how fire sparked out from the eyes of Saracens, and how they had tails under their tunics.

They'd been on the march through France for three weeks when they came at last within sight of Vezelay, the city set on a hill where the kings of Britain and France had met to assemble their vast armies. For days past the Fortis men had been passing through deserted villages, bare fields and trees stripped of fruit. No cattle grazed on the common lands, no chickens pecked round cottage doors and the folds were empty of bleating sheep.

'The country's sucked dry,' Adam heard Hugo de Pomfret complain to one of his men. 'A hundred thousand people living off the land, and for months past – it's impossible. The villagers hereabouts have hidden everything left to them, if they have anything left, that is.'

It was clear, when they halted before the gates of Vezelay, that the vast armies had already gone. The wreckage of a huge camp lay on the plain below the towering walls. The earth was beaten flat and hard by thousands of feet and hooves; there were circles of ashes from cooking fires, and here and there, among the heaps of stinking filth, were smashed wagon wheels, discarded worn-out shoes and broken earthenware jars. Their stomachs rumbling, the Fortis expedition looked round in dismay. It had been days since they'd been able to buy food from the villages they had passed, and their own supplies were running low.

They had been seen. The black hammers that decorated their shields and fluttered from their banners had been recognized by a Fortis knight, who came trotting down through the city gate on his palfrey to meet them on the plain below.

'You'll camp here tonight,' he shouted. 'Make shift as best you can. The kings have gone on to the south. We follow them tomorrow.'

The Fortis Crusaders, crawling slowly like a giant caterpillar down the high roads of France, had marched through Lyons and, following the course of the river Rhône, were now only a few days away from the great Mediterranean port of Marseilles.

The fields they'd passed through were already harvested, and grapes hung in heavy clusters in the vineyards. The summer was drawing to an end, but the heat was still too fierce for Englishmen. They marched doggedly on through the hottest hours of the day, not resting till the sun was lower, as the local travellers did. They left their heads bare too, so that the skin peeled off their sunburned noses, and the less hardy among them even collapsed with heatstroke.

Adam noticed with wonder how, little by little, everything had changed as they'd moved further south. The houses were built in a different way. There were richly decorated, big churches, made of fine carved stone, everywhere. The people here were smaller and darker-skinned, and the food they ate had a strange taste and smell. He noticed something else too. Jacques was keeping up with the Crusader band. He didn't march with them every day, but appeared from time to time, flitting in and out of the convoy like an evil spirit, charming money out of purses with his trinkets, medicines and false remedies.

It wasn't until they were two days' march away from Marseilles that the truth finally dawned on Adam.

'You're going to have a baby, Jenny, aren't you?' he said, voicing his thought out loud, then flushing with embarrassment.

They'd been walking silently together up a steep hill and had paused at the top to catch their breath.

'Yes,' she answered simply, and turned her head away, but he saw her shoulders shake and guessed she was crying.

He didn't know what to do.

'Lord Robert will look after you,' he said awkwardly, after a pause. 'You'll be all right.'

She said nothing and didn't turn round. He took her arm and shook it.

'You've told him, haven't you?'

'Yes.'

'What did he say?'

She spun round, and he noticed for the first time how haggard she'd become. Her face had lost its rosy freshness. It was thinner, and her skin was pale under her sunburn. Even her curls, once so bouncy, lay lank and heavy now over her shoulders.

'You wouldn't understand,' she said flatly.

'I would! Go on. Tell me.'

'Well, then. He says it ain't his. He says I'm a lying slut. He won't let me come near him no more.'

Adam stared at her, appalled.

'I don't think he wanted to turn me off,' she went on miserably. 'It was Father Jerome. He came sliding into the tent, in that creepy way he has, while I was telling Lord Robert. Father Jerome's the only person in the world apart from Lord Guy that Lord Robert's scared of. If it hadn't been for Father Jerome, he'd have done all right by me, I know he would.'

Adam bunched his fists.

'He wouldn't! I could kill him!'

Jennet ignored him.

'It was my fault too. I've got to admit. And he *would* have looked after me, but he was scared, like I said, and he just sort of burst out that he hardly knew who I was, I was only the washerwoman and he didn't know what I was talking about and I was taking liberties. Father Jerome looked at me as if I was mad or something, then he made Lord Robert swear by Our Lady that he'd never laid a finger on me.'

'He's perjured himself then. He'll burn for that,' Adam said savagely.

'Then Father Jerome told me I was a wicked woman, and I ought to be whipped at the cart's tail and thrown off the Crusade to fend for myself, because I was corrupting the holy mission, and – and polluting everyone.'

She was crying properly now. Adam looked away, helpless and embarrassed, not knowing how to comfort her.

'They didn't whip you, though, did they, Jenny?' he said at last. 'And they didn't turn you off. You're still here.'

'Only because Lord Guy came into the tent where we were and heard. He didn't believe Lord Robert, I know, because he's seen us together before. He slashed him across the face with his mailed fist and called him a whole lot of things. And then he said something about atoning for past sins, and I wasn't to be whipped or cast off, but I was to keep myself to myself, out of the way of everyone, and live decently from now on. Then he gave me a bit of money and sent me away, but when I was outside the tent I heard him yelling at Lord Robert, and Father Jerome going on in that horrible cold way he does.'

He couldn't think of anything to say.

'Don't,' she said, suddenly fierce. 'Don't say you warned me. I know you did. Come on. We'd better get walking again if we don't want to be right at the back with the wagons.'

'I wasn't going to say I warned you.' He leaned down to free Mirre's lead, which was entangled with one of the brachet hounds', and when he stood upright again his face was set. 'I was only going to tell you I'd – I'd look after you. You can count on me for anything.'

She laughed bitterly.

'Look after me? You? Grow up, Adam.'

He bit his lip and flushed.

'I would. I'd go with you if you ran away.'

She touched his arm.

'Thanks all the same but I wouldn't let you. They'd catch you and cut your nose off for being a runaway serf. Anyway, you've got to go to Jerusalem to fight for Christ and Our Lady. You took the cross, didn't you? You made a vow. And you've got to save your ma.'

At four o'clock that afternoon, the long snake of a convoy halted, and the camp was set up as usual. The round, high-roofed tents of the lords and knights were pitched in a circle, with the de Martel banners fluttering from their crests. The animals, from the pack-donkeys and wagon-mules to the palfreys and huge cavalry chargers, were led away to be watered and groomed, the squires busied themselves around their knights, parties were sent out to forage for wood and fodder, men-at-arms were picketed on guard duty, fires were lit, sore feet inspected and supplies of food brought out.

Adam, busy removing a thorn from Ostine's front paw, looked up to see Lord Guy standing in front of him. He scrambled to his feet and stood with his head respectfully bowed.

'Lame? Have you let Ostine go lame?' Lord Guy said testily, bending down to pull at the greyhound's ears.

Adam cleared his throat nervously.

'No, my lord. It's just a small thorn. I've got it out now.'

Behind Lord Guy he could see Lord Robert and a couple of knights who were unwillingly following the baron on his evening tour of inspection.

'What's this?' Lord Guy was frowning down at Faithful, who, in spite of Adam's restraining hand, was growling, his hackles raised.

'My mastiff, my lord. Master Tappe gave him to me.'

Lord Robert had muscled his way forward.

'*Your* mastiff? Since when did a serf own his master's dog? What right did Tappe have to make free with it?'

Lord Guy, ignoring him, was staring down at Faithful.

'By Powerful, I suppose. A good guard dog. Tappe was right to send him with you. Teach him to know my scent.' He took a scarf off his neck and threw it at Adam. 'I may need him later.'

He walked on, carving a majestic path between his cringing serfs.

Adam, seething, watched them go. Jennet was by one of the wagons, helping old Joan lift out a heavy bag of flour. He saw Lord Robert leer at her and say something to the knight next to him. The other man laughed uneasily. His smile looked forced, and the look he gave Lord Robert was full of disdain.

They know what he's like. They don't think much of him either, Adam thought with satisfaction.

As the sun was setting on the following day, the Fortis convoy came at last within sight of Marseilles. Beyond it, hanging like a blue curtain from the sky, the Mediterranean sea stretched into infinity. Its waters, unlike the cold grey of the English Channel, were a deep, sparkling blue.

It wasn't Marseilles, however, which made Adam gasp, but the vast camp outside the city walls. Thousands of tents, tens of thousands of men and hundreds of thousands of horses were crammed on to a few acres of land. Even from this distance it was possible to pick out the grand, colourful pavilions of the Kings of France and England, surrounded by small tented towns containing their vassals, soldiers and servants.

The sight of so many strangers in one place made the Fortis people nervous. They bunched closer together as they streamed down the road towards the camp.

The stench, a foul miasma of human and animal waste, hit Adam's nostrils when the camp was still half a mile away. The noise came next, an overwhelming cacophony of shouts, barking dogs, the clash of metal, smiths' hammers and the braying of donkeys.

'Stick by me, Jenny,' he said, taking a firmer grip on the dogs' leads. 'It'll be easy to get lost. People will take advantage if they don't know who you are.'

The nobles on their horses halted when they were still some way from the camp, and there was a flurry of activity as the knights ordered their equipment to be dragged out from the wagons. They were clearly determined to look their best, fastening on their coats of mail and covering them with their white surcoats emblazoned with crosses. Helmets were donned, their crests flowing in the breeze. Even the horses were being smartened up. Gaudy caparisons were thrown over them and plumes were attached to their heads. The de Martel banner floated from the point of every knight's lance, so that, held upright, they made a little forest of bright flags. The hundred or so foot soldiers, barked at by their sergeant-at-arms, were rummaging in their packs for showy buckles and buffing up their round-rimmed basin-like helmets with their sleeves.

'Got to show 'em, haven't we?' Adam heard one of the grooms say, as he rubbed at the flank of Vigor, Lord Guy's gigantic warhorse, to make his black coat shine. 'De Martel's as good as any of 'em. Better.'

Lord Guy had sent a knight ahead and he now came trotting back with a middle-aged official, who was dressed in a gown and cloth headdress. A younger civilian rode at his side.

Adam had let the dogs loose to run about while the column had halted. They'd dashed off towards Lord Guy, hoping for the titbits he often gave them, and he was bending down to pet Mirre when the official arrived. Adam, hovering nearby to take control of the dogs again, heard the official say, 'The de Martel contingent, I presume? Good journey? Excellent. His grace the King is expecting you.'

Lord Guy stepped forward.

'Guy de Martel at your service,' he said, bowing with a pompous flourish and making his chainmail rattle.

'William Scriveson,' the official said, running a harassed eye over the de Martel people.

'We come at the King's command,' Lord Guy was beginning, standing with his feet apart, clearly about to embark on a formal speech. 'Our finest knights, bowmen and infantry have answered the call, ready to—'

'Yes, yes,' William Scriveson said hastily. 'How many in your group?'

'Ten knights,' Lord Guy said, and Adam could see that he was put out at being interrupted. 'Twenty experienced bowmen, eighty or so men-at-arms, and others who have pledged to fight and die for—'

'The total number, please. A round figure will do.'

'Two hundred, more or less,' Lord Guy said huffily. 'You are very hasty, sir.'

William Scriveson waved an apologetic hand.

'Forgive me, Lord – Guy, is it? The business of organizing our forces – there's a crisis to be resolved ten times a day. The King has been out of the camp today and is expected back at any moment. I must be at his pavilion when he arrives.' He turned to the younger man behind him. 'Two hundred from

Martel of Fortis, including ten knights. You have that down, Richard?'

The younger man had pulled an inkhorn and quill from his satchel and was writing, resting the parchment on the pommel of his saddle.

'Yes, Master William,' he said.

'Richard will show you where the English camp is,' Scriveson went on. 'It's appallingly crowded, I warn you. There are several thousands of us already and more arriving every day. You'll have to find places for yourselves as best you can. The Germans and Flemings have hogged the best spots, and as for the Burgundians . . .' He broke off as Mirre, approaching his horse, took exception to the flicking of its tail and began to bark. Adam ran forward, leashed Mirre and began to round up Ostine and the lymers, thankful that he had left Faithful tied to a wagon.

'Hounds, Lord Guy?' Master Scriveson was saying disapprovingly. 'Dogs are forbidden, or didn't you know? The King and the bishops are very firm on the point. We're engaged on a holy mission, not a glorified hunting expedition.'

Lord Guy had flushed a deep red at the schoolmasterly tone of the other man's voice.

'I hunt where I choose,' he said grandly. 'My dogs travel with me.'

'Oh, take it up with the King, if you must,' Master Scriveson said wearily. 'Show them the way to the English camp, Richard. I must be off at once.' As he turned his horse, Adam heard him say, 'These rural barons from God knows where – very touchy. Try to keep him sweet.'

Adam had just managed to leash the last lymer when a stinging whiplash across his face sent him reeling backwards, half stunned.

'Dolt! Scum!' Lord Guy was shouting. 'Showing me up before the King's marshal! Did I tell you to let the dogs loose?'

Another cracking blow from the whip toppled Adam to his knees. Keep them close from now on, do you hear? Now get out of my sight. Out of the way! Why am I surrounded by such idiots?'

The welts the whip had made on Adam's face were showing up as scarlet slashes when he went back to the wagons to fetch Faithful, who jumped up at him with ecstatic barks of welcome. He had hoped for sympathy from Jennet, but she was too busy helping Joan climb into a wagon that was already lumbering off.

As the de Martel convoy entered the great Crusader camp, Adam forgot the pain of the whip marks on his face and looked round eagerly, astonished by the sights and sounds.

The tents, wagons, tethered horses and sheer mass of people were so tightly packed that it was hard to force a way through them. Everyone seemed to be shouting; there was loud laughter and louder arguments. Metal clattered, canvas flapped in the breeze and somewhere in the distance a drum was beating.

The Fortis people could only pass in single file, taking care not to trip up on the guy ropes of the thousands of tents, and several times Adam was afraid he'd lose them and be wandering forever in this vast crowd, trying to find them again. Then he would catch sight of the black hammer on its white background fluttering from the upright lances of the knights leading the way. It stood out boldly from the mass of other bright escutcheons that were painted on shields, floated from tents and were held aloft on a forest of lances.

There was a commotion nearby and a group of knights in foreign-looking gear cut across the convoy at a reckless gallop, beating people out of their way with the flats of their swords.

'Damned Frisians!' he heard a foot soldier mutter angrily. 'Treating us like riff-raff.'

'Make way! Make way!' someone shouted, pushing Adam

aside. Everyone stood by respectfully as a troop of knights all dressed in white surcoats with red crosses emblazoned on them trotted by.

'Who do they think they are?' the same foot soldier called out. 'Going round like they own the place!'

'Shut up, fool,' the man beside him said. 'Don't you know anything? They're the Knights Templar. They're the best.'

Adam could see, as they progressed, that this was not one camp, but many. There were different groups, strange languages, odd kinds of armour and weapons.

'Germans here,' someone would say, as they passed through a camp of blond giants. A little later on it was Flemings, then Burgundians. All had tents for their nobles and knights, all had their long lines of warhorses and palfreys, packmules and donkeys, and all had their poor hangers-on, tattered people with thin faces, but bright crosses worn proudly on their threadbare cloaks.

They'd just passed a makeshift tented church, where priests were intoning a mass within billowing clouds of incense, when Adam heard English voices around him. A space opened up, and one of the knights rode back down the Fortis lines.

'We make our base here!' he called out. 'Bring up the wagons. Captain, keep your men close in the camp. There's to be no fighting with any other contingent. The grooms will be shown where to water the horses.'

He had barely finished speaking when a drum sounded not far away and a trumpet blared. Everyone turned as a glittering procession of tall men on high-stepping horses, whose glossy backs were covered with scarlet and gold caparisons, rode out from the crowds into the open.

'Richard! It's the King! The Lionheart!' Adam heard the people around him say. Everyone had moved back to let the King's party pass, and all those on foot fell to their knees.

Lord Guy swept off his helmet and spurred his horse forwards to intercept the leading horse.

'Your grace! My lord!' he began, but the rider turned indifferent eyes away from him and rode on.

'Later, Fortis, later,' one of the cavalcade called back to him. 'The King's grace is not to be interrupted. He'll receive you tonight in his pavilion. Bring your knights.'

As soon as the King's procession had clattered on, everyone rose to their feet.

'Did you see him? That was him, wasn't it? I didn't know he was so tall. And did you see his horse?' they were all eagerly telling each other.

Adam had been too concerned to keep the dogs out of sight to look closely at the King, but for a moment the calculating blue eyes in the fair handsome face had swept over him, and he had sensed something he had never experienced before, a radiant power, a kind of glory that frightened as much as impressed him.

CHAPTER SEVEN

Salim glowed with pride as he trotted with the Mamluk troop towards the camp of Sultan Saladin. It was a bright morning and the sun, rising behind Saladin's position on the eastern hills, set the white walls of Acre shining against the blue of the sea beyond. In the plain below it was easy now to pick out the details of the Crusader army. It ringed the city on the landward side in a half-moon of tents, wagons, milling horses and men.

'There aren't very many of them,' Salim said cheerfully to Ismail, who was being carried on a litter between two horses.

Ismail didn't answer. It was only two weeks since his accident with the lance. His eyes were shut and his face pale with pain, but Dr Musa, bumping uncomfortably along on his mare on the far side of the litter, had heard.

'The sea, boy. Where are your eyes? Look at the sea!'

Salim's heart sank as he followed Dr Musa's pointing finger and saw yet another fleet of ships bending into the breeze, approaching the beach to the north of the city where clusters of men were waiting.

'Reinforcements,' the doctor said, shaking his head. 'God forsake them! They're sowing the wind and shall reap the whirlwind. Where's your water bottle? Give the poor patient a drink, or do you want him to die of thirst? Don't choke him! A little at a time now, that's the way.'

Salim bent across his saddle at a perilous angle and dribbled a little water from his bottle into Ismail's mouth. As he straightened up, the Mamluk troop reached the top of a low rise and he gasped at the sight of Saladin's camp stretching ahead.

It seemed at first sight to go on forever. Round tents with pitched roofs were strung like beads along the brow of the hill and between them thronged a mass of people, horses, mules, camels and oxen, tripping over wagons, boxes, bales and sacks of provisions. Bright banners fluttered from the tent poles.

'Ha! Turcomans here, I see,' Dr Musa said, as if to himself. 'Kurds and Turks, of course. Some Syrians – and Bedouin! Any man who can hold the reins of such a mob . . .'

Salim stopped listening. He'd seen the great marquee of Saladin in the centre of the line which was ringed by soldiers.

Captain Arslan, slowing his horse to a steady walk, was advancing through the camp, his men following him. Guards stopped him as he approached the Sultan's enclosure. He dismounted, exchanged a few words with them in rapid Turkish, then they parted to let him through. One or two of the men tried to follow him.

'Not you!' the guards said roughly.

Dr Musa, with a grunt of relief, had scrambled down off his horse and was laying his hand on Ismail's forehead. Salim dismounted too.

'Can I get something for him, *ustadh*?'

'Some water only for now. Then fetch Suweida and make sure she's—'

He was cut short by a high voice nearby singing out the call to prayer. The camp stilled at once. Prayer mats were unrolled on the rocky ground and set down to face south towards Mecca.

Captain Arslan returned to his troop soon after prayers were over. He looked unusually excited.

'You're wanted, doctor,' he said. 'I've seen Saladin himself, peace be upon him. I told him of your olive trick.'

'My what?' The doctor spluttered.

The captain tapped him on the arm by way of an apology.

'He wants to see you now. In his tent!'

For once the doctor was struck speechless.

'Yes!' Captain Arslan was smiling. 'This is your chance. It's your reward for your goodness to my man. You'll be a rich man!'

'Riches? Pah!' said the doctor, recovering. 'Boy! Make yourself presentable. Clean hands and a pure heart. Wash.'

'Excuse me, *sidi* Musa, but your turban is knocked a bit sideways,' Salim said, drying his hands on his tunic.

'If Sultan Saladin cares one jot about crooked headdresses he's not the man I take him for,' the doctor said testily, but he pushed his turban back in place.

Salim's heart thumped as he followed the doctor past the guards and approached the great pavilion. The sides of it were open, and the interior was so shady that for a moment he could see nothing as his eyes adjusted from the brightness outside.

The tent was comfortably furnished with cushions and rugs while overhead a saffron silk canopy cast a dim yellow glow. A black-robed cleric sat with a Koran open on a little stand, reading from it in a quiet monotone. A bare-footed servant carrying a copper tray moved aside and Salim saw a short, middle-aged man sitting cross-legged against a scarlet-and-gold striped cushion. He knew at once that it was Saladin. He dropped his eyes, not daring to look.

'You are the doctor?' Saladin's voice was husky and he spoke Arabic with a Kurdish accent.

'Yes, my lord,' Dr Musa said calmly.

'Sit down. Sit here beside me.'

Saladin waved a hospitable hand. The doctor obediently gathered in his robe and lowered himself to the floor. As he did so, Saladin caught sight of Salim.

'Your son?'

'No, my lord. My apprentice.'

'A Jew?'

'He is Muslim.'

Salim dared to raise his eyes, and in the seconds before he lowered them again the Sultan's hawk-like face, long greying beard and deep-set piercing eyes were printed on his memory.

'Wait over there, boy,' Saladin said, waving his hand again.

For the next ten minutes Salim watched awestruck as messengers came and went, mailed knights hovered respectfully and chieftains from Asia waited like servants for a word of command from Sultan Saladin. He quivered with pride at the sight of the doctor – *his* doctor – sitting like an equal on a cushion beside the Sultan, holding his wrist as he took his pulse, while Saladin talked confidentially into his ear, pointing now to his stomach and now to his chest.

At last Dr Musa struggled to his feet and beckoned Salim.

'I'll send my boy to you with a draught, my lord. If God wills it will relieve the symptoms.'

Saladin smiled.

'I hope you're right, doctor. But I fear I'll never be at ease again until the day we send these infidel barbarians back to the lands of snow and ice where they belong.'

'May the Lord bring that day soon,' Dr Musa said fervently.

'Extraordinary people, the Franks,' Saladin said, as if to himself. 'Superstitious as children, believing all kinds of foolish magic and fairytales, unwashed, drunken, uneducated – terrible manners! – but their faith! Their courage! To risk all, to travel across the sea, and fight like lions for their religion! You have to admire them after all.'

Salim was shocked.

How could anyone admire the Franks? He thought. *They're wicked and hateful. All of them.*

A servant led Salim and Dr Musa back out into the bright sunshine.

'A tent's being prepared for you,' he said respectfully. 'By our lord's command. Over there, under the tree, close to the Sultan, peace be upon him. I'll send a man for your belongings.' He hesitated, then put his head on one side to look round into the doctor's face. 'Doctor, can I ask you something? My piles – they're agony! You don't have anything you could give me?'

Dr Musa cast his eyes up.

'Here it begins,' he said despairingly. 'Oh Jerusalem, Jerusalem! When will I see you and my Leah again?'

'I'm sorry, sir,' the servant said humbly. 'I didn't mean . . . Don't tell Lord Saladin that I was so presumptuous . . .'

'No, no, my good fellow,' Dr Musa said hastily. 'Your piles, of course I can help you. Diet first. A correct diet – that's the root of all good health. And something to soothe the – ah – the area. Come to me later this afternoon. First let an old man rest and wash and pray.'

'Yes, of course,' the servant said eagerly. 'I'll bring water. And for prayer – there are other Jews in the camp. Did you know? They pray together in the morning and evening. They have their own cook too.'

Dr Musa's round cheeks creased as he smiled.

'Other Jews? God be praised! Salim, go and find the medicine chest and that mule of perdition. And tell them to look after Ismail. He's not to get up yet. I'll visit him later. Why do

I bother, when all's said and done? As soon as I've patched him up I've no doubt he'll try to kill himself again.'

Salim squared his shoulders and hurried away, proud of the doctor's confidence. The Mamluk troop had moved some way off and he had to pick his way carefully through the crowd. Strange languages were being spoken all around him, and there were devices painted on shields and stitched to banners that he'd never seen before.

They've all come, he thought admiringly. *Everyone's answered the call of Saladin.*

He stood back to let a couple of laden camels pass, and as he did so a voice speaking in Arabic came disastrously loud and clear out of the din around.

'Those poor devils in Acre,' the man was saying. 'Thank God my family's not there. I counted five more Frankish ships landing on the beach this morning and there are more arriving every day. This won't be over tomorrow, I tell you. Months, this siege is going to last. The Franks will starve the city out. It's the kids I feel sorry for. They always die first.'

Zahra! thought Salim.

In his imagination he saw his little sister growing pale and thin, not grizzling like a spoilt baby but crying real tears of pain and hunger. He could see Mama, Baba and Ali too, their eyes sinking into their skulls, their hands becoming claw-like, the flesh withering on their arms and legs, till they looked like the beggars who scavenged for food around the edges of the city.

I've got to do something, Salim told himself. *I've got to get them out of Acre. Why didn't Baba leave when he had the chance? Maybe he did. Maybe they're out already. I've got to find out. I must!*

He hobbled on, scarcely looking where he was going.

He was nearly sent flying by a hearty clap on the shoulder.

'Hey, little brother,' said a cheerful voice. 'Where do you

think you're going, walking right past us? Forgotten your old friends already, have you? Did you see the Lord Saladin? What does he look like?'

He'd reached the Mamluk troop's quarter. Other soldiers crowded round him.

'Are you coming back to us again?' one asked.

Salim, forgetting his troubles, shook his head proudly.

'No. The doctor's been advising the Sultan on his health. We're to stay close to him.'

'*Wallahi!* Our own doctor! He's a great man, little brother. You will be too one day.'

One of them led Suweida up to him. The old black mule, with her rough coat and simple leather tack, looked so humble after the magnificence of Kestan, the chestnut thoroughbred that Salim had so loved riding, that he felt ashamed of her. One of the soldiers saw him look longingly back towards the tethered horses.

'You ride well,' he said encouragingly. 'You're a quick learner, anyway. You'll never be a Mamluk, exactly, but you're better than most Arab boys. Come and see us again soon. When we've killed all the Franks and looted all their stuff, we'll have a feast. A couple of roasted sheep, rice with almonds, the best fruit – what do you think of that, eh?'

Another had brought up the medicine chest. Salim tied it on Suweida's back with care, then, with the men's good wishes in his ears, he led the mule away through the camp towards his new home beside the great tent of Saladin.

Salim lay awake that night, staring up into the conical roof of the tent. The doctor lay on a mat nearby. His whistling snores were so like Baba's that tears pricked Salim's eyes.

They'll have got out of Acre, all right. They must have done, he told himself. *Baba's ship probably came in the day we left. They'll have packed up and gone at once. They'll be in Damascus by now, with Aunt Aliyah.*

He almost smiled as he imagined his mother's frantic packing, her shouts to Selma the servant girl, the delving into chests, then Ali's grumbles as she made him carry bundles out into the courtyard.

Ali! He won't have gone. He'll have stayed to fight, he thought, half enviously.

If only he could be sure! If only he could find out where his family really was!

The camp outside was quiet. Sentries posted round Saladin's enclosure coughed from time to time, and Salim could hear the clink of weapons as they patrolled. Further away, voices were raised in argument, and a goat bleated in startled protest. Just outside the tent a stone rattled, dislodged by a mouse, perhaps, and in the tree above an owl's claws scratched against the branch. Otherwise, the great camp of Saladin was quiet.

I could creep down to the city, Salim thought. *I could go round by the sea and sneak past the Frankish army. I'd find a way in, I know I would, if I could just get up to the walls.*

He imagined everything: slipping out of Saladin's camp past the sentries, borrowing Kestan from the Mamluk troop, picking his way down the hill, then galloping across the plain to the sea. Under his cloak, which he'd wrapped round himself, his fists were clenched.

I'd be caught for horse-stealing. And I'd never get that far on foot. Even if I did, the beaches are all covered with Frankish boats. There are hundreds of infidels there.

But what if he didn't go round the Frankish army, and instead tried to worm his way through it? What if he crept up to the enemy camp in the middle of the night and darted from behind one tent to the next, sliding silently through it till he came to the walls of Acre? He'd pretend to be a Frankish boy if someone accosted him.

He rehearsed phrases from the half-remembered language in his head.

What do you want, you little bleeder? What are you doing here?

I'm – I'm John, he'd say, thinking of one of the boys he'd once played with. But he knew he wouldn't be able to keep it up for long.

My clothes are all wrong, anyway, he told himself. *They'd think I was a spy. They'd stone me.*

It was a relief to accept that the whole idea was crazy. He yawned, turned over, and went to sleep.

The next morning he had fetched milk for the doctor's breakfast and was crouching over a fire, boiling water, when he became aware of a knot of men silently watching him. He looked back at them warily, afraid he was doing something wrong. One man, a Kurd by the look of him, came up to him, and Salim saw with surprise how nervously he was fingering the wooden scabbard of his sword.

'Are you the doctor's boy?' he asked.

Salim nodded.

'Will he see us? Me and my friends – we all want to consult him.'

He fumbled inside his gown, brought out a coin and pressed it into Salim's hand.

Salim heard a familiar grunt and shot up to his feet. Dr Musa was standing behind him. Salim read the look in his eye, and put the coin back into the Kurd's outstretched hand.

'Bribe my servant, will you?' the doctor said, his voice rumbling with menace. 'No need for that. Come and see me in my tent after noonday prayers.'

Salim watched the men file away.

'Pennies from poor soldiers, that's no way to get rich,' the doctor said reprovingly. 'It's as I thought it would be. We'll have every blister and stomach twinge standing outside the tent by this afternoon. Are you ready for work, boy? You'd better be. You know what I think of laziness? It's to be punished! Mercilessly! There's a shocking lot to do. My poor medicine chest wasn't kitted out to service an army. It'll be emptied in a day. Replenishment! Fresh supplies! Thanks be to God, his marvellous creation bountifully supplies. Heads of mice.'

Salim, whose mind had wandered, looked up, startled.

'Mice, *sidi* Musa?'

'You heard me. Heads of mice, kneaded in honey. Extraordinary properties. And herbs! I shall need everything! Chicory! Poppy! Henbane! Deadly nightshade! Oh where, where is Sayed, my old pharmacist?'

'In Acre, *ustadh*?' Salim ventured.

'Of course he's in Acre! At least, I hope he's fled by now. The point is that he's not here, and neither is his storeroom. We must do what we can. You'll go out into the highways and byways and bring back the fruits thereof.'

'Fruits?' Salim was becoming more puzzled by the minute. 'You mean figs?'

'Figs? Did I say figs? Fresh fruit is an abomination to the digestion. No, you'll seek out plants and bring them to me. You'll start now, on the slopes behind the camp. Not a word of argument! Chicory first. You know a chicory plant?'

'I – I don't think so.'

The doctor rolled his eyes.

'Belladonna? Hemlock?'

Salim shook his head.

'Asphodel? Thistle? Sage?'

Salim said nothing.

'Ignorance! Well, we must start somewhere. You will go out now and collect one of every kind of plant you find. I'll teach you what they are, and what I want you to look for. Off!

Now! What are you waiting for?' Salim had already hobbled away. 'And mice!' the doctor's voice floated after him. 'Bring me mice!'

Salim, brought up in the narrow, crowded streets of Acre, had never roamed about on the rocky hillsides above the city. At first he stumbled around aimlessly, not knowing what to do. He'd never really looked at plants before. He'd never noticed that some were small, some large, some bushy, some spiky, some grey-green, some fleshy and some brittle. He began to pull them up and, half an hour later, pleased with himself, hobbled back to the doctor with his haul.

Dr Musa scowled when he saw the roots dangling from the bundle.

'You want to turn the hillside into a desert? Is that it? Did I say uproot? Pluck! Pick! Leave the plant in place to grow again! Now what have we here?' Quickly he sorted through the wilting leaves. 'This one, yes. And this. The others are useless. More! I need more! Go further. Look harder! Don't neglect the little things that creep upon the ground.'

Salim hurried off again. He had picked a dozen new kinds of leaves when he saw, out of the corner of his eye, a mouse whisk itself under a stone. He lunged for it, dropping his load. The mouse shot out from its hiding place and with incredible speed raced up a short incline from the dip where Salim had been looking for plants and disappeared over the top. Salim stumbled after it, but when he came to the top he forgot the mouse and his mouth dropped open in surprise.

He'd come further than he'd thought and was looking right down into the Crusader camp. It ringed the city in a great horseshoe, both ends of which ran right down to the sea. All along the outer rim, men were at work digging a huge trench and throwing the earth from it up on to a high bank. Archers were stationed along the length of the trench, arrows ready on the strings of their bows, watching out for a Saracen attack.

Fascinated and afraid, Salim crawled further forward. The nearest point of the earthwork was a good half-mile away, but the sun was behind him and he could see clearly in the bright morning air. Behind the bank the camp was much the same as Saladin's. Tents sprouted everywhere, some small and simple, others large and magnificent. Several had crosses raised above them.

Churches, Salim thought.

Horses were tethered in lines. Banners with different devices fluttered from dozens of poles. There were wagons and cooking fires and piles of wood and blacksmiths' forges. He could even make out a huge haystack and the two men who were pitchforking bundles of hay into a barrow.

A bird in the tree above him squawked noisily, and although the Franks were too far away to hear it, Salim instinctively ducked his head, afraid of being spotted. If he was seen the Franks would send a volley of arrows towards him. Even at that distance, one could kill him.

On his way back to the Saracen camp he was distracted by a crow that was tussling with something on the ground. He went to look. The crow flapped away, and Salim saw that it had killed a mouse. Triumphantly, he scooped it up.

Dr Musa nodded with satisfaction when he saw Salim's haul.

'Achillea. Excellent,' he said, laying the plants aside one by one. 'First-class for healing wounds. And valerian for nervous disorders. What's this? A mouse! Your industry has been richly rewarded!' His brows twitched together in a look of the utmost ferocity. 'You didn't stray towards the Frankish camp, boy, eh? You didn't risk capture by those murdering fanatics?'

Trying not to look guilty, Salim shook his head.

The doctor's scowl would have stopped a lion in its tracks.

'If you allow yourself to be snatched by the enemy, believe me, I shall pursue you like a fury! You think I want to see my investment wasted? Is that it?'

Salim shook his head.

'No, *sidi* Musa. Would you like me to make you some mint tea?'

The doctor rolled his eyes.

'Mint? On an empty stomach? Now you want to kill me! But a light meal – some bread, a little cheese, a few olives and then a rest, for us both, in the shade of our tent – a good idea, my boy. See to it.'

The days quickly settled into a pattern. In the afternoon a respectful crowd assembled outside the doctor's tent, bringing with them every kind of ailment, as well as countless little gifts of gratitude, until the tent was overflowing with eggs, flasks of rose-water, small bags of nuts and bottles of olive oil. Often the doctor was called away to Saladin's marquee to attend to one of the chieftains or to the Sultan himself. Salim would go with him, watching everyone, learning the names and characters of the great men, becoming a familiar presence so that he could slip in and out of the compound past the guards without a challenge.

It was the mornings, though, that he enjoyed most. He spent hours every day out on the hillsides looking for the plants the doctor needed. He would start on the inland side, away from Acre, but always he was drawn back to the seaward side, to the little outcrop where he'd first looked down into the Crusader camp, and he would lie there for as long as he dared, watching people come and go, anxiously assessing the new arrivals from Europe pouring in off the ships, counting the tents springing up in the ever more crowded space, shuddering at the sight of the wagons full of weapons, and the knights in their heavy chainmail, puzzling over the Crusaders' odd clothes and strange habits and, more and more as the weeks went past, wrinkling his nose against the stench that built up into an unspeakable foulness as the Crusader camp became more squalid and dirty day by day.

He watched anxiously as strange contraptions rose from the ground near the city walls. Immense beams of wood were hauled to strategic points by teams of oxen. The men who were working on them from dawn to dusk were slowly building gigantic catapults. Salim shuddered as he watched, his heart in his mouth, as the first one to be finished swung back its great arm and sent a huge rock crashing into the city wall. It took a second or two for the dull thud to reach him, but he had already let out a sigh of relief. The wall had stood firm but the rock itself had disintegrated. He could see, even from this distance, the splash of white it made against the masonry.

The ditch grew deeper and the bank grew higher day by day. There were gaps in it here and there, cleverly designed with inner walls so that it would be easy for knights to charge out and attack, but possible also to defend against an assault from outside. Quite often, he saw Franks emerge through such gaps from behind their great mud wall. Horses cantered along the length of it, and soldiers often foraged for wood and grass.

The cool winds of autumn, blowing in off the sea, brought violent storms of rain, which drenched the Saracen and Crusader armies alike.

'What's the Sultan waiting for?' Salim heard one of the patients mutter outside the doctor's tent, holding his shield above his head against the rain. 'Why doesn't he attack and sweep the infidels into the sea? There are more arriving every day.'

'Short memory you've got,' another retorted. 'He tried, remember? Months ago. A farce it was too. Satan himself must fight for the barbarians. How else could they have beaten us back? They fought like demons, curses on them.'

'He's settling in for the winter,' someone else chipped in. 'We'll be here for months. Starving them out, that's what he's trying to do.'

The first man spat.

'It won't work. Look at all their ships coming in to supply them. And while we're trying to starve them, they're starving Acre. I wouldn't be in the city now, not for the hope of Paradise.'

Salim shivered, looked up and caught the eye of the doctor who was pounding dried seeds in a mortar with pungent cloves of garlic. He put his pestle down, stuck his head out of the tent and waved a dismissive hand at the soldiers.

'Idle gossip!' he fumed. 'I won't stand for it! At my very door! Keep your ignorant thoughts to yourselves. Next patient!'

Salim had explored every inch of hillside by now, both behind and in front of Saladin's camp. The doctor's chest was well stocked with the commoner herbs, but the rarer remedies were still missing, and he had to go foraging further and further afield.

One cool December morning he was crouching down behind a large boulder, trying to decide if the dried seed heads scattered on the ground were useful or not, when he was suddenly seized from behind by a pair of powerful hands and wrenched round to face two scowling men. His heart leaped with terror.

Franks! he thought. *They've caught me! I'm dead!*

But an instant later he saw the Arabic inscription chased into the metal rim of one of the men's helmets, and gasped with relief.

'Please,' he said. 'Let me go. I'm the doctor's boy. I'm—'

'Shut it,' one of the men growled, cuffing him painfully over the head. 'We've been watching you. A spy, that's what you are. Caught red-handed checking the lie of the land.'

'What are you talking about? I'm one of you! I'm not a Frank! Look at me!' Salim cried indignantly.

'You're a Christian,' the other man said, as he tied Salim's hands efficiently behind his back with a leather thong. 'Spies, all you dirty Christians. Selling our secrets to the Franks, may Allah destroy them. Execution's too good for the likes of you.'

Salim stared at him in disbelief.

'What do you mean? Are you crazy? I'm Muslim. Same as you are. I told you, I'm Dr Musa's assistant. He's the physician of the Sultan himself!'

The men looked at each other for a moment, then simultaneously shook their heads.

'Tell that to the birds, you little sneak,' the older one said. 'You're not getting away with clever talk like that.'

He brought the flat of his sword across Salim's shoulders in a blow so hard it nearly felled him.

By the time Salim had been prodded and kicked back to the camp he was a mass of bruises and his legs were badly grazed from the many times he'd fallen. He was not afraid, but furiously angry. Every now and then he'd been unable to hold back and had burst out in protest, only to receive another violent blow.

'Fools! Idiots!' he kept muttering under his breath. 'Wait till the doctor hears about this!'

As he was pushed and kicked through the camp, everyone turned and stared.

'He's a spy,' one of his captors said proudly. 'Caught him, didn't we, out on the hillside. Dirty little Christian. Paid a fortune by the Franks to tell them all our secrets.'

Salim, not daring to speak, flushed with helpless rage as

curses were spat at him and he ducked to avoid swinging punches from the crowd.

He was wondering if this nightmare would ever end when a familiar voice rang out above the angry buzz around him.

'Salim! Is that you, Salim? Hey, little brother, what have you been up to? Why have they tied you up like that?'

'Ismail!' he yelled. 'Ismail! Please!'

A blow in the stomach winded him and he doubled over, gasping for breath. As if from far away he heard voices rage above him.

'He's not a spy, you damn fools. He's the doctor's boy!'

'Nah – he fooled you too. We saw him. He—'

'He belongs to the Sultan's own doctor! Are you crazy? He lives in a big tent in Saladin's own enclosure! The doctor healed me of my lance wound. With an olive!'

Jeers broke out. Salim, recovering his breath, looked up to see Ismail, pale yet determined, facing the hostile crowd.

'A lance wound healed with an olive? You believe that, you'll believe anything!' someone shouted. 'Grab him. He's a spy too!'

'Me? What did you call me?' roared Ismail, beginning to draw the sword from his scabbard. 'I am a Mamluk! Come and get me then, if you dare!'

Salim hardly saw what happened next. There was a sudden bustle and scramble around him. Someone was slashing through the strap binding his wrists, and now he was sur-rounded by his old friends from the Mamluk troop, while beyond them the crowd seemed to have melted away.

'What happened? Who were they? Who did this to you?' the Mamluks were asking.

Breathlessly, Salim tried to explain, but his head was aching furiously and speech wouldn't come.

'Look at him! He's gone the colour of cold soup. Catch him!' he heard Ismail cry out, and then he fainted clean away.

When he came to, he was lying on his own mat in the doctor's tent, and Dr Musa was sponging his face with vinegar.

'*Ustadh*,' Salim tried to say, struggling to sit up, 'I . . .'

The doctor's hand pressed him gently back down again. Salim, looking up, saw with amazement that the doctor's eyes were wet.

'I'm to blame!' he said, striking his chest. 'Sending you out, a defenceless child! If the Lord had taken you from me . . .' He turned away, and Salim heard the sound of liquid being poured out. A moment later the doctor was holding a beaker to his lips. His hand was trembling.

'A sip at a time. No more! You want to choke? Slowly, that's it. Good. This will help the headache.'

Salim smiled up at him weakly.

'How did you know I've got a headache?'

'Two bumps the size of ducks' eggs on your skull and you don't have a headache? The Lord's to be praised that there's no fracture. I felt carefully while you were unconscious. Quiet now. Rest. Sleep. You'll be completely better four days from now. Completely, do you hear? I will accept nothing else.'

It was in fact only three days later when Salim received a summons that astonished him.

'The Sultan wants to see me? Me, *sidi* Musa?' he said, staring up at the doctor. 'I didn't do anything wrong. You told him, didn't you? I'm not a spy. He knows that, doesn't he?'

'He knows! Of course he knows,' the doctor said testily, but Salim saw with alarm that he was anxiously chewing his lower lip. 'There's nothing to worry about. Nothing! Now put this on.'

'A new tunic! Is it really for me?' Salim touched the green linen gingerly.

'Who do you think it's for? Suweida? If I must have an assistant, at least he should do me credit.' He lifted the fresh green cloth over Salim's head. 'Now the belt. A little better than the old one, eh? No, not your old sandals! You want the Sultan, peace be upon him, to think I employ a ragamuffin?'

Delighted, Salim tied on his new sandals and wrapped round him the warm cloak that Dr Musa was now holding out.

'You've grown,' the doctor said, looking him up and down. 'In wisdom as well as stature, let it be fondly hoped.'

In spite of his new clothes, Salim's heart knocked inside his chest as he entered Saladin's great marquee. He had been inside it many times before, but never before had he been the focus of attention. Now he was pushed forwards until he was standing in front of the bank of cushions on which Saladin sat cross-legged. The Sultan's dark, deep-set eyes were closely watching him.

'You are the doctor's boy? Your name is Salim? You have been roaming about the hillsides, collecting herbs, I believe.'

'Yes, sire.' Salim's voice was barely audible. He cleared his throat and tried again. 'Yes, sire.'

'You have ventured to both sides of our position, so I'm told. Towards the Crusader camp as well as away from it?'

'Yes. The plants are not all . . . Some grow better on the Frankish side, sire.'

Saladin was fingering his silky black beard.

'You have observed the infidels? You have watched them?'

Salim shuffled uneasily, not knowing what answer would be best.

'Sometimes.' A wave of Saladin's hand forced him on. 'There is a place,' he said unwillingly, 'a sort of rocky bit, with bushes growing on it. I can hide there. I can see a lot from there.'

'You haven't been noticed? The Franks have never seen you?'

'A boy, sire, wandering about on the hillside,' one of the men standing by a nearby tent pole put in. 'Who would suspect him of anything? A cripple too. They'd think he was a shepherd boy looking for his sheep.'

'What did you see?'

Saladin's eyes had never left Salim's face.

Salim tried furiously to think.

'Nothing much, sire,' he began. 'It's just a camp.'

'Give me a picture of it,' Saladin encouraged him. 'Tell me every detail.'

Salim swallowed, and began hesitantly to describe the Crusader camp. Seeing the interest in the Sultan's eye, he told him of the wagons, the shape of the fortifications behind the gates, the men with barrows pitchforking the hay.

'But last time I looked the hay had all gone,' he said, 'and there are more tents crowded in on top of each other, every time I look. And a – a very bad smell, sire. They foul the place everywhere.'

'Good. Very good.' Saladin waved a hand. 'I've had dozens of men reporting on the camp but none has given me so much detail. It takes the eyes of a boy. Information, intelligence, that's what's required. The smallest details are of importance. If the Franks are running out of fodder for their horses, I need to know. If their filth is piling up to cause disease, I want to hear about it. You are to resume your watching, Salim. Put aside these new clothes. Dress like a simple boy again. Spy for me. Get as close to the infidel army as you can without being caught.'

'Oh yes, sire!' Salim was on fire with enthusiasm.

'Better! Even better! Do your best, Salim. This is jihad, you understand, Salim? We're fighting to cleanse our land of the foul invaders, who wish to take from us the holy city of Jerusalem, the very place to which the Prophet himself, peace be upon him, came on his great night journey.'

'Yes, oh yes, I understand!' Salim, who was half mesmerized by the Sultan's steady gaze and his rich compelling voice, would at that moment have been content to be run through by a Crusader's lance if Saladin had required it.

A groan made him turn his head. Dr Musa was wringing his hands in distress.

'The danger, my lord, think of the danger to the boy! He's a child, and lame! How can he run if he's pursued? And if he's caught . . .'

'For the greater good, doctor, we must all make sacrifices,' Saladin answered calmly. 'The boy is sent by Allah to be our eyes and ears. You have your commission, Salim. Go out and fulfil it.'

CHAPTER EIGHT

A week had passed since the Fortis contingent had arrived in the camp outside the walls of Marseilles, and it had been a worrying time for Adam. He knew that Jennet would be safe most of the time with Lord Guy's people, who still felt awed by her link with Lord Robert, although when the men-at-arms started drinking the mood could turn ugly. It was the mass of strangers all around that concerned him most. He didn't dare speak to her, afraid that she would laugh at him and call him a kid again, but he stayed near her as much as he could, alert to danger, setting Faithful to guard her whenever he had to be away.

The worst thing, though, was a mysterious sickness that was affecting all the dogs. It had started with one of the lymers, who had gone off his feed and kept scratching at a sore eye. His nose was dry and hot to the touch, and Adam could tell that he had a fever. Two of the other lymers showed the same symptoms the next day, and by the end of the week all Lord Guy's dogs, except for Ostine, seemed ill. Faithful, who had been most of the time with Jennet, seemed unaffected.

Adam nursed the dogs as best he could, cleaning out their

running eyes, coaxing them to eat and drink and stroking their flanks when they twitched in uncontrollable convulsions.

Since they'd arrived at Marseilles, Lord Guy had been too busy waiting around the royal pavilion in the hopes of catching the eye of the King to take much notice of his own people, but the thing Adam dreaded happened at last. Returning from a dinner with an earl from Suffolk, Lord Guy almost stumbled over Mirre, who was lying at Adam's feet turning her head away from the titbit he was holding beneath her nose.

'Mirre,' Lord Guy said, clicking his fingers, expecting the dog to jump up and greet him as she usually did. Mirre flapped her tail once wearily against the ground, but didn't lift her head.

'Sick? Is she sick?'

Lord Guy's eyes were glazed with too much wine, but focused them angrily on Adam.

'Yes, my lord.' Adam's heart was thumping. 'I've been trying to feed them and give them water, but—'

'Them? What is this? The others are sick too?'

'Yes, my lord.' Adam's voice was so low he was almost whispering. He made himself speak louder. 'The lymers are bad, but not Ostine. And – and the mastiff puppy is well.'

Lord Guy bent down and lifted Mirre's head with a hand that was surprisingly gentle.

'I know this sickness,' he said, straightening up unsteadily. 'It kills them. All my dogs! Only Ostine left!'

Adam waited, trembling, for a blow to fell him. When it didn't come he dared to look up. Lord Guy was running a bleary eye over the other dogs, who, limp and miserable, were lying panting in the shade of a wagon.

'It's a curse,' Lord Guy said at last, as if to himself. 'It's that low-born son of scribbler, William Scriveson! Keeps me away from the King, and now the scoundrel's cursed my dogs!' He lifted his head. 'Robert! Where's my idiot son gone now? Robert! My sword! Bring me my sword!'

He stumbled off in the direction of the King's pavilion.

Adam, watching him go, let out a sigh of relief. Jennet appeared at his elbow, a pile of freshly washed linen hanging over her arm.

'What happened, Adam? What did he say?'

'He says the dogs are cursed. That's why they're sick.'

She took a step backwards, her eyes widening fearfully as she looked down at Mirre's heaving, sweating flanks.

'Witchcraft! Why? Who?'

'The King's marshal,' Adam shrugged. 'Lord Guy hates him. But I don't believe it. They started going sick before we got here. They caught the infection from some village dogs a couple of weeks ago. Mirre looks just like the dog lying by that crossroads at the top of the hill. You remember that place. It was where we passed the bodies hanging up on the gallows.'

Jennet shuddered.

'I do remember. I wish I could forget. Did you tell Lord Guy?'

'Of course not. If he thinks they're cursed he won't blame me.' He flexed his shoulders as if a weight had rolled off them. 'It's a relief and all. I thought I'd be whipped, or worse.'

'They won't die, will they, poor things?'

He shrugged.

'I'll do my best. None have died yet. Who knows what'll happen tomorrow?'

'I do. I've just heard. The ships are ready. We're out of here in the morning. Sailing first thing. And you know what? Even if the dogs don't die I reckon I will. It makes me heave just to think about the sea. The first little wave and I'll be wishing I was never born.'

'The ships are ready?' he said, looking disbelievingly at the vast numbers of men and horses that surrounded them. 'For everyone?'

'No, only a few. Us Fortis people, and one or two other English groups.' She grinned. 'Joan heard Hugo de Pomfret talking about it when she was carrying him his clean linen. The King wants to get the most quarrelsome barons out of the way because they're causing too much trouble.'

Adam, thinking of Lord Guy staggering off to fight dry old Master William Scriveson, began to laugh, and once he'd started he couldn't stop. Jennet stared at him.

'What's got into you? I haven't heard you laugh for months.'

He wiped a sleeve across his streaming eyes.

'I don't know. It's just the thought of Lord Guy, I suppose, getting into fights with everyone.'

But he knew it was more than that. With the news that they were leaving, he'd felt an uprush of joy and confidence. The dogs might be ailing, and he was worried about Jennet, but the thought that they were at last to set off on the final leg of their journey had warmed him with the same glorious certainty he'd known on the night when he'd taken the cross. The great city of Jerusalem, salvation for himself and his mother, the beginning of a new and marvellous life, floated in a golden cloud in front of him. He had only to step forwards and it would engulf him. He knew that from now on, whatever happened when the Crusade was over, nothing would ever be the same again. Even if he had to spend the rest of his life bonded in serfdom to the lords of Fortis, subject forever to their whims, inside he would be free.

Adam felt almost like a hardened sailor when he stepped on to the ship that was to carry him to the farthest end of the Mediterranean. The vast empty expanse of water still frightened him, but the little waves lapping against the stone walls of the quay seemed almost friendly compared to the vicious breakers which had crashed with such force against the coast of England.

He found to his dismay that he was on the second ship, with Lord Robert and five of the knights, their attendant squires and grooms, and fifty of the men-at-arms. Lord Guy and the rest of the knights and fighting men were on the leading ship. He would be separated too from Jennet, who was in a smaller ship following behind with the baggage train. Six other ships were in the convoy, carrying men from different parts of England to the port of Acre on the coast of Palestine.

'I'll be all right,' Jennet said to him bravely, as they stood on the quay ready to embark. 'There's all the odds and ends on our ship – us women, and the armourers, and some of the hangers-on. You're going up in the world, Adam. You'll be with the knights and squires.'

He'd tried to leave Faithful with her, partly to guard her, and partly to keep him away from the sick dogs, but the young mastiff had seemed to panic when Adam had tried to part from him and had even given Jennet a nasty nip on the hand.

'You take him. He's a little monster,' she said, shaking her hand to relieve the pain and frowning down at Faithful, who was hanging his head with guilty shame. 'A crazy dog's all I need.'

They'd been separated then, but as he was lifting the last of the sick lymers into a shady corner of the deck, he'd caught sight of the unwelcome figure of Jacques slipping up the gangway behind Jennet. He shaded his eyes to look properly and saw that the pedlar was making up to her, contorting himself like a cat in an effort to please.

Don't fall for it, Jenny, he muttered to himself. *Keep clear of him.*

They were well out at sea by the time night fell, and the sun had not long slipped over the purple horizon when Mirre died. Everyone else on board had gone below to stretch out between the chalk lines that marked their sleeping places on the bare boards, but Adam sat on beside the greyhound as she stiffened in death. He didn't know what to do.

I ought to tell Lord Robert, he told himself. *I can't just throw her into the sea.*

The decision was taken out of his hands by a sailor, who saw Mirre's dead body, drew in a sharp breath, crossed himself nervously and looked over his shoulder, as if expecting the devil to appear. Then he picked the body up and with one swift movement flung it over the side of the ship. Adam didn't even hear the splash Mirre made against the swish of water cresting against the bows.

Two lymers died the following day. It was almost a relief when the last of the six died. The sickness had been horrible to see and nothing Adam had done had helped. Now only Ostine and Faithful were left. He kept the mastiff tied up in the bows of the ship as far away from Ostine as possible and visited him there whenever he could.

After two weeks at sea Adam was quite used to the motion of the ship, the creaking of the timbers and the flapping of the great white sail with its huge emblazoned cross. Ostine was the only hunting hound left. To his great relief, the dog showed no sign of illness, and Adam was confident enough to release Faithful from his tether and bring him back to share the corner he had found for Ostine.

I'll have one dog to show Lord Guy, anyway, when we get there, he told himself.

Now that he had only two animals to care for, and no Jennet to talk to, Adam began, for the first time, to feel more at ease with his fellow travellers. It was impossible to stay aloof from them anyway. At night everyone was crammed together in the stinking, stifling lower deck, and by day they crowded above in the open air, spending their time picking lice out of their clothes, grumbling about the food and trying to clean off the sticky tar which clung to every surface of the ship and made black stains on their hands and clothes.

Three or four of the younger men were particularly friendly, though Adam still felt an outsider in their group, as they cracked jokes he couldn't understand about their officers, or bragged about the targets they'd hit with their arrows.

Lord Robert and the knights spent their days above in the stern forecastle, the coolest and roomiest part of the ship, with their squires running up and down the narrow stairways to provide them with all they wanted. They would lean on the rail to look down on the lower orders on the open deck below, but seldom went down among them, unless they were on their way to the bowels of the ship below the waterline to look at their horses, who were somehow enduring this long voyage in the frightful heat and filth and darkness of the hold.

A build-up of violet clouds on the western horizon was the first sign of the sudden summer storm that roared down upon the little fleet, sending the ships bobbing about on the waves like peas in a pot of boiling water. Struck with terror, the Crusaders huddled together, calling upon the Virgin and the saints for protection. Adam, convinced that he was about to die, sat for hours with his head buried in the soft folds of Faithful's neck, while Ostine pressed himself against his back, whining and shivering with fear. With each pitch of the ship, Adam had to brace himself against a bulwark, and once, when a huge green wave curled up and over the ship's side, he was almost washed overboard. The storm seemed to last for hours and Adam, drenched and terrified, was almost ready to give up and let himself roll right over into the sea. But suddenly, the storm was over as quickly as it had come, leaving the decks slippery with vomit.

'We made it then! We cheated Old Nick,' Roger Stepesoft,

one of Adam's new friends, said, stepping over a stinking pud-
dle and slapping Adam heartily on the back.

The others had crossed themselves swiftly at the mention
of the devil. Adam gave Roger a wavering smile.

'Thought I was done for,' he said. 'Specially when that big
wave came over and sent the barrels flying about.'

Roger shuddered.

'Me too. Can't believe we're alive. A miracle, really, ain't it?
Our Lady's looking out for us. Must be.'

'Stands to reason,' his friend, Treuelove Malter, chimed in.
'We'd be dead otherwise. All of us.'

Adam nodded. He knew they were right. It could only have
been by a miracle that they'd been saved. He felt as if he'd
come through a great battle with death itself, and that somehow the life to which he'd been returned stretched ahead full
of promise.

It wasn't until two days after the storm that dreadful news
ran round the ship. Most of the convoy, scattered by the
winds, had managed to straggle together again, but the ship
Jennet was on hadn't reappeared. Treuelove Malter heard
about it from one of the squires and came to tell Roger, who
was showing Adam how to splice feathers on to an arrow.

'Gone to the bottom, I'd bet on it by St Christopher,'
Roger said with gloomy relish. 'Pity. There was good helmets
in them baggage weapons, not to mention spare pikes that
we'll be needing.'

Adam stared at him, filled with dread.

'What do you mean? What are you saying? The ship's
sunk? You mean everyone on it's drowned?'

Treuelove softened at the misery in Adam's face.

'Could have just been blown off course,' he said. 'They'll
end up on some island or other, if there are any in this crazy
ocean.'

Roger laid a brotherly hand on Adam's shoulder.

'Chances are that your girl's ship . . .'

'She's not my girl!' Adam burst out. 'You don't understand anything! She's – she's my family!'

'. . . that your girl's ship is just fine,' Roger swept on. 'Just bobbing along a bit more slowly than us, that's all. Now, are you going to come and shoot at seagulls, or what?'

Adam tried to smile.

'No, thanks. I'll stay with Faithful. He's still all on edge, the daft mutt.'

He settled himself against a bulwark, one hand on Faithful's collar, needing to think. He made himself go through everything that could possibly have happened to Jennet's ship, trying to imagine wrecks, survivings, pirates, drownings, rescues, sea monsters and heavenly interventions by angels. All of them seemed equally possible. His thoughts were circling more and more desperately, when to his astonishment he heard someone call out, 'The dog boy! Fetch the dog boy!'

Adam jumped to his feet. A squire was looking over the rail from the raised deck at the stern of the ship into the crowded open deck below. Adam stood up and pushed his way to the foot of the ladder-like stairway.

'You mean me?'

The squire, who looked no more than thirteen and was a whole head shorter than Adam, nevertheless managed to stare him down haughtily.

'If you're the dog boy, of course I mean you. Lord Robert wants you. Bring the mastiff.'

His pulse quickening, Adam followed the squire up the stairway to the shaded upper deck. Lord Robert was sprawling against a cushion in the centre of a circle of three of the knights. The fourth, Sir Raymond de Pommeroy, was quietly strumming a lute and singing as if to himself, while Sir Ivo de

Chastelfort, the oldest of the five knights, was sitting upright on a chest, staring thoughtfully down into a goblet.

'Behold, the dog boy! I summon him and he appears!' Lord Robert cried, waving Adam back with a disdainful gesture of his hand. 'By the rood, how these people stink.'

Adam obediently stepped back, keeping Faithful on as short a leash as he could. He could hear the low growl in the dog's deep chest and sense his unease.

'I told you, Ivo, what a fine mastiff I have,' Lord Robert said, his voice high-pitched and excited. 'You can't refuse the wager now.' His thin fair face was flushed. Although it was still morning, it was clear that he was already half drunk. He clicked his fingers towards Faithful. 'Here, boy.'

Faithful bared his teeth. Adam stood still, not knowing what to do.

'What's the dog's name?' Sir Ivo asked Adam. He spoke quietly and slowly, as if to calm the tension which Adam could feel crackling in the air.

'Fai—' he began.

'Cutthroat. His name's Cutthroat,' Lord Robert said, taking a deep pull at the tankard a squire had been holding out to him. 'Now, Ivo. You can't refuse. Your second destrier for my mastiff. One last toss of the dice to decide it.'

'A dog for a warhorse, Lord Robert, is hardly—' Sir Ivo began.

'Then I'll throw in the laundry slut!' Lord Robert looked round at the three recumbent knights who let out dutiful guffaws. 'If her ship is ever found she shall be yours.'

Rage sent a tremor down through Adam's hand and along the leash to Faithful's collar. It upset the mastiff even more and his growls turned to deep snarls.

'You see?' Lord Robert said delightedly. 'You'll make a fortune from him. He's full of fight. Look at him. Made to bait bears. Three good matches and you'll win enough to buy two more destriers at least.'

No, no, not the bear pit! I won't let them. I'll set you free to run away. I'll save you, Faithful, I promise! Adam was telling the dog silently in his head.

Sir Ivo turned to hand his goblet to the squire and Adam saw disgust in his face. Without a word he scooped up the pair of dice lying on the boards of the deck and cast them with a casual hand. Lord Robert leaned forward eagerly.

'A four and a two. I'll better that!' he crowed, and threw the dice himself.

Adam couldn't see what he had thrown, but Lord Robert, having stared disbelievingly down at the dice for a moment, pushed them aside with a petulant sweep of his hand.

'Take the dog away, and take yourself off too,' he muttered, a little too loudly. 'Your long face is depressing me.'

Sir Ivo got to his feet. A tall man, he towered over the lounging knights.

'You'll excuse me in future from such games, Lord Robert,' he said coldly. 'I took the cross to fight for our Lord and his mother, not to gamble and wench.'

Lord Robert said nothing, but Adam saw the wounded dignity in his face turn to a scowl.

'Go away, dog boy,' he snapped. 'Tie the dog to the chain there. Get back to the filth where you belong. The dog needs breaking in. I'll see to it myself before I hand him over.'

Adam, stumbling down the stairway, half blinded by the sun, could not take in this fresh disaster that had befallen him. He walked stiffly across to where he had left Ostine. The greyhound whined in welcome, but Adam barely noticed. Ostine wasn't Faithful. Faithful had gone. His own dog. His own friend. Like Ma and Jennet, Faithful had been snatched away. Nothing was left to him now. His throat tight with unshed tears, he dropped his head on his knees and clasped them tightly.

He was jerked back to awareness ten minutes later by a cold nose thrust into his face and a long tongue licking his chin.

'Faithful!' he said, starting up. 'No, no, you have to go back! They'll beat you senseless! Go back, Faithful!'

'So that's his name, is it? Faithful?'

Adam looked up. His jaw dropped at the sight of Sir Ivo standing in front of him, and he scrambled to his feet.

'Yes, it's Faithful, sir, at least that's what I call him. And he isn't a fighter. He wouldn't do anything to bears. He looks fierce, but he isn't. Soft-hearted, he is, useless for anything except guarding. You could use him to guard your tent, sir.'

He stopped, aware that he was babbling.

'I'm not sure that you're right about the fighting bit,' Sir Ivo said with a half-smile, backing away from Faithful who, having finished his rapturous reunion with Adam, had turned to snarl at him again. 'Since you left the upper deck not more than ten minutes ago this dog has wrenched his chain out of the bulwark, bitten two squires and knocked over at least one flagon of wine.'

'Yes, but that's only because he's – he's still a puppy, sir. He's not used to other people yet. But if he saw a bear he'd run a mile, I know he would.'

'Then it'll have to be guard duties after all,' Sir Ivo said with a sigh. 'There is one problem still to be solved, however.'

'What's that, sir?' Adam said cautiously.

'He clearly refuses to be separated from you, and since I hear that all except one of Lord Guy's hunting dogs have died, you're likely to be underemployed. I shall have to take you on as my – my what shall we call you now? Ah yes. My dog's boy. It's clearly to Faithful that you belong. He'll have to stay with you, of course, and you'll continue to care for Ostine.'

A grin spread across Adam's face.

'What about Lord Robert, sir?' he asked daringly.

'Not your concern,' Sir Ivo said with a disapproving frown. 'It so happens that I need another servant in my little household. My groom took sick in Marseilles and I had to leave him there. If you're half as good with horses as you are with dogs, you'll do. Now stop your dog – or rather, *my* dog – from looking at me in that hungry way. He's obviously planning to take a piece out of my leg.'

It was a fine morning in late October when a long falling cry came from the crow's nest, halfway up the mast of the leading ship.

'A-a-a-cre!'

Everyone on board rushed to the ship's side to look.

Adam, desperate to see, shinned up a piece of rigging to get a better view. Acre was still only a grey smudge, miles away, but the coast was quite near.

That must be the Holy Land, he thought. *Right there.*

The rocks, beaches, low hills, grass and trees looked strangely ordinary, and yet, Adam felt sure, a kind of light shimmered across the shore. He shivered, half with excitement, half with fear. He almost expected Christ himself to come walking towards him on the water, and to hear choirs of heavenly angels singing. On those very rocks, those ones, not half a mile away, the Virgin herself might be standing, her arms held out in love and welcome, strands of her black hair escaping from her blue cloak and floating freely round her face.

He took a firmer grip on the ropes and shook the foolish thoughts away. Of course Mary and her son could not appear to him. They'd been imprisoned by the evil Saladin. They were chained, weeping, waiting for rescue. Instead of Christ and his Mother on the shore there were enemy infidels prowling, day and night, their eyes flashing fire, their fangs dripping with blood. They had tails, so someone had said, like monkeys. And they ate Christian children. Or was that the Jews? He couldn't quite remember.

Little by little, in the distance, the city of Acre was growing as the ship approached. The high walls and massive fortifications looked so daunting that the watchers on the decks fell silent. A ragged cheer went up as the banners of the besieging Crusaders came into view along the shore, but it died away as they saw the vast Saracen camp on the hillside above, poised like a hawk above its prey. Murmured prayers could be heard over the swish of water against the ship's prow, and the sign of the cross was made on every chest.

The sun was setting when the convoy of ships dropped anchor at last in the shallows. The doors in the hull swung open and, not waiting for a gangplank to take them to the beach, the eager men jumped into the water and waded ashore. Adam, with Faithful and Ostine on tight leashes, was one of the first to set foot on firm ground. As soon as he was out of the water he sank down to his knees and kissed the sand, picking up handfuls of it and holding it reverently in his two hands. He sensed, rather than saw, that others all around him were doing the same. Then, feeling the excited dogs tug eagerly at their leashes, he jumped up and let them run, dashing wildly after them, hardly able to believe that he had survived the long journey and the perils of the sea and had landed in the very country whose soil Christ had once trod.

A year and a half later . . .

CHAPTER NINE

It was springtime again at last, and nineteen long months had passed since Salim had been bundled so suddenly away from home and had unwillingly walked out of Acre behind the doctor. He had grown a full ten centimetres since then, his voice had deepened and he had acquired broader shoulders and a fine rim of dark hair along his upper lip. It seemed to him sometimes as if he'd been in the Saracen camp forever, and his life at home was a dream from long ago.

From time to time, the city would mount a surprise raid. The gates on their rusted hinges would creak open and some of the defenders would rush out. They'd snatch a wagon-load of food, seize some horses and set fire to a few tents, then race back behind the shelter of their walls. Whenever this happened, Salim would remember his family in a rush of anxiety and live for days on tenterhooks, not knowing whether Ali was among the ones who hadn't run back in time, imagining his body lying with the others in the ditch below the city walls, unburied and foul with swarms of flies. But it was impossible to live in an agony of worry for too long, and soon enough the pain of not knowing would turn once more into a dull, permanent ache.

From the beginning, Salim had taken to spying with enthusiasm. He'd stuck to his old routine in the first few months, moving around in the dead ground between the two armies, pretending to collect leaves and seed heads for the doctor. By the end of the first winter there had been little enough to find. Foraging parties of Franks, desperate to feed their horses, had ventured beyond their earthworks and, long since, stripped the hillside bare of every green thing, as well as every stick to light their fires. The bushes had even gone from the old spying place above the outcrop, where Salim had first hidden to watch the Franks. It was still possible, by crawling up to it on his hands and knees, to approach without being seen from below, but he rarely bothered now.

In a way, the armies had become used to each other. Saracens from one side and Crusaders from the other would even meet in the ground between them, leaning on their lances as they tried to converse without a common language. There was an odd kind of peace. The catapults were still silent, their long arms lying idly in the dust.

Salim, in his old tunic, bleached to a faded grey by the sun, would make himself almost invisible as he squatted on a stone, watching with amazement as a group of Frankish knights, their faces shaved in the strange European manner, would beckon to a group of Saracens, greet them politely and usher them right into their camp, into their very tents, offering them food, and showing off the finer points of their warhorses, some of which, as big as camels, were beyond anything even the Mamluks had ever seen.

Salim would shake his head with disgust. What was the point of him being a spy when the soldiers of Saladin could saunter into the Christian camp at their ease, look around them and stroll back home to report on every detail?

Once or twice, he'd dared to attach himself, like a shadow, to a pair of Syrian knights, who seemed to be friendly with a group of Franks from Tyre. Slipping quietly behind them, he had overheard their conversation as they met on the open ground between the camps. These Franks spoke some Arabic. They were the old type of Crusader, ones who had been born in Palestine and lived in the country all their lives. They had even, thought Salim, become quite civilized, with their clean clothes and proper manners, unlike the loud, rough newcomers fresh from Europe, with their wild manes of hair and their roaring fighting drunkenness.

Increasingly, though, Salim's expeditions outside the camp of Saladin had become rare. There was nothing new that he could report about the Crusaders, and there was scarcely a plant remaining to be harvested. In any case, Dr Musa seldom let him run free. Solomon, a pharmacist from Damascus, had arrived in Saladin's camp. He had taken up residence in a tent next to the doctor's, and the two men worked together. Salim was constantly at their beck and call.

'Where do you think you're going?' the doctor would say every time Salim tried to slip away. 'Salves to be prepared! Seeds to grind!'

Now that it was spring again and the days were getting warmer, the stench from the Crusader camp was becoming even more unbearable. Saladin, suffering constantly from fevers and stomach pains, and afraid that the foul miasma was making him ill, called Dr Musa frequently to his tent. Often Salim went with him, but sometimes he had permission to slip away. When he was feeling like company he would seek out Ismail who, completely recovered now from his lance wound, would sometimes let him mount Kestan, and the two of them would ride off into the hills a little way, their horses restless from the long inactive days in the camp.

At other times, though, an awful homesickness would overcome Salim. This happened one March evening, when the smell of a bubbling stew suddenly brought to mind the courtyard of his Acre home so vividly that he could almost hear his mother's voice calling him to supper. The doctor was with Saladin. Salim slipped out of the camp and went to sit on a favourite rock from which he could look out across the plain, teeming with tents and men and horses, towards the walls of Acre.

The spell of homesickness turned, as it often did, into anger.

They sent me away, he thought. *Baba sold me, like a piece of cloth. He never loved me. Why didn't Mama stop him? She doesn't really care about me either. It's because of my leg. They only ever wanted Ali and Zahra. They couldn't wait to get rid of me.*

Self-pity threatened to overwhelm him. He felt shameful tears run down his cheeks and wiped them savagely away. Then, from one moment to the next, his mood changed. He saw his father's anxious frown, and remembered how he'd wanted Salim to be sent to safety. He remembered how Mama had packed the honey cakes for him, and how Ali had been almost affectionate when they'd said goodbye.

'If only I knew you were all right!' he said out loud.

Dreadful scenes tumbled one after another into his mind: Zahra, pale and weak with hunger, Mama hunting around for something to eat in empty storage jars, Baba's fingers fretting and fretting over his worry beads.

And Ali! he thought. *He might be dead by now. I'd kill every one of these mad foreigners if I could. I hate them. I hate them! Why did they have to come here? Why don't they go back home and leave us alone?*

In a feeble gesture of defiance, he picked up a pebble and threw it, with as much force as he could, towards the Crusader camp. It landed out of sight, further down the hill. There was a yelping sound and the scuffle of paws on stones, and suddenly, as if from nowhere, a huge dog appeared. It raced up to him, the low growl in its throat turning to deep, hostile barks. Salim jumped to his feet and put out his hands to protect himself. The dog's lips were drawn back from its teeth in a hideous snarl, and it seemed to be about to launch itself at him, to tear out his throat, when a voice from below yelled in the language of the Franks, 'No! Faithful! Down! Come *here*!'

The mastiff dropped down obediently on to its haunches. Salim backed way. This seemed to infuriate the dog all over again and it jumped up, but before it could attack, the boy had run up, grabbed it by the collar and wrenched it backwards.

Whining, the dog subsided at the boy's feet.

'He wouldn't have hurt you,' the boy began. 'He's—'

Then he took in Salim's appearance, his hooded cloak and the skullcap on his head. His eyes narrowed.

'Infidel!' he said, crossing himself.

'Infidel you!' Salim shot back, the half-remembered language of the Franks coming back to him. 'Barbarian! Get out of my land! Go back to *Farang*!'

'What? What do you mean?' the boy clearly didn't understand. 'Go where?'

His hold on the dog's collar was loosening. Salim, afraid he would release it, bent down swiftly, picked up another stone and flung it at the boy. It missed. He backed hastily away up the hill.

'Go home! Go you home to Frankish land!' he yelled, and without looking round hobbled back to the camp as fast as he could.

The endless months of siege had passed slowly for Adam too. He had also grown. His face had lost the roundness of childhood and had slimmed and firmed to become handsome under its thick thatch of dark hair. He was unaware of this, since he had no means of looking at himself. He took pride, though, in the increasing strength of his arms and back, and his skill in handling a sword and mace, honed by constant practice with the men-at-arms.

No one had thought the siege would last so long. After the

first winter had passed, everyone had expected that King Richard of England, Philip of France and the Emperor of Germany would sweep into the harbour of Acre at the head of their mighty fleets, leap on to their horses and, riding at the head of the glorious band of faithful Crusaders, sweep aside the God-hating Saracens with the sheer force of their righteousness. Then, after a swift battle, they would enter Jerusalem to the sound of trumpets.

Instead, the different factions of the camp quarrelled and grumbled among themselves. Knights from all over Europe tested their skills against each other, keeping more or less courteously within the rules of competition. The countless priests and bishops conferred together in the Latin of a dozen different national accents, while the high-born nobles and princes eyed each other jealously, each one hoping to outdo the other in rushing first to glory on the day of victory, when Jerusalem would be their prize.

Adam had frequently hugged to himself the thought of that tremendous day. Once there, in the holy city, he was sure that the knowledge of divine salvation would lift his soul to bliss. He had certainly never expected to be trapped in a crowded camp, stuck in one place month after month, spending long days digging the ditches and embankments, and even longer ones in weary idleness, while the food grew more and more scarce, people sickened and died, and the rising tide of filth threatened to overwhelm everyone.

The English contingent had made their camp with the few other English troops, who had come out in advance of King Richard. It was to the east of the city walls, in a spot nearest the low rim of hills beyond, which Saladin commanded.

Adam had given up all hope, months ago, that the lost ship which Jennet had been on would arrive. During the whole of the first summer he had spent hours looking out to sea, hoping against hope to see a sail with the familiar scarlet cross emblazoned on it. Once the storms of November had closed in, however, all sea traffic had stopped, and he had had to accept that Jennet had gone.

As the second autumn approached, news had come that King Richard had been detained in Sicily and would remain there for the winter until it was safe to put to sea again.

'If I'd known he'd take this long I'd have stayed at home another year,' Adam heard Lord Guy grumble. 'I may be saving my soul, but I'm certainly losing everything else! I'll have spent my last groat before this is over, just on bread and beer for my lazy vassals.'

Father Jerome, not wishing to rebuke the baron in front of his inferiors, had nevertheless allowed a frown to cross his austere face.

'Those that wait upon the Lord, they shall inherit the earth,' he said, speaking in Latin which no one else could understand. Then, turning to address everyone close by, he had informed them that a mass was about to be said in the huge tented church in the centre of the camp, and that constant devotion to Christ and his Mother was the only way to ensure victory over the evil forces of Islam.

In spite of the fleas that infested the straw-strewn ground inside the church tent, Adam attended the masses as often as he could. He squeezed his eyes shut as he prayed, trying to feel again the passionate conviction of the night when he'd taken the cross. He begged the Virgin to save his mother from purgatory, and pleaded with all the saints whose names he knew to rescue Jennet from hell.

Adam was used to hunger, but as the second winter came to an end, even he was desperate for food, and the job of keeping the two dogs alive was becoming harder and harder. There was still just enough money in Lord Guy's coffers to save his people from absolute starvation, but with a single egg going in the camp for a silver penny, even the baron's fortune was fast running out. Already half the precious horses had been slaughtered and eaten. The prized warhorses had been saved, but the other animals had all gone, their flesh devoured and their bones chewed and chewed again.

Adam knew he was luckier than many. Sir Ivo made sure he had enough to keep body and soul together. Some of the Crusader army, who had answered the call to take up the cross without the protection of a lord, were gaunt with hunger and scarcely had enough strength to wield a sword or a bow. They had come from every part of Europe, from German, Italian and Spanish lands, from France and the Low Countries. They stayed together, each in their own small patches of ground, begging from their neighbours, wondering why they'd come, each of them longing for the spring, and the hope that reinforcements from Europe would arrive and the final push to take Acre would begin.

Every time he went to mass, Adam thanked the Virgin for Sir Ivo. The knight had been as good as his word and, with Lord Guy's agreement, had taken Adam on as his groom. It hadn't been hard to look after Sir Ivo's four horses – Grimbald, his massive charger, the two riding palfreys and the slower, older packhorse. He'd been sorry when first the packhorse and then the palfreys had had to be slaughtered for their meat, and he watched anxiously as the fodder available to Grimbald diminished day by day, and the horse grew thinner.

Disaster struck Sir Ivo's little household shortly after the second Christmas. A severe bout of dysentery had laid low his squire. The knight had sat up with him for three nights, but on the fourth day the squire had died. Sir Ivo had placed him in his grave with his own hands and hadn't been ashamed to cry like a child.

'His father trusted him to me,' Adam heard him say, as he stared down at the low mound of earth. 'How shall I face him when we go home?'

Adam hadn't known what to say. The squire had been a moody, arrogant boy, who had taken pleasure in ordering Adam about. He couldn't pretend to mourn him. At last he said awkwardly, 'His soul has gone to Paradise, sir. He died on Crusade.'

'Yes, but that won't comfort his mother,' Sir Ivo sighed. 'And it's not much comfort to me. His father's my oldest friend.'

He walked on with Adam at his heels.

'What will you do for a squire now, sir?' Adam dared ask a little later, as he took the squire's soiled blanket out of Sir Ivo's tent, ready to take it to the river for a wash.

'Sir Baldwin's boy will help me out,' Sir Ivo had said indifferently. Then a smile had lit his face. 'But there's you! Why, yes. Adam the dog boy becomes Adam the groom, and now it seems he'll have to be Adam the page. You're going up in the world. It's an unlikely promotion for a serf, I grant you, and temporary of course, but these are exceptional times. You'll have to learn new tricks, dog boy. You'll have to master the art of dressing me in my coat of mail, and keeping it clean and in good repair.'

'Yes, sir, yes!' stammered Adam.

'You can start,' Sir Ivo said drily, 'by washing yourself and your clothes. I'm going to have to teach you manners, young Adam. It's not exactly easy, in this infernal dung heap, to survive with any decency at all, but standards must be maintained. You will, for example, kindly stop scratching yourself in that distressingly primitive manner.'

Adam, quick to learn, had not taken long to master his new duties. Sir Ivo, strict but fair, had been patient with his fumblings. When he had demonstrated the intricate business of how he had to be dressed in the complicated armour of war – the padded under-jacket, the iron-ringed hauberk that covered his body down to his knees, the chainmail leggings and mittens, the bright white linen surcoat, secured by a long leather belt, and lastly the massive box-like helmet with its narrow eye slits – Adam had concentrated with frowning intensity. He hadn't needed to be shown again.

The other pages had been scandalized at first by the sight of an illiterate serf doing the noble work of a squire. They'd taken it out on Adam, poking at him with the sharp ends of their swords, mocking the way he spoke and sending him on useless errands. Sir Ivo had let well alone, until Adam's leg was almost broken when a group of squires had kicked and beaten him. He'd knocked a few heads together and reminded them of the sacredness of their mission. As he was the most respected of Lord Guy's knights, most of them had settled down to a grudging acceptance of Adam's new role and one had even offered tips on the tricky business of attaching spurs to a mailed foot.

Adam, discovering for the first time that it was impolite to pick his nose, belch or spit on the ground, covertly watched the squires. He noticed how straight they stood, and how they never hung their heads obsequiously in the presence of the knights. Without copying their swagger, he unconsciously began to move through the camp with more assurance, holding his own head high.

It was a strain, though, to live up to the demands that Sir Ivo made on him, and whenever he could, Adam slipped away. He scrambled over the earthwork defences and roamed about on the hillside above the camp, going as near to the Saracen camp as he dared, looking for anything edible. He'd been lucky enough once to snare a couple of birds, but after he'd shared them with the dogs there was no more than a mouthful or two left for him.

Soon after that, at least one responsibility fell from his shoulders. Ostine disappeared. Adam hunted for her everywhere but she didn't answer his call. He guessed that she'd been caught, killed and eaten by the desperate hangers-on who were dying of hunger and disease on the fringes of the camp.

After that, he feared for Faithful, but it was clear that the mastiff still had the strength and ferocity to keep any hunters at bay. It was a long time since Adam had been able to feed him, and he often wondered how Faithful was managing to remain so strong and healthy. He let him loose to roam at night, and he suspected that the dog trotted up to the Saracen camp and foraged for scraps. Often, Adam wished he could do the same.

He'd been surprised to run into the Saracen boy. He'd never been so close to one of the enemy before. He'd half expected other infidels to leap out at him from behind the nearby boulders and hack him to pieces with their swords. Even worse, he'd wondered for one petrifying moment if the boy would summon up a demon, something of hellish wickedness, who would try to snatch his soul away.

Then he'd seen the fright in the boy's eyes.

He was scared of Faithful, he thought afterwards. *There was something wrong about his leg too. Cursed at birth, maybe.*

Then there had been the stains he'd noticed, making runnels in the dust on the boy's cheeks.

He'd been crying, Adam thought, surprised by the discovery.

The realization was uncomfortable. He hadn't expected a Saracen to feel or look like a real person. He shook his head, trying to dispel the memory, and thought about the boy no more.

Trumpets and the beating of drums woke Adam one morning before dawn. He had been sleeping as usual beside Grimbald, under the rough awning that covered the Fortis warhorses, and he started up in fright, thinking that the Saracens were attacking. Faithful was barking furiously, his hackles raised.

Sir Ivo came stumbling out of his tent.

'My sword! What have you done with my lance? Hurry up, boy!'

All over the Crusader camp the alarm was being sounded. Foot soldiers were groping in the darkness for their helmets and bows, warhorses were being saddled and squires were easing knights into their coats of mail.

Then, through the din, came an unexpected sound. Cries of joy were rippling backwards through the camp from the beach.

'Ships!' people were shouting. 'Ships!'

The light was growing brighter, minute by minute.

'Sounds of joy, I think, rather than conflict,' said Sir Ivo, in his usual light way. 'Mail coat in readiness, however, just in case. And saddle Grimbald.'

He disappeared in the direction of Lord Guy's large tent nearby, and Adam saw the grey shapes of the other knights gather to confer.

He set about his duties, starting with Grimbald. The great black stallion, excited by the clamour, was tossing his head and blowing noisily down his nostrils.

'No call for all that,' Adam said, as he flung the heavy saddle up on to the horse's back. 'No fighting today, not by the looks of things.'

Faithful was still barking and Adam went across to quieten him. The first shafts of sunlight were making stripes across the eastern sky. In a moment the sun would be up over the horizon. He could see the knot of knights clearly now, as they stood at the entrance to Lord Guy's tent. Some were looking up anxiously towards the Saracen army on the hill above. Others were pointing the other way, towards the sea.

Adam bent over Faithful, stroking his head and reassuring him quietly. He could feel the bones of the dog's skull sharp through the lank folds of his skin.

I'm not much more than a scarecrow myself, he thought, licking his dry lips. *If that's more Crusaders arriving, I hope they've brought their own food. There won't be a bite left to eat in this camp soon.*

The very thought of food made saliva well up inside his mouth. He swallowed it, felt for his belt and tightened it round his waist. Half a cupful of watery porridge was all he could hope for today.

He was about to trot back to Sir Ivo's tent to start laying out his armour when he caught sight of Lord Robert, who had emerged blinking into the new dawn light and was fixing plumes into the crest of his father's great helmet. Adam grinned.

Noble you might be, he thought, *but you're still only a squire. I heard your pa bawl you out yesterday for ripping that pennant on his lance. Careless, you are.*

He'd never have a made a mistake like that. He handled Sir Ivo's knightly gear with reverence, and knew he was skilled in managing it.

At that moment, Lord Robert looked up and stared straight across the rough intervening ground into Adam's eyes. He scowled, as if he had read Adam's thoughts. Adam's grin disappeared at once, and he hurried into Sir Ivo's tent. One day, he knew, when Lord Guy was no longer there, he'd become the property of Lord Robert, his bonded serf, completely in his power. The thought of it chilled him and he shivered.

He was taking a freshly washed surcoat from the small chest by Sir Ivo's pallet bed when he heard shouts and cheering coming from the direction of Lord Guy's tent. He hurried outside, the surcoat in his hands.

'The lost ship!' he heard someone call out. 'It's come! It's a miracle! A miracle!'

Shocked with joy, Adam stood still for a frozen moment. Then, hardly knowing what he was doing, he shouted, 'Jenny!' and flinging the surcoat aside, he dashed off in the direction of the sea. Ruthlessly using his elbows, he tried to push his way through the crowd hurrying in the same direction. Eager Fortis men were pressing up against him on all sides, barging their way through a camp full of protesting Burgundians, tripping over their guy ropes and dodging round their wagons.

He reached the front, where the crowd had thinned out, and found himself running alongside Roger Stepesoft, his old shipmate.

'What did I tell you?' Roger panted, beaming at him. 'Come back to you, hasn't she, safe and sound.'

He didn't bother to answer. Weakened by weeks of hunger, he was painfully out of breath.

''Tain't all good news, if it is our ship.' Treuelove Malter had trotted up on the other side of him. 'They'll have eaten up all their own food by now. Hundreds more sharing what we got – there won't be a mouthful left for anyone.'

Adam put on a spurt and left the other two behind. If Jennet was alive, it would be miracle enough for one day. There'd be time enough to think about food later.

There was not one but three ships at anchor just off the beach, which was crammed with people. Men were splashing out through the shallow water, returning to the shore with heavy sacks weighing down their shoulders.

'Corn! They've brought corn!' someone shouted. 'Food for everyone! We're saved!'

As the news spread, people dropped to their knees on the sand and looked up at the sky, their hands clasped in thankful prayer. Some began to sing, their weak voices strengthened with hope, while in the camp behind, the bells outside the tented churches jangled with violent joy.

Adam had eyes only for the lost Fortis ship, beached a little way apart from the other two. The huge door in its bows had swung open, and horses were mincing delicately down the gangway. After them rumbled wagons, pulled by teams of mules. Adam, barely taking in their sleek, well-fed appearance, was scanning the heads that crowded along the rail of the upper deck, searching for Jennet.

The faces peering down from above were solemn, awed, lit from within by holy joy. Adam, remembering how he'd felt when he'd first arrived in the Holy Land, was sorry for them. They were expecting glory and salvation. They had come to hunger and squalor.

He almost didn't see Jennet. She had drawn a shawl close over her head and was slipping off the ship half concealed by one of the wagons. Adam, catching a glimpse of her, ran forward, then hesitated as he saw her more clearly. Was this Jennet, this stooped, stumbling creature? Could anyone have changed so much?

Then he saw the child she was carrying on her hip.

Of course! The baby. It'll have been born by now. It'll be a child, not a baby, by now.

'Jenny!' he shouted.

She looked up and her face, white and drawn, broke into an exhausted smile. A moment later he was beside her.

'I thought you were dead,' he said. 'I gave up hope. Everyone said the ship had gone down.'

She shuddered.

'It nearly did. More than once. Sometimes I wished it had. Another week at sea and the sickness would have killed me off. I feel terrible, Adam. And the ground keeps heaving under my feet. I thought it would stop when I was back on dry land. But am I glad to see you! I was afraid you'd have been sliced in half by now by one of them wicked Saracen swords. But what have you done to yourself? You're nothing but skin and bone! Grown, though, haven't you? Not a kid any more, are you?'

He was looking curiously at the child, a little girl, with a tangle of dirty blonde curls on her head.

'Food's run out, nearly,' he said.

Jennet shifted the child from one hip to the other.

'What are you grinning like that for, then?'

'I'm pleased to see you! And these other ships, they're full of supplies, aren't they?'

She was no longer listening but was standing still, looking round at the teeming, crowded camp, pulling a face at the foul stench wafting down from it.

'This is the Holy Land, then, is it? I thought it would be – oh, I don't know. Beautiful. Not ordinary, anyway. What's that up there, on the hill?'

'It's them. The Saracens,' Adam said. 'Stalemate, that's what this is. We've been sitting it out, staring at each other for a year and a half already. We hoped the King would be here by now. They've got a cunning devil of a king on their side, I can tell you. Saladin his name is. He calls on the powers of darkness, they say. It'll take a hero like King Richard to get the better of him.'

'And that's the city, is it? That's Jerusalem?' Jennet nodded towards the walls of Acre.

'No,' he said, feeling pleasantly superior. 'Jerusalem's miles away. That's Acre. We've got to take it first, before we can even think about Jerusalem.'

She pulled down the corners of her mouth.

'Look at it! Those walls – they're massive! No one could ever get in there.'

'They'll give up soon,' Adam said cheerfully. 'Starving them out, that's what we're doing.'

He wanted to tell Jennet about the dogs dying, and Sir Ivo taking him on, and how he was now doing the work of a squire, but the little girl was kicking Jennet's hip, her mouth turned down at the corners as if she about to cry.

'How old is she?' Adam asked awkwardly.

'Just on a year. Walking already. It's a job keeping up with her, I can tell you.' She dropped a light kiss on to the fuzz of pale hair. 'Her name's Matilda. It was my ma's name. I call her Tibby most of the time.'

He looked down briefly at the child's pink face. 'I don't know much about children.'

Jennet smiled.

'I didn't either. I know more than I ever wanted to now. Lovely, though, she is.'

She's changed again, Adam thought. *I suppose the baby's the main thing with her now.*

It was hard keeping up with Jennet.

She was looking eagerly around her as they walked up through the crowded camp.

'Where's the English then?' she said, hearing the strange languages all around. 'Look at this lot. They're all foreign.'

'We're further on. The other side of the camp, nearest the hills. Right up by the bank at the edge.' Adam was becoming worried. He could see too much interest in the faces of the men they passed. A young woman was a rare thing in the Crusader camp and the thousands of men cooped up there had been without their wives and girlfriends for too long. His shoulders tensed. Jennet needed someone to protect her, but there was nothing much he could do. The thought made him feel useless and half resentful.

Anyway, I'm working for Sir Ivo now, he told himself.

Sir Ivo! He remembered with a jolt how he'd thrown the surcoat aside and run off without permission.

'Come on, Jenny,' he said, tugging at her arm. 'We've got to hurry. I'm with Sir Ivo now. His groom got left behind, and his squire died. I'm sort of doing their work.'

'Squire's work? You don't mean it!' She stared at him admiringly. 'Adam, that's amazing! I remember Sir Ivo. He's the nice one.'

'Yes, but I ran off without telling him when I heard your ship had come in.'

'You didn't, did you?' She stopped walking and pointed forwards. 'You'd better go on ahead. I'll go back down to the wagons and come in with the other women.'

He frowned.

'Be careful. A woman can't go anywhere in this camp on her own. It's dangerous.'

'Listen to you, ordering me about!' she marvelled. 'Go on, Adam. If you get into trouble I don't want it to be my fault. I can look after myself anyway, thank you very much.'

Her mocking tone offended him, and he stood still, glaring at her. And then behind Adam came a silky voice that he remembered only too well. He spun round, and grimaced at the sight of the pedlar, Jacques.

'My young friend! I should say my *dear* young friend. Well! Very neat and tidy-looking for a dog boy you are, I must say. Gone up in the world, I can see that. New tunic, new sandals – quite the young lord. Rich opportunities there are for all of us in a camp like this. I feel my horizons expanding. I'd say I could smell success if it wasn't for the stink of something different.'

Jacques lifted his foot and looked with disgust at what was clinging to the sole of his shoe.

'Jacques!' said Jennet, sounding pleased. 'Good thing you're here. I want to go on with the wagons. Adam's got to hurry on. He's Sir Ivo's squire now.'

'I'm not a squire,' Adam said hastily. 'I'm his servant, that's all.'

Jacques whistled admiringly.

'A squire! Where will it end? Glory beckons, young man. Now go on. Scarper. I'll look after Jenny here. Be all right with me, won't you, lovey?'

Jennet was already hurrying back towards the beach. In the distance, Adam could see the wagons making their slow, laborious progress.

Jacques met Adam's scowl with a wide, innocent smile.

'Trust me, my boy!' He winked and turned to follow Jennet, his eyes darting everywhere as he took in the large possibilities the camp offered to his talents. He caught Jennet up and flung his cloak protectively round her shoulders.

Adam watched doubtfully, then ran on towards the Fortis camp.

She's only been here the space of a half-hour and we're going on at each other already, he thought ruefully. *She doesn't see that I'm older. She's only a woman, after all, and I'm a man now, almost. She needs me.*

He bit his lip with anxiety as he saw Sir Ivo standing at the opening to his tent, slapping a leather belt against one hand.

'My surcoat lying in the dust. My horse saddled but unbridled. My coat of mail all in a heap. You run off like a gaping fool, at the first hint of excitement. I'm disappointed in you, Adam. I took a risk with you.'

Adam searched his mind for something to say, and found nothing.

'I'm sorry, sir,' he managed at last.

'To be trustworthy,' Sir Ivo continued in the same biting tone, 'is the first lesson any servant must learn, much more a page. I should have known better than to expect such a quality in a serf. I shall be forced to look elsewhere, I can see.'

Adam stared at him, the blood draining from his face.

'Sir Ivo, please . . .' He stopped, seeing in Sir Ivo's face that pleading would only make matters worse. He took a deep breath and tried to keep his voice from trembling. 'I understand,' he said. 'I'm very sorry.' He stopped. There was no change in Sir Ivo's expression. A little defiance crept into Adam's soul. 'If you find another boy,' he said stiffly, 'tell him to look out for Grimbald's left forehock. There's a tick bite there looks like it might become infected.'

Exasperation replaced the anger on Sir Ivo's face.

'You stupid boy! What did you run off like that for?'

'No reason, sir.' Adam was staring woodenly ahead. 'I was just stupid, like you said.'

He flinched as the belt Sir Ivo was holding flicked painfully across his face.

'Don't take that insolent tone with me! Why did you run off?'

Adam felt Faithful's wet nose push against his hand. The dog, sensing that he was in trouble, was growling softly.

'Stop that,' Adam whispered fiercely. Faithful whimpered, backed obediently away and flopped down nearby, watching intently.

'It was because of Jennet,' Adam said unwillingly at last, a dark flush mounting his face.

'*Jennet*? A *girl*?'

There was disgust in Sir Ivo's voice.

'She's a laundry maid.' Adam saw recognition in Sir Ivo's eyes, and hurried on. 'It's not – that sort of thing, sir. She's like my big sister. Her father was always kind to me, after mine died.'

'Go on.'

Adam hesitated, not knowing if he dared criticize Lord Robert.

'She was got into trouble,' he plunged on recklessly, 'by Lord Robert. She's got a baby now. Lord Robert, he said it wasn't his, but it was. He wouldn't do anything to help her. It's put her in danger. The men-at-arms, they think she's no better than a – you know what I mean, sir.' He was trying to read Sir Ivo's face, but the knight's expression gave nothing away. Adam went doggedly on. 'When I thought the ship she was in was lost, it was like my whole family had gone. It's what she is to me. My family. There's no one else. And I thought of her coming up here through the whole camp, with all the foreigners, not knowing her, just seeing a girl, with no protection, and when I thought what they might do, I just ran, sir. I had to look after her. I'm – she's my responsibility.'

'You know, of course, young Adam,' said Sir Ivo after a pause, resuming his normal light tone, 'that the duty of a knight is to protect women and the fatherless? I have some authority in this camp, I believe. I shall warn the sergeant-at-arms that if any harm comes to her there'll be the severest punishment. She'll be safe enough if she stays within the confines of the Fortis camp.' He coughed. 'She's been wronged, I know.'

Adam's heart lightened.

'Thank you, Sir Ivo! That'll make things go all right.'

'And now, the matter of my surcoat,' Sir Ivo said severely, picking up the crumpled bundle of once-white linen which was streaked with dirt. 'You'll wash it immediately. And the next time you rush off on a chivalrous quest you'll refrain from throwing my belongings in the path of your scabrous hound. His paw marks are all over it.'

It took Adam a moment to digest Sir Ivo's meaning.

'Then am I – you're not going to—'

'You stay in my service. Yes. On trial. You understand?'

'Oh yes, sir!' Adam beamed at him. He'd never known any-one as good and generous as Sir Ivo before. His heart was swept with devotion.

Something else occurred to him.

'I didn't tell you, sir. There were two other ships came in with ours. Full of food. They're unloading sacks of corn off them now.'

Sir Ivo clapped him joyfully on the shoulder.

'Wonderful news! Christ be thanked! I had begun to believe that we were destined for a most inglorious and uncomfortable martyrdom.'

The new arrivals from the recovered ship were stream-ing into the Fortis camp by now. Lord Guy stood with his hands on his hips, his chest thrust out, nodding with pleasure and satisfaction as one by one his long-lost vassals came and bowed in front of him. Their adventures, as they were retold by one person to another, became more and more fantastic, including as they did frightful storms, the sighting of great sea monsters, hostile islanders, appearances of saints and the blessing of the Virgin in the form of a friendly coastal village, who had taken them in and supplied them with food and water. Adam gave up trying to make head or tail of it all.

He was kept busy all day helping to unload the wagons, store the precious supplies of food and make sure that Grimbald had his fair share of the animal fodder the new arrivals had brought with them.

'You can count yourself lucky, old boy,' he said cheerfully, nudging aside Vigor, Lord Guy's horse, as he rubbed Grimbald down with a wisp of straw. 'Tomorrow you'd have been everyone's dinner, same as all the rest.'

There was a festive atmosphere throughout the whole Crusader camp that night. The new supplies had given everyone hope. It was clear now that the sea was navigable again after the storms of winter, and more ships would soon be arriving. The business of war would start up again in deadly earnest. The catapults were already back in action, and the dull crump of their missiles hitting the city walls frequently echoed out across the camp.

In the Fortis section, everyone was jubilant.

'Christ and his saints haven't deserted us after all,' Adam heard someone say. 'I was having my doubts, if I'm honest with you.'

'Aye, we'll be all right now,' his companion answered. 'The King's grace will be here any day soon. Damned infidels. The wrath of God, that's what they'll feel.'

Ale and wine, unloaded from the recovered ship, were drunk in great quantities that evening. Lord Guy, uncommonly genial, walked about among his Crusaders, his face scarlet with alcohol and pleasure. Adam, having been excused by Sir Ivo, went off to find Jennet, with Faithful padding at his heels.

She was sitting behind a wagon, with Tibby drowsing in her lap. To Adam's relief, Jacques was nowhere to be seen.

'Are you all right here?' he asked her. 'Where are you sleeping?'

'In the wagon. It's not bad there.'

'Sir Ivo says he'll speak to the sergeant. He'll make him keep the men in order.'

She touched his arm and he thought he saw a new respect in her face.

'Thanks, Adam. You done a lot for me. Don't think I'm not grateful. I truly am.'

Adam smiled.

'That Jacques,' he said feeling more confident. 'You want to watch him. He's a cheat, Jenny. I know it for a fact. You mustn't trust him.'

'Jacques?' She shook her head. 'No, you've got him wrong. He's all right. He's given me things. Charms and that. He's lovely with Tibby. He takes an interest.' She yawned. 'What a day! I'm glad we got here in the end, though I can't say it's like I thought it would be. There's just one thing though, Adam, that I wanted to ask you. We didn't have no priest with us on our ship, so Tibby's never been baptized. I was so scared she'd die before we got here. I'll have to pluck up my courage tomorrow and go and see Father Jerome. You'll stand godfather to her, won't you?'

Adam felt a flush of pride.

'Godfather? Of course I will. I'd be pleased.'

CHAPTER TEN

The arrival of the second spring brought a restless feeling to the Saracen camp. Saladin had watched and waited throughout the winter, not wishing to throw his men against difficult odds, hoping that hunger and disease would force the Crusaders to give up and withdraw.

'Such cruel, fanatical people,' Salim overheard him say to Dr Musa. 'But you can't deny that they're brave.'

'As for courage, sire, there's too much of it around, in my humble opinion,' Dr Musa had answered. 'Sticking swords into people – it only leads to trouble. Better to sit down and talk things over quietly.'

The surrounding courtiers exchanged horrified glances at this audacious speech, but Saladin laughed.

'I'm glad you're not one of my soldiers, Musa. But you can take your anti-courage message to the barbarians with my goodwill and pleasure. May Allah frustrate their wickedness!'

The arrival of the Crusaders' supply ships had roused a new anxiety in the Saracen camp.

'It's only the beginning,' one of Dr Musa's patients grumbled, as he waited outside his tent. 'The Sultan of France will be here soon, and the devil of England, curse him. There'll be thousands more Frankish knights and soldiers. Why doesn't Saladin attack?'

Another, nursing his infected hand, said, 'He's waiting for more troops to join us. They'll come. Don't you trust him? Saladin always wins. He ran the Crusaders out of Jerusalem, didn't he? He'll drive this lot into the sea.'

Salim, on edge like everyone else, had taken to going back to his old vantage point, and whenever the doctor let him go, he'd lie on his stomach, trying to make out what the enemy was doing. The boom of the catapults made him shudder when he thought of how frightening the sound must be inside the city itself, but he took comfort from the many buryings that took place every day. Several times he'd seen the boy with the fearsome dog. He'd started watching out for him. They'd only been face to face once, for a few moments, but there had been something unforgettable about the boy. He had a strange intensity about him, like an animal crouched to spring.

He looked as if he was really scared of me, Salim thought. *But he was bigger than me and he had the dog too.*

He watched the new arrivals off the ship come into the Fortis camp, and he tried to count the wagons they'd brought with them.

'Seven or eight, I think,' he told Ismail, who always wanted to know exactly what he'd seen.

'Could you see what was inside them?' Ismail asked.

'Of course not! They were too far away. Anyway, they were covered.'

'Weapons, probably,' guessed Ismail. 'Arrows, for sure. And food maybe.' His eyes lit up. 'Didn't you say they put the wagons at the very edge of the camp, right under the earth bank? Why don't we make a raid, little brother, and go in and fetch a couple out?'

'Are you crazy? You couldn't possibly. You'd never get past the gate, never mind get out again. There are always hundreds of soldiers and knights on guard. You wouldn't stand a chance. I've seen them. You couldn't do it.'

But Ismail wouldn't let the idea go.

'Not a raid then. An ambush. I'll talk to Captain Arslan. It's a great idea. He'll love it. You'll see.'

The next day Salim was busy with Solomon, pounding herbs in a mortar to make a healing paste, when to his surprise Captain Arslan came to the pharmacist's tent and called him out.

'This near section of the camp that you've been watching,' he said. 'Describe it to me.'

'Well,' Salim said hesitantly, 'there are big tents for the lords, and smaller ones, and shelters for the horses, and—'

'I know all that.' The captain looked impatient. 'How many knights? How many soldiers? What kind of horses?'

'About twenty-five knights altogether, I think, just in that small section. I don't know where they're from. There's a device with a black hammer on a silver background, and another shows a bear with an axe. There are three or four more banners besides those.' Salim was frowning as he tried to remember. 'I don't know about horses. There were more in the beginning, but they've killed most of them. There are only a few left now.'

'Warhorses? Chargers? The big ones are still there?'

'Yes. Some of them have been killed, but not all.'

'Twenty-five knights . . .' the captain repeated thoughtfully. 'Good.' He tapped Salim on the shoulder by way of thanks and strode off towards Saladin's great tent.

Later, as thousands of little cooking fires sprouted like orange flowers along the lines of Saracen tents, Ismail came to seek Salim out. His face was alive with excitement.

'We're actually going to do it! We're going to set up an ambush. We're going for those twenty-five Frankish knights, the ones you told the captain about. Brilliant, isn't it? And it's all my idea!'

Salim's heart had skipped uncomfortably.

'What do you mean? You're going to attack the camp? But you can't, Ismail! There are too many of them. They'll kill you!'

Ismail slapped his chest.

'What, you think I'm scared? What do you take me for? Some little girl from Cairo? I'm a Mamluk, don't forget. Anyway, you don't have to worry. We're going to set up a trap. It'll be great. Make sure you're watching, little brother, when the Franks come charging out to chase us. It'll be a fantastic sight!'

Blood rushed to Salim's head. He grabbed Ismail's arm and shook it.

'Let me come with you. Please, Ismail! Let me ride Kestan. I won't let you down. You know what a good shot I am. Just let me come!'

'You? Shoot arrows?' Ismail laughed. 'You don't know what you're talking about. Sorry, Salim, but you've never seen us in action. I've been training since I was ten years old for this: riding without hands, shooting backwards while galloping forwards – it's difficult. Captain Arslan wouldn't let you anywhere near the real action.'

Salim raged with frustration as the Mamluk troop slipped quietly out of the camp that night, ready to set up the ambush. He'd watched enviously as they'd gone about their preparations, putting on their coats of mail and studded brigandines, sliding daggers inside their belts, filling their quivers with arrows and checking the edges of their swords. He cursed his fate in being cut out of the real action.

He watched from a distance as the ambush party melted into the night, and when the sound of their horses' hooves had died away, he limped back moodily to the doctor's tent. Dr Musa raised a massive eyebrow as he saw the look in his eyes.

'So. A tragedy has taken place? You've received news of your imminent death? You have some dreadful crime to confess to me?'

Salim summoned up the ghost of a smile.

'No, *sidi* Musa.'

'Good. Then go and tell Solomon that we'll need more rose-water and sugar ointment. There have been five cases of eye inflammation today, and there are sure to be more tomorrow. And kindly stop looking as if you've come from a funeral. Do you want to scare all the patients into fits of depression?'

That night, battle cries and the clash of swords echoed through Salim's sleep. As dawn broke, he found himself standing in the path of a silver-armoured knight who was thundering towards him on a gigantic black horse. He was unable to move. Something was clinging to him, wound round his legs, paralysing him. Just as the knight's lance was lowered to kill him, Salim saw, through the slits of the man's helmet, that there was nothing there. No eyes. No face. No head. He woke with a sob of terror and lay sweating in the darkness, trying to shake the nightmare away.

Even if they let me go with them, I'd never be brave enough to be a soldier, he thought miserably. *I couldn't ever be like the Mamluks.*

He had served the doctor his breakfast and was eating his own portion when shouts made them both look up.

'Yes, yes,' Dr Musa said testily, seeing the eager look in Salim's eye. 'Go and see what's happening.'

Salim was off already, hobbling as fast as he could towards the sound.

A large number of soldiers had gathered at the edge of the Saracen camp and were hurling insults down towards the Crusaders. Salim could see helmeted heads bob up from behind the bank as puzzled Franks tried to see what was going on.

This is it. The trap's being set, thought Salim. *They're trying to lure them out into the ambush.*

Sliding along the hillside, he came to his lookout place, and lay down, propping his chin in his hands.

A small troop of five or six Kurdish horsemen now appeared, trotting towards the embankment. They were whirling their swords above their heads and shouting, *'Allahu akbar! Allahu akbar!'* at the tops of their voices.

Salim could see a ferment now among the English tents. Squires were running about with helmets and coats of mail. Drums were beating. Grooms were saddling the few remaining warhorses. More and more heads were appearing above the earthworks. One archer raised a bow and shot an arrow towards the nearest Kurdish horseman. The arrow missed, but a hail of others followed. The Kurds pulled away out of range, then fitted arrows to their own bows and from their greater height began to shoot back towards the camp.

There was a roar of anger as an English soldier, pierced through the face, fell backwards off the bank. Salim could see a kind of frenzy among the Crusaders now. Knights weighed down with their heavy chainmail, their heads encased in metal helmets, were lumbering towards their horses. Their squires stood by to hoist them into their saddles, then handed them their swords and lances. It was easy to see who their leader was. Heavier than the others, he carried the longest sword and was the only one to wear plumes in his helmet. A white pennant with a black hammer embroidered on it fluttered from his lance. His horse cavorting under him, he raised his sword and shouted something. Salim was too far away to make out the words, but the circle of knights around him, raising their own lances, shouted in response. Then the big man rode his horse straight through the gap in the bank, whose heavy doors had been hastily pulled open. He waited until all the rest were through after him, then shouted an order. The knights formed themselves hastily into a line, then began to charge.

The hair rose on Salim's head as he watched them. The knights rode as one, their lances held straight out in front of them, their banners and the tails of their huge horses streaming out behind. They were a solid wall of power and fury, terrifying, invincible. The very ground seemed to shake with the thunder of their hooves and the air quivered with their battle cry as from every mouth came a scream of 'God wills it! God wills it!'

It seemed to Salim that nothing could ever stand in the way of them, as if they would ride over and annihilate the few lightly armed Saracen horsemen, who were racing just ahead of them on their smaller mounts.

It wasn't a good idea, Ismail. It wasn't! he thought. *They'll go straight through the ambush. Get out of their way! You didn't know what they'd be like!*

The charge was so fast that a few moments later all that was visible was a cloud of dust in the knights' wake. The place of the ambush, where Ismail and the Mamluks were waiting, was out of sight, over a ridge, more than a mile away. Salim longed to run there, to see what would happen, but he knew it was too far. He had no choice but to go back to the doctor and tell him what he'd seen. There'd be the wounded to care for later, perhaps. He'd have bandages to make and healing draughts of medicine to prepare.

He was up on his feet, recklessly forgetting to keep himself concealed, when he saw that more people had burst out of the Crusader camp. Foot soldiers, their helmets clapped hastily on to their heads, their bows ready in their hands, were running after the knights. Among them he saw the boy with the dog, and the dog itself, loping along beside him.

*

After the excitement of recovering Sir Guy's lost ship, bitter disappointment afflicted the Fortis camp. The wagons which the new arrivals had brought with them were full of weapons, tools and spare clothing, but what everyone longed for was food, and of that there was very little. The supply ships too, which were meant to feed the whole vast Crusader force, were disappointingly inadequate for tens of thousands of hungry men. There was a little more porridge and bread to go round for the lower orders, and a few extra luxuries for the nobles, but there was nowhere near as much as people had hoped for. Every day, the burying of starved bodies continued.

Discontent made everyone irritable. Tempers flared easily and several men-at-arms in the Fortis camp had been flogged on Lord Guy's orders for brawling.

'Christ has deserted us,' Adam heard people mutter. 'We're being punished for our sins.'

No one took much notice at first of the jeers and catcalls coming from the Saracen camp until a look-out ran in from the bank, shouting that heathen horsemen were approaching. News spread quickly that something was happening. Everyone stopped what they were doing and hurried to the open space outside Lord Guy's tent.

Another scout ran into the circle.

'They're holding a cross upside down!' he yelled. 'They're spitting on it! They're insulting our Lord!'

Lord Guy's face flushed darkly.

'I won't stand for this!' he roared, throwing aside the goblet he was holding.

Adam, who had been grooming Grimbald, edged to the front of the crowd in time to see Sir Ivo walk up to Lord Guy and say something quietly to him.

Lord Guy stared back at the knight, his bloodshot eyes bulging.

'A trap? An ambush? What are you saying? Are you a

coward, Ivo? The enemies of Christ are asking for a fight, and by his holy blood we'll give them one.' He raised his voice so that everyone could hear. 'King Richard will soon be here. Do you want us to tell him that we've sat here all this time, trembling with fright like a bunch of milkmaids? Archers! Take position on the banks. Fire in volleys. Grooms, saddle up. Knights, arm yourselves! To the charge!'

A drum began to beat, sending the hairs rising on Adam's chest. He clenched his fists with excitement.

He's right, he thought. *We've got to show them.*

He had recognized in Lord Guy's face something he'd often felt himself – a frustration longing to burst out, a suppressed rage that demanded action. He was still staring at the baron when Sir Ivo rushed up to him.

'Hurry up!' he began, then stopped as if struck by the expression on Adam's face. He turned to look back at Lord Guy, then shook his head, as if dismissing a strange idea.

Adam's hands trembled as, piece by piece, he handed Sir Ivo the thick padded lining to his mailcoat, the coat itself with its chainmail hood, the surcoat and mailed gloves. He'd practised for this moment time and again, and had often rehearsed it in his head. He'd kept everything in perfect readiness, stored so that there would be no muddle when the rush to battle came. Even so, he was flustered, holding the coat of mail out the wrong way round, and almost letting the huge helmet slip out of his hands when the moment came to pass it to Sir Ivo.

'See to Grimbald, quickly.' Sir Ivo's voice echoed oddly from inside the closed metal box of the helmet on his head. 'No, leave the sword and lance. I'll bring them. But my shield! Find my shield!'

Adam was only half aware of the trumpets braying nearby, and the shouts of rage when a dying archer was brought back down from the bank, shot through the face by a Saracen arrow. He was fumbling frantically to buckle on Grimbald's padded protective coat.

The knights were ready at last, armoured and mounted. Their horses, sensing battle, pranced nervously as they mustered behind the gap in the embankment, where men-at-arms were pulling aside the upturned wagons and other debris that blocked it.

'God wills it!' yelled Lord Guy, holding his lance high.

All his life, Adam had feared Lord Guy, and sometimes, when his sense of helplessness had overwhelmed him, he had hated him. Now, as he saw his lord in the glory of his armour, riding his gigantic black stallion towards the breach in the bank and the enemy beyond, shouting his battle cry and urging his knights to follow him, he was struck with admiration.

A moment later, the ten Fortis knights and the fifteen others from the larger English camp had spurred through the gap and were out of sight.

'God wills it! The Holy Sepulchre!' Adam heard them yell.

He made for the bank, intending to watch the charge from the top, but he saw that the men-at-arms had hastily struggled into their protective jerkins and, ramming their helmets on to their heads, were streaming out in pursuit of the knights. He stood for a moment, not sure what he was supposed to do, then saw that the squires had scrambled into their coats of mail and were running with the men-at-arms.

He wanted to bolt straight after them, but common sense made him run to fetch his own thickly padded jerkin and the helmet Sir Ivo had given him. It wasn't until he'd nearly caught up the last of the squires that he became aware of Faithful galloping up after him. He skidded to a halt.

'Go back! Go back, Faithful!' he shouted fiercely.

Faithful whined, stretched out his front legs and dropped his head on to them, looking up at Adam pleadingly.

Adam struck him across the nose.

'No! Go back!'

With a reproachful look, Faithful turned and began to walk away towards the camp. Adam sprinted off again, not realizing that Faithful, unable to resist the temptation, was following him again.

Adam had never seen a full cavalry charge against an enemy, though he'd watched the knights practise often enough on the flat ground by the river that ran alongside the walls of Acre towards the sea. He'd heard endless discussions, though, among the men-at-arms, about the likely outcome.

'It's like this, Adam,' Roger Stepesoft had kindly explained one long, slow afternoon on the ship last summer. 'Your knight and your charger, they're like battering rams, see. Go straight through the enemy, they do, like a – a . . .'

'Mad bull through a herd of cows,' Treuelove had put in.

'Yes.' Roger hadn't been pleased at the interruption. 'They scares the enemy. Terrifies him. *But* –' he'd paused impressively – 'your knight, he's nothing without his foot soldiers. Why?'

'I'll tell you.' Treuelove had become impatient with Roger's slow style. 'Knight gets knocked off his horse – he's useless. Can't hardly move in all that armour. Can't see nothing with that box on his head. And if some bleeding Turk nobbles the horse, he's done for.'

'And that,' Roger had concluded impressively, 'is where your man-at-arms comes in. Protecting our knights, that's what we do. Form a ring round them, once the charge is over. Stop them horrid little heathens from pulling them down.'

Adam had forgotten this conversation, but one sentence was ringing in his head as he ran.

'Protect my knight!' he chanted to himself. 'Protect my knight!'

Gasping for breath, he ran into the cloud of dust which the horses' hooves had churned up and heard, very close now, the unearthly din of battle, the banging of an infidel drum and the strange, blood-curdling war cries, the clash and grind of metal and the whistling scream of a wounded horse.

He had overtaken the last few squires by the time he'd reached the top of a small ridge, and he drew in his breath at the sight below. There were far more Saracens than he'd expected.

Sir Ivo was right, he thought, with a lurch of fear. *It was a trap. We've fallen right into it.*

The charge must have faltered here. The enemy must have been waiting for it. Their deadly hail of arrows had killed at least four knights. Three others, their helmets removed, were lying bound across Saracen horses and were being led away captive. In the middle of the confused mass of struggling men and horses, Lord Guy was waving his sword as if he was trying to form the knights up for another charge. Circling round, like hounds scenting blood at a bear baiting, the Saracen cavalry pranced on their dancing horses. They wore no heavy coats of mail and had nothing over their faces. Agile and fast, they darted into the crush to deliver a deadly stab with a knife-sharp sword, or to fell a knight from his horse with a crushing blow from a studded mace.

Adam caught sight of Sir Ivo at last. He was on the edge of the battle, couching his lance under his arm ready to launch Grimbald towards a Saracen ahead of him, but Adam, with a gasp, saw that two other Saracens were closing in on him, one on each side.

'No!' he yelled, and a moment later he was in the thick of the fighting, dodging trampling horses and flailing swords, ducking under lances, forcing his way through to where he could see Grimbald's blood-streaked flank and the arrow embedded in his side.

With a final shove, he reached Sir Ivo just as one of the Saracen knights grabbed Grimbald's bridle, and the other lifted his mace to lash out at Sir Ivo's head. It was clear that Sir Ivo, who could see only straight ahead through the slits of his helmet, was unaware of the danger he was in.

'On your left! Watch out!' Adam yelled.

He thought, for a sickening moment, that Sir Ivo hadn't heard him, but at the last moment the knight looked round, saw the mace descend and ducked. The massive weapon struck him on the back, but lightly, ripping his surcoat with its spikes, but glancing off the coat of mail underneath. The Saracen, caught off balance, swayed in his saddle and had to back away while he brought his horse back under control. Adam let out his breath, but now he saw that the other Saracen, who was holding Grimbald's bridle, was jerking it violently, trying to make the horse rear. If he succeeded, Sir Ivo would fall and be easy prey.

Diving under Grimbald's tossing head, Adam scrabbled at the Saracen's hand, trying to prize it off the horse's reins. The other man was closing in again, his mace held high. Sir Ivo, twisting in the saddle to take aim with his sword, had already lost one stirrup and seemed in danger of losing the other.

'Get off! Get off!' Adam screamed, shoving at the second Saracen's horse with all his strength.

And then, just as Grimbald laid his ears back and skittered violently, preparing to rear, a yellow ball of fur launched itself at the Saracen holding his bridle, and the man howled with pain as Faithful's teeth sank deep into his hand.

A savage blow in his side sent Adam reeling as the Saracen's horse, terrified by the mastiff, lashed out with his hooves. Ignoring the pain, Adam leaped for Faithful's collar, dragging him off just as the Saracen, with his free hand, tried to drive his dagger into Faithful's head. Faithful, confused and enraged, turned snarling on Adam, and knocked him off balance. Adam struggled to stand up and put up an arm to protect his head against the flailing hooves, the trampling, shouting and bludgeoning above him. His other hand, clammy with sweat, lost its grip on Faithful's collar, and the dog disappeared between Grimbald's legs. Another violent blow in the shoulder almost knocked Adam to the ground again, and he looked up to see Sir Ivo lean forward in his saddle and thrust his sword at the older Saracen, who was raising his mace, ready to bring it down on Adam's head. The blow caught the man on the neck, and Adam caught a glimpse of his face, and saw there an expression of surprise, almost of wonder, as he slumped forwards on to the pommel of his saddle, and his frightened horse carried him away.

Then, suddenly, the fighting was over. The English men-at-arms, hastily regrouping, sent a hail of arrows after the fleeing Saracen horsemen.

A ragged cheer went up from the English side.

'Follow! Follow!' Lord Guy bellowed. 'Don't let them get away!'

Adam watched as the knights jostled to separate themselves and settle their swords and lances. Then, with a gasp of horror, he saw that Faithful, wild with excitement, and attracted by Lord Guy's waving lance, was snapping at Vigor's hind legs. Worming his way between the sweating flanks of a dozen warhorses, he reached Faithful, grabbed his collar and yanked him back just as Vigor kicked out.

This time, Faithful gave into him without a struggle. Exhausted, his tongue hanging out, his yellow fur streaked with the Saracen's blood, he let Adam drag him away, out of the press of horses and men.

'Go back, Faithful, go *back*!' Adam ordered desperately, cuffing Faithful hard across the nose and pointing towards the camp.

To his relief, Faithful dropped his tail between his legs and limped away. But as Adam watched him, groans and shouts of dismay from the mass of knights made him turn his head.

The knights were pulling their horses back and looking down at something on the ground. Men-at-arms were shouting and rushing forward. Lord Guy had disappeared.

'He's down! Lord Guy's fallen!' he heard someone shout.

It wasn't Faithful's fault. It can't have been, Adam told himself. *I got him away. Lord Guy wasn't falling then.*

But he had seen, in those few fraught seconds, how Vigor's panic had made Lord Guy rock in the saddle, and how his feet had slipped out of the stirrups.

He looked over towards the Saracen camp.

What if they've seen him go down? he thought. *If they have, they'll come back and finish us off.*

But to his relief the Saracens hadn't noticed the Crusaders' confusion. They were out of sight already.

'Back! Retreat!' he heard Sir Ivo call out. 'Retrieve the wounded! Men-at-arms, form up around the horses. Keep your arrows on your strings. Knights, a walking pace!'

Adam, his heart in his mouth, fell in beside Roger Stepesoft, who had taken off his helmet to wipe the sweat off his forehead. He looked worried.

'This is bad,' he said.

'What happened? Did you see? Is Lord Guy hurt?' Adam asked him.

'Don't know. I seen his face, though. Horrible grey colour.'

'He's not . . .'

'No. His eyes was open. He was groaning.'

'Was he bleeding? Where's the wound?'

'Didn't see no blood. It was a bad fall off Vigor, though. Came down on his neck with a thump they'll have heard in Acre.'

Adam said nothing as nightmare visions chased through his mind. Why hadn't he just tied Faithful up?

'Treue, he was close by,' Roger went on. 'Seems Vigor was restive. Not surprising. There was a slash across his rump would have felled most horses. Hey, watch out! Look up there, on the ridge! More of them devils. Don't you doze off now, young Adam. Dangerous moment, a retreat. We'll be shooting our way out of this one, more 'n likely.'

But there were no more attacks from the Saracens that day and the sombre English troop plodded the mile or so back to the camp without a single arrow being loosed from their bows.

The first thing Adam saw, as he stumbled wearily towards Sir Ivo's tent, was Faithful lying across the threshold. The dog lay so still that for a moment Adam was afraid he was dead, but Faithful, recognizing his step, lifted his head and let his tail flop a couple of times against the ground.

'Adam!' Jennet was running towards him. 'What's happening? They're saying Lord Guy's been killed. It isn't true! It can't be!'

He stared at her, horrified.

'Dead? It's not what I've heard. A fall off his horse, that's all.' His voice was gruff with anxiety. 'Give Faithful some water for me, Jenny. I've got work to do.'

Sir Ivo, who had been at the rear of the troop, had appeared on foot, leading Grimbald by the rein. The horse's breathing was laboured and his head hung low. There were so many arrows sticking into the protective padding on his chest, flanks and rump that he looked like a hedgehog. Sir Ivo had taken off his helmet and was carrying it under his arm. His fair hair, dark with sweat, was plastered against his forehead, and Adam was shocked to see the weariness in his face.

'Get me some water,' Sir Ivo croaked.

He drained the goblet that Adam fetched for him in great gulps, and threw Grimbald's reins over the post outside his tent.

'Get me out of all this quickly, then see to him,' he said to Adam. 'An arrow's got through under the padding. Low down.

Nasty to get out. You'll need advice from one of the older grooms. I must go to Lord Guy.'

He's not dead, is he? Adam longed to ask, but didn't dare. *And if he is, it wasn't my fault, was it?*

'Hurry, can't you?' Sir Ivo was impatient as Adam helped him struggle out of the unwieldy coat of mail. 'Never mind about a clean robe. Any one will do.'

A few minutes later he was hurrying out of the tent.

Adam, his heart thumping, watched him push through the group of younger knights and squires, who were talking in hushed voices outside Lord Guy's great tent. He paused for a moment at the entrance, and Adam saw Father Jerome come out and usher him inside.

What's the penalty for causing the death of your lord? Adam asked himself. *It must be death, but how will they kill me?*

He had a wild urge to run and hide, somewhere, anywhere, away from the Fortis people. But where would he go?

He began automatically to tidy the gear of battle away, arranging it in readiness to be put on again in a hurry if the need arose. The familiar activity was comforting.

No one's said anything about me yet, he thought. *Perhaps they didn't notice. Anyway, who said Lord Guy's going to die? He'll have a few bruises, that's all.*

'You in there, Adam?' came Jennet's voice.

He went outside.

'What's going on? Have you heard anything?' he asked her.

'Course not. Who's going to stop and talk to me?' She frowned at him. 'You look like death. Not wounded anywhere, are you?'

'I got a thumping kick in the ribs,' he told her. 'Nothing serious. Just bruising, I think. Hurts when I breathe, though.'

'Grimbald don't look too happy,' she said, walking round the charger, who was standing with his head drooping, lifting one trembling back leg towards the wound. 'Here, look! An arrow's gone right into him!'

'I know. Sir Ivo says I'm to take him to one of the grooms.'

He unbuckled the horse's padding and peeled it carefully off him. One or two of the arrows had pierced it and nicked Grimbald's back, but the wounds were slight. One unlucky shot had found the gap between the edges of the padding near Grimbald's tail. Adam drew in his breath at the sight of it, embedded half way up the shaft, and the slick of dark blood sliding down the horse's flank. He lifted the reins off the post and clicked his tongue.

'Come with me, boy. We'll put it right.'

Jennet took the reins out of his hand and slipped them back over the post.

'Wait!' she said. 'I'll get it out.'

'Don't be daft!' Adam scowled at her. 'You want to get me into worse trouble than what I'm in already? What do you know about horses, anyway?'

'A lot more than you do. Or half the grooms at Fortis, come to that. My dad used to treat every horse and cow and donkey in the valley, remember? I've watched him get a spike like a spear out of the side of a mad bull that no one else dared go near.'

He said nothing. He remembered now Tom Bate's healing way with animals. He'd been famed for it, even beyond Ashton. He walked round to Grimbald's head and put a light hand on his bridle, then talked to him gently, stroking his long black nose. He didn't want to watch what Jennet was doing.

Grimbald suddenly snorted with pain and trampled backwards, rolling his eyes till the whites showed and laying back his ears. But Jennet was crowing with triumph and holding the arrow above her head.

'See? You didn't believe I could do it, did you? It's a nasty one too. Barbed.'

She leaned forward to examine the wound.

'Not as bad as I thought. He'll do now.'

Adam smiled at her. Jennet was so practical and steady that his worries suddenly seemed exaggerated.

'You're a marvel, Jenny. I think I know all about you then you pull some new thing and knock me flat with surprise.'

She sniffed.

'I've had enough surprises in my life, thank you. Don't wish any more on me, whatever you do.'

CHAPTER ELEVEN

Salim couldn't conceal his pride and excitement as he watched the Mamluk troop trot back into camp. He cheered them, and joined with everyone else in the hoots and jeers of derision at the sight of the four Frankish knights who had been taken prisoner. Helmetless but still in their coats of mail, they were trussed up like chickens and lying across their saddles.

There had been one death. The body of the Mamluk was carried reverently in on a pallet, wrapped in a simple linen cloth, and arrangements were made for his immediate burial. Everyone stood in silence as the little cortège passed by. No one had expected the Franks to fight back quite so fiercely. There was a feeling that the ambush had been worth it, but only just.

It had not been the only action that day. Saladin had ordered small raids and attacks all along the Crusader lines. The action had come as a relief to everyone.

'The sooner we show these criminals what they can expect, the sooner we can all go home,' the soldiers muttered, but without much conviction. In spite of their half-starved, miserable condition, the Crusaders had resisted ferociously, and there had been Saracen casualties, with fewer Crusader prisoners than had been expected.

A steady trickle of wounded had been coming in all day. Most of the wounds were from arrows, but there were also men with hideous gashes from swords and lances. They had been sent straight to the field hospital, where surgeons, summoned by Saladin in readiness for the coming season of war, had set up beds and trained orderlies in the care of wounds.

'God be thanked,' Dr Musa said, as the injured were carried past his tent. 'A doctor is a doctor and a surgeon is a surgeon. Fish is not fowl, nor fowl fish.'

'But none of them could have saved Ismail, the way you did,' Salim objected. He had secretly imagined himself sharing the glory of Dr Musa's amazing exploits in the saving of heroes' lives.

'Patching up fools so that they can rush back into battle again – so that's what medicine means to you, is it? No, my boy. The inner workings of the body, its humours, its marvellous mechanisms – understanding and regulating – that's our art. Art, do you hear me?'

Ismail, nursing a mangled hand, had been taken to the hospital, but had walked straight out of it again, and come to find Dr Musa. He looked pale and sorrowful.

'I don't trust them in there,' he said. 'You fixed me up brilliantly last time. Please, *ya-hakim*, help me.'

Dr Musa, sighed, pushed his turban straight, then took the hand Ismail was holding out to him and bent to study it.

'What's this? Teeth marks? The Christians bite when they fight? I knew they were barbarians, but this . . . !'

'No, no.' Ismail shook his head. 'It wasn't a man. It was a dog. A monster! The size of a lion, honestly. I had hold of an infidel's horse by the bridle. Hassan was trying to get him with his mace. But the dog come from nowhere like – like an evil spirit. He bit me so hard, I had to let the horse go. Then the knight lifted his sword and –' he demonstrated, raising his sword arm and thrusting upwards – 'he caught Hassan in the neck, like this. He didn't have a chance.' He wiped a sleeve across his eyes. 'Hassan was always a good friend to me. He was like my older brother.'

Salim looked down. He couldn't bear to see Ismail cry. And he remembered Hassan well.

'You mustn't mind too much, Ismail,' he said gruffly. 'Hassan was a martyr for Islam. He's in Paradise now.'

'Where you will be shortly if we don't clean up this hand,' Dr Musa remarked drily. 'Dog bites infect easily. Water, Salim, and oil of woundwort. Only barley soup for the next few days, young man. And chicken. No mutton or goat meat.'

Ismail smiled weakly.

'Chicken? There haven't been any chickens for us lot for months. The food's lousy now.'

The doctor was gently feeling the injured hand.

'No bones broken. It will mend soon enough if you follow my orders. I'll need to bleed you in a few days to balance the humours. You lead a charmed life, Ismail, though I fear it will be a short one if you don't take more care.'

Ismail drew himself up.

'Whoever heard of a Mamluk *taking care*?' he said, bowed his thanks, and walked away.

The rest of the day dragged for Salim. He longed to go to the Mamluk camp and hear more about the ambush. Secretly too he wondered about the Frankish boy and his huge dog. He hurried through his duties, tidying away the doctor's instruments, fetching water and sweeping out the tent, but just when he was about to ask permission to slip away, Dr Musa said, 'A clean tunic now, and kindly wash your face. I have an audience with the Sultan, and I want you to come with me.'

Salim tidied himself up as quickly as he could, while the

doctor muttered over the medicine chest, 'Oil of thyme. Fennel seeds . . . Are you ready, boy?'

Saladin's tent was crowded with the captains of the various troops that made up his huge army, all waiting their turn to tell the Sultan of their exploits that day, but the doctor was well known to the guards and they ushered him in at once, allowing Salim to follow.

Instead of the imam who usually sat on a rug near the Sultan's dais, reading from the Koran, there was a musician plucking at the strings of a lute. His song rang out above the buzz of voices.

> *This is war! This is war!*
> *The white sword's point*
> *Is red with blood*
> *And the iron of the lance*
> *Is stained with gore.*
> *It is war! It is war!*

Saladin was sitting cross-legged, as usual, his face lined with pain. In sharp contrast to the silk robes and turbans of his courtiers, he was wearing the simple, rough gown of a holy man.

'Doctor!' he called out, catching sight of Dr Musa. 'You've brought my draught?'

'Yes, sire. But first let me check your pulse.'

There was a commotion by the entrance as the doctor bent over Saladin's wrist. Turning, Salim saw the four Frankish knights stumbling in, their feet and hands shackled. Their coats of mail had been stripped off and they were wearing their simple padded under-tunics. They seemed smaller without their armour and held themselves stiffly. Their heads high, they looked directly ahead. Salim thought he could almost smell their fear, though they were doing their best to hide it.

Saladin drank down the beaker of medicine the doctor had given him and waved him aside.

'Let the prisoners come near,' he ordered.

The knights shuffled forwards, their chains clanking, until they were standing in front of the Sultan. They looked round, as if expecting a much more glorious personage than this simple middle-aged man in his rough gown and plain black turban. Then the oldest knight felt the hand of a guard press firmly down on his shoulder, and he obediently sank down to his knees. The others knelt too.

'Your names and rank?' Saladin asked. 'Where's the interpreter?'

A man stepped forwards. He said something unintelligible, and the knights looked back at him, puzzled.

'They don't know Italian, sire,' the interpreter told Saladin.

'Speak to them in French.'

The interpreter tried again. The knights understood.

'My name is Reynauld Croc Venator,' the oldest one said stiffly. 'I fight for Christ and his Mother under the banner of Baron Guy of Martel, who is my liege lord.'

The others spoke one after the other.

'Raymond de Pommeroy, knight vassal of Martel.'

'Baldwin le Blond, knight vassal of Martel.'

'Tancred de Bohon, knight vassal of Martel.'

'What is this Martel?' Saladin asked, without waiting for the interpreter, who translated his question for the knights.

'Martel is the name of a noble and puissant lord, baron of England, vassal of Richard, King of England and Duke of Aquitaine,' Sir Reynauld said proudly.

Saladin stared down into his eyes.

'Sir Reynauld,' he said softly. 'You are a brave knight, and I respect your valour. You'll be treated here with courtesy. But

I am asking you, now, all of you, to renounce your false religion and become followers of Islam. If you do, honours will be heaped on you, and you'll be free to go wherever you want.'

A flush of indignation burned in three of the knights' faces when they understood this, though Sir Tancred looked sideways round the tent, as if he was assessing it.

'I speak for us all,' said Sir Reynauld boldly. 'You may use us as you will, torture us, sever our limbs or burn our bodies, but you may not have our souls. We will never betray our Saviour.'

Saladin, who had been leaning forwards, sat back wearily.

'You are misguided, but courageous. If your lord is as noble as you say, no doubt he will pay your ransom money, which I set at three hundred dinars for each of you.'

The knights looked at each other, shocked at the size of the sum.

'But my lord,' Sir Reynauld said, 'Martel has no money left. He's broken himself to pay for this campaign.'

'Then he would have done better to stay at home,' Saladin said shortly. 'No doubt King Richard, if he ever arrives, will be interested in your fate.'

Sir Tancred leaned forwards and whispered in Sir Reynauld's ear. Sir Reynauld shook him off roughly.

'What do you mean, pretend to convert?' Salim heard him hiss. 'I don't want to burn in hell forever. Go your own way if you must, but don't dishonour the rest of us.'

Saladin was watching with interest, sensing the strains between them.

'Think it over,' he said. 'I'll speak to you individually tomorrow. You've invaded our land, insulted the Prophet, peace be upon him, and brought death and misery to our people, but vengeance is not the message of Islam. Your lives are not to be forfeit. You'll be held in a safe place and treated with courtesy until your ransoms are paid.'

'By God's blood, twenty years in a stinking dungeon in Damascus,' Sir Tancred said angrily, under his breath. 'Is that what you want, Sir Reynauld?'

Saladin had waved his hand in a dismissive gesture, and the guards were hauling the knights to their feet. But as they turned to shuffle away, a messenger, dressed in the simple clothes of a shepherd, came into the tent, went boldly up to Saladin, and spoke into his ear.

'Wait,' Saladin called out to the departing knights. 'Your lord, what was his name? What is the name of his lands?'

'Fortis,' Sir Reynauld said.

'I fear I have bad news for you.' Saladin sounded genuinely sorry. 'Your lord has fallen badly from his horse. It appears he has fractured his skull. He lies between life and death.'

A gasp broke from the knights. They stared back at Saladin, shocked and astonished. Saladin questioned the messenger quietly, who whispered to him again.

'I hear,' Saladin went on, 'that your lord is not a young man, but has great courage, and has led his people nobly.' He turned to dismiss the messenger, and as he did so he noticed Dr Musa. 'This is not the time to rejoice in the downfall of an enemy. The way of Islam is to spread rose-water rather than blood. I'll send my own doctor to him, as a symbol of the mercifulness of Allah. Dr Musa, you'll take the boy as your interpreter and attend the English baron. I'll be most interested to hear your account of him when you return. It's one thing for hot-headed young men to go adventuring far from home, but in an old man it shows true faith and nobility, however misguided. Come tomorrow, and bring me more of this draught. I can feel its calming effect on my stomach already.'

Dr Musa was barely out of the great tent when he began to give vent to his feelings.

'What have I done, O Lord, to deserve this? To send me forth into the lion's den! Me, a peaceful, God-fearing Jew, who has observed Thy laws and walked in Thy ways all my life!' His eye fell on Salim. 'And why should the punishment fall on this innocent child?' He tugged distractedly at his beard. 'So this is what we're expected to do, is it? We walk up to their fortified bank, ignore their blood-crazed archers and call out, "Saladin's doctor to see the injured lord," and they answer, "Oh yes, you're very welcome, we don't have a single doctor of our own, come straight in. We've been waiting for you." I tell you, Salim, my boy, this is a bad turn our master's played us.'

'Doctor!' One of Saladin's captains was hurrying up to them. 'Do you need anything to take with you? Fetch it now. You must go at once.'

'He means it then?' Dr Musa's usually deep voice rose almost to a squeak. 'Saladin really wants to send us to our deaths?'

The captain laughed.

'It's not that bad. You'll be fine. One of the English knights will go with you. He's pledged his oath to take you there safely and bring you back again. He knows full well, anyway, that if any harm comes to you, and if he doesn't come back himself, his friends will be beheaded. Anyway, I and my men will escort you as far as the camp. Really, you mustn't be afraid. Saladin values you far too much to send you into danger.'

Dr Musa's laugh rang hollow.

'Excellent, captain. You make it sound just like a pleasant little outing. And suppose this lord dies under my treatment? What will his followers do then? Will they blame me? I rather think they will. What happened to him, anyway? A bad fall, wasn't it? While wearing all that heavy Frankish armour? If his injuries are as severe as I imagine, there'll be little enough I can do for him. My one comfort is that those ignorant barbarian doctors will no doubt have killed him by now. But I'll obey. I must, after all. I'll put a few things by to take with me.

Salim, we may have to cauterize wounds. Find the irons. Pack them in my bag.'

The reappearance of Sir Reynauld caused a sensation in the Fortis camp. He was surrounded at once by a jostling crowd as everyone hurled questions at him. Dr Musa and Salim, ushered through the gap in the bank behind him, were almost unnoticed, except by Adam. He stared at them curiously, recognizing Salim with surprise, before turning back to listen to Sir Reynauld.

'Where are Raymond and Baldwin? What's happened to Tancred?' people were shouting.

Sir Reynauld lifted a hand and they fell silent.

'They're prisoners of Saladin, like I am myself,' he began with a wry smile. 'Though seeing me here, you may not believe it.'

'Why's he let you go? What's he like, anyway?' someone yelled.

'He's treated us so far with courtesy,' Sir Reynauld said. 'Though he did ask us to renounce our faith and follow his cursed prophet.'

'Heretic! Blasphemer!' the crowd shouted.

'But there's to be no force.' Sir Reynauld had to raise his voice to be heard. 'We've chosen freely, and with his respect, to remain faithful to the cross. We've been well fed too.'

This provoked envious murmurs, but everyone was now settling to listen.

'What's he saying?' Dr Musa muttered to Salim. They were standing uneasily on the edge of the crowd. More people had noticed them now and puzzled glances were being cast in their direction.

'He's describing the Sultan, and his tent, and how many captains there are, and what they gave him to eat,' Salim whispered back. To his relief, he was following the knight's speech more easily than he'd expected. 'He's saying that the Sultan doesn't look like a king because of his clothes.'

'Hah!' burst out the doctor, more loudly than he'd intended. He dropped his voice again. 'Foolish men look on the outward appearance, my boy, remember that. But the Lord looketh upon the heart.'

'And then, to crown it all,' Sir Reynauld was saying, 'someone came in to tell him of Lord Guy's fall, and how he was lying near to death.'

'Who? How? How did they know?' The buzz of voices had broken out again. 'There's a spy in the camp! No – it must have been witchcraft. The work of the devil! The devil tells secrets to his own!'

Sir Reynauld raised his voice again. He was speaking with impressive earnestness.

'I don't know how he knew, but there was no smell of witchcraft about it. Saladin said that he admired the courage of Lord Guy, him not being a young man, and so full of faith. He seemed quite sorry to hear he was so badly hurt.'

The murmurs died down. Adam, who was listening intently, felt a glow of pride.

Even the fiend Saladin, the son of hell, respects Martel, he thought.

'Saladin said that the way of Islam is to spread rose-water rather than blood,' Sir Reynauld went on, almost unwillingly. 'That's why he's sent—'

He was interrupted by hoots of derision, even though some in the crowd were silent and looked puzzled.

Everyone turned as Lord Robert, who had run out of Lord Guy's tent, pushed his way through to the front of the crowd. His face was tight with strain. Though he was still some inches shorter than most of his father's vassals, Adam could see that he was making himself look as tall as possible.

'What is all this?' he said in his high thin voice. 'How dare you make this noise when my father's so ill? Sir Reynauld! What are you doing here? How did you escape?'

Everyone tried to explain.

Lord Robert frowned when at last he'd understood the gist.

'You ought to be ashamed of yourself, Sir Reynauld,' he said, trying to speak gruffly in his father's voice. 'You shouldn't have listened to that heathen. Why did he send you back here, anyway? Charmed you, did he? What are you trying to do – turn us all into infidels?'

'No, my lord.' Sir Reynauld spoke with outward respect, but he looked down into Lord Robert's face with contempt. 'Saladin was sorry to hear of your father's accident. He's sent his own doctor to attend him.'

Eyes swivelled round to Dr Musa, who looked back at the crowd with what dignity he could muster. Salim, seeing him through their eyes, was horribly aware of his master's crumpled gown and untidy turban, the tail of which was escaping as usual down the doctor's back.

'His doctor? You believe that?' Lord Robert said furiously. 'It's a trick! A trap! Saladin's sent the man here to murder my father. Seize him! Take the boy too. Look at him – a cripple touched by Satan! Torture will get the truth out of them. Put out their eyes!'

Salim's heart bounded in his chest as soldiers lunged forwards to grab him. He set his face, trying not cry out, or shut his eyes, or show the terror he was feeling.

The lion's den, he thought. *Sidi Musa was right. We're in the lion's den. Ali would be brave if this was happening to him. I've got to be too.*

'Stop! Don't touch them! Lord Robert, please!' The urgency in Sir Reynauld's voice made everyone draw back. 'If you harm the doctor or the boy in any way, your three knights will die. And so will I. I've sworn an oath to return to my imprisonment and take these two back safely.'

Father Jerome appeared in the centre of the crowd, a crow among pigeons with his beaked nose and black hooded cloak.

'Did I hear you right, Sir Reynauld? You swore an oath to an infidel?' He looked shocked. 'You realize, I suppose, that no promise is binding to any but a Christian? You need not regard it. An oath to a Saracen can be broken without any sin.'

Sir Reynauld frowned.

'My honour, Father, lies in my word. I wouldn't break it to anyone, Christian or Saracen, or even to a Jew.'

'What's that? What did he say?' Dr Musa hissed in Salim's ear.

'He says he can't break his promise, even to a Jew,' Salim whispered back.

On the other side of the crowd, Sir Ivo, who had been watching closely without participating, muttered, 'Sir Reynauld's a good man. I always knew it.'

Father Jerome, however, was clearly not impressed.

'No infidel understands honour, Sir Reynauld, and that you would do well to remember.'

'I believe that Saladin does,' Sir Reynauld said defiantly. 'In any case, do you want me and your three other knights to die? You must treat this man with courtesy! If it's all a trick, he won't know anything about medicine, and our doctors will soon find him out. But I've seen him with my own eyes give Saladin a draught of medicine to drink and how it revived him. If this is a true act of chivalry on Saladin's part, think of the shame if we reject it ungraciously!'

The crowd had been looking uncertainly by turns at Sir Reynauld, Father Jerome and Lord Robert. Adam, however, saw that Father Jerome had looked over their heads to Sir Ivo, the senior and most respected knight of all, and he saw Sir Ivo nod, and bow politely in the direction of the Saracen doctor. Father Jerome considered for a moment and then said, 'Very well. Don't let it be said that a Christian could be outdone in nobility by an infidel. And it's true enough, I've heard that the Saracens' doctors are uncommonly skilled. What if Our Lady herself, in her mercy, sent this man, unpromising though he looks, and we were to turn him away? We may be witnessing a miracle here. Let the doctor go in.'

'How dare you? You can't do that!' Lord Robert shouted shrilly. 'I'm the master here now. You all have to do what I say.'

'You're not the master yet,' Father Jerome said severely. 'And by the terms of your father's will, which is still unknown, you may not become so at all. In any case, the authority in such matters rests with the Church. Sir Ivo, kindly accompany the man into Lord Guy's tent and explain his presence to our doctors there.'

Adam, watching the doctor's boy, noticed how stiffly he was holding himself, and how his eyes darted from one speaker to another as he tried to follow the twists and turns of the mood in the crowd.

He's brave, Adam thought, with grudging admiration. *I'd be scared half out of my wits if I was him. He's doing his best not to show any fear.* He remembered how frightened of Faithful the boy had been. *Can't think why I was afraid of him too*, he told himself. *He looks younger than me. And that leg – it's like Margaret's at the mill in Fortis. It doesn't have to mean he's a limb of Satan. Margaret wasn't.*

The doctor was prodding the boy, saying something in his ear, then pushing him insistently forward. Unwillingly, the boy cleared his throat and said, 'Thank you, sirs. My master hope your lord not too sick. He will help him if is possible.'

'He can speak! Listen to the lad! 'Ow come a Saracen talks the language of a Christian?' Adam heard men round him saying, as they parted to let Dr Musa and Salim go through.

The sun had dipped below the horizon, and as Salim and Dr Musa entered Lord Guy's tent his servants were lighting branches of candles.

The baron lay on a trestle table, which had been covered with a white linen cloth. He was obscured from Salim's view by the people crowding round him, and Salim had time to look round the tent. There were no woven cushions, as in Saladin's marquee, no silk hangings or fine brass trays, only a few chests, a simple chair, a couple of low pallet beds and a crude table with a crucifix on it. A pile of chainmail, shields and weapons had been thrown roughly into a corner, though the baron's sword and lance had been propped carefully against the canvas of the tent. There were no rugs on the floor. Instead it was strewn with beaten-down straw. Salim's legs itched at the thought of the fleas that must be in it.

A couple of bystanders moved back, and Salim saw the baron properly for the first time. He had been stripped to the waist, so that his broad muscular chest, covered with fine curly red hair, was exposed to view. His face was deathly pale, the heavy jaw hanging open, and the hooded eyes closed. Salim had to suppress a gasp of horror at the sight of his head. A section of his scalp, from which the hair had been hastily shaved, had been cut open and pulled back to expose the bone of the skull. Part of it had been shattered, and slivers of bone protruded from it.

Two men, wearing the caps and gowns of civilians, stood by the baron's head. They had been arguing in low voices, but turned when Father Jerome entered the tent, with the two strangers in tow.

'You'll be surprised to hear,' he announced to them, standing aside to let Dr Musa approach, 'that this person is no less than Saladin's personal physician, whom he has sent to help you in your efforts. The boy speaks our language. He can interpret for you.'

222

The English surgeons' mouths gaped open in astonishment. The oldest was the first to recover.

'No need for translation,' he said, starting forward. 'I can converse in the doctor's own language.' He put out a hand to shake Dr Musa's. 'What an opportunity!' he said, switching to Arabic. 'Let me introduce myself. Dr John Fleetwood of Sidon at your service.'

Dr Musa's face lit up.

'This makes things much easier,' he said. 'May I ask, sir, how you come to speak my language so fluently?'

'I was born in this country,' John Fleetwood said. 'I've lived here all my life. I shall be most interested to hear your opinion of this case. I've heard so much about the skill of you Saracen doctors.'

'I must explain,' Dr Musa said, looking at him fixedly, 'that I am in fact a Jew.'

You didn't have to tell them that, Salim thought silently.

Consternation spread across Dr John's face.

'Sir, what can I say? The violence done to your people in England has revolted those of us who . . . I mean to say . . . And now you're here, in this situation, which is so extraordinary! Belonging, as we do, to opposing armies! But we professional men must draw together. In the circumstances, it's particularly good of you to . . . A tricky case, as you observe. The fall was very bad, from a height, and the helmet rim shifted and penetrated the skull, which, you can see, has been badly fractured.'

Salim, relieved that he didn't have to translate after all, was watching the other doctor, who had turned half away and was shooting Dr Musa hostile glances from over his shoulder. Now he plucked at John Fleetwood's sleeve.

'Are you out of your mind, John? The man's a pagan! An emissary of the devil! Surely you're not going to let him anywhere near Lord Guy? He'll kill him on the spot. He might even spirit his soul away to eternal damnation with some demonic trick.'

Dr John sighed, exasperated.

'My dear Nicholas, this is ridiculous! Heaven has sent us this chance to learn something of great value to us as doctors. Whatever else the Saracens may be, and I share your view of them, of course, as our natural enemies, I have to say that their medical knowledge is extensive. I've long hoped for just such an opportunity. Besides, this man is a Jew, not a Muslim, so—'

'A Jew?' hissed Dr Nicholas. 'A murderer of Christ? This is typical! How can you be so lax? You refuse to see the wider implications of this case. I keep telling you, we should lose no time in bleeding Lord Guy. It's perfectly clear that the opening up of the skull has caused an evil spirit to enter his body. It's the only explanation for the shaking of his limbs, which was so severe just now, and the way he lies so limply.'

Salim, trying to understand, could grasp only the bare bones of this exchange.

'What are they saying?' Dr Musa whispered to him.

'This other one says the lord's got a demon in him,' he whispered back, 'and they ought to bleed him.'

'What folly,' snorted Dr Musa. 'The man has clearly lost too much blood already.'

Dr John had turned back to him.

'I must explain,' he said, looking embarrassed, 'that my colleague came with the expedition from England and has little experience of . . . Well, we're losing valuable time. Please, doctor, look at the patient and give us your opinion.'

It seemed for a moment as if the man called Nicholas, who was standing close to Lord Guy's head, would refuse to step aside so that Dr Musa could examine the wounded skull, but Father Jerome, who had been listening closely, unexpectedly intervened.

'I believe,' he said, in his usual measured tones, 'that the arrival of this doctor is by the direct agency of the Virgin. I counsel you, Dr Nicholas, not to stand in his way. Heaven sends us many instruments, strange though some may appear. Let the man look. He can't do Lord Guy any harm.'

As Dr Musa looked down to examine the horrible mess of Lord Guy's head, Dr Nicholas crossed himself ostentatiously and whisked the hem of his gown away with a flourish. But before Dr Musa could say a word, Lord Guy's eyes fluttered open and his lips began to move.

'Look! He's recovering consciousness!' Father Jerome exclaimed. 'What did I tell you? Our Lady is already intervening here.'

Lord Robert had come into the tent. He stood at the foot of the table, biting his bottom lip and twisting his hands.

'Water!' Lord Guy moaned suddenly. 'For the love of Christ!'

Lord Robert darted round to the head of the table and held a beaker to his father's lips.

'Not like that!' Dr Musa said hastily. 'He'll choke!'

Gently, he removed the beaker from Lord Robert's hands. Lord Robert looked as if he wanted to strike him, but Father Jerome put a restraining hand on his arm.

'A sponge, Salim, quickly!' Dr Musa said.

Salim reached into the bag and brought out a little sponge. Dr Musa dipped it into the beaker of water and held it to Lord Guy's lips. The baron opened his mouth and sucked at it gratefully. Salim felt some of the tension go out of the watchers, as they saw the gentle care in Dr Musa's skilled hands and the concern in his eyes.

The touch of water in his mouth seemed to have revived Lord Guy. He was unable to turn his head, but his eyes were moving, as though he was looking for someone.

'I'm here, Father,' Lord Robert said, leaning over him.

Lord Guy ignored him.

'Jerome,' he croaked.

'Yes, Lord Guy.'

'Confess, I must confess!' Lord Guy's voice had grown stronger. 'To you alone. No one else here.'

Father Jerome straightened up.

'Clear the tent,' he said, in his most commanding voice.

'But there's no time!' Dr John protested. 'To leave the skull open for more than a few minutes – the risk of infection . . .'

'Do you know what you're saying?' Father Jerome said coldly. 'Do you place a man's physical comfort above the salvation of his soul? If he doesn't confess now, and receive absolution, while he's conscious, his soul is condemned to the everlasting fires of hell.'

Salim, translating rapidly, heard Dr Musa sigh with exasperation.

'And condemn his body to a rapid death!' the doctor muttered. 'There's still a chance, but with every moment of delay it lessens.'

Dr John, though, had nodded with resigned agreement, and ushered Dr Musa out of the tent.

It was quite dark outside. The flaps of the tent had been tied back and light from the candlelit exterior fell on the ring of anxious faces as the men of Fortis waited for news of their lord. Dr Musa and John Fleetwood stood together, conversing amiably, while Dr Nicholas stood alone, his head bowed, his lips moving, as though he was praying.

'How very interesting,' Salim heard Dr John say. 'I've never heard that gold dust could be efficacious in such cases before. You've seen its effects with your own eyes, you say? Now, I had a most extraordinary case last week . . .'

Salim's mind wandered. He was aware that curious eyes were upon him and he slipped out of the light to one side, where he would be less visible. To his surprise, he heard a baby cry, and peering into the gloom saw a girl standing there with a small child in her arms.

'Oi, don't you give me the eye, you pagan,' she said indignantly. 'I don't want no cursing, thank you very much.'

He smiled placatingly.

'No cursing. Look at the baby. Is a little boy?'

'No, she's a girl,' she said, surprised that he could speak a language she understood. 'She's a good little Christian too.'

He sighed. It had been a long time since he'd seen a small child. He couldn't help thinking of Zahra.

The girl had heard his sigh.

'What is it?' she said, less aggressively. 'Something the matter?'

'Your baby, she make me think my little sister,' said Salim. 'Her name Zahra. She is in Acre. She very hungry, I think. Maybe not alive now.'

There was a silence as the girl took this in.

'Poor little thing,' she said at last, real compassion in her voice. 'Your ma and pa, are they in there too?'

'Yes.'

'Did you hear that, Adam?' the girl said, turning to a boy standing in the dark behind her. 'His folks are all banged up in Acre. Must be horrible in there.'

The boy called Adam stepped forwards into the half-light.

'I met you before,' he said. 'Up there.' He jerked his chin in the direction of the hillside.

'Yes. You got very big dog.' Salim stepped back nervously, afraid that the dog was with him.

'It's all right. He's tied up. Anyway, he's all wore out. He had a busy day.'

'Your dog, he bite my friend's hand, bad,' Salim said, then wished he hadn't. It wouldn't be wise to antagonize anyone, surrounded as he was by potential enemies.

'Your friend?' Adam was frowning. He couldn't imagine

the ferocious Saracen on his prancing horse, sword raised to kill Sir Ivo, as anybody's friend.

'Yes. He is Ismail. Very good, very brave Mamluk.'

'Mam what?' said Jennet, wrinkling her nose.

Salim didn't try to explain. He had seen, behind Lord Guy's great tent, the row of warhorses, and everything else went out of his mind.

'Please,' he said to Adam, 'you show me horses? Big horse, much bigger than Mamluk horse. I never see one close.'

'All right.'

Adam was glad to move on to less treacherous ground. He led the way, the other two following.

'Very big, very fine,' Salim said, looking up admiringly at Vigor's long nose, and daringly putting up a hand to stroke it.

'See his back?' said Adam, proud to show off the charger's finest points. 'He's a special one, he is. Lord Guy's own. He's got the weight, see? And look at the muscles in his legs. A beauty, isn't he?'

Salim nodded, impressed.

'You ride him?'

Adam laughed.

'Ride? Me? No. I'm nothing but a—'

He was about to say 'dog boy', but Jennet chimed in, 'He's a squire, or nearly. He's servant to a good knight. Looks after his armour an' all.' She shifted Tibby from one arm to the other. 'What's it like, then, up there in your camp? You got anything to eat?'

Salim nodded.

'Not so good food as before. No more meat. Too many mens now. Only eating bread and vegetables.'

'Only!' Jennet laughed enviously. 'Give all my teeth for a good hunk of fresh bread, I would.'

'Shut up, Jenny,' Adam said roughly, afraid that she might be giving secrets away.

The three of them stood awkwardly, not knowing what to say next.

'I'm sorry about your folks,' Jennet said at last, nodding towards the massive walls of Acre, half a mile away, which shone white in the light of the rising moon.

'Me too,' grunted Adam. 'I hope they come through all right.'

The sympathy he was feeling confused him and made him feel ashamed. This boy was an enemy, an infidel, an insulter of the Virgin. He had no business feeling sorry for him.

Jennet was rocking Tibby, whose grizzling cry was distressing Salim.

I didn't know there were babies here, he thought. *It sounds hungry too. But I shouldn't feel sorry for them. They're barbarians. Unbelievers. They've brought all this on themselves.*

'What's her name?' he asked.

'Tibby,' said Jennet. 'And I'm Jennet.'

'I'm Salim,' he responded. 'Salim Ibn Adil.'

'Sal what?'

'Salim. It means "safe".'

'Oh. That's nice.'

He was astonished by the way she spoke back at him and looked him straight in the face. The Muslim girls in Acre would never dare speak to a stranger as she was doing. But he remembered how bold the Frankish women had been in the old days, when Acre had been in Crusader hands. The mothers of the boys he'd played with had gone about unveiled, chatting like men with men, scandalizing his own mother. He felt a blush rise when he remembered the things she'd said about them. He was glad it was too dark for the others to notice.

Father Jerome appeared at the entrance to the tent.

'The doctors can come in now!' he called out. 'And the

knights. Adam, son of Strangia – is he here? Fetch him quickly! Lord Guy wishes to speak to him.'

Adam's heart gave a great bound inside his chest when he heard his name called out. Jennet gasped and put a hand over her mouth.

'What you done, Adam?'

'Nothing,' he said firmly. It was too late to explain anything to Jennet.

He'd been frightened many times before in his life, but had never felt as terrified as this. Walking out of the dark shadows into the circle of light streaming from the tent, and seeing the eyes of the whole Fortis contingent on him, was the hardest thing he'd ever done. He felt like an animal being herded to the killing place.

They're on to me, he thought. *I'm to get the blame for Lord Guy's fall.*

He took a last look round the familiar faces, hoping to see a friendly smile, or a nod, or any sign of encouragement at all. There was nothing but gaping mouths and blankly curious eyes. Only one face, at the back of the crowd, looked at him with any expression. Jacques, his cloak wrapped round him, was shaking his head with an air of assumed sorrow, like a father disappointed in a child.

To Salim, Lord Guy's tent had seemed simple and crude. To Adam it was unimaginably luxurious. The branched candlesticks cast what was to him a brilliant light, and the very carelessness of the richly coloured robes trimmed with thick fur, piled higgledy-piggledy on one of the chests, seemed magnificently casual.

The doctors were standing by the head of the trestle table on which the wounded baron lay. The Saracen boy, Salim, hurrying in after Adam, had taken his place beside his master. The knights and squires had filed in too, and were standing in a quiet respectful ring round the walls of the tent. Adam tried to catch Sir Ivo's eye, but the knight was talking in a low voice to his neighbour. They were both looking at Lord Robert, who seemed half frantic with anxiety.

Father Jerome, standing tall and black beside the blood-flecked white linen sheet on the table, cleared his throat and everyone fell silent.

It's coming now, thought Adam. He wanted to blurt out, *I didn't mean to let the dog go. It wasn't my fault, or his either. Anyway, he saved Sir Ivo's life*. But he didn't dare open his mouth.

'Lord Guy has made his confession,' Father Jerome said. 'Before he can receive absolution, he must speak out publicly. He must make amends for an old sin, and put right a past injustice.'

Complete silence had fallen in the tent. Adam's ears, unnaturally sharpened with fear, were painfully aware of the adenoidal snuffle of a young squire, and the rustle of straw as the foreign doctor's boy shifted his weight from his short leg to his good one. He had barely taken in Father Jerome's words. He was waiting for someone to seize him and drag him off to be punished.

'Make it brief, Father Jerome, I beg you,' Dr John urged quietly. 'With every moment's delay . . .'

Father Jerome nodded curtly.

'This won't take long. Lord Guy wishes it to be known to you all assembled here that Adam, known as the son of Gervase, is in fact his own son, born from an adulterous union with the woman Strangia. He acknowledges him in front of witnesses, and begs your regard and protection for him in the future. The boy, to be known henceforth as Adam Fitz Guy, is no longer a serf but a free man, and the demesne of Brockwood in the vale of Ashmere is to be given him and his heirs in perpetuity as his inheritance.'

A muted gasp had greeted this declaration, and every eye was turned towards Adam. He stood quite still, paralysed with shock, incapable of unravelling Father Jerome's words. The only thing he understood was that it seemed, after all, that he was not to be blamed for Lord Guy's fall.

'So it's not . . . I'm not . . . it's not because of Faithful . . .' he stammered at last.

No one heard him. Lord Robert, the first to recover, had stormed up to Father Jerome and was shouting in his face.

'It's a lie! You're lying! You always hated me. You're trying to steal my property from me! What's his hold on you? I won't take this. I'll have his eyes put out. I'll have him hanged.'

An inarticulate moan from the table silenced him.

'It's the truth,' Lord Guy whispered. 'Adam son of Strangia is my son. He's your brother. I make him free.' There was a long, agonizing pause, then the faint, laboured voice spoke again. 'Swear to me, Robert, on your knees, that you will never hurt him. I should have told you – acknowledged him – long ago . . .'

His lips went on moving, but the sound died away.

'Please!' interjected Dr John. 'There's no time!'

Father Jerome ignored him.

'You heard your father, Robert,' he said coldly. 'On your knees. Swear.'

'No!' Lord Robert looked round wildly. 'This animal can't be my brother! Look at him! He's a cunning little serf! My father's demented. An evil spirit's entered his head. Dr Nicholas said so. It must be exorcized!'

Father Jerome frowned.

'There's no evil spirit. Your father's speaking a truth which I've known for a long time. Until you swear, the doctors can't continue their work, and if he dies from the delay the guilt of his death will be on your soul and you will have to do penance for the rest of your life. Get down on your knees!'

Salim, spellbound, saw the rage in the young lord's eyes turn to bitter animosity, and then to reluctant obedience as he sank down stiffly to his knees.

'I swear by Christ and his Holy Mother,' Father Jerome said swiftly.

'I swear by Christ and his Holy Mother,' Lord Robert mumbled resentfully.

'That I will acknowledge Adam Fitz Guy to be my father's son.'

'That I will acknowledge Adam Fitz Guy to be my father's son.'

'And that I will never harm him or despoil him of his inheritance.'

'And that I will never harm him or despoil him of his inheritance.'

'It's done,' came a faint sigh from the table.

Father Jerome lifted his right hand and made the sign of the cross.

'*Indulgentiam, absolutionem, et remissionem peccatorum tuum,*' he intoned. 'May the Almighty and Merciful Lord grant you pardon, absolution and remission of your sins. Amen.' He paused, then made a sign towards the doctors. 'Dr John, the salvation of Lord Guy's soul is assured. Do what you can to save his body.'

Dr Musa had been the only person in the tent to ignore the drama swirling round the lonely figure of Adam, who was still standing motionless at the foot of the table as if he'd been turned to stone. Resting his delicate tapered fingers on the white linen sheet, he'd been bending down to closely examine the horrible wound and the shattered bone of Lord Guy's skull.

'I think I can see the best way to proceed,' he was saying to Dr John as the astonished crowd left the tent. 'With your permission, I'll withdraw that smaller splinter first, if you can be on hand to staunch any flow of blood. I have to say that my hopes aren't high. This extraordinary delay . . .'

The soft incomprehensible Arabic voice faded as Adam was borne outside the tent in the middle of the flow of knights and squires. He didn't notice that everyone was staring at him. He felt as if he was living in a dream.

A sudden unexpected clap on the shoulder nearly overbalanced him.

'You're a dark horse, Adam. What a surprise, eh? You must have known! Of course you did! Having us all on like that.'

It was one of the squires, who had never deigned to notice him before.

Adam was so bemused that he could say nothing. He shook his head, trying to clear it. The other squires were crowding round him, talking and laughing, half mocking, half congratulatory, watching him curiously.

'Master of Brockwood, eh?' one of them said, friendly but envious. 'Very nice too. My father's hunted in the forest near there. You're a rich man, Adam.'

'You think Robert'll let him get his hands on anything?' another said. 'Did you see his face? He'll find a way round his oath, if he possibly can. I'll be amazed if . . .'

'Adam Fitz Guy! Who'd have thought . . .'

The voices buzzed on.

He's my father. Lord Guy's my father. I'm his son. The words came into Adam's head as if from nowhere and rang around in it like a peal of bells. They made a strange clamouring sound, without meaning. Dazed, he was barely aware of the noisy squires all around him. At last he felt a hand on his shoulder.

'Come with me, Adam,' Sir Ivo was saying.

Relieved to be told what to do, Adam stumbled after him to his tent.

Sir Ivo let down the flaps at the tent's entrance, lit the wick in his little oil lamp and sat down on his folding stool. He pointed to the floor, and Adam sat down opposite him, hugging his knees.

'You had no idea about this?' Sir Ivo said. 'You look shocked.'

'Is it true? It can't be!' Adam burst out, able to speak at last.

'Yes. Lord Guy is your father. It's come as a great surprise to everyone. I wanted to bring you away, to give you time to think. And to warn you. You're not in an easy position now, Adam. The way you behave is very important. Your future – even your life – depends on it.'

Adam couldn't listen.

'Is that why Ma was so alone? Is that why no one in the village was nice to her?' he asked wonderingly. 'And why Father Gilbert and – and everyone said she was such a sinner?'

'Maybe. I didn't know your mother. But no one in the village could have known who your real father was, or you would have found out long ago. Secrets like that are never kept for long.'

'But they might have known I wasn't Gervase's son.' Adam was frowning with concentration, slowly piecing things together. 'I'm glad of that. He hated me. I didn't ever find out why. I tried not to hate him back, but I did.'

'Adam,' Sir Ivo began. 'Listen. Lord Robert will try to—'

'She was Lady Ysabel's maid,' Adam went on. 'She must have gone with Lord Guy then. He must have made Gervase marry her, when he found out I was on the way. Not like Lord Robert. He just abandoned Jenny and Tibby.'

Sir Ivo, watching the process of Adam's slow realization, gave up trying to hurry him and sat back, allowing him the time he needed.

'But Ma had nothing!' Anger sparked in Adam's eyes. 'Poorer and poorer we got, after Gervase died. It wasn't much better when he was alive. Always drunk. Hitting us. Why didn't Lord Guy tell me sooner? He could have helped her! If

I'd been able to give her meat . . .' He stopped. 'Is he really my father? My real father?' he said, as if he'd heard the news for the first time.

'Yes, Adam,' Sir Ivo said patiently.

'Then he did her wrong, and me too! He should have kept her better, and seen we weren't hungry. Why didn't he? Ashamed of her, I suppose. And me too.'

'I don't think so.' Sir Ivo was watching him closely. 'I wondered why he didn't punish you when the dogs died. I'd expected him to.'

'He said they were cursed. By that old man in Marseilles.'

'He didn't really believe that. And I saw how he watched you.'

'Watched me!'

'Yes. He was interested in you.'

'Why didn't he help us then?'

'I think,' Sir Ivo said hesitantly, 'that he wished to keep all knowledge of you from Lady Ysabel. Lord Guy has many faults. What man doesn't? But he's been a kind husband to her.'

Adam remembered the first meal he'd eaten in the great hall at Fortis, and how Lady Ysabel had stared at him.

She suspected him, he thought.

'Lord Robert doesn't like all this.' Adam's thoughts had at last reached the point Sir Ivo had been waiting for. 'He went mad. Did you see him? He'll hurt me if he can. He hates me already because I stood up to him for Jennet.'

'He *will* harm you if he can,' Sir Ivo repeated, giving his words a solemn emphasis. 'That's why I want you to be careful, Adam. To think before you speak and act.'

'Careful?' Adam was hearing him at last. 'How can I be, sir?'

'Things will change for you now. Think.' Sir Ivo leaned forwards and tapped Adam's knee. 'The position of the – I shall put it bluntly – the bastard son of a nobleman is never easy, especially as Lord Guy has no other legitimate son beside Robert. There are many people in the Fortis camp who dislike Robert. They dread his taking over from his father. They'll see you as an opportunity. They'll try to use you. They'll make you a focus for their discontent.'

'Me?' Adam looked bewildered. 'I don't want anything like that.'

He stopped. He didn't know what he wanted. He'd never thought about it. He'd had no choices in his life, anyway. To serve Sir Ivo while the Crusade lasted had been his highest ambition up to now. To return to Ashton, take the lease of a little piece of land, work it with the help of Tom Bate – that had been all his expectation.

'You'll have a good manor when you return home. A fine piece of property,' Sir Ivo put in, watching the struggle in his face. 'It'll be yours. You'll own it.'

'A manor? Me?' Adam looked disbelieving. 'Yes – I remember. Father Jerome said something. What is it? Where is it?'

'Brockwood. A good place. Some forest, a fine house, a mill, fertile strips of land near the river, a village of fifty serfs or thereabouts—'

'Serfs! I'm to own serfs? And a mill?' The thought was so alarming that Adam recoiled. 'I can't own serfs! What would I do with them? They'd never respect me. I'm a serf myself. The poorest of them all.'

'You're a free man now. You'll have to get used to the idea. But there's no need to think of all that at present. You'll have to be careful, Adam, as I said, if you are ever to come into your property. People in the Fortis camp will come to you, flatter you, try to use you for their own ends. Don't be drawn in. Behave quietly and respectfully as you always have done. Keep to yourself. Don't choose friends, and don't make enemies. I'll help you. If you agree, I'll let it be known that you're no longer my servant, but my squire. That you have no wish to be anything else for the time being. Stay close to me. I'll show you how you should go on.'

Adam suddenly felt as if his feet, which had been dangling helplessly over a deep abyss, had found a rock to rest upon.

'It's the truth, sir. I have no wish to be anything else. To be your squire, your real squire, it's more, miles more, than I'd ever thought of.'

He sat for a while in silence.

'Is Lord Guy going to die?'

'I don't know, Adam. It's in the hands of Our Lord.'

'Because I'd like to see him again. Not to say anything much. I'd just like to look at the man who's my father, and have him look at me.'

CHAPTER TWELVE

S alim had watched the operation on the English baron's head with revolted fascination at first, and then with increasing interest and admiration as Dr Musa and Dr John, the Frankish surgeon, worked together, delicately removing splinters of bone. The man had lost consciousness as soon as the doctors had started work. His eyes were shut and he lay quite still, his face deathly pale. Several times, Dr Musa had paused in his work to take his pulse and check that he was still breathing.

The other Frankish doctor, the angry one, had withdrawn to a corner of the tent and was arguing in an enraged undertone with the tall, cold-looking priest. Outside, Salim could hear the low voices and chanted prayers of the Fortis people, who seemed determined to stay as near to their lord as possible. Once or twice, through the silence of the night, Salim winced at a distant crash, as one of the Crusaders' vast catapults pounded the walls of Acre with boulders the size of sheep.

There wasn't much for him to do. After he had lit a little brazier and heated on it the irons needed to cauterize the edges of the baron's skull, he was required only to stand by and pass the doctors anything they needed. There was plenty of time to think, and he kept going over in his mind the extraordinary scene he'd witnessed: the boy Adam, his face so white, hearing for the first time the true identity of his father, discovering that he was in fact the son of a noble lord.

Why didn't the lord take his mother as his second wife? Salim thought disgustedly. *How could he abandon her like that, and ignore his own son? A Muslim would never do such a thing.*

Christians, he knew, had strange customs when it came to marriage. They could take only one wife at a time, and if they had concubines they hid them away, as if they were a shameful secret.

How would I feel if Baba turned out not to be my father at all? he thought. *Suppose I was the son of someone really famous? Saladin himself, maybe?*

The thought was so ridiculous that he smiled.

'So you find all this amusing, do you?' Dr Musa suddenly shot at him. 'Wake up, boy, and pass me another swab.'

At last, Dr John carefully stitched the flaps of the baron's scalp together, and the two doctors straightened up, flexing their shoulders to relieve their cramped muscles. Salim held out a bowl of water to them in turn so that they could wash their hands. They examined Lord Guy's pulse for the last time, gave orders that he should be left absolutely quiet to rest and walked out of the tent together.

'It's been a privilege to work with you,' Dr John said enthusiastically. 'If the outcome of this campaign is successful, perhaps we can meet again in Jerusalem.'

A peculiar look crossed Dr Musa's face.

'You'll forgive me if I don't look forward to that outcome,' he said drily. 'Last time Jerusalem was taken by the Franks the outcome for us Jews was, let us say, unfortunate.'

Dr John flushed with embarrassment.

'I'm sorry. I was forgetting for a moment. This situation

has brought us together in such an unexpected way! It would have given me great pleasure to invite you to take a glass of wine with me, but I regret that we're reduced here to such straits that all I could offer you would be a beaker of water and a husk of dry bread.'

Dr Musa shook his head.

'This suffering! So needless! A period of calm reflection – some negotiation – I've urged such a course on the Sultan, peace be upon him.'

'What was his response?' Dr John asked eagerly. 'What kind of man is he? One hears so many . . .'

They passed out of Salim's earshot.

The circle of people outside moved forwards when they saw them coming.

'How is he, doctor?' someone called out. 'Is he going to live?'

'It's in the hands of God,' Dr John called back. 'Pray for him.'

Dr Musa took hold of Salim's arm.

'It's time we went. Find the Frankish knight, the prisoner.'

Salim, peering at the unfamiliar faces in the gloom, couldn't pick out Sir Reynauld. As he stood wondering what to do, a soft voice behind him made him jump.

'My dear young man! I should say, my *clever* young man. I'm sorry, did I alarm you? No need to be scared. I'm only Jacques, the pedlar. A harmless fellow. The friend of everyone! And I know – I'm *sure* – that you've done miracles in there, with our poor Lord Guy. What a strong man! Amazing, wouldn't you say? Sure to live. Is that what your master thinks? There's no secret about it. You can tell me.' Salim, not sure what to say, said nothing. 'How sad it would be,' the coaxing voice went on, 'how *tragic* if such a man was to die, leaving us all without our leader! But your master – a wonderful doctor – a brilliant man, so I'm told – will have been certain to save his life. Yes, I feel sure that you would like to tell me so.'

Salim, twisting round to look at the man, felt a stir of recognition. Wasn't this the same strange, thin fellow, in his tattered colourful cloak, that he'd seen outside the Saracen camp, on more than one occasion, talking to a couple of camel drivers? He stepped sideways. There was something about the pedlar, in spite of his caressing, flattering voice, that he instinctively disliked.

'I not know anything,' he said shortly. 'You know as good as me. Is time now for me to go back.'

'Of course, my dear! And with our poor Sir Reynauld too! A very noble knight, is our Sir Reynauld. Not a man to go back on his word, or leave his friends in the lurch. Now, where was he? I saw him just a minute ago, passing all the secrets of your sultan, no doubt, to that odious – I should say that *excellent* man, Sir Ivo. He's over there. Do you see?'

Salim, only half understanding him, followed his pointing finger with his eyes. He saw Sir Reynauld and hobbled off to fetch him.

'Goodbye, my young friend,' Jacques called out softly after him. '*Such* a pleasure to meet you.'

'Praise be to God that we've been safely delivered from the clutches of our enemies,' Dr Musa said fervently, as he and Salim passed through the opening in the Crusader embankment to find their escort of Saracen soldiers impatiently waiting for them.

'But Dr John was nice, wasn't he?' Salim said. 'He liked you, anyway.'

'A good man in his way, no doubt. But naive. A wishful thinker. No grasp of the painful realities of war. How could he possibly believe that I would welcome this rabble of barbarians back into Jerusalem?'

'What did you mean,' Salim asked curiously, 'about the last time the Crusaders took Jerusalem? Did they do even worse things than usual?'

'Ha!' barked Dr Musa, then was silent for a moment. 'It depends,' he said at last, 'on what you think is usual, I suppose. They made all the Jews gather together in the synagogue, then set fire to it. Every one of them was burned alive. What do you think, Salim? Was that "worse than usual"?'

'Oh,' Salim said in a small voice. 'Oh, I see.'

'Well, well,' Dr Musa said, with a weary sigh. 'It was nearly a hundred years ago, and there've been atrocities on all sides. Saladin himself, peace be upon him, is no saint. He's slaughtered Christian prisoners with his own hands.'

Salim said nothing, but in his head he was passionately disagreeing.

'And spare a moment of pity for that sad knight,' Dr Musa said, interrupting his thoughts and pointing to Sir Reynauld, who was walking stiffly ahead of them. 'I wouldn't choose to spend the best years of my manhood in a stinking dungeon, as he is likely to do. You see his back? How straight he holds it? Courage, Salim, that's what you're seeing. Take a good look. It's a noble thing, even in an enemy. War's a horrible business. It brings out the worst in men, but sometimes you see the best too.'

Salim, knowing that Dr Musa couldn't see him in the dark, shook his head. He refused to admire Sir Reynauld. Dr Musa was wrong. Saladin was the best there had ever been. Jihad was the noblest of all pursuits, and the cause of Islam was right. The Crusaders were violent, greedy, fanatical invaders, who deserved nothing but death.

And yet, at that moment, there came into his mind the softening memory of the girl he'd met, holding her little daughter in her arms. There was something so ordinary about her. And then there was the boy, Adam, and his extraordinary story.

What's he feeling like now? he kept asking himself. *What's he going to do now?*

It was late by the time they arrived at their own small tent. Nearly everyone in the Saracen camp was asleep, except for the sentries and Solomon the pharmacist, who was pacing up and down, wringing his hands with anxiety.

'Thank God, you've returned!' he said when he saw the short, stout form of the doctor and the slim figure of Salim emerging from the shadows. 'I was so afraid! How could the Sultan, peace be upon him, have exposed you to such danger? I've imagined every kind of fate – torture – death . . .'

'My dear Solomon,' Dr Musa said breezily. 'You shouldn't have distressed yourself. We've had a most interesting time. Quite a succession of dramas, in fact. No doubt Salim will give you a highly coloured version of it all in the morning.' He yawned. 'Time for bed. Fetch my prayer shawl, Salim. And if any other barbarian lords with holes in their heads need my services, you can tell them to stand outside my tent and wait till the morning.'

The story of the wounded Frankish baron and the astonishing revelations at his deathbed sped round the Saracen camp.

'And you know what?' the soldiers told each other. 'Those ignorant Frankish doctors thought they'd heal the wound by smearing it with pig fat and waving crosses over it! It was only Dr Musa arriving just in time that saved his life.'

Salim wanted to contradict the stories, but he knew they wouldn't listen. The story of the poor boy discovering that he was the son of a noble lord, and being granted land and freedom, while the lord's heir looked on with hatred in his eyes, was too good to leave unvarnished. It was told and retold round a hundred fires in a dozen different languages, and grew more fantastic with every telling. It ended every time on a note of self-congratulation.

'It all goes to show how merciful the Sultan is, peace be upon him,' one after another concluded. 'That'll show the barbarians. Civilized behaviour, that's what they'll learn from us. Such generosity! Sending his own doctor! And the man was only some small lord, not even a king or a prince.'

The story had created an even greater sensation among the Crusaders. It had spread beyond the Fortis part of the camp to the other English troops, and even into the territory of the French and Burgundians, who were camped alongside. In the days that followed, Adam became quite an attraction. Visitors kept strolling around the Fortis quarter, asking for the lucky boy to be pointed out to them.

Adam hated the fuss. He felt like the midget man at the Ashton fair, who people paid to see.

'I wish they'd all just leave me alone,' he grumbled to Roger Stepesoft. 'I can't turn round without falling over someone who's come to look at me.'

Roger, who'd become self-conscious in Adam's presence, had disappeared and returned a moment later with Hugo de Pomfret.

'Unwanted visitors, eh?' the sergeant-at-arms had said. 'Very unpleasant. I'll warn the sentries. Make sure they're kept away. You won't be bothered again, Master Adam.'

Adam, stunned by the attention and respect, and by being addressed as 'master' by such an important personage, had been quite unable to reply.

Sir Ivo, keeping him close by his side, made sure he didn't hear half the stories about him, which, growing more colourful all the time, were circulating round the camp.

'Heard the latest?' Roger said to Treuelove Malter one morning, a week after Lord Guy had been wounded. 'It seems like Lord Guy wants to disinhcrit Master Robert and make

Adam his heir. It'd suit me. Nasty little piece of work, Robert is. We'll be thanking all the saints for this, Treue. We befriended that boy, when no one else took no notice of him. He won't forget us, when he's got the power.'

Treuelove, who had been squatting over a precious hoard of lentils, carefully picking out the little stones, squinted up at Roger disbelievingly.

'Nah,' he said at last. 'Ain't never going to happen. A man can't do that – set aside his rightful son for the sake of a bastard. And look at Adam. I ask you. Not brought up to it, is he?'

'Stranger things have happened,' Roger said, tapping his nose meaningfully, as if he knew more than he was telling.

While the gossip swirled about him, Lord Guy lay deep in a coma, breathing but scarcely alive, while John Fleetwood and Dr Nicholas hovered over him, disagreeing furiously on how he should be treated.

'Let nature take its course!' Dr John kept pleading. 'The shock to his system has been severe. It's a miracle there's no infection in the wound. See how nicely it's healing! He'll be restored to consciousness at the time of Our Lord's choosing, and not before.'

'He'll be restored when the evil spirit in his head is let out,' Dr Nicholas snapped back. 'The skull must be reopened, I tell you! I should have insisted on it long ago.'

Robert, scowling at Dr John, sided with Dr Nicholas.

'Why the delay? Why?' he would say. 'It's as clear as day that there's a demon infecting my father. It's a creature of that devil, the dog boy, who's a witch, if ever I saw one. There was some story I heard about a fiend, with a long tail and fiery eyes, that attacked Vigor and made him rear. The fiend must have entered him when he fell off his horse. It was the same demon speaking through my father's mouth when he said the boy was his son. Go ahead and bleed him, for the sake of the Virgin! When the demon's let out, my father will come back to himself and tell the truth.'

'There's no fiend,' Dr John countered patiently. 'Your father was hurt in battle, like the noble soldier he is. His state now, after such a severe head wound, is quite normal. I've seen many such cases before. Properly treated, there's a good chance that he'll make a full recovery.'

'There's only one way of finding out the truth!' Robert answered furiously. 'Put the dog boy to the test! Apply hot irons to the flesh. If they burn him, we'll know for sure he's guilty.'

'That,' Dr John said, exasperated, 'is a matter for the Church. Speak to Father Jerome. He'll have to bring it up with one of the bishops in the camp. Correct procedures will have to be followed.'

Robert had only muttered in reply.

It was during a lull in these arguments that Lord Guy, temporarily alone in his tent, opened his eyes and moved his head.

'Water!' he croaked.

A page, idly tossing a handful of dice at the tent's entrance, heard him. He started up and shouted, 'He's come round! Lord Guy wants water!'

Adam, kept busy by Sir Ivo at his daily tasks as squire and groom, was inspecting Grimbald's rear hooves, wondering if the horse needed to be reshod, when he heard shouts and saw people running towards the great tent.

That's it, he thought. *He's died. I've missed my chance. I'll never talk to him now.*

He stood motionless, the patient horse's huge hoof held in his hand, dreading what might happen next. Lord Guy, even as he lay unconscious, had still been at the centre of the Fortis camp, the pivot on which everything had turned. He had been all that stood between Adam and the fury of Robert, which would, Adam knew, be unleashed on him as soon as he had managed to gather up the reins of his father's power.

Then, in the confusion of noise, he heard someone shout, 'He's alive! He's speaking!' and he dropped Grimbald's hoof and straightened up.

'Thank God,' he whispered. 'Thank God.'

Jennet, attracted by the noise, hurried past. He'd seen her only in the distance since Lord Guy's accident. He'd guessed she was keeping out of his way.

'Jenny!' he called out.

She stopped and turned, but didn't step towards him.

'What's going on?' she said, looking at him guardedly. 'What's all the fuss about?'

'It's Lord Guy. He's woken up. I heard someone shout it.'

'Oh. That's good. I'll be getting on, then.'

'Jenny!' he called out sharply. 'Don't go! Why are you avoiding me?'

She shifted Tibby on to her hip.

'Too grand for the likes of me now, ain't you? Going up in the world. A real squire already, so I've heard. You'll be made a knight next. And a man of property. You don't want to go associating with the likes of me.'

He stared at her, shocked.

'How can you say that? Are you off your head?'

'No, I'm not, thank you very much. Anyway, it's you that's avoiding me. I thought at least you'd come by the wagons and tell me all about it.'

'I'm sorry, Jenny. I haven't had a minute to myself!' he said contritely. 'There's all kinds of fools pestering me all day long, and Sir Ivo's keeping me so close to my work I can't get away. I'm glad of that, mind you. Stops people getting at me.'

'Getting at you, am I?' she said huffily. 'I'm sorry, I'm sure. I'll be on my way.'

'Jenny! Don't! Come back here!' He ran forward and

grabbed her by the arm. 'Of course I didn't mean you. You know I didn't. Come and sit down for a minute. I need you more than anyone else. You know I do.'

They went across to the mounting block beside the line of horses. She sank down on to it, rocking Tibby up and down automatically on her knee, and smiled up at him, mollified.

'It's true then, is it? Lord Guy really is your pa?'

'I suppose so. I can't believe it. I wake up in the morning and think I've been dreaming.' He frowned. 'But you knew something, didn't you, Jenny? When Tibby was on the way, you said something about how I ought to understand, of all people. I've thought and thought about that. Why didn't you tell me?'

She looked away, embarrassed.

'I didn't like to speak ill of your ma. I knew Gervase wasn't your father. Pa let it out one day. I asked him who your real father was, but he didn't know. No one knew. I can't wait to see Pa's face when I tell him. I'm longing to go home, aren't you, Adam? I wish I'd never come. I'm sick to death of all this. I never thought much of life in Ashton, but it seems like heaven now.'

'It's going to be heaven,' he said, taking her hand. 'I can't believe it all yet, Jenny, but if Father Jerome was right, and Lord Guy meant what he said, and I do get Brockwood, it'll be lovely, you'll see. It's a proper manor. Sir Ivo described it to me. It's got a big house, and a mill and all. First thing I'm going to do is buy your freedom, yours and Tom's. You can come and live with me.'

She looked at him, awed, as if he was no longer the little boy she'd always ordered about, but had become someone quite different.

'Thank you, Adam,' she said, dropping a kiss on Tibby's matted curls. 'I'd like that, if we ever make it home.'

*

Although Lord Guy had recovered consciousness, it was clear to everyone that he was a changed man. The muscles of his heavy body, which lay motionless on his pallet bed, had already lost their hardness and seemed weak and flabby. He barely spoke or moved, and dribbled like a very old man, plucking feebly at the sheets, his cheeks and mouth slack. Father Jerome, Robert, the doctors and knights bent over him whenever he stirred, trying to understand his few slurred, mumbling words. It was clear to everyone that he was unlikely ever to be himself again. Only Robert and Dr Nicholas held out the hope of a full recovery.

Slowly, the mantle of power was falling on Robert's shoulders. Though everyone knew that he would have to wait until the King arrived before he could be confirmed as the rightful heir of Martel, they were beginning, in a hundred small ways, to look to him as their leader. Unsure of himself, desperate to be respected and to stamp his authority on his father's people, Robert was forced for the time being to rely on the counsel of the Martel senior knights, and was even prepared to listen to Sir Ivo, though there had never been any trust between them.

It was two weeks now since the fateful night when Adam had learned the truth about his birth. He woke every day determined to see Lord Guy and speak to him, wanting only to be near him and to look him in the face.

His chance came late one afternoon when the sun was setting behind the white walls of Acre. A mass had been arranged for all the Fortis people in order to pray for Lord Guy's recovery. Adam slipped out of the tented church before it was quite over and hurried to Lord Guy's great tent. The two sentries at the door stepped aside to let him in. A page, left to watch over the baron, was playing with Lord Guy's dagger, lunging it at an imaginary enemy. He jumped guiltily when he saw Adam and dropped it.

'Sorry,' he mumbled. 'I didn't . . . I wasn't . . .'

'That's all right,' Adam said, embarrassed. 'You can go out now. I'll stay with him.'

He wasn't used to giving orders and was surprised and gratified when the boy obeyed.

He tiptoed up to the still form on the low bed. Lord Guy's eyes were shut and he was breathing slowly and noisily. Adam stared down at him. This broken man, his head roughly shaved and bandaged, with many days growth of beard on his chin, his cheeks pale and puffy, was quite different from the arrogant nobleman Adam had always feared, remote and powerful, swaggering above his serfs on his huge horse. He seemed like another person altogether.

The baron's hands were crossed on his chest. There was something pathetic in their soft stillness. Then Adam noticed, with a start of surprise, that there was a kink in the little finger of his left hand, and a ridge running down the centre of the nail. He spread out his own left hand and looked at it. Yes, the kink and ridge on his own little finger were exactly the same. Unexpected tears pricked his eyes.

'Please, sir,' he whispered. 'Wake up. I've got to talk to you.'

The heavy eyelids fluttered and lifted. Lord Guy was looking directly up at him. His brow creased as he recognized Adam, and his lips moved.

'You really are my father, aren't you?' he said desperately. 'Tell me it's true!'

Lord Guy rolled his eyes sideways. Following them, Adam saw a beaker of water and a sponge. Remembering what the Saracen doctor had done, he dipped the sponge in the water and held it to Lord Guy's mouth. The baron sucked weakly, then pushed the sponge away with his lips.

'It's true.' His voice was weak but clear. 'You are my son. I should have . . . long ago . . .'

His voice faded.

Adam knelt down beside the bed. He was afraid that at any moment other people would come bursting in, find him there and send him away. This might be his only chance.

'I want you to forgive me,' he said urgently.

Lord Guy stared back at him, puzzled.

'Forgive?'

'It was the mastiff made you fall from your horse. Faithful. I ought to have kept him tied up. He followed me. I didn't see him till it was too late. It's my fault that you're like this.'

The corner of Lord Guy's mouth twitched, and Adam was astonished to recognize a smile.

'Ah. The dog. So I am punished.'

'Please,' Adam said. 'Forgive me. I want you to bless me. I don't want anything else. I want your blessing.'

Lord Guy's hand moved. He seemed to be trying to lift it.

'Put your hand on mine,' he said.

It took all Adam's courage to touch the heavy swollen fingers, from which the massive rings had been removed. The flesh was cold to the touch. He looked up at Lord Guy's face and saw to his amazement that a tear had welled up in the corner of one watery blue eye.

'No need to forgive. You have my blessing.'

A hundred questions raced through Adam's mind.

What about Ma? Did you never think of her again? he wanted to ask. *Why didn't you help her when she was so poor and sick? That man, Gervase, you must have known he was no good. Why did you make her marry him? You've got a granddaughter, you know that? She's called Tibby. Robert, he's going to treat her the same way you treated me. What are you going to do about it, then?*

He couldn't say a word. His fingers closed almost involuntarily round the hand that was so like his own. He felt a choking mixture of anger, pity, and at last a certainty that the hand he was touching was indeed flesh of his own flesh.

It was enough. He stood up quickly and hurried out of the

tent without a backward glance. He felt like a different person. Stronger. Angrier. More confident.

No one's going to do me down any more, he thought. *Not any more. Not Robert, nor any of those sniffy squires.*

The sun was setting over the distant sea. He stood and watched as it dipped down into the golden water.

Am I like him? he wondered. *Not just my fingers, and little things like that. I suppose I've got a temper like he has. Robert, he's like his ma. He's a cold fish. Not like us.*

The pride welling up inside him almost frightened him.

But I won't be like him, he told himself, *not in the things that matter. I'm going to keep promises, and be faithful, and not betray people or let them down when they need me.*

Then, as the sky turned a rosy pink, mirroring itself in the sea, he felt a burst of joy.

He must be sorry for what he did to me and Ma. He cried. He forgave me for Faithful worrying his horse. I don't need to feel bad about that any more. And his blessing. He gave me his blessing, like a real father.

Adam, now being rigorously trained in squirely duties by Sir Ivo, was present as usual as the knights ate their evening meal, which, although pitifully meagre, was served with as much ceremony as if it had consisted of the half-forgotten sides of beef and haunches of venison they had been used to eating in the great hall at Fortis. Like the other squires, he held the bowl for his knight to wash his hands, served him on bended knee and stood behind him while he ate. And like the other squires, he listened to the knights' conversation.

Robert, who, until the accident, had been his father's squire, had taken to sitting down with the knights. Eyebrows were raised at this, as he had yet to be knighted himself, but in the odd circumstances it was allowed to pass.

The talk that evening was of a courteous message that had

arrived during the day from the Saracen camp, enquiring after the progress of Lord Guy.

'It's too much,' Sir Henry de Vere said irritably. 'Why are they loading us with these obligations? There must be some ulterior motive. Tricky as monkeys, these Saracens are.'

'On the contrary,' said Sir Ivo. 'It's pure courtesy. Their doctor performed a marvel, John Fleetwood told me. We're under an obligation to him.'

'Exactly. An obligation,' snapped Sir Henry. 'To an infidel! It's what I dislike about the whole situation. It's not natural.'

'We should try to repay the favour,' Sir Ivo said thoughtfully. 'I agree that the position's an uncomfortable one. We could send a message back to the doctor, maybe, and ask if there's anything we can do for him. It's not likely to cause any difficulty. What could he ask us to do, after all?'

'If you feel so strongly about it, Ivo,' Sir Henry said waspishly, 'why don't you march up to the pagans' camp yourself and offer to give the man whatever he wants?'

'Do you know,' Sir Ivo said, a smile lighting his face, 'I might do just that. At least it would be something to do. Anything's better than this endless waiting for the King.'

The next morning the sentries at the edge of the Saracen camp were surprised to see two men and a boy, without armour, shields or weapons, walk slowly out of the Crusader camp and approach their own outposts.

'Halt! Don't come any further! What do you want?' they shouted in Arabic.

'We have a message for the Sultan's doctor, in reply to his own,' John Fleetwood called back. 'I'm accompanied by Sir Ivo of Fortis, knight of the wounded baron, and Adam Fitz Guy, his squire. We come without arms or malice.'

'Stay there!' the sentry called back. 'Wait.'

It was mid-morning, and the Mediterranean April sun was

already hot. Adam, running his tongue over his dry lips, looked round with interest. It was a pleasant change to be outside the confines of the overcrowded Crusader camp. He breathed in the almost forgotten scent of clean air with gratitude.

A full half-hour passed.

'Where the devil is the fellow?' Sir Ivo said, slapping at the flies hovering round his head. 'I'm beginning to regret this whole idea. Pure folly to expect honourable behaviour from an infidel.'

'He'll come. He's a man of honour, I'd swear to it. He must be at the other end of the camp.' John Fleetwood shaded his eyes against the sun as he scanned the endless lines of tents and the vast numbers of men and horses, which occupied the entire hillside as far as the eye could see. 'Look at them all! They seem to have multiplied like a plague of locusts. How can we ever expect to beat them off and get through to Jerusalem? The thing's impossible.'

'Defeatism won't make it any easier,' Sir Ivo said. 'Have you forgotten that Christ and Our Lady fight on our side? Once the King arrives, everything will change. You'll see.'

'Look, sir,' Adam said. 'They're coming.'

Dr Musa and Salim had appeared some way above them.

'You can approach!' the Saracen sentries called out.

'You bring news of our patient?' Dr Musa called out, as he recognized Dr John. 'He's doing well, I hope?'

'Recovering, but slowly,' said John Fleetwood. 'Gaining strength. The pulse is regular. There's been some fever, but that's to be expected.'

The medical talk, in Arabic, flowed on between the doctors as Adam and Sir Ivo stood by uncomprehendingly.

Salim, glad of another opportunity to see the Frankish boy whose story had become so famous, smiled shyly at Adam. Adam smiled back.

'You're very good, sir,' Dr Musa was saying. 'A favour, eh? Now then. I can't think – no, there's nothing at all I . . .'

Salim, waking up suddenly to what was happening, was struck by a stupendous idea.

'Excuse me, *sidi* Musa,' he said, plucking at the doctor's sleeve. 'I think you've forgotten.'

'Eh? Forgotten what? Don't meddle, boy.' The glare that was turned on him would have turned to stone anyone who didn't know the doctor.

'The family in Acre,' Salim pressed on bravely. 'The merchant's family. Adil's family. They need a safe conduct, *sidi* Musa, out of the city.'

The doctor stared at him for a long moment.

'Correct!' he exclaimed at last, turning back to Dr John, who had rapidly translated the request to a disconcerted Sir Ivo. 'A safe conduct! Yes! An elderly merchant. His wife and small daughter. Another son also. Harmless people. Non-military types. They lived under the Franks for many years. A noble act of rescue.'

Sir Ivo bowed.

'Naturally, doctor,' he said stiffly, 'we'll do what we can. I'm sure it'll be possible. You'll need to accompany us, of course, to the city walls to parley with the garrison.'

'I? Parley?' The doctor looked thunderstruck. 'Impossible! I can't leave the Sultan, peace be upon him, at this critical time. His stomach . . .'

He stopped, aware that he might be revealing important information to Saladin's enemies.

'Your boy, then,' Sir Ivo said, when Dr John had translated. 'Let him come with us. We'll take care of him. He's known to this merchant, I presume?'

'Known? To Adil?' The doctor spluttered. 'Oh yes, he's known to him. Very well indeed. Take him, then, if you must. An imp of Sat— I mean, an excellent boy. Very full of – of ideas. It's mighty good of you. Not putting you to too much trouble, I hope. A favour indeed. Yes, indeed.'

Sir Ivo and John Fleetwood conferred for a moment.

'We'll get the authorities to issue a safe conduct and come back tomorrow morning at about this time,' Dr John told Dr Musa at last. 'The boy can walk as far as the city walls, on that leg?'

Salim flushed.

'Thank you for your concern. I've walked much further than that,' he said stiffly.

CHAPTER THIRTEEN

S alim barely slept that night. Although Dr Musa had been irritable all evening, Salim knew that he wasn't angry but anxious.

He tossed and turned on his sleeping mat, trying to imagine what it was like in Acre. His parents were suddenly tantalizingly close, almost at his fingertips. They'd been there, a constant nagging worry, since the day he'd left, although he'd managed to push them out of his thoughts most of the time. Now the memory of their faces surged back, so real that he could almost speak to them.

But what if they're too sick to move? he thought. *What if they're dead already? Not Mama! Please, not Mama!* He shut his eyes for a moment, willing himself to fall asleep, but his thoughts churned round, tying themselves into ever more uncomfortable knots. *What if they managed to slip out months ago, by sea through the harbour? Perhaps they escaped up the coast, and they're living all together in Damascus? Never giving me a thought, probably. A real fool I'll look, if I get into the city and find they've gone.*

He must have dozed off at last, because the muezzin calling the camp to prayer woke him with a start. Dawn was already greying the eastern sky. Salim sat bolt upright, the knowledge of what the day would bring rushing back to him.

Mama won't be able to walk all the way up to here, he thought, a new anxiety besetting him. *She'll never make it.*

He decided that he'd think about that problem later, stood up, folded his bedclothes and sleeping mat and stowed them neatly away. The doctor had left the tent already. His prayer shawl was missing. He must have already joined his fellow Jews in their morning worship.

Quickly, Salim scrambled into his tunic, belted it round his waist, strapped on his sandals, groped for his skullcap, quickly performed his ritual wash and hurried outside, his prayer mat rolled up under his arm. Thousands of others were already obeying the call to prayer. On many mornings, Salim merely parroted the familiar words and went through the actions so automatically that afterwards he could not have said if he'd prayed or not. Today, however, he meant every word.

'In the name of Allah, the Merciful, the Compassionate,' he recited, and added in his heart, 'be merciful and compassionate to my family today!'

The sounds from the Crusader camp, so familiar that he usually ignored them, seemed strange and almost sinister today. The bells announcing the start of early mass seemed to mock him. The trumpet blasts and shouts of the heralds, passing through the camp and issuing the orders for the day, sounded like warnings. In the distance, near the city walls, the catapults were creaking into action. He flinched as he heard the crash of a boulder against the stone masonry.

I must have been crazy! Salim thought. *How can I possibly go down there? We'll be smashed to pieces by a flying rock. I'm stupid! So stupid! Why didn't* sidi *Musa just tell me to shut up?*

Salim was almost dancing with impatience by the time Dr Musa returned.

'What are you standing there for?' the doctor snapped.
'You can't expect a mule to saddle herself.'

'A mule?' Salim gaped at him.

'And where are your wits this morning? You think your
poor mother will enjoy struggling all this way on foot? And
your little sister, she'll manage it too? Or were you proposing
to carry your family here on your back?'

Embarrassing tears of gratitude threatened to choke Salim.

'Thank you, *sidi* Musa. I didn't expect . . .' he said gruffly.
'I never thought of taking Suweida. It was wrong. I shouldn't
have – well – tricked you like that. I should have kept my big
mouth shut.'

'Wrong?' the doctor roared. 'Wrong? It was magnificent!
If the Lord had ever given me a son, I would have wished
for . . . Now stop all this nonsense. You think if we're late
these ill-mannered Christians will wait for us? And you
intend, I suppose, to go among the barbarians looking like a
guttersnipe from the bazaar in Aleppo! A clean tunic, if you
please! And take off your skullcap. You could pass for an
Italian or a Spaniard without it. There's no need to make
yourself a target for some ignorant hothead from the back-
woods of Europe.'

No one was waiting at the meeting place when Dr Musa
and Salim, who was leading Suweida, arrived. Saladin, who
had followed the story with interest, had sent a small detach-
ment of Kurdish troops to accompany the doctor and his boy
into no-man's-land. They stood well back, not wishing to pro-
voke the enemy, but ready for action if anything untoward
should happen.

Salim squinted up at the sun to check the time. His palms
were clammy and he felt an ignoble hope that the infidels had
gone back on their promise and were not intending to come.
It would be so easy and comfortable to go back with the

doctor to his tent and spend a quiet, ordinary morning assisting at the day's surgery.

Dr Musa was harrumphing impatiently, and Suweida was flicking her long ears and swishing her tail to distract the flies, when at last a bustle could be heard at the gap in the embankment. A narrow path appeared through the obstacles and the barbarian doctor, the knight and the boy Adam appeared. After them came ten men-at-arms, helmets on their heads and swords hanging from their belts. Like their Saracen counterparts, they stood back to let the doctor and the knight go through, eyeing the enemy in case of a surprise attack.

'So sorry we're late,' puffed Dr John, hurrying towards Dr Musa and waving a parchment in the air. 'A few hitches in acquiring the permit. So many signatures needed! I had no idea.'

Salim's heart had given a great thump at the sight of the document.

It's going to happen! he thought. *I'm going to rescue them! Ali will never be able to kick me around again.*

The doctor's hand was on his shoulder.

'God go with you,' he said gravely. 'And if you get yourself killed you'll have me to reckon with, do you hear?'

Salim felt unexpectedly confident as he walked through the English camp. The place seemed almost familiar from their last visit. The knight and Dr John led the way, with the posse of men-at-arms following. He and Suweida were sandwiched between them, with the boy Adam walking at his side. People looked up as they passed, calling out questions and staring at him. He even saw the girl, bending over a tub of water, scrubbing at some cloth. She smiled and nodded at him.

They were soon beyond the English part of the camp, working their way along well-trodden paths between tents and grander, brilliantly decorated pavilions, from whose crests fluttered banners with strange patterns on them. The men-at-arms had drawn closer together. There was no banter now.

'They're French here,' Adam said to him, as if an explanation was needed. It meant nothing to Salim. The Franks all looked the same to him, with their bare shaven chins and dirty matted hair.

'Your father, he is getting better?' he asked, trying not to sound too curious.

Adam looked self-conscious.

'My father, yes. He's even eating a little bit.'

Salim was longing to ask more, but there was something in Adam's silence that put him off.

'These people in Acre we're going to fetch out,' Adam said. 'Who are they? Why do you want to get them out of there?'

There had been much speculation round the English campfires the night before. Sir Ivo had frowned on it, saying that it was unchivalrous to enquire too closely into a favour that had been requested by a man who seemed to be honourable, even if he was a cursed Jew, but Adam couldn't resist asking the question.

They were stepping over a complicated web of guy ropes as he spoke, and Salim, guiding Suweida, was reluctant to answer, afraid that if the Crusaders knew how unimportant the objects of this rescue mission were, they might draw back from it. There was something about the boy Adam, though, something quiet and serious, that made him feel he could trust him.

'They are my father and my mother,' he said at last.

'I thought so. I thought they were your relatives.'

For the first time, Adam smiled at him, and Salim was surprised by how different he looked. He smiled back, with an answering glow of friendliness.

The little procession was halted suddenly by a couple of soldiers who stood in front of them, blocking the way. Salim's nervousness returned. What if he was being led into a trap? What if he was to be taken prisoner, and some huge ransom demanded before he would be let go?

Sir Ivo and Dr John were trying to talk to the soldiers, but it was clear that they had no language in common. The soldiers brushed their efforts aside. They were pointing at Suweida, holding up their fingers to show numbers, and pulling coins out of their leather pouches. Their meaning was quite clear. They wanted to buy the mule.

Salim pulled Suweida's reins closer and put a hand on her stiff, bristly mane. How could he ever face the doctor again if he returned from this adventure without the beloved mule?

Other strangers were joining the two soldiers now. They were running hungry, sunken eyes over Suweida, and a couple even came right up and prodded her rump, as if assessing how much meat covered her bones.

'Please, Dr John!' Salim called out anxiously, 'They can't buy Suweida. She's not for sale!'

The doctor turned and glared at him. Salim dropped his head and looked at the ground. He wanted to kick himself. How could he have been such a fool, shouting out in Arabic like that? What better way could he have chosen to draw disaster down on his head?

Sir Ivo had pulled out the precious document and was showing it to a man who had just appeared, and who seemed to have some authority. This person barked a command, and the crowd reluctantly withdrew, though as Salim clicked his tongue to make Suweida walk on he felt greedy eyes boring into his back.

The walls of Acre were approaching all the time, seeming to grow above the huge camp with every step they took. Salim, knowing he was being absurd, kept looking up at the ramparts, almost expecting Ali's brush of black hair to appear between the crenellations. The sight of the city shocked him.

It looked completely unfamiliar. The walls were festooned with bulging sacks, mattresses and bundles of cloth let down from above on ropes, and in the unprotected gaps between, wherever the Crusader missiles had found their mark, the stonework looked battered and crumbling. The elegant battlements, which used to stand out so crisp and white against the blue sky, were damaged and broken, like a mouth with ugly gaps and jagged, broken teeth.

They were almost at the border of the camp now, and it was possible to look along the edge of it, set back as it was from the walls out of range of the garrison's archers. Salim gasped at the sight of a row of huge, slender wooden siege towers, as high as the ramparts, ready on their wheeled bases to be pushed forwards to the walls. He had looked down on them often enough from above, but had had no idea how frighteningly tall they were. He shivered as he thought of how it would be when the great push for the city came. The barbarians would swarm up to the top of the towers, the drawbridges at the top would swing down on to the battlements and the Crusaders, screaming their hideous battle cries, would rush across the gap, swords flailing. He could almost see Ali bravely facing them, trying his best to fend them off, with nothing but a blunt old spear in his hands.

Adam, who hadn't been this near the walls of Acre for many weeks, was looking sideways at the siege towers too. He was imagining how he would feel when the moment came to climb the rickety wooden ladders to the top, and what it would be like to run across the narrow bridge, over the sickening gap, right into the swords and arrows of the enemy.

I'm a Martel, he thought, tightening his lips. *Adam Fitz Guy. I'll have to show that I'm up to it.*

He was surprised by how different the camp was down here near the city walls. Up in the English section the danger was from Saladin and his vast armies, but though the sentries had to be vigilant all the time, the threat wasn't constant. Here, though, the danger was from the embattled city itself. Scorch marks on the ground showed where fireballs had landed. There were workshop areas, where planks and tools lay around huge wooden constructions – battering rams, mangonels and catapults. One of these was already in operation, its long arm swinging round with ever increasing speed until it released a hail of pebbles which flew in a deadly shower over the city walls. Shouts and jeers from inside answered it, and something foul was thrown back, to land with a splatter in the ditch below.

Adam, used to the stench of the Fortis camp, nevertheless almost retched at the foulness of the air here. To the stink of latrines was added the terrible, all-pervasive, cloying smell of the dead, whose bodies lay unburied below the walls, black with clouds of flies. Sir Ivo and the doctor were holding up their hands to cover their noses and mouths, and the Saracen boy, Salim, looked pale and sweaty, as if he was about to be sick.

They were now standing on the very front line of Crusader tents. Ahead of them was the littered, empty ground of the fighting zone. To walk straight out into it was to invite instant death from the archers on the ramparts above.

What happens now? Salim thought, looking at the huge city gates ahead. They had been closed for so long that sand had drifted up against them, and clumps of grass and even young bushes were sprouting from the once beaten-down earth of the road leading into the city.

A yell from behind made them all turn round. A huge man, his fair face battered by the sun and wind to a coarse redness, his straw-like hair hanging long and lank to his shoulders, was shouting at them. Above the din of the camp, the hammering of workmen in a battering-ram shed, the creaking of wheels, shouts, yells and raucous singing, it was impossible to make out any words. Adam saw Sir Ivo and Dr John exchange shrugs.

'Flemish, I think,' Dr John said. 'Let's hope the fellow speaks something we can understand.'

The Fleming marched up to them aggressively and stood staring down at them, his vast forearms locked across his chest. Sir Ivo nodded at him politely and offered him the document. The Fleming brushed it aside with the back of his hand and talked at them loudly, as if he could make them understand simply by raising his voice. He seemed so threatening that the English men-at-arms moved closer to Sir Ivo and massed themselves round him, laying their hands meaningfully on their sword hilts.

The impasse might have continued if Dr John hadn't caught sight of a priest hurrying past behind the aggressive Fleming.

'*Pater!*' he called out in Latin. '*Adiuve nos!* Help us!'

The priest turned, shading his eyes against the sun to see who was calling him, and came forward.

'*Quis es? Quod vis?*' he answered. 'Who are you? What do you want?'

The men-at-arms, looking to Sir Ivo for guidance, obeyed his curt nod and relaxed as the priest and the doctor conferred in Latin. At last the priest spoke to the Flemish captain, who listened respectfully, eyes cast down. Then he nodded, and without looking at the English contingent raised one huge hand and shouted an order. Heads turned towards him. Tools were laid down. A drum beat rolled out. A boy was sent scampering across to the nearest catapult. Its huge arm, already rising into the air, slowed, then drifted back down till it was pointing once more at the ground.

Cautious heads appeared on the ramparts above.

'Now?' Sir Ivo said.

Dr John raised his brows at the priest, who looked at the Fleming. The man nodded.

'Good.' Sir Ivo lifted his lance. The white flag took the breeze and fluttered out to its full extent. 'I go forward first,' Sir Ivo ordered, 'with the boy and my squire. Doctor, this is no task for civilians. Please don't come any further.' He raised his voice to address the men-at-arms. 'Stay here, boys. Look relaxed, but be ready in case there's a rush from inside when the gate opens. If there is, form up and attack, but only at my signal. Peter Doggett, I'm putting you in charge. Keep an eye on the mule.'

Salim was so nervous that he had barely understood a word of this, but a nudge from Sir Ivo propelled him forward. There was a strange quietness as he stepped out into the open ground, followed by Sir Ivo and Adam. A voice floated across from on top of the city wall ahead.

'Halt! Who are you? What do you want?'

Salim cleared his throat.

'I'm Salim Ibn Adil, the merchant's son!' he shouted as loudly as he could. 'I have a safe conduct here for my family!'

It was clear that he hadn't been heard.

'Don't move!' the voice shouted again. 'Don't come any closer! Identify yourself!'

'Salim! Salim Ibn Adil!' Salim yelled at the top of his voice. 'Ali's brother!'

Daringly, he took a few steps further forwards, hoping that his limp would be seen and recognized.

'Adil's lame son?' the man called back at last. '*Wallahi!* You can approach on your own. Tell the two Franks to stay where they are.'

The distance to the city gate was no more than two hundred metres, but it seemed like a mile to Salim. His back tingled at the thought of the hostile army of Crusaders that must be watching him from behind, and his chest crawled at the knowledge that the suspicious men ahead might panic and fell him with a sudden arrow.

At last he stood so near the huge city gates that he could have counted the nicks in the wood cut by Crusader axes on their first assault. Voices were calling down to him again.

'What are you doing here? What do you want?'

'I've come for my family!' he shouted back. 'I've got a safe conduct for them. Please, quickly, open the gate and let me come in and fetch them.'

'It's a trap! You're acting under duress! They want to spy on us!'

'No, no! I swear it! The Sultan gave permission himself. Let me in before someone shoots me!'

'If we open the gate they'll storm in.'

'Look at them! There are only a few armed men behind me, and they're just an escort. Please, I beg you, let me in. It's my family's only chance.'

The heads disappeared for a moment, then a new voice called out, 'Have you brought any food with you?'

'No. They wouldn't let me. I was searched.' Salim's voice was growing hoarse.

It's hopeless. They'll never believe me. It's all going wrong, he thought.

There was another long pause, then a deeper, more commanding voice shouted, 'Wait by the postern gate. Be ready to come inside quickly, as soon as it opens.'

Salim did as he was told. The postern was a small door set into the huge double doors, which could open independently, allowing only one person through at a time. He put his ear against the crack, listening for approaching footsteps. It seemed as if an hour had passed, but it was only a few minutes before he heard the patter of many pairs of sandals on the other side, and then a scrabbling sound as the heavy bolts, rusted into their sockets from long disuse, grated back. Then, just as the door swung open, Sir Ivo's voice shouted across the empty ground behind him: 'Boy! You have one hour, do you understand? One hour. After that, we'll have to leave, and anyone coming out of the city will be attacked.'

One hour? Salim repeated desperately to himself. *Only one hour?*

Stepping through the gate into the narrow street beyond was like passing into another world. The rough stone paving slabs underfoot, the overhanging upper storeys, the curved doorknockers, the carved stone lintels were all achingly familiar, but the strange emptiness, the rubble in the streets, the bars across the upper windows and the heavy shutters over the lower ones made the place so eerie that it was if the city had become a ghost of itself – as if it was the setting for a strange, unsettling dream.

There was no time, though, to look around.

Captain Qaraqush, the commander of the city's garrison, was hurrying towards him, pushing through the small crowd that had already gathered.

'What's all this about? Is it a trick? What are you doing here?'

'No, no. No trick, sir. Please, listen,' began Salim, his words falling over themselves in his haste. 'I've got a safe conduct, look here, for my family.' He pulled the document out of his belt and showed it to the captain. 'It's in return for a favour the Sultan did for a Frankish lord. He sent his own doctor, Dr Musa, to him. The doctor asked for Adil's family to be released in return.'

'Give me that.' Captain Qaraqush took the document and began to turn it round and over in his hands with agonizing deliberation. He scratched his beard and frowned, unable to decipher the strange foreign writing.

Salim watched in an agony of impatience.

'Sir, I have only an hour. Please let me go to them.'

'What's this thing here?'

The captain was peering at a scarlet wax seal which hung from the bottom of the document.

'It was to show the Franks, so they'd let us through.' Salim was hopping from his good leg to his bad. 'Sir, please . . .'

The captain seemed to suddenly make up his mind.

'Go on then. At least it'll mean fewer mouths to feed. You'd better hurry.'

Salim was about to run off into the maze of streets when he remembered Ali.

'My brother, Ali. Is he still here? The safe conduct's for him too.'

Qaraqush's brows snapped together.

'Ali Ibn Adil is a serving soldier. He may not desert his post. Every man's needed here, or didn't you know?'

'Can I see him, sir? Just for a minute?'

'I don't know where he is. Go on and fetch your parents now, quickly.'

The distance from the main gate of Acre to Adil's house had never seemed so far. Salim ran as fast as he could, dodging over fallen beams and piles of rubble, while a growing crowd of thin, hollow-eyed people gathered behind him. News of this astonishing visitation from the world outside had spread like wildfire. Everyone wanted to ask for news.

'The Sultan, when's he coming?' voices from all sides asked. 'When's he going to relieve the city?'

'Doesn't he know we're starving in here?'

'Tell him we're desperate! My daughter's dying!'

'When's he going to break the sea blockade?'

'We can't hang on much longer. Make sure and tell him.'

It seemed an age before he arrived at the familiar door in the bare stone wall. He tried to open it, but the bolt was drawn on the inside. He pounded on it with his fists.

'Mama! Baba! Open up quickly! It's me, Salim!'

There was no sound from within. He screwed his eyes shut with anxiety.

They're not there. They're at someone's else's house. I'll never find them in time. Or they're sick. They've died already. I've come too late.

At last he heard the quavering voice of an old man call out, 'Who is it? What do you want?'

'Is Adil there? Open up, quickly! It's me. His son. Salim.'

The door swung open. Salim stepped inside and closed it behind him, shutting out the curious onlookers.

He stared with dismay at the old man who had opened the door. Could this stranger, this shrunken old man, with his sparse grey beard, hollow cheeks and dull eyes, be his father?

'Baba?' he said at last. 'Is it you?'

The eyes filled with tears.

'Salim! You're so big! I was afraid you were dead!'

His father's trembling arms were around him. Salim struggled free.

'Baba, listen. You must listen! I've come to get you out, you and Mama and Zahra. Quick. There's no time! We've got to leave at once. Did you hear me, Baba? Did you hear what I said?'

His father's eyes were worryingly vacant.

'Leave?' he said vaguely. 'Go where? How can we leave? Your mother—'

'Mama! Where is she?'

Salim couldn't bear to look at his father any longer. The person of authority, of action, of discipline and certainty had gone, and in his place was this defeated, famished, lost old man.

Salim hobbled across the courtyard at his fastest pace.

'Mama! Quick! Mama!'

His mother was lying on a mat inside the kitchen door, her white muslin coif pulled over her face. It looked almost like a shroud, and for a sickening moment Salim thought he'd come too late. Then she stirred, pulled the cloth away and looked up at him.

'Salim! *Habibi!*' Joy sharpened the eyes in her skeletal face. 'What's happened? How did you get here? Tell me! The infidels have been defeated! Saladin's taken the city! We're saved!'

'No, Mama. You've got to listen to me.' He knelt beside her and took her face between his palms as he used to do when he was very small and wanted her whole attention. 'There's no time. I've got a safe conduct for you and Baba and Zahra. I can get you out of Acre. But we have to go now. At once. Get up, Mama. Come with me. We've got to hurry. Please, Mama. Get up.'

To his intense relief she had understood. She struggled to her feet, staggered and put her hand against the wall to steady herself.

'Are you all right? You're not sick?' he said, noticing how her clothes hung off her body.

'I'm all right. It's only weakness. There's been no food for so long. Where's your father?'

'In the courtyard. I can't make him understand. Tell him, Mama. Make him come. If we don't go at once, this minute, our chance is lost.'

She set her shoulders back.

'Zahra's in the other room,' she said, with a shadow of her old decisiveness. 'Go and wake her up.' She was looking vaguely towards the chest in the corner of the room.

'Mama, there's no time for packing!'

'Packing!' she almost laughed. 'You think we have anything left to pack? Everything, every scrap of cloth, every dish, gone to buy food. Where's Ali?'

He'd been dreading this question.

'I don't think – Mama, the garrison commander said – I don't think that Ali can come with us.'

Her burst of energy left her.

'You want us to leave Ali behind? In Acre?'

'I don't want to, Mama! It can't be helped! Think of Zahra! Think of Baba!'

She shook her head from side to side and closed her eyes.

'Aiee! What have we come to? What curse has fallen on us?'

His heart sank. He knew that wailing tone. When once his mother started in that vein, she could go on for hours.

'Mama!' he shouted, shaking her arm. 'There's no time!'

She pulled herself together with an effort.

'Zahra. I told you. Fetch her,' she said. 'What are you waiting for?'

His little sister was lying on her back, fast asleep, her arms above her head, her soft black hair spread out on the mat, as still as an abandoned doll. He was so shocked at the sight of her stick-like arms and pale little face that he could hardly bear to touch her in case she broke in his arms.

'Zahra!' he whispered. 'It's me, *habibti*. Salim. Wake up. Come on, now. We've got to go.'

She opened her eyes and then her face puckered, and the corners of her mouth turned down.

'Not Salim,' she said crossly. 'Salim gone away.'

He scooped her up, shocked at her lightness, and settled her against his shoulder. To his relief she relaxed against him and snuggled her head into his neck. He knew that her thumb had wandered towards her mouth.

He hurried outside. His mother was tottering across towards his father.

'Where are you taking us?' she asked fearfully as they crossed the courtyard. 'What's going to happen to us? When are we coming home again?'

'Come on, Mama.' He grabbed her hand. 'Baba, come.'

It seemed an age before he had coaxed his parents out into the street, and another before his father had locked the door with shaking hands and fumbled the key into a pocket of his cloak.

The crowd of thin, desperate people outside the door had grown.

'Salim, take us too! My daughter, look at her!'

'Just take the baby, the little one, Salim. You remember me, how I used to give you honey cakes?'

He ignored them all. Dragging his mother by the hand, holding Zahra over his shoulder and praying that his father was following, he pushed his way through, murmuring, 'I'm sorry. Forgive me. You'll be saved soon, *inshallah*. The Sultan, peace be upon him, hasn't forgotten you.'

He had no idea how much time had passed. It seemed as if he was in a nightmare, his feet weighed down so that he could only drag them slowly.

The gates were ahead of him at last.

'Leave her alone, Auntie!' he shouted to a woman who was clinging, sobbing to his mother's arm. 'Let her go!'

Suddenly, Ali was there, pushing through the crowd.

'Salim! What's happened? How did you get in here?'

'Ali! *Al hamdi l'illah!* Thank God! I thought I wouldn't see you. I've got a safe conduct for Mama and Baba.'

Ali's eyes opened wide.

'You've got a *what*?'

'A permit. Listen, there's no time. If we're not out of here in the next few minutes we won't be able to go at all.' He grabbed Ali's arm. 'Come with us! Don't ask the commander. Just come!'

Ali bit his lip in a moment of agonized indecision.

'Idiot,' he said at last. 'You know I can't. There aren't nearly enough of us as it is. It'll be touch and go at the next big assault.' He shook his head, as if trying to rid it of the thought of escape. 'Anyway, we're working on a new thing. A new method of shooting with Greek fire. It's going to slaughter them. Dozens of barbarian devils up in smoke in one go. You'll see.'

His enthusiasm was feverish. His eyes burned in his thin face. Salim was struck with a cruel pang of guilt.

'I ought to be here with you!' he cried, putting Zahra down. 'I should be helping! Look, I'll stay. We'll all be together.'

'Ali! My son!' Khadijah, who had been embracing her neighbour, was clinging to Ali now and crying. Zahra had been quiet up till now, but she sat down on the ground and began to cry, her voice a pale, weak thread.

'Don't be such a fool, little brother,' Ali said, trying to detach his mother. 'You're being a bigger hero than me. Getting them out of here's a miracle.'

He picked Zahra up and put her into Salim's arms. From the other side of the great wooden doors, came a drum roll and distant shouts.

'Go on! Just go!' Ali was shoving Salim towards the postern, which someone had opened.

Salim was about to step out of the narrow door when an idea struck him. He pulled the safe conduct out from his belt and thrust it into Ali's hands.

'Take it. It's the permit. Your name's on it. It might be useful later.'

Ali grinned as he took it.

'Well done, little brother.' There was admiration in his voice. 'Go on. Quick.'

The drums were beating again on the Frankish lines.

'Look after yourself,' Salim called back to Ali. *'Ma'a salama.* God go with you.'

'And with you. Hurry, Mama. Goodbye, Baba.'

Pulled from the front by Salim and pushed from behind by Ali, Salim's parents were over the threshold at last and the postern gate was shut behind them. His mother, facing the entire Crusader army in front of her without the protection of the massive city walls, staggered and seemed about to fall.

'*Ya haram*,' she kept saying. '*Ya haram!* God be merciful!'

'Come on,' Salim said, his voice sharp with anxiety. His father was standing in a daze, looking round the wide open space like a lost child. Zahra, twisting in his arms, had set up a high-pitched wail. Salim shifted her higher up his shoulder. 'Help Baba, Mama. Come *on*!'

With a visible effort, Khadijah summoned up her courage.

'Go on ahead of us, Salim,' she said in an almost steady voice. 'Show us where to go. Look after Zahra. I've got your father.'

The few hundred metres to the Crusader front line seemed even further to Salim now. The brief ceasefire was over already. The Flemish captain, ignoring the slow-moving little band of escapees, had already lifted his sword in signal. The long arm of the catapult was moving once more, gaining momentum as it swept upwards.

Adam watched the little group make its way painfully across the open ground. He saw the feeble figure of the man behind Salim totter and fall. The woman bent over him, helplessly talking to him. Without thinking, Adam dashed forwards into no-man's-land, bent down, picked up the man and slung him over his shoulder as easily as if he'd been a sack of flour. He ran back with him towards Sir Ivo.

'Young fool,' Sir Ivo said crossly, as Adam set Adil back on his feet, but he put out his arm to steady Adil, who seemed unable to stand unaided.

Adam had already run back out to help Khadijah, but she

had broken into a lumbering trot and was keeping up with Salim. He was concentrating on holding Zahra, who, in spite of her weakness, was thrashing about in his arms in panic.

The men-at-arms watched stony-faced as the little family reached them.

'All this trouble for them?' Adam heard Peter Doggett mutter, as he raised his helmet to scratch at a wandering louse. 'Two old crocks and a screaming kid? I thought at least it'd be someone noble.'

Salim had put Zahra down and was already trying to help his father on to Suweida's back. Sir Ivo, seeing him struggle, picked Adil up bodily and hoisted him into the saddle. The man seemed on the point of collapse. His face was grey and his eyes half shut.

'We'll be safe soon, Baba,' Salim was murmuring to him. 'Don't worry. There'll be a good meal waiting for you. Dr Musa, he'll put you right. Just hold on, Baba. It won't be long.' He turned to his mother. 'You can ride behind Baba,' he said. 'Come on. I'll help you.'

To his surprise she shook her head.

'And make a spectacle of myself in front of all these infidels? Like an old woman going to market? Your father needs more help than me. Give me your arm, Salim. I'll manage on foot. Zahra, behave yourself. Stop making that noise or the Christians will get you.'

Terrified, Zahra stopped crying mid-sob. Her eyes opened wide with fear and she wrapped her arms round Salim's good knee.

'The woman intends to walk?' Sir Ivo said to Salim, surprised.

'Yes, sir,' Salim answered. 'She can, I think. She will lean on my arm.'

'Adam, carry the child,' Sir Ivo said briskly. 'We must get

moving. We've been here long enough. The mule's attracting too much attention.'

Adam bent down towards Zahra.

She shuddered, shut her eyes tight and clung to Salim's leg with even greater ferocity.

Salim bent down too.

'You've got to let him carry you, *habibti*,' he whispered. 'The big knight says so. I can't manage you any more. The boy, he's called Adam. It's an Arabic name. He won't hurt you.'

Zahra dared peep round at Adam.

'Nasty,' she said. 'Christian.'

'How can he be? He's got a Muslim name! He must be Muslim!' Salim said soothingly, glad that Dr John was out of earshot and no one else could understand.'

'Adam,' Zahra said experimentally, and when Salim picked her up and passed her into Adam's arms, she subsided without more fuss.

Curious looks followed the party all the way back through the camp. To Adam's relief the little girl quickly settled down. The woman, Salim's mother, had set her face in an expression of impassive dignity as she walked between the tents of her enemies, leaning on Salim from time to time, or holding on to the mule's saddle, but always holding her head high.

She's brave, Adam thought, trying to imagine how Jennet would feel if she had to march right through the camp of the Saracens.

They reached the English quarters at last. The men-at-arms dispersed, shaking their heads over the folly of the exercise. Salim turned round as they reached the embankment and bowed formally to Sir Ivo. He'd been preparing a little speech of thanks and he wanted to deliver it.

'Sir knight,' he said politely. 'My father and mother want thanks to you. Very great . . .' He paused, forgetting the word for 'obligation'. 'Very good and kind. *Inshallah* one day I can pay you in my thanks and my families also.'

Sir Ivo grinned.

'So these are your parents, eh? I suspected as much. You're an enterprising lad, I must say. I admire your courage. Good luck to you. I hope your father gets his health back soon.'

Salim bowed again.

'And your lord,' he said. 'With Allah help, he make good repair.'

'Go on with you now.' Sir Ivo's eyebrows had twitched together at the mention of Allah. He slapped the mule on the rump. 'Greet the doctor for us. Tell him again how grateful we are.'

Adam led Suweida by the bridle through the gap in the embankment.

'*Ma'a salama*,' Zahra called out to him, waving her hand as she'd been taught. 'Goodbye!'

'You very kind boy. Very good,' Salim said to Adam, grasping his hand. His smile radiated such joy and relief that Adam felt warmed by its glow. 'I see you again one day maybe, when . . .'

He stopped. His smile faded. *When we've liberated Acre and this war is over*, he'd wanted to say.

Adam was no longer smiling either.

When what? he was thinking. *When we've taken Acre and Jerusalem and driven you infidels out?*

The abyss had opened between them again.

But Adam watched half regretfully as the Kurdish troop, who had been waiting all this while, ran down from the Saracen camp to escort the family to safety.

CHAPTER FOURTEEN

I t was April again. The nights were cool but the days were already hot. The Crusaders were thankful that the endless rain had stopped, and the mixture of mud and sewage in which they'd lived all winter was drying up, but they dreaded the return of summer, the searing heat and the dust storms, the scorpions and biting flies and the epidemics of sickness that they knew would afflict them.

'A few more months of this and we'll be so weak that the Saracens will walk all over us,' Adam heard Sir Ivo mutter, in a rare moment of depression.

'King Richard's on his way. He *must* be here soon, sir,' Adam reminded him, anxious to cheer him up.

But it was Philip, the King of France, who arrived first. His eight ships made a magnificent show as they scudded on the spring breeze towards the beach, their pennants flying. The French camp celebrated their king's arrival long into the night, with fanfares of trumpets and raucous singing. For days afterwards dukes, earls, counts, barons and bishops from a dozen different nations donned their most impressive armour and went to pay him homage.

Sir Ivo, though, was not impressed.

'He's no more use than a glass sword,' he said, shaking his head. 'Richard's the only man who can take Acre. He'll crack it like a nut. If he ever gets here.'

Nothing worried Adam more than Sir Ivo's pessimism. He had come to rely on the knight absolutely. In all his life, he'd never known a feeling like it.

It was eighteen months now since Sir Ivo had taken him under his wing, and Adam thanked God for it every time he heard the bell ring outside the church tent. He'd shared a tent with the knight all that time, had seen him shiver with fever, wake with a hangover, fume with rage, grumble at the weather and heap curses on the infidel Saracens, but he had never known him do a mean thing, or lose faith in the Crusade, or join in the malicious gossip that ran round the camp, or unjustly accuse anyone to cover up his own fault. He had never seen him lack courage, or shirk a difficult, boring or dangerous task.

He was watching Jennet one afternoon, as she draped a batch of fresh linen over the poles of a wagon, when Jacques suddenly appeared. To Adam's disgust, Tibby raised her arms and crowed when she saw him, displaying two rows of pearly new teeth. Jacques reached inside his cloak, which was now so tattered it hung from his shoulders in shreds, pulled out a little cake and gave it to her.

'Why if it isn't me old friend Adam Fitz Guy,' he said, bowing with a flourish. 'Not too proud yet to talk to your humbler acquaintance, I do trust?'

Adam had almost lost his fear of Jacques, but the man still made his flesh creep with disgust.

'Didn't I see you, last week, up by the Saracen camp, talking to a pair of Turks? Crooks they looked too,' Adam said suspiciously.

Jacques laughed.

'A pair of Turks? My, how wicked you make them sound!

Trading gentlemen, they was, my dear boy. Base unbelievers they may be, but every man must live. They buys and sells, sells and buys, same as your humble servant.'

'Buys and sells what?' Jennet said eagerly. 'They haven't got any lotions, have they? Only Tibby's got a rough patch on her neck she keeps scratching at.'

'Lotions? Why didn't you tell me before, my darling? Got to keep little miss here in prime condition, haven't we?'

There was something about the way he patted Tibby's yellow curls that made Adam's gorge rise.

It's like he owns her, he thought.

'You still haven't said what you were buying,' he said, scowling. 'From the Turks, God curse them.'

Jacques's eyes narrowed till they looked like splinters of green glass.

'Still as narrow-minded as ever, I see! And I thought you were so friendly with that Saracen boy. It's the Martel blood coming out. Norman blood. You need to take care, young Adam. Hot-headed and blinkered as a packhorse, that's your typical Norman lord. I can see it now. You'll go charging into battle alongside that priggish knight of yours and get yourself spitted on a Saracen lance. While I, like a sensible man, will add my mite to the cause by sending up prayers to Christ's Mother from the safety of the baggage train.'

He laughed mockingly at the disgusted look on Adam's face.

'Duty calls, my dear ones. Business is business. Someone has to keep the art of honest trading from dying out.'

The next moment he'd gone as suddenly as he'd come.

Adam felt confused. Unwelcome thoughts, which had recently been bubbling up from deep down in his mind, rose again to the surface.

I'm not friendly with that Saracen boy, he told himself. *He's an infidel. It would be a sin.*

But an uncomfortable feeling pricked at him as he thought of Salim's family.

Is it really right to starve old people and children? I know what Sir Ivo would say, that they ought to recognize Christ as their saviour, and worship him, and give up their wicked religion. But they're foreigners. You can't expect them to know what's what. It doesn't seem fair.

He tried, as he so often did, to recapture the glorious certainty of the night at Fortis when he'd taken the cross. It was harder and harder to warm the ashes of the fire that had burned in him then.

It'll be different if we ever get to Jerusalem, he told himself. It must be like heaven there. The Holy Sepulchre, where Christ was buried, and the place where he walked, carrying the Cross, and the garden where he wept tears. If only I could see all of that this would be worth it.

It was nearly two months since Lord Guy had fallen from his horse, and his anxious people were beginning to despair of his recovery. The baron sat all day in the entrance of his pavilion, smiling vaguely at those who came near him, a trickle of saliva running down his chin. Every now and then a flash of his old self returned, and he barked out orders, demanded explanations and was so much in control that he seemed on the brink of a complete recovery. But after an hour or two the listlessness would return, and he would sit rubbing the stubble on his head, as if he was wondering where his thick hair had gone.

It was well known in the camp that Lord Robert and Dr Nicholas still clung to the theory that a demon had entered the baron through his wound and that he wouldn't become his old self again until it was let out. They'd begged Father Jerome to perform an exorcism, but the priest had steadfastly refused.

'There are no clear signs of demonic possession,' he said sharply to Lord Robert. 'Confusion and weakness after a head injury are to be expected. I haven't noticed you doing penance for his recovery. Do so, and let Christ perform his healing task in his own time.'

'That priest never liked me,' Lord Robert muttered to Dr Nicholas, as Father Jerome stalked away. 'He's always been against me.' He looked up, saw that Adam was nearby and shot him a spiteful look. 'The dog boy's no more my father's son than you are, Dr Nicholas,' he said, raising his voice so that Adam would be sure to hear. 'Witchcraft, that's what this is about. If we could only let the demon out of my father's head he'd be his old self again. They'd believe me then. The boy would burn for a witch, like he deserves.'

It was lucky for Adam that no one else in the Fortis camp seemed to share Lord Robert's view. He became more and more aware, as the weeks passed, of the wisdom of Sir Ivo's advice. He followed it carefully, working quietly at his squire's duties, keeping away from flatterers and treating everyone the same, copying Sir Ivo's respectful manner towards the high-born and lowly alike. He could feel, as he walked through the camp, how right this approach had been. Even the rowdy squires now treated him with calm respect. It was the best he could ask for.

The crisis, when it came, took everyone by surprise. It began on a Saturday afternoon in the middle of May. The catapults and mangonels which King Philip had brought with him had stepped up the assault on the walls of Acre, and the dull thuds of stone battering stone in the distance, and the screams of wounded men, were so commonplace that the English camp had learned to take them for granted.

It was just after tierce, the hour of afternoon prayer, when the baron fell into a sudden fit. His limbs went rigid, his eyes rolled up under his eyelids and froth came out of his mouth.

Unluckily, Dr John Fleetwood had walked over to the Burgundian zone, half a mile away, to visit a fellow doctor. The way was left clear for Dr Nicholas.

Adam knew nothing about what was happening until it was all over. Sir Ivo came to find him, making him sit down while he told him the news.

'He's gone. Your father's soul is now in Paradise,' he said sorrowfully.

Adam looked back at him, his feelings strangely blank.

'Just like that? He died?' he asked. 'But he was all right this morning. I saw him sitting there when I passed his tent.'

Sir Ivo shook his head in puzzlement.

'Dr Nicholas is a learned man. Lord Guy went into a fit, which as everyone knows is a demonic sign. Nicholas opened up his head wound, to let the evil out. I didn't see what happened then, but Sir Baudoin told me that one minute Lord Guy was shaking all over in his fit, and the next minute, as soon as the wound was opened, his soul took flight and left his body. Sir Baudoin said he almost saw it go. I'm sorry, Adam. If he'd lived, your father would have put right the wrongs he did you, I'm sure of it.'

'Maybe he would have,' Adam said quietly. 'Maybe.'

News of Lord Guy's death reached Dr Musa's ears two weeks later. It made him furiously angry.

'Such a crime! Such wickedness!' he raged. 'That man Nick-las, or whatever he calls himself – he's no more a doctor than my poor Suweida. Cracking open the man's head? To let a demon out? Did you ever hear anything so stupid? And the operation we'd performed, the good John and I, it was a masterpiece. I tell you confidently, *ya*-Adil, without false modesty, it was a masterpiece.'

Salim's father, who was sitting cross-legged outside the doctor's tent, took another sip of sage tea. Since his family's spectacular escape from Acre he had regained weight. The fingers clicking over his worry beads were no longer as thin as chicken bones, and his eyes had lost their vague, vacant look. But his hair, once so black and glossy, was now thin and streaked with grey, and his manner, which had been so confident, was still uncertain.

'Simple-minded, that's the problem with the Franks,' he said, watching Salim who was dressing the sore on a Bedouin soldier's knee. 'Just like children.'

'Such misplaced faith!' Dr Musa shook his head. 'It would make you laugh if they weren't so violent. To call the Prophet Jesus, peace be upon him, the Son of God! As if the Lord God could father a son!'

'Sheer blasphemy,' Adil agreed. 'But if only our people had half their faith and persistence. There's the Sultan, may God prosper him, desperately trying to keep the chieftains and all their troops here, but they keep slipping away. And the Egyptians and Turks and all the Faithful promise every day to send more men, but never do it.' He paused, looking across at the walls of Acre. 'If this isn't resolved soon . . .'

A tear welled up in the corner of his eye and ran down his wrinkled cheek.

Dr Musa patted his hand comfortingly.

'Ali is a strong young man. And you told me yourself that what food there is in Acre goes first to the garrison. He'll come through this all right. Don't give up hope, my dear friend.'

'Hope!' Adil laughed bitterly. 'What else have I got left but hope? My home gone, my business ruined . . .'

'But you still have your family. Your wife, Zahra and that young villain Salim,' Dr Musa chided him.

'Yes, yes, Salim!' Adil brightened. 'It was a good day's work that, eh, doctor, when I brought him to you? The little rascal. He didn't want to come, did he?'

Salim gave the neatly tied bandage a final pat, and as the soldier went away he looked up at his father and smiled. Things had been different between them since the rescue from Acre. Salim, who was now nearly as tall as his father, was no longer the spoilt mother's darling, whom Adil had so often tried to discipline. He was the acknowledged saviour of the family, the experienced campaigner, known and respected throughout the army, a friend of Mamluks, a frequenter of Saladin's own pavilion. Sometimes, Adil's humility made Salim feel uncomfortable, and he half wished that his father would resume his old authority, and shout at him, and tell him what to do.

It's as if they think I'm responsible for them now, he told himself. *But they can't stay here forever, living off the doctor. If only Ali was here. I wish I could talk to him.*

Zahra came running up to him. Two weeks of good food carefully prescribed by the doctor had turned her back into an energetic child.

'Leave your brother alone, Zahra,' Khadijah called out from inside the tent that had been pitched for the family. 'Can't you see that he has his work to do?'

'Your wife is well, Adil. Better every day,' Dr Musa remarked cheerfully.

'*Al hamdi l'illah*. Thank God,' Adil said fervently. 'And thanks to you, doctor. How we can ever repay—'

'We can never repay,' Khadijah called out, surprising both the men by butting into their conversation. 'But once we're back on our feet, in Damascus, our home will be your home, doctor, whenever you come that way. And our family will be in debt to yours forever.'

'In Damascus?' Adil looked astonished. 'What are you talking about, woman?'

Khadijah emerged from the tent and put down the tray of rice she'd been picking over.

'We're going to my brother,' she said with calm authority. 'He'll take you into partnership in his business. We'll live in his house in Damascus until we get settled.'

'Oh? And how will we get there? Walk all the way with nothing to eat but leaves plucked from the trees? It takes money to travel. Don't you understand, woman? We're destitute! There's nothing left at all!'

'We'll use this,' she said, taking off her belt. She turned it over and showed him the row of gold coins stitched along the inside.

'But this is – there's a fortune here!' Adil said angrily. 'Why didn't you tell me about this before? Where have you been hiding it? It would have bought us a week's supply of corn!'

'Umm Fares gave it to me as we were leaving Acre,' she said. 'She's owed me this money for fifteen years and always avoided paying me back. She caught up with us as we were leaving. She said she'd accepted that her death was approaching, according to the will of Allah, and she wanted to have this money off her conscience.'

Salim had limped over from the bench where he had been tearing strips of cloth to make bandages.

'I needed time to think things over,' she went on. 'This gift's a miracle. It came straight to me from Allah. We've got to use it wisely. A new life in Damascus, where trade is always good and we can make a new start – that's the answer.'

'Damascus – after all, it's not a bad idea,' Adil said reluctantly.

Salim watched him as he looked up at Khadijah and meekly handed the belt back to her.

It's as if she's the husband now, he thought. *She's the powerful one.*

Adil stood up and put the worry beads into his pocket.

'We'll leave tomorrow,' he said, trying to sound decisive.

'You can't, Baba, you have to wait for the next caravan,'

Salim told him. 'There are too many robbers on the road. You can't possibly go alone.'

'Tomorrow?' Khadijah was vehemently shaking her head. 'Not tomorrow! Not until Acre is relieved. How can we leave while Ali is still there? How can you think of leaving your son?'

A turbaned servant, his silk sleeves flapping, came running up to the doctor.

'The Sultan needs you, *ya-hakim*,' he panted. 'His stomach pains have returned.'

'Ah, poor man, may God preserve him. How he suffers!' Khadijah murmured. 'Did you hear that, Salim? Hurry! Put your cap straight. Let me tie your belt.'

'Not now, Mama.' He pushed her aside and hurried into the tent to fetch the bag which the doctor kept permanently in readiness for a call from Saladin's tent.

King Richard of England arrived at last, on a blazing day in June. Seagulls screamed round the twenty-five galleys of his fleet, and the ecstatic Crusaders, watching from the shore, were half dazzled by the brilliantly coloured pennants fluttering from his masts and the rows of painted shields decorating the ships' sides.

It took all that day and several days more to unload the enormous numbers of horses and wagons, the vast quantity of food and arms and the massive beams and blocks of stone that would be transformed into the greatest catapults and siege towers the citizens of Acre had ever seen.

Huge fires were lit in the Crusaders camp to celebrate the King's arrival, and all night there was singing and feasting.

'We'll see it through now. He'll pick Acre like a plum,' Adam said exultantly to Jennet, as they shared a couple of salted herrings, the finest food they'd eaten in more than a year.

She jerked her chin towards the walls of Acre.

'I know I shouldn't, them being infidels, but I feel sorry for them, when you think what's coming. That little girl, the boy's sister. Skin and bone she was. They'll all be like that in there by now. And worse. And what they'll get when our army goes in, I don't like to think of it.'

Adam didn't want to cloud his excitement by feeling sorry for the enemy.

'All they've got to do is admit they're wrong and that their religion's wicked. If they get baptized they'll be allowed out free,' he said, quoting Sir Ivo.

Jennet said nothing.

'You ought to take a look at the King's horses,' Adam said, anxious to change the subject. 'The chargers are the biggest I've ever seen. Poor old Grimbald, he's no bigger than a donkey beside them. And their helmets! When they all came riding in, the King and his knights, and all the earls and princes – so tall, with their flags, and the sun shining on their armour, and the drums rolling . . .'

He fell silent, unable to express the glory of it.

'Changed your mind, have you?' Jennet said drily. 'Want to be a knight then, after all?'

He grinned.

'Who wouldn't want to be one of them? But I couldn't do it. I'm not like them. Fighting scares me stiff. Don't tell anyone, though. Don't want to look a fool, do I?'

In the Saracen camp the arrival of Richard of England cast everyone into a gloom.

'Malek Richard's as brave as a lion, so I've heard. His false faith burns like a dozen fires, curses on him!' Ismail told Salim as they sat cracking a bowl of walnuts together. 'He wants Jerusalem like a man wants a beautiful woman. He'd sell his kingdom for it.'

'He's rich too,' Salim said unhappily. 'And a famous soldier. He's taken dozens of cities the size of Acre, Baba said. And cruel. Shows no mercy to anyone.'

'Not like Saladin, Allah defend him,' Ismail sighed. 'Our Sultan's too noble for his own good.'

'But he's powerful. A great leader too,' objected Salim. 'Look how he's beaten the Crusaders every time. They've never got the better of him before.'

Ismail shook his head.

'This time, little brother, I am not so sure.'

They were interrupted by the distant sound of frantic drum beats and the wild braying of trumpets. Ismail lifted his head.

'It's from their side,' Salim said uneasily. 'They've been banging away all night.'

'No, no. They're ours. It's coming from the garrison in Acre.' Ismail jumped to his feet, scattering walnut shells. All around, soldiers were running for their helmets and weapons, captains were shouting to their men, cavalry troops were scrambling to saddle their horses and goats bleated in fright, straining at their tethers.

What's the point? Salim thought miserably, as he limped back to the doctor's tent. *It'll be impossible now that king of theirs is here. We've missed our chance. They're too strong for us.*

A pattern of actions had set in now. The Crusaders, filled with fresh hope and confidence, launched attack after attack on the city walls. Whenever they did so, the desperate garrison of Acre, as their towers tottered, their walls crumbled and their men were hit by flying rocks and hails of arrows, beat their drums and made as much noise as they could to warn Saladin. He would marshal his troops and counter-attack along the rear of the Crusader army, trying to turn his enemy away from the city to face and fight him.

But he never breaks through! Salim thought despairingly. *He never gets over all their banks and ditches. If we don't get to Acre and rescue everyone, Ali won't get out alive. I'll never see him again. I know I won't.*

The knot of worry, always present in his stomach, pulled itself even tighter. He stepped back hastily as a column of Kurds, led by their turbaned captain, clattered past him at a trot, almost knocking him over in their haste.

This time the attack would be a big one, he could tell. The troops had lined up all along the escarpment, the cavalry already mounted, the archers with their arrows in position, the lancers and swordsmen ready.

What are they waiting for? Salim thought, biting his lip. *The walls of Acre might have fallen by now!*

Then he saw a familiar figure riding along in front of the massed ranks of the army. It was Saladin himself, his sickness put aside, his black robes flowing out behind him as he trotted up and down in front of his men, calling out, 'Be lions, my men! Look to Allah for victory! There is no God but God. *Allahu akbar!'*

Salim gasped with admiration at the sight of him. This was not the familiar statesman in his silk tent, or the sick man with the stomach pains, or the generous prince dispensing justice. This was a warrior, a great soldier, his whole body taut with purpose, controlling his high-stepping horse with the deft hand of the brilliant polo player he had once been. The eyes of every man in his vast army were on him. As Salim watched, Saladin brought down his sword, and pointing it directly at the enemy roared, 'Cast down the infidel! God is great!' Then he set off at a gallop down the slope towards the Crusader embankment, which was bristling already with the helmets and lances of tens of thousands of defenders.

Salim, shading his eyes against the sun, lost sight of Saladin, engulfed as he soon was by the tide of his own men. He was hugging himself in anguish.

If only I was with them! I ought *to be with them!*

He started as a hand was laid on his shoulder.

'No intelligent man fights, Salim. Remember that,' Dr Musa said.

Salim watched, his heart in his mouth, as the Saracen army tried to clamber up the high bank into the terrifying wall of lances.

'Look! We never break through! They always turn us back!' he said despairingly. He gasped with horror and turned away at the sight of a heroic Syrian who had leaped up on to the embankment only to fall back and lie still with an arrow embedded in his neck.

They watched for a long time, unable to tear themselves away from the dreadful sight, unable to block their ears against the screams of dying men and the groans of the wounded, until the Saracen army at last gave up the attempt and straggled, bleeding and exhausted, back into their camp.

'All for nothing,' Salim said furiously. 'It's always the same. They're stronger than us. They win every time.'

'You think so, do you?' said Dr Musa, raising his eyes to heaven in exasperation. 'Listen, Salim! Can't you hear the difference?'

'Listen to what?' Salim asked unwillingly.

'The catapults, boy! The bombardment of Acre! It's stopped! Our troops may have been thrown back, but at least they've forced the barbarians to turn away from the city. Your Ali has no doubt had a chance to rest and regain his strength for the next assault. Now go and saddle Suweida. There are wounded men out there to be picked up. Not too near the infidel camp, mind, unless you want to come back stuck all over with arrows like a porcupine.'

King Richard was ill. He lay in his tent, his rough blond hair coming away in clumps from his reddened scalp. But streams of instructions still poured from his great pavilion, and the Crusaders, filled with good food at last, and vibrant with hope and purpose, dashed to obey. Day and night the carpenters were working on the King's new and terrifying machines of war. Just to look at them made Adam shudder.

It won't be long now, he told himself. *I'll have to really prove myself soon.*

Sir Ivo seemed untroubled by doubts and fears.

'Christ's blessed Mother has returned to us at last,' he told Adam one morning, as they walked together towards the church tent for matins. 'I'll confess to you that there have been times when I was afraid she'd deserted us.' He slapped one long-fingered hand against his thigh. 'But our cause is just! To rescue the Holy Sepulchre from the filth of the pagan! All doubt must be sin. I'll pray that she'll beg Christ's forgiveness for me. I've felt her presence around us since the King has arrived, haven't you, Adam?'

Adam muttered something unintelligible and threw a sideways glance at him. Sir Ivo's face was serene and joyful.

I wish I was so sure, Adam thought. *I don't know about anything. Only that I've got to fight and prove I'm brave. And Jerusalem. That's all I want. To get there, and get the dust for Ma, and go home.*

The Fortis men were now being sent by King Richard down into the thick of the assaults to join in the desperate attempts to scale the high city walls.

'Have you heard? Four gold pieces the King's promised for every stone you can drag from off them walls. Think of it! I ain't never seen so much money in my life!' Roger Stepesoft called out cheerfully to Adam as they prepared to go down into the stinking heat at the heart of the camp.

'Adam don't need no gold pieces,' Treuelove Malter muttered. 'He's a Martel. Fighting's in his blood.'

Adam felt his stomach rise with nausea but he managed to force a cheerful smile.

'See you later,' he called back to Roger. 'Last one to get a stone buys the others a good dinner with his money. Agreed?'

Sir Ivo called him into the tent.

'Hurry up, Adam. Do you want Acre to be taken before we get there? Put this on.'

He had pulled something from the bottom of his chest which clinked and rattled as he laid it over Adam's arms.

'Chainmail? For me?' Adam looked up at him, astonished. 'But I've never worn it before.'

'No, you haven't. But there'll be dangerous work today. This belonged to my poor squire. I'll return it to his family when we go home, but there's no point in it lying there unused. You were too small when you first came to me, but now it ought to fit you well.'

'Thank you, sir!' Adam wanted to say more, but couldn't find the words. He held up the coat of mail and looked at it with awe. A thing like this, so costly and noble, was for the knightly class. He had never imagined he would wear one himself.

He helped Sir Ivo into his own armour, then, feeling shy, pulled over his head the inner lining of soft padded linen. It smelled musty, of old sweat, and he repressed a shudder as he thought of the dead boy who had worn it. The suit of mail slid easily over his head and fitted him well enough. The tunic fell below his knees, and the leggings, though loose round the waist, were of nearly the right length. He put on the inner cap, and Sir Ivo pulled the chainmail hood up over his head and handed him a surcoat.

'You'd better borrow this one,' he said. 'And tie the belt securely. There's nothing worse than flapping cloth getting in the way of your sword arm. Talking of swords, take my second one. You had it sharpened, didn't you?'

Adam nodded. His neck felt stiff and heavy in its metal casing. Everything felt heavy, in fact. His arms were weighted down and his legs seemed pinned to the ground.

I'll never be able to move in all this stuff, he thought, *let alone fight, or run.*

Already he was stiflingly hot. Sweat had broken out on his back and was trickling down between his shoulder blades.

'You'll get used to it,' Sir Ivo said, strapping on his own sword and picking up his shield and lance. 'Come on, Adam. Remember, it's God's work we'll be doing today.'

He looked calm and cheerful, as if he was preparing to set out for a day's hunting with his friends. Adam bit his lip, trying to breathe deeply to calm his pumping heart.

The men-at-arms, ignoring Hugo, their captain, were already running out of the Fortis camp, fired up with the thought of the gold pieces they'd been promised and eager for action after the long months of waiting. It was now that the loss of Lord Guy was keenly felt. The baron would have been in command, directing everyone, keeping his men together as a fighting force. Lord Robert, his thin face flushed, was trying to take his father's place, shouting orders in his reedy voice and threatening dire punishments to all who disobeyed, but no one was paying him much attention. Eyes were turning to Sir Ivo, who called out at last, 'Go after your men, Hugo. Round them up and keep them together. Find a herald and see what orders have come through from the King. See who's in command down there and take your lead from him.'

'Thank you, sir,' Hugo said, with heartfelt relief. He shouted an order to the remaining men-at-arms and a moment later they had marched away, singing:

> *You need have no fear of Hell*
> *If it's for God you raise your sword!*

Your souls will live in Paradise
With the angels of our Lord.

Lord Robert turned furiously on Sir Ivo.

'What is this?' he shouted. 'Giving orders to my people? Are you a coward, sending the foot soldiers into action and staying back yourself?'

'Chaos will serve no one, my lord,' Sir Ivo said peaceably. 'We can't move without orders from the King's herald. We must wait.'

Adam was distracted by a tap on his shoulder.

'Jenny!' he said, and drew back away from the circle of knights and squires to talk to her.

'This is it, then,' she said. Her eyes were wide with a mixture of fear and excitement. 'You're going in to take the city. And look at you. I almost didn't know you.'

He was about to answer when a yellow streak shot out at him from between two tents and two huge paws hit his chest, almost knocking him over.

'Faithful! Here, get down boy. Where have you been all this time?'

Faithful was ecstatically licking his face. Adam grabbed his front legs and held him off, then lowered him to the ground.

'Look, he's been tied up,' Jennet said, eyeing the mastiff with her usual mistrust.

A rope was tied tightly round Faithful's neck, biting into his flesh and leaving a raw, bloody wound.

'He's bit through it,' Jennet said, holding up the chewed end.

Adam, clumsy in his armour, took off his mailed mitten and knelt awkwardly. He bent over Faithful's neck and started working at the knot.

'Where have you been, boy? I thought you were a goner,'

297

he said, pulling lovingly at one of Faithful's long ears. 'I thought I'd never see you again.'

The knot gave way at last. Faithful shook himself, whined happily and licked Adam's hand.

'I don't want him getting in the way again down there,' Adam said anxiously. 'Look what happened last time. Keep him with you, will you, Jenny?'

'Can't you tie him up again?' Jennet said. 'That dog's a menace, Adam. It's only you doesn't realize it.'

Adam was already hurrying to the heavy wooden mounting block which still stood where the long-dead packhorses had once been stabled. Deftly, he tied the rope round Faithful's body, then attached the other end firmly to the block.

'Stay, Faithful. Stay,' he said firmly, wagging a finger in the dog's face. To his relief, Faithful circled round, then sank down on to his haunches. 'Listen. There's the herald. I'd better go.'

Jennet threw a sudden arm round his shoulder and kissed his cheek.

'Look after yourself, Adam. Don't go and get killed. I'm not sure I can manage without you.'

He shook her off.

'You? You'd manage anywhere,' he said with a grin.

Then he landed a kiss on her ear, and went off without a backward glance.

Marching in chainmail was easier than Adam had feared. The weight of it was bearable after a while, and it was surprisingly flexible. The worst thing was the heat. The sun was already high and there was not a breath of wind. The surcoat kept the sun off the mental links on his chest and back, but there was no material covering the armour on his arms, neck and head, and it was soon almost too hot to touch. Underneath the thick

padded lining he was drenched with sweat and already longing for another drink.

The herald had ordered all the Fortis contingent to assemble facing the northern tower of Acre and to wait for the
personal orders of the King, who had risen from his sickbed
and taken charge. By the time the other knights and squires
had arrived at the waiting point, the assault on the walls was
in full swing. Foot soldiers from all parts of the Crusader
camp, desperate to earn the promised gold pieces, were out-
doing each other in mad acts of courage, racing across
the debris-strewn ground below the city walls, leaping over
the bodies of those already killed and scrabbling furiously at
those parts of the wall where the stones had been loosened in
the bombardment, trying to prise out a loose one before a
lethal object was hurled down on them from the battlements
above.

Adam, waiting beside Sir Ivo for orders, watched with
admiration. He saw Roger race forward, hack out a stone and
stagger back with it, whooping with triumph, an arrow sticking harmlessly into the padding of his thick leather jerkin.
Treuelove, frowning fiercely, hesitated for a long moment,
then dashed out into the killing zone below the walls. He was
only halfway there when a heavy piece of wood thrown from
above hit him with sickening force on the head, stoving in his
metal, basin-shaped helmet. He swayed once to the side, then
fell and lay still.

'Treuelove, you fool!' shouted Roger. 'Get up! Come back
here!'

Adam's view was obscured by a platoon of Germans pushing a massive battering ram in the direction of the city's gates.
When they'd passed, he saw Roger running back to the Fortis
men with Treuelove slung over his shoulder. Adam screwed
his eyes shut, wanting to block out the sight. Treuelove

Malter's head had been cracked like an egg. He was clearly dead.

An unexpected tide of anger and courage swept through Adam. He wanted to run out there himself and claw at those unyielding walls with his bare hands.

Sir Ivo was restlessly fingering the pommel of his sword.

'Soldiering – nine parts boredom, one part frenzy,' he said lightly, though Adam could tell that he was fretting with impatience. 'And ten parts thirst. What I wouldn't give for a drink of cold water!'

A ragged cheer from nearby made Adam turn his head. The unmistakable figure of King Richard was approaching. He was on foot, a page following close behind leading a huge horse by its bridle. An attentive stillness fell on the Fortis knights. On every face was an expression of awe.

'Who's leader here?' the King called out before he had reached them.

Lord Robert darted forwards.

'I am, sire. Robert, Baron Martel of Fortis.'

'Baron, eh?' said the King, raising an eyebrow. 'Not yet, young man, until I see fit to confirm your title and you have paid your dues. How many knights are at your disposal?'

Lord Robert had flushed with embarrassment.

'Five, my lord. And their squires. And a troop of men-at-arms. They're engaged now, pulling out stones from the walls.'

King Richard threw back his handsome head and laughed.

'The wonderful power of gold working on the simple mind! It never fails. Martel, take your knights to the nearest siege tower. The groundsmen know where to push it. Once it's hard up against the walls the drawbridge on top will be let down. There are fifty other knights waiting there. You'll be under the command of the Earl of Leicester.'

He paused, and his brilliant, commanding eyes swept

round the circle of knights. 'The glory of this day will live forever. Christ is with us! Who can be against us?' He pointed to the banner of a bishop floating nearby. 'Feast your eyes on the Cross, then go out, my men, and fight!'

A thrill of wild joy coursed through Adam. He fell to his knees, as the others were doing, and crossed himself ardently. His eyes never left the glowing face of the King.

Richard passed on. The Fortis knights rose to their feet and began to run towards the siege tower.

'God wills it!' they were shouting through cracked lips. 'Saint George!'

A kind of madness had seized Adam. All fear forgotten, he wanted only to leap at the enemy and fight. He tried to elbow aside the others, who were already pushing against the dozens of men crowding round the base of the siege tower as it lumbered slowly towards the walls of Acre. He wanted to be the first to climb to the top, fight his way on to the battlements across that narrow drawbridge and enter the city at last.

'Jerusalem!' he shouted, his voice catching in his dry throat. 'Jerusalem!'

There were dozens of other English knights already round the siege tower, all eagerly trying to crowd inside. The Fortis men, the last to arrive, hovered impatiently behind them.

'Hurry up, can't you? Get on in there!' they were shouting.

But the wheels of the siege tower had caught on a stone. The groundsmen pushing it raced forwards to free it. Arrows rained upon them, but few could pierce their thick padded jerkins and metal helmets.

'Water!' a cheerful voice shouted from close by. 'Who needs water?'

The red mist cleared from Adam's head.

Jenny? he thought. *What's she doing here?*

He turned and saw her. She was standing by a barrel of water, ladling it into beakers. The knights waiting to mount the tower, desperate with thirst, were crowding round her. Adam elbowed his way through them.

'Are you mad? You can't stay here. You don't have any protection. One arrow and you'll be finished!'

'Water!' she shouted, turning away from him to pass a beaker into the hands of a gasping squire.

'Jenny!' Adam yelled, shaking her hand, so that the ladle almost slipped from it. 'Go back to the camp! Go away!'

She turned on him.

'Go away yourself! I've had enough of doing nothing. There's men here fainting with thirst. How can they fight like that?' She put a beaker of water into his hands. Without thinking he raised it to his lips and drank it down in one long, greedy gulp. 'See?' she said. 'Feels better, don't it?'

Someone grabbed the beaker from his hand and thrust it at Jennet. It was Lord Robert. She filled it and he drank quickly, recognizing her only as he handed back the beaker. His face, already scarlet with heat, flushed even more.

'And I hope it chokes you,' Adam heard her mutter as he turned away.

The siege tower was moving again, rolling bumpily towards the city wall. The crowd of waiting knights disappeared into it, up the narrow stairway. Soon it would be the turn of the Fortis men. Missiles from the desperate defenders on the city walls were hurtling towards the tower. Its leather-covered sides were already bristling with arrows, and some rips were beginning to appear in the hides.

'Fire!' someone shouted. 'They're throwing Greek fire!'

A pot, trailing a long tail of sparks and whistling like a demon as it flew overhead, landed on the base of a catapult some distance away. It smashed and exploded in a ball of flames. Men nearby shouted in panic and ran frantically away, beating at their burning clothes.

Adam, in the first row of Fortis men, had worked his way

to the front of the crowd and was now in the entrance of the siege tower, his foot on the lowest step, his hand on his sword, his heart pounding in a frenzy of excitement.

'God go with you, Adam!' he heard Jennet cry from behind him.

And keep you safe too, he said silently, without turning round.

Then came the unearthly sound of terrified yells as two explosions ripped into the tower. Looking up, Adam saw that two pots of Greek fire had hit the sides, and their deadly substance was rolling down the leather walls, engulfing the whole structure in flames. The dozens of men already inside, pressing up the narrow wooden stairs, were now trapped in a furnace. The leather split as some burst out from within, leaping to their deaths on the ground far below. But most, caught inside, had no way of escape. Their desperate shrieks knifed through Adam's head. He stood as if paralysed, unable to move.

A hand grabbed his surcoat and wrenched him backwards.

'Quick!' Sir Ivo shouted at him. 'It's going to fall! Get out of the way!'

The knights not yet inside the tower were stumbling away from it, looking back fearfully at the terrible sight, shielding their faces from the intense heat. With the awful deliberation of an animal sliding to its side in the slow agony of death, the tower heeled over and began to fall.

'Jenny!' screamed Adam. 'Get out of the way! Jenny!'

As the tower hit the ground, the flames burned brighter all the way along its length, and smoke and dust billowed out over the ground. Only the few men still on the first few rungs of steps had been able to dash outside to safety.

'Jenny!' Adam yelled again, peering through the smoke. 'Where are you? Jenny!'

But there was no sign of her. All he could see was her barrel. It had been knocked over by one of the siege tower's upended wheels, and the water that had poured out of it was rapidly turning into steam in the violent heat of the blaze.

Almost faint with shock, Adam ran forward towards the fire, but the heat had already made the metal rings of his armour blisteringly hot. They were scorching his cheeks and hands.

'What's that fool doing? Who is he? Come back!' people were yelling at him.

Adam could go no further. He stopped and stared helplessly into the roaring flames. The screams inside the wreckage of the tower had stopped minutes ago. Nothing, nobody, could have survived in such an inferno. Jennet had gone. She must have done. He had been within a few arms' length of her, but he hadn't been able to save her.

The ardour that King Richard had inspired only a few minutes before had entirely drained away. He had no wish to fight anyone, now or ever. The thought of more death and injury sickened him.

'To me!' Lord Robert was shouting excitedly. 'Fortis! To me!'

Once again, Adam felt a hand grasp his shoulder. Sir Ivo spun him round.

'It's over for them, poor souls,' he said. 'They're glorious martyrs now. No time for grieving, Adam. Come on. We must avenge them. Our holy work is still to be done!'

Pushing Adam from behind, he broke into as fast a trot as the weight of his armour would allow, following the other knights who were already some way ahead, running towards the place where the most daring men-at-arms were still pulling at the stones in the crumbling city walls.

'Back! Get back all of you!' Hugo de Pomfret was shouting at them. 'The wall's going! Get back!'

With a sound like a rumble of the loudest thunder, a section of the great wall of Acre began to collapse, the huge blocks of masonry crashing down on top of each other, rolling outwards in a tide of stone amid a cloud of choking white dust.

All along the Crusader front line, shouts of triumph were raised.

'Forwards!' commanders were shouting. 'Into the breach! For the Cross!'

Adam, his feet leaden, his heart lying like a dead stone inside his chest, found himself pounding towards the enemy. Surrounded by the knights and squires, he was barely aware of what he was doing.

Jenny's dead, he repeated over and over again in his head. *Jenny's dead*. But the words were meaningless. Nothing made sense any more.

They had crossed no-man's-land now, an area littered with missiles dropped from above and the bodies of the Crusader dead. In front was the pile of rubble where the breach in the wall had been made.

'Death to the infidel!' Sir Ivo was roaring beside Adam.

Adam turned his head for a fleeting moment and was astonished to see a fierce joy burn in the knight's face.

He can't realize that all those men are dead, he thought.

They'd reached the collapsed wall. The pile of rubble rose above them, higher than the tallest house in Ashton. Knights were scrambling up it, using one hand to climb and holding their swords aloft in the other. Adam caught a glimpse of a row of scarecrow heads appearing on the other side of the rubble, a line of thin, grim faces under ragged turbans. Here was the enemy. He was face to face with him at last. Kill or be killed. This was the moment. Victory or death.

Copying the others, he had already pulled the sword from his scabbard. He pointed it forwards. He must go on now. There was no turning back. But he had to look round once more at the place where Jennet had died. He had to turn back and see the tower, still blazing on the ground below.

He never saw the stone, flung from the claw-like hand of an Acre defender ahead, which hit him a glancing blow on the side of his forehead. He barely felt pain, just a sense of unreality, a strange dreaminess, a sudden absence of sound and a slowing of all his muscles.

The last thing he saw was Sir Ivo bounding over the top of the rubble ahead, straight at a tall thin Saracen, who was whirling a huge double-edged axe round his head. Then he fell backwards, and everything went black.

CHAPTER FIFTEEN

All day, rumours had been circulating around the Saracen camp. A message had arrived from the besieged city, brought by a heroic swimmer, who had managed to dive under the chain blocking the harbour and slip between the anchored ships of the Crusader fleet without being seen. His words, passed from mouth to mouth, were being chewed over by everyone in the Saracen camp within an hour.

'I bet you know more than anyone, little brother, seeing you're in and out of the great pavilion all the time,' Ismail said to Salim, as they stood together looking out towards the city and the sea.

'Honestly, Ismail, I don't know more than anyone else. Just that the walls are crumbling all over the place, and the Franks keep attacking. Everyone's totally exhausted. The garrison are begging the Sultan to rescue them by tomorrow morning, or they say they'll surrender.'

'Surrender?' Ismail sounded shocked.

'It's all very well for you,' Salim burst out. 'They're desperate! They don't have any food! They must be running out of weapons by now too. And there's women and little children in there!'

'I'm sorry. I didn't mean anything.' Ismail braced his shoulders, as if shaking off an unpleasant subject. 'What about the Sultan? Has he answered? Are we going to attack again tonight?'

'He got the scribe to write at once. He said they had to hold on down there. He can't attack yet. He's waiting for fresh troops. They're supposed to be coming from Egypt. He sent the message by carrier pigeon. I saw it fly off myself.' He lost the effort to sound controlled and his voice rose in anguish. 'What'll they do to everyone in the city if it surrenders, Ismail? What'll they do to Ali?'

Ismail shook his head sympathetically.

'You know, when a city surrenders, the people, they're like goods. Something to bargain with. The Franks won't just kill them. They'll try to swap them for something from us. Frankish prisoners, or their precious true cross, or something.'

Salim turned hopeful eyes on him.

'Really? Do you really think that's what they'll do?'

'I'm sure of it, little brother.'

Salim felt comforted.

Ismail's right, he thought, as he washed for the time of prayer. *Bargaining chips, that's what the garrison will be. They'll be too valuable just to kill.*

He lived through the night and the next day veering between hope and despair. Messengers kept coming and going round Saladin's pavilion. No one knew what was happening. Everyone's eyes were straining towards the city and the sea, listening to the relentless boom and crash of the catapults, watching the brilliant flashes of Greek fire exploding, and wincing at the sounds of battle and the screams of the wounded.

And then, at last, came the moment that everyone had been dreading. A great groan went up from the whole Saracen camp as the anxious watchers saw the banners of Muslim Acre being torn from the masts, and in their place fluttered the hideous, garish flags of the Franks, decorated with their hateful crosses. As the evening sun sank into the sea, baying shouts of triumph, the ugly clatter of wooden bells and a horrible cacophony of drums and trumpets told the story. The city of Acre had fallen. The Crusaders had entered and taken it.

'*Ya haram! Ya nakba!* It's a disaster!' everyone was saying. 'Satan has defeated us!'

Salim, unable to bear the wails of his mother and the disappointment and grief he saw on every face around him, slipped into the doctor's tent and sat hugging his knees, rocking backwards and forwards in misery.

I'll never be able to go home again, he thought. *Our house'll be taken over by a Frank. They're probably in there already.*

The thought of filthy strangers infesting his home, lolling on the carpets where his father had sat with Dr Musa, scratching their fleas on the verandah upstairs where he had always liked to spend the afternoon, using his mother's water jars, wearing the old slippers from the pile by the door . . .

He wanted to be sick.

Thieves! he raged. *Murderers!*

Where was Ali now? Had he been taken alive, or was he one of the dying whose dreadful cries had now been stilled? And if he was alive, had he been given something to eat at last?

They'll have put him in the dungeons, I suppose, he thought with a shudder. *With all the rats and scorpions.*

Dr Musa, who had been looking for him, came into the tent and found him at last.

'So, the sick are to look after themselves from now on, are they?'

'I'm sorry, *sidi* Musa.' Salim scrambled to his feet, realizing too late that he should have been accompanying the doctor on his afternoon rounds.

Dr Musa's voice had been rough but his eyes were sympathetic.

'Now it begins. The real business,' he said.

'What begins?' Salim asked fearfully.

'The comings and goings, the embassies, the talks, treaties, negotiations, we'll give you this, you'll give us that. Most tiresome. At least your brother will be safe.'

Salim's heart lightened.

'He will?'

'Of course. I'm sure. A most tiresome delay there'll be now. We'll be stuck here for months, no doubt.'

'What then?' Salim asked. 'Will we go on to Jerusalem?'

Dr Musa heaved a sigh.

'How I long for it! My house, my books, my dear Leah, her wonderful cooking! But I fear my home may go the way of yours. Malek Richard will be heading for Jerusalem now. It's what he wants most, after all. And we have seen what a man he is. It will take all of Saladin's strength and cunning to keep him at bay. No, Salim. For the time being we'll have to stay with the army.'

It was several days before Adam learned of the triumphant taking of Acre. He had lain, concussed and unconscious, on the pile of rubble while the battle had raged around him. Someone must have picked him up at last and carried him here, into this strange room, and laid him on this mattress. He was vaguely aware of other beds in rows along the wall nearby, the moans of other men, and white-robed monks moving quietly between them, but it was too much effort to look round. He kept his eyes closed most of the time, trying to block out the ferocious pain in his head. He slept the days and nights away, rousing only to drink a little of the water or broth pressed to his lips.

When he came to properly, he was aware of someone sitting beside him. He turned his head, regretting it at once as daggers of pain shot through his skull, and saw Sir Ivo. The knight seemed to have been talking for some time. Adam, his mind slowly clearing, tried to pick up the thread.

'Even then,' Sir Ivo was saying, 'when you'd have thought no one could have gone on resisting, they wouldn't give up. They beat us back again and again. You have to admire the Saracens, devils though they are. Their courage is amazing. They fight like Christians.'

'Where am I?' Adam managed to ask. 'The city, is it taken?'

'God's bones, boy, don't you know? Of course the city's taken. You're inside it, in this excellent hospital!' Sir Ivo exclaimed, raising his voice to a pitch that made Adam wince. 'The pagans took us by surprise in the end. They surrendered. It was the very day after you fell.'

Adam tried to smile.

'Oh. That's good.'

'The churches in the city are already being restored. The pagans in their wicked pride had torn down the crosses. They'd even scratched out the faces of the Holy Mother and Christ himself on the sacred pictures!' He shook his head, as if unable to believe such wickedness. He paused, then said awkwardly, 'Glad to see you restored to your wits, Adam. You'll be your old self in a day or two, I expect.'

Through the open door leading out of this large vaulted room came the sound of monkish chanting.

'The Templars,' Sir Ivo nodded. 'Singing another *Te Deum*. Every mass is a true celebration now. The saints have blessed us. We'll be in Jerusalem before the year is out, I'm sure of it.'

The music was so soothing that Adam's eyelids drifted down. When they opened again Sir Ivo had gone, and the light penetrating through the narrow pointed windows had turned from the bright white of midday to the soft gold of evening. Someone brought him a bowl of thick lentil soup. He drank a little of it, closed his eyes and slept again.

The next couple of weeks passed in a blur. From the streets of Acre, outside the hospital, came the sounds of drunken carousing as often as the chanting of monks. Titbits of news penetrated his muzzy brain, without making much sense. The King of France, sick and disillusioned, had gone home, though his knights had begged him, with tears in their eyes, not to abandon the quest for Jerusalem. Saladin had agreed to pay huge sums of money, give back the True Cross and free all the Frankish prisoners taken to Damascus in return for the release of the prisoners of Acre, now languishing in the city's dungeons. Jennet had miraculously walked out from under the burning tower, her clothes unsinged, and was even now coming through the door to visit him . . . No, that wasn't right. That was only a dream. Jenny was dead. She was dead. She was dead.

He was too weak to wipe away the tear that trickled out of the corner of his eye and ran past his ear on to the straw pillow.

Slowly, Adam's strength began to return. He found at last that he could lift his head from his straw pillow without fainting. Then the feeling of sickness in his stomach began to go. One day, he managed to sit up for a few minutes, though the effort exhausted him.

A few visitors came. Roger Stepesoft, his normal cheerfulness gone, staggered in one morning in the grip of a blinding hangover, his eyes bleary, his voice cracking when Adam stupidly asked after Treue, forgetting in his confusion the dreadful sight of Treuelove's dead body slung over Roger's shoulder. A few of the friendlier squires dropped in briefly to ask how he was, and one day even Jacques appeared, his eyes roving round the sick men in the ward, like a cat sizing up a cageful of birds, until he was sent packing by a monk.

Sir Ivo came regularly, but to Adam's surprise the knight's visits depressed rather than cheered him. There was something about Sir Ivo's diamond-bright faith in the Crusade, his restless energy and his evident relish for the battles to come, that wearied and confused Adam.

I must be a sinner, he told himself guiltily, lying on his back and watching the motes of dust dance around in the ray of sunshine glancing across the room from the window. *I don't even hate the Saracens now. If I'd been one of them, I'd have fought for my city too.*

He tried to fan the flames of indignation with thoughts of the old churches of Acre which the Saracens had turned into mosques, and the crosses they'd torn down.

'It's the blindness of evil that closes their eyes to the truth of the gospel of Christ!' he remembered Sir Ivo saying, as he lovingly polished the haft of his lance. 'They cling to their prophet and worship their book of lies because they're children of Satan himself.'

But that boy, Salim, answered a small rebellious voice in Adam's head, *he didn't look like a child of Satan. He didn't have a tail, or anything like that. And his ma, she was like anyone's ma, and really brave, walking through the camp. And Saladin himself, he's supposed to be a demon but he sent his own doctor to Lord Guy, to my father. Even Sir Ivo admits that that was true chivalry.*

He was wrestling with these thoughts one hot afternoon when Dr John stopped beside his bed.

'It's Adam, isn't it?' he said, a smile crinkling the corners of his eyes. 'Adam Fitz Guy. I hardly recognized you when they brought you in. White as your surcoat you were.'

Adam tried to sit up.

'No, no. Stay still. You had a bad crack on the head. The skull's fractured. It takes a while to mend, and until it does you must stay where you are. You'll be on your feet again soon. No long-term ill effects, I trust.'

'I'm going to get better?' Adam gave up the struggle to lift himself and smiled waveringly up at Dr John. 'I was beginning to think – I mean, my head aches all the time and I feel all confused. I can't think straight about anything. I keep forgetting stuff and get in a muddle.'

Dr John leaned down to feel his pulse, then drew up a low stool and sat down beside him.

'What do you mean, muddled? You have delusions? Hallucinations?'

'I don't know.' Adam didn't understand the words. 'I think it's the devil coming into me, Dr John, to make me sin. I'm not sure about anything, not even the Crusade. Whether it's right or not, I mean. I still want to get to Jerusalem, because of my ma, to save her soul from purgatory, but I don't want to kill anyone. It's not just being a coward, though I am one, I suppose. I just don't think it's right . . .'

He stopped, not daring to express the true wickedness of his thoughts.

'You don't think what's right?' Dr John prompted gently.

'Well, it's like – I mean, it's not like . . .' Adam stopped, then started again. 'The way the monk told it, back in England, when I took the cross, it sounded so simple, that the Saracens were all evil, and killing them was a holy task. But they're not all evil! Not the ones I've met. And the monk, he went on about Our Lady's tears falling because infidels were trampling on the grave of her Son. I've tried to see her. I've prayed to her again and again, but when I do I just see my ma. She used to say, "Treat people nice, Adam. Don't hurt anyone, whoever they are. That's the right way. It's worth more than a hundred masses." And then I remember all the dead people, theirs and ours, and the wounded, and how they screamed in pain, and I don't think it can be what Our Lady wants.'

He stopped, afraid that he'd shocked the doctor. There was a short silence.

'What an amazing thing,' Dr John said at last, 'to hear my own thoughts in the mouth of a squire, whose whole life ought to be dedicated to fighting. I fear it's the knock on the head that's made a philosopher of you. Once you're back in shape, wielding your sword, putting on your armour and trying to win your spurs and become a knight yourself—'

'I don't want to be a knight!' Adam interrupted, his brow puckered with the effort of trying to think things out. 'I'm not even a squire, not really. I'm just – I was – a serf. A nothing. Then a dog boy. Then Sir Ivo's servant. None of it seems real to me.'

'Sir Ivo's a good man,' the doctor said. 'You were lucky that he took you on.'

'I know!' Adam looked more worried than ever. 'Sir Ivo, he's the best knight in the world. He's kind and wise and fair to everyone. I love him! I owe him everything! And his faith in our mission here, his love of Christ, it's so strong it makes me ashamed because I can't feel the same as him.'

Dr John leaned forwards.

'Sir Ivo's a warrior,' he said. 'He thinks like a soldier. For a military man like him everything's clear and simple. Black and white. He has one goal, the taking of Jerusalem, and he never lets his mind stray from the task. But I've lived in this country all my life. I grew up here, Adam. I've known many Jews, and followers of Islam, as well as Christians. Some of them are my good friends. When all this started, I was glad to think that Jerusalem might be taken back into Christian hands, but when I see all the suffering that this campaign is causing, then, like you, I'm not so sure that it is the will of God. In fact, I no longer believe it is.'

'So the Saracens, then, the infidels, you don't think they're demons from Hell and the children of Satan?' Adam asked anxiously.

'I think they're people like us, created by God. Loved by God. I'm content to respect them and wish them well.'

'So if you were me you wouldn't want to fight and kill them either?'

Dr John laughed.

'I've never wanted to fight anyone! I'm a doctor. My job is to save life, not to destroy it.'

Adam, suddenly exhausted, closed his eyes. The doctor stood up.

'That's enough mental exercise for one day,' he said. 'Rest now, Adam. I'll see you again soon.'

It was three weeks before Adam, still shaky on his feet, but clearer in his mind, was able to leave the hospital and resume his duties with Sir Ivo. He still loved and admired the knight, but he felt detached from him too. He would never again try to share Sir Ivo's belief in the rightness of this Crusade, and he would never again feel guilty about it. His head still ached, often, and Dr John still made him drink disgusting daily brews of herbs, but he was recovering. He was thankful too to be living within four walls again. It was stiflingly hot inside the narrow streets of Acre, but it was better than the filth and discomfort of the camp.

The Fortis people had taken over a series of houses near the harbour, at the end of a small narrow street, and Sir Ivo had been allocated a pleasant little room off a courtyard, where the horses were tethered. It would be time, soon enough, once the negotiations over the prisoners had been completed, to set out for Jerusalem, but in the meantime it was pleasant to rest here.

Several times, Adam had seen King Richard himself. He strode about, restless with purpose, exuding an energy that seemed almost to scorch those around him. Adam had been among the knights and squires in the Fortis train when Lord

Robert had paid a formal visit to the King. The large hall in the principal building of Acre, where the King was seated, was hung with gorgeously coloured banners. Richard sat on a great chair, surrounded by princes and nobles from all over Europe. He had received Lord Robert graciously. The matter of succession to Lord Guy's land and title would be handled once the usual fee had been paid. Father Jerome would thrash out the details with the King's scribes. In the meantime, Richard had heard how valiantly the young lord had fought for the cause, and he would knight him himself before they left Acre. Lord Robert had better purify his mind and thoughts, fast and keep vigil, in preparation for the day.

Adam, uninterested in the career of Lord Robert, was far more concerned with Tibby. Without Jenny to look after her, what would become of her? He assumed that Joan was caring for her, for the time being, at any rate. And Faithful? Was Joan looking after him too, or had he bounded off, as he'd done so many times when food was scarce, to forage on his own?

He had gone in search of them as soon as he'd been able. It hadn't been hard to find Joan. The poor hangers-on of the Fortis contingent had packed themselves into a couple of old booths in the bazaar area. It was a stone's throw from the main Fortis quarters. Adam, coming round the corner, was shocked to see Tibby on her own in the middle of the busy covered street, filthy from head to foot, staggering about with a piece of ragged grey cloth in her hand.

'Oh, so you've decided to grace us with your presence, then, Master Adam?' Joan said, appearing suddenly from the shadows. 'Thought we'd seen the end of you, now young Jen has gone. Silly girl! I told her what would happen if she went down there.'

'I couldn't come before,' Adam said. 'I was wounded. I've only just got out of the hospital.'

Joan's face softened. 'Glad to see you looking all right now, anyway.' She sighed. 'You're like me, I suppose. Missing her. And what's to happen to the little one? Worries me sick, it does.'

Tibby had seen Adam. She came running towards him on unpractised feet.

'I can't keep an eye on her all the time,' Joan said defensively. 'Got me own work to do. Toddles off, she does, soon as my back's turned.'

Tibby hurled herself against Adam's legs and clasped him round his knee. He patted her awkwardly on the head and she stared up at him, still clutching her rag.

'Jennet's old coif that is,' Joan sniffed, nodding at it. 'Don't try to take it off her. She'll scream the walls of Acre down, what's left of 'em.'

Tibby let go of Adam's leg and stepped back. Though her eyes were as blue as Lord Robert's, and her hair, unlike Jennet's, was fair, he saw a gleam of Jenny's old expression in her eyes. 'I suppose it's up to me now,' he said gruffly. 'I'll have to look after her,' he said. 'When we go home I'll take her back to Jenny's pa.'

'*You'll* look after her?' scoffed Joan. 'And how will you do that, mister squire? I think I see it. "Oh, sorry, Sir Ivo. I can't polish up your armour right now. I've got to fetch the babby out of the fire."'

Adam grinned at the picture she'd conjured up, then frowned, trying to think things out.

'If I can get money to pay you,' Adam said, almost breathless at the thought of the responsibility he was undertaking, 'so that you don't have to do the laundry any more, but could spend all your time just looking after Tibby, would you do it?'

Her lined old face broke into a wistful smile.

'Would I do it? And not break my back and rub my hands sore every day? Of course I would! Anyway, it breaks my heart to see her so neglected.'

Adam nodded, and summoned up a smile for Tibby.

'I'll come back tomorrow,' he said. 'I'll have sorted it out by then. She's my family, after all.'

'So she is!' Joan agreed happily. 'Your niece, in a manner of speaking, seeing you're brother to Lord Robert.'

Adam didn't answer. It wasn't what he'd meant. To him, Tibby was family because she was Jenny's child, not Lord Robert's. But the realization that she was in fact his own blood relative pleased him.

I'll do it, he thought. *I'll look after her. All my life.*

'You haven't seen – you don't know where Faithful is, do you?' he asked, feeling almost timid, knowing how much Joan had always disliked the dog.

She put her hands up in a defensive gesture.

'Oh so that's it, is it? No, no, Master Adam. I'm not looking after that brute of yours too.'

'I don't want you too,' Adam said hastily. 'I just want to find him, that's all.'

'In and out of here he is, all day long,' Joan grumbled. 'Getting in the way, stealing food, howling at night like a soul in torment. Surprised he ain't found you yet. He goes off searching every day.'

A few hours later, Adam broached the subject of Tibby with Sir Ivo, as the knight was leading Grimbald out of the city to take him for a gallop on the open land near the river.

'She's alone in the world now, you see,' he said nervously, not sure how Sir Ivo would react. 'Lord Robert'll never admit she's his, and I'm her uncle, I suppose, as well as her godfather. I feel I ought to – well, it's like she's my responsibility.'

Sir Ivo listened in silence, his brow creased. Adam waited, hanging back while Grimbald shied at a group of noisy soldiers who were throwing stones at a scorpion.

'It does you credit, Adam,' Sir Ivo said at last. 'And I'd like to help. But my own finances, I fear, are in a very bad way. I'm living on credit as it is. Until we return home and I can get back the income from my own small manor, I don't have a penny to spare.'

'I'll keep a careful account!' Adam said desperately. 'I'll pay you back every groat, I promise, once my own – well, when Brockwood is made over to me.'

'You mean it hasn't been yet?' Sir Ivo raised his eyebrows. 'I think you'll find it has. Go and see Father Jerome. He'll tell you what's what. He should advance you any money you need.'

Adam walked thoughtfully back to the city, glad to be out of the blinding August sun. He had found the heat even harder to bear since the injury to his head.

'Ah! So pensive!' came a fluting voice ahead.

He looked up. Jacques was hurrying towards him, his lips parted over his dirty broken teeth in an insincere smile.

'What a miracle you are, young Adam or – *Master* Adam, as we must now call you. Given up for dead! Carried lifeless from the battlefield by the upright Sir Ivo! Hovering – yes, *hovering* – for days, between life and death, only to return to us, full of strength and vigour.' He leaned forwards to peer more closely. 'Though still pale as a Scotchman's backside,' he said with satisfaction. 'Not surprising, seeing as how you was knocked flat, and your head split right open. Dear me! What a tragic loss you would have been to all your dear friends! How we would have mourned!'

'Get away from me, you cheat,' said Adam, through gritted teeth.

A flash of pure hatred sparked in Jacques's eyes, to be extinguished at once with another false smile.

'Tut tut, my dear. No need to be so very sharp. A good boy like you too. Quite the little saint, I hear. Not that there's any need. Tibby has other opportunities you know. Very much in demand. Shame, don't you think, to take her back to drudge her life away in England, like her poor ma?'

'What do you mean? What are you getting at?'

Adam scowled at him, suddenly uneasy, hearing menace in Jacques's silky voice.

'Mean? Me? Nothing at all! What should I mean? You should get out of the sun, my dear young master, before it boils you alive.'

He was gone before he'd finished speaking. Adam stood watching him, one hand shading his eyes, as the pedlar flitted away across the open ground, making for a gully near the river. Adam was about to turn away when he saw two men, wearing the turbans of Turkish merchants, step out from behind some fallen rocks. They raised hands in greeting, and Jacques hurried over to talk to them.

I've seen him talking to them before, Adam thought. *What's he up to now?*

It took all Adam's courage, the following morning, to visit Father Jerome in the monk-like cell he inhabited close to Lord Robert's much more magnificent rooms, but the result of the meeting astonished him. Father Jerome frowned at the mention of Jennet, but looked thoughtful when Adam pointed out that her daughter was now destitute. No mention was made of Lord Robert, but it was clear that Father Jerome understood the situation perfectly.

'This is a charitable impulse, Adam, and it does you credit,' he said, his voice sounding almost warm. 'I shall certainly make available the money you need for this purpose, and it will be set against the revenues from Brockwood, which are already piling up, no doubt, and will be at your disposal when you return home.'

Adam, not knowing how to answer, felt dazed by the large

ideas these words had opened up. He looked up to see that Father Jerome was actually smiling at him.

'And I'll take this opportunity to congratulate you on your behaviour since discovering the truth about your birth. You've been wise and cautious. Go on like that, Adam, and you'll do well.' He had one last surprise in store. 'Lord Robert's to be knighted tomorrow, by the King's grace. There's something he wishes to say to you before he begins his vigil tonight. He's in his quarters now. I suggest you go there at once.'

Two of the least pleasant of the Fortis squires were sitting on the steps leading down into the courtyard of the house next door, which was the Fortis headquarters.

'What do you want?' one said to Adam rudely.

The other stood up unwillingly.

'He's to go straight in. Don't you remember?' He called in through the open door, 'The dog – I mean, Adam Fitz Guy here to see Lord Robert!'

To Adam's amazement, Lord Robert was sitting in a large tub of water having his back scrubbed by a servant. He looked uncharacteristically anxious when he saw Adam.

'Turn your back,' he commanded sharply.

By the time Adam had turned round again, he was out of the bath and a cloth was wrapped round his lower half.

Adam waited in silence.

'I'm to be knighted tomorrow,' Lord Robert said. He spoke with none of his usual swagger and sounded almost thoughtful. He nodded towards the empty bath. 'The purification of the body. And tonight, there's my vigil.'

Sir Ivo's words came back to Adam.

To become a knight, a man must be clean in body and mind, he'd said earnestly. *All wrongs must be put right. At his vigil, a knight is naked before Our Lord.*

Lord Robert was licking his lips nervously.

'I acknowledge that you are my father's son,' he blurted

out, all in a rush. 'And that therefore you are my brother.' He wasn't looking at Adam, but at someone behind him. Turning, Adam saw that Father Jerome had followed him in, and that he was nodding with approval. 'And I swear,' Lord Robert hurried on, 'that, unless you seek to harm me, I will never seek to harm you, and that your inheritance is assured by me.'

He sighed with relief, as if he'd spat out a bitter mouthful. Adam knew what he had to do. He dropped down on one knee.

'I swear,' he said gruffly, 'that you are my liege lord. I won't ever take up arms against you, or harm you in any way, or ask for any more than what Lord Guy – our father – left to me.'

Lord Robert had flinched at the words 'our father', but he was ready to finish the business off. He leaned down, took Adam's hand and pulled him to his feet, not quite managing to hide his grimace of distaste.

'We're agreed, then,' he said, shaking Adam's hand.

'Yes. We're agreed.'

Adam could tell that Robert was longing for him to go, but he knew he had to talk about Tibby.

'There's the child,' he said in a low voice, which only Robert could hear.

Robert flushed again, a much deeper red this time. There was guilt in his face, and uncertainty.

'I'm going to take her,' Adam said, sounding much older than he felt. 'I'm going to look after her. Jenny, she wasn't my real sister, but near enough to it. That makes Tibby my niece twice over.'

Robert stared at him in amazement, tried to speak and failed.

'I'll pay you,' he whispered at last.

'No need for that,' said Adam, feeling wonderfully power-ful all of a sudden. 'There's something you can do, though.

She's your serf, and so's her grand-daddy, Tom Bate. Make them both free.'

'I will. I promise, by the Holy Cross. I will.'

'Tell Father Jerome now then,' Adam went on stolidly, afraid that, when this moment passed, the promise would be conveniently forgotten.

'There's no need. I heard,' Father Jerome said, behind Adam's shoulder. 'It will be done. Go away now, Adam. There's more to be done tonight before the knighting tomorrow.'

Lord Robert's knighting was, after all his anxious preparations, a hurried affair. Hollow-eyed from his all-night vigil and edgy from his fast, dressed with scrupulous care in his polished chainmail and carrying one of his father's great helmets, he presented himself at the King's apartments at the appointed time.

King Richard wasn't there. He hurried into the great hall a quarter of an hour later, his face troubled.

'There's no other way out,' Adam heard him mutter to one of his earls. 'Saladin hasn't paid up. He's trying to keep me trapped here. What else can I do?'

He went through the motions of knighting Lord Robert automatically, with a distracted look on his face, and almost dropped the ceremonial spurs as he handed them over.

As soon as he had tapped Robert's shoulder with his sword, called him 'Sir Robert' and told him to rise from his knees, he hurried away, calling out to his commanders to bring the Turkish prisoners out of the dungeons, take them out of the city to the open ground and do what they had to do.

CHAPTER SIXTEEN

T ension had been mounting in the Saracen camp. Salim felt it crackle in the quarrels breaking out between the different factions of the army. He read it in the lines that scored the doctor's forehead under his unruly turban, and he heard it in the fretting of his mother, who worried endlessly about Ali.

He was seldom admitted now to Saladin's great pavilion, though Dr Musa attended the Sultan almost every day, but like everyone else he saw how the chieftains were slowly melting away, taking their troops with them, and he heard the rumours that, for all his efforts, Saladin was unable to raise the vast sums of money he had promised to pay Malek Richard for the lives of the garrison of Acre.

The white heat of July had long since turned into the sultry heaviness of August and it was now nearly September. The Crusaders rested and celebrated inside the city walls, waiting for the negotiations over prisoners and ransoms to be resolved. Saladin, trying to assemble the money he'd promised to pay, waited to see what would happen. One day, soon, he knew that Malek Richard would lead his army out of Acre and set out on the road to Jerusalem. He'd be ready when that happened. Acre had been lost to the Franks, but Saladin would never give up Jerusalem.

'It's tomorrow,' Salim's father said, as he held out a glass to Khadijah with a trembling hand. She filled it with hot mint tea from the kettle Salim had found for her.

'What's tomorrow, Baba?' Salim asked.

'The deadline! The devil Richard's demanded his money by tomorrow.'

'What'll he do if the Sultan doesn't pay?' Salim asked anxiously.

'What'll he do? Nothing!' exploded Dr Musa. 'He'll wait! He must! The prisoners are safe. If he harms them – just think of it! The whole world will fall on his cursed head. Now then! We must occupy ourselves. You will restore some order to the medicine chest, which you've allowed to fall into a deplorable condition. We'll need it any day now. We'll soon be back on the road again.'

The next day began as usual with the normal routine of prayers and chores, though dread could be seen on every face. Messengers ran urgently in and out of the Sultan's great pavilion, and everyone kept a watchful eye on the distant gates of Acre.

As morning turned to afternoon, a shout went up.

'The gates are opening! They're coming out! The prisoners are coming out!'

Salim, his heart in his mouth, hurried as fast as he could to his old vantage point. It was still early in the day and the sun was behind him. He could see the city clearly, the phalanx of armoured Frankish knights on their great horses, the men-at-arms with their pikes and swords and the ragged, stumbling remnants of the garrison of Acre, nearly three thousand souls, with their children trotting behind them. From inside the city came the sinister sound of church bells tolling.

'They're going to free them! Malek Richard's a man of honour after all.'

Salim turned. Ismail had come up behind him. Salim felt so happy he wanted to grasp Ismail's arm and pump it up and down, but he managed to restrain himself.

'See those pikes they're carrying?' Ismail was saying, pleased to show off his professional knowledge, as he screwed up his eyes to focus into the distance. 'Very good weapons they are. In battle, I'd rather meet a sword than a pike any day . . .'

His voice petered out as his mouth dropped open in incredulous horror. Cold terror was turning Salim's heart over in his chest.

'No!' Salim said. 'It can't be! Ismail, it can't be! They're killing them! They're killing the prisoners! And their children! They're killing the children too!'

Ismail had already turned and was running back towards the camp.

'It's a massacre!' he was yelling. 'The prisoners are being murdered!'

Shouts of anger and dismay rang out along the long line of the Saracen army. Drums pounded out a call to arms. Orders were shouted and horses saddled. Salim balled his fists in desperate hope as he watched the Saracen troops stream down the hill to launch a frantic attack on the Crusader outposts.

'Allah go with you!' he shouted at the top of his voice. 'Hurry! Hurry!'

But it was no good. The Saracens were as always beaten back by the sheer numbers of the enemy.

Helplessly, Salim watched as, in full view of the Saracen camp, the brave defenders of Acre were slaughtered one by one.

'Ali!' he was screaming in his head. 'Ali!'

He sank to his knees, unable to look away from the terrible

sight of swords and pikes flashing down on the helpless prisoners, or to block his ears against their distant screams.

That evening, as the sun went down, the rage and hatred boiling in Salim's heart almost suffocated him. Even though the Sultan's forces had been beaten back, he wanted to mount a one-man assault, grab a handful of weapons, mount Kestan and ride as close to the nearest Franks as he could get.

I'd just hurl everything at them, he told himself, *and kill as many as I could, and I wouldn't care when they killed me for it.*

He couldn't bear to look at his mother. She was sitting outside her tent, rocking backwards and forwards and keening like an animal.

Soldiers and messengers were running into and out of Saladin's great pavilion, which was buzzing like a hornet's nest.

'What's going on? What's going to happen now?' people shouted at them.

'We're fetching the Frankish prisoners,' one called back. 'The Sultan wants to see them. He'll have them executed tonight.'

Salim remembered the four Frankish knights kneeling in front of the Sultan. There were many others like them in the camp now. He was filled with loathing for them.

'I hope they all die slowly,' he said through clenched teeth.

Dr Musa, grinding seeds nearby, raised his eyebrows.

'And what, may I ask, would that achieve?'

'It'd show them! It'd teach them!' Salim answered savagely.

Dr Musa sighed wearily.

'An eye for an eye,' he said thoughtfully. 'A tooth for a tooth. It's the Law of Moses, and yet . . . The Sultan, peace be upon him, is a greater man than their Malek Richard, because he has shown much greater chivalry and mercy. It would be a sad day if he became vengeful now.' He cleared his throat.

'Your brother – I'm sorry. He was a fine young man. You and he were very close to each other, I'm sure.'

Honesty made Salim shake his head.

'No, we weren't. We never stopped fighting. But he was Ali. He was my brother.'

Without waiting for permission, he ran out of the tent and stumbled away. He found himself near the horses. He went over to Kestan, put his head against the horse's sweet-smelling chestnut neck and let his tears fall.

Some time later, a hand was roughly shaking his shoulder.

'Salim!' Ismail was saying. 'I've been looking for you everywhere. Haven't you heard the news? What are you doing here?'

'Leave me alone,' Salim muttered thickly.

But Ismail was dragging at his arm.

'Listen, Salim! *Al hamdi l'illah!* Your brother's come! God be thanked, he's alive!'

Salim's head jerked up.

'Ali? *Alive?* What do you mean?'

'Come and see.'

Salim, his head spinning, covered the ground back to his parents' tent as fast as his leg would let him. His heart was beating wildly.

It's not true. It can't be! Ismail's made a stupid mistake, he kept telling himself.

It was only when he came through the last of the forest of tents and saw the familiar figure of Ali sitting cross-legged between his parents, heard his husky voice and saw the tears of joy on his father's cheeks that he understood.

'Ali!' he shouted, plunging forwards. 'Ali, you're alive!'

Ali turned, and Salim stopped when he saw how grey Ali's face was, and how his whole body was trembling.

'They let me go! Only me. Everyone else – all of them! – are dead. Butchered! I ought to be there with them. We were comrades. We fought together. I ought to have died with them.'

Khadijah was patting his knee, on and on.

'Ought to have died?' she said, her face alive with happiness. 'What is this – ought to have died? Allah has spared your life! Be grateful!'

Ali sprang up.

'You don't understand, Mama. You'll never understand.'

'I don't understand either,' Salim said, bewildered. 'Why did they let you go?'

Ali pulled a worn parchment from his belt and waved it in Salim's face.

'Don't you recognize this? The safe conduct you wheedled out of those – those sons of hell? It was you who got me out of there. And it's thanks to you that I'll be ashamed for the rest of my life.'

Salim stepped back. This was Ali all right. Unfair, unreasonable and angry. He could feel the old familiar outrage and helplessness surge up inside him as hostility crackled between them. Years ago, when they'd been younger, he'd have cried, and gone to complain to Mama. Now, he stared back at Ali and said nothing.

Ali shook his head and dashed his sleeve across his eyes.

'I didn't mean it. I'm grateful, really I am. At least, I will be. But not yet. What they did today . . . Their faces – those Franks, their savage triumph! I can't bear to think of it now, of what a coward I was. I should have stood and died with the others, but I pulled out that – that thing, and showed it to one of the soldiers. He just laughed and threw it back at me, then he lifted his axe and swung it back. I could see he was about to cut me down. I shut my eyes and prayed. But then a knight on a horse called out something in Frankish, and the soldier put his axe down and showed him the paper. He was angry, I could tell! He'd been dying to kill me! And the knight made him cut off the ropes round my hands and gave me a shove in the back to make me run away. So that's what I did. I just ran away.'

'What good would it have done if you'd stayed and got yourself killed?' Salim said, more angry than sympathetic. 'How do you think I've been feeling all this time, not able to fight at all, just watching while everyone else makes heroes of themselves?'

'You!' Ali sounded amazed. 'You saved Mama and Baba and Zahra! You're the biggest hero of them all! How you ever managed it I can't imagine. When I saw you that day, walking up to the gates of Acre, on your own, as bold as a lion, I couldn't believe it. And afterwards, knowing they were safe and being fed, it was the only thing that kept me going.'

Salim said nothing. There was no point in going on explaining to Ali how he felt. He'd never understand.

'The whole world knows how brave the garrison was. Everyone was amazed that so few of you kept that huge army out for so long,' he said at last.

'What do they know?' Ali said sourly. 'Everyone's dead who could tell what it was like.'

'Except you. That's your job. You've got to tell them,' Salim said triumphantly.

'It's the will of Allah, my boy,' Adil butted in piously. 'You have been saved. It's not for you to question it, but to be grateful.'

'But our home's gone, Baba,' Ali said, shaking his head. 'Acre's gone. We tried so hard to save it. We failed.'

'Oh, there's no call for regrets!' Adil astonished the brothers by sounding almost carefree. 'Your mother's hatched a completely new idea. We're to go to Damascus. You and I, Ali, will set up in partnership with your uncle Hamid. There's nothing to keep us here now.'

'What about Salim? Isn't he coming too?'

'I'm staying with the doctor, if he'll have me,' said Salim.

'I'm going to be a good doctor too, the best in Palestine, in fact.'

'The best?' roared Dr Musa, his eyebrows twitching comically. 'Better than me? We'll see about that, young man. Anyway, how do you know that I'll keep you on, you impudent young lazybones?'

Salim's jaw dropped open in dismay.

'Oh, *sidi* Musa, you wouldn't – oh, please . . .'

'That's better,' the doctor said, exchanging pleased nods with Adil. 'A little humility at last. Well, well, I was going to let you go, but I might change my mind and keep you, if you make a good job of the medicine chest. *After* we've celebrated with a feast in honour of your brother, of course.'

The Fortis men were not among the soldiers selected by King Richard to carry out the slaughter of the Saracen prisoners. For that grim task he had chosen soldiers closer to him, whose loyalty he could trust, but nobody in Acre had been unaware of the terrible deeds taking place just outside the city walls.

Adam couldn't bear it. When he'd heard what was happening he put his hands over his ears to blot out the screams of the victims and ran out on to the harbour quayside, through the empty customs house, hoping that the vast stone bulk of the city between him and the killing field would block out the ghastly sound.

He found Sir Ivo already there. The knight was pacing up and down along the quay, a look of great distress on his face.

'To kill defenceless prisoners! And even their wives and children!' he exclaimed. 'It's against all the rules of chivalry!'

'We've got to do something! Perhaps there's still time to save some of them,' burst out Adam. 'Can't we ask someone – one of the princes – someone near the King – to plead with him to stop it?'

Sir Ivo didn't seem to hear him.

'The honour of our whole Crusade brought down. This is a sin, a grievous sin. After this, Our Lady will desert us. We can't ever hope to take Jerusalem now.'

He sank down on a wooden block near the edge of the harbour wall and put his head in his hands.

'Sir Ivo! There might still be time! To save even one of them!'

The knight groaned.

'It's too late. The King must have decided on this last night. He won't turn back from it now.'

Not even the mass of the stone city was enough to quite muffle the sounds of the slaughter. Long minutes passed. At last, Adam could hear no more screams, only the shouts and jeers of the triumphant killers.

'Murderers!' he whispered. 'Wicked murderers!'

He felt sick with shame and guilt. He wanted to rip off his surcoat and tear to pieces the crosses it bore on the front and back.

Forgive us, Blessed Mary, he prayed. *I wasn't a part of this. I wouldn't ever have wanted this.*

His feet dragged as he walked slowly back through the customs house and into the city.

'Master Adam! I've been looking for you everywhere!' Joan was running towards him, her hair flying out from under her coif. 'Is she with you? Tibby, have you seen her?'

He stared at her.

'Tibby? Have you lost her?'

Joan was holding the front of her skirt, wringing it between her hands as if it was wet.

'Disappeared! Gone, two hours ago! One minute she was there, good as can be, playing with that pedlar man, then I looks round and she's gone!'

'The pedlar? You mean Jacques?' Adam felt his stomach turn over. 'Did you see him after she'd gone?'

She thought for a moment.

'No. No, I didn't. You think he took her? But why would he? What would a man like him want with a babby?'

'I don't know. I don't know!'

Adam put up a hand to his aching head and tried to think.

'If it's Jacques took her, maybe he'll just bring her back,' Joan said doubtfully.

Adam remembered the two men Jacques had been talking to. And what was it he'd said about Tibby? *Other opportunities.* That was it. What had he meant?

Dr John, he thought. *He knows what goes on here. I've got to find him!*

He ran off towards the infirmary.

'Where are you going?' Joan called after him. 'Here, don't just run off! What are you going to do?'

Dr John was washing his hands in a bowl of water, scrubbing at them with savage vigour. There were tears in his eyes when he turned to look at Adam.

'Our men *enjoyed* it!' he said with loathing. 'Did you hear them shout? The lust of killing defenceless people. I'll never get over it!'

'Please, Dr John,' Adam broke in. 'You've got to help me. The little girl I told you about, Tibby, she's disappeared. I think the pedlar's taken her.'

Dr John shook his head.

'That ragged fellow? Nasty piece of work. I'm very sorry to hear it, Adam.'

'But why? What would he want with a baby? She can only just walk.'

'Pretty little thing, isn't she? Blue eyes? Blonde hair? I fear she'll be on her way to a slave market by now. In Jerusalem most probably.'

'A *slave* market?'

Adam gaped at him, appalled.

The doctor patted his arm kindly.

'On second thoughts it's not likely. Even if the pedlar was wicked enough to steal the child and sell her, he's a stranger in this country. It's not likely he'd know any traders to sell her to.'

'Oh, he does!' Adam said bitterly. 'I've seen him talking with two Turks. You're right, Dr John. Sold her, that's what he's done! I'm sure of it. He doesn't care about anything except money. I've got to go after them and get her back.'

'Adam, don't be foolish!' Dr John looked alarmed. 'You can't go running about the countryside on your own. There are Saracen troops everywhere. And after this massacre their anger will be uncontrollable. You'd be picked up at once. You don't even speak a word of Arabic. You'd end up on the point of a sword, or spend the rest of your life chained to an oar of a galley ship.'

'I don't care,' Adam said stubbornly. 'I've got to get her back.'

CHAPTER SEVENTEEN

S alim was taken by surprise the next morning. The doctor, who had gone early to the great pavilion to pay his daily visit to Saladin, came hurrying back with a smile wrinkling the corners of his eyes.

'Be quick, boy! Quick! Pack everything up, everything, do you hear? We're leaving at once! Now!'

'Leaving? Where are we going?' Salim asked, startled.

'To Jerusalem! This instant! The Sultan – may his head be crowned with blessings! – has heard an old man's pleas at last. Ah, Leah, my dear wife! One more arduous journey, then home!'

'We're leaving the army?' Salim asked stupidly, shocked at the thought of saying goodbye to the camp, and the Mamluks, and Ismail, and all the people he'd lived with for the past two years.

'Yes, yes! Where are your ears?' the doctor said impatiently. 'In any case, the army's deserting us. Malek Richard will leave Acre any day now and march on Jerusalem. The Sultan will keep pace with him and attack whenever he can. Not a tent pole will be left standing here a week from now!

We'll move fast, ahead of the army. We'll be in Jerusalem before their wagons have gone ten miles.'

'How far is Jerusalem?' Salim asked, trying not to sound anxious. He had only a hazy idea of the distances in his native land, never having been more than a few miles away from Acre all his life, and he was afraid that his bad leg would seize up if he had to walk too far.

Dr Musa had read his thoughts.

'Horses,' he said, the corners of his mouth turned down with distaste. 'The Sultan, in his mercy, is giving me two. Quiet creatures, I'm assured, but all four-legged beasts of burden are instruments of evil, including my wicked Suweida, and no one will ever persuade me otherwise. And a groom. We're to have a groom. A strong fellow, to be our bodyguard, as much as anything else. Now why are you standing there, Salim? Pack everything! Then say goodbye to your parents. We must be off in an hour, before it's too hot to move, or Saladin suffers another attack of stomach ache and changes his mind.'

The Saracen camp was already in a ferment of activity. Tents were being struck all the way along the hillside. The ground where they had stood was covered in a strange, mosaic pattern. Round patches showed where they had been, while between them was the beaten bare earth of trodden-down paths. It would need only the rains of autumn and a fresh sprouting of green to mask the site of the camp, and soon only the piles of broken pottery, worn, discarded shoes and heaps of mutton bones would show where the vast army had lived for so long.

Salim, daring to disobey the doctor, slipped away and hurried as fast as he could to where the Mamluks were rolling up their tents and packing their saddlebags.

'Ismail!' he called out. 'Are you there?'

Ismail emerged from the cooking tent, a bunch of grapes in his hand.

'Hey, Salim! Want to see my new helmet? I've just bought it off Mahmud. My old one's so dented it's—'

'No, Ismail, listen! I've come to say goodbye. I've only got a minute. We're leaving today. Now. Me and the doctor.'

Ismail nodded without surprise.

'Where are you going?'

'To Jerusalem. Saladin's given the doctor leave to go home.'

'Oh.' Ismail dropped another grape into his mouth and offered the bunch to Salim. 'We'll all be on our way to Jerusalem tomorrow or the next day, I suppose, following the demon Richard. I'll see you there, *inshallah*, little brother.'

'Yes, yes, I suppose so.' Salim felt deflated by Ismail's matter-of-fact tone. The break-up of the camp, which had become strangely like home in the past two years, seemed like a huge upheaval to him, but it was clear that to Ismail, used as he was to the life of a soldier, it was nothing out of the ordinary. He turned to go.

'Don't forget, Salim, I promised to teach you to play polo!' Ismail called after him. '*Ma'a salama*, little brother. Goodbye. Allah go with you!'

Dr Musa was fretting with impatience by the time they were ready at last to leave. He had been held up by a group of disconsolate patients, who had heard that he was about to go and had crowded round with requests for last-minute advice and supplies of medicine. Tewfik, the groom, a muscular, silent man, led up two small, stocky horses just as Salim was cording up the last bundle of the doctor's possessions from his now empty tent. Suweida, who had grown fat and lazy after months of inactivity, was shaking her long black ears irritably at the feel of the heavy chest strapped to her back.

Adil had given Salim his final blessing. Ali, unusually quiet, had actually hugged him. Zahra had burst into tears and his mother, between heavy sighs, was delivering incoherent instructions regarding diet, clothing and manners to which Salim was paying no attention.

Salim mounted the smaller horse with relief. Goodbyes were always awful. He felt a tightness in his throat as he looked down at his family.

'I hope it goes well in Damascus,' he said awkwardly.

The horse under him skittered nervously at an unexpected clatter from a nearby tent. Salim, barely noticing, controlled it with a firm tug on the reins.

'Where did you learn to ride a horse like that?' Ali asked.

The admiration in his voice steadied Salim.

'A Mamluk taught me. I've been riding one of their horses. He's going to teach me polo.'

The flash of respect in Ali's eyes warmed Salim as the little procession set off, the horses picking their way delicately through the chaos of the disintegrating camp.

It was odd to be riding boldly down the hillside to the overgrown path at the bottom, which ran just above the huge mound of earth the Crusaders had thrown up. To have gone that way only a few days ago would have invited instant death from a hail of Frankish arrows. Salim couldn't help feeling a chill as he passed under the huge bank. There had always been armoured guards posted along the top of it before, and from behind it had come the shouts and curses of the Crusaders, and the clatter of pots and weapons. Today there was silence. The only sign of life was a pair of crows tussling over a shred of gristle.

And then, suddenly, a head appeared over the top of the bank, and someone was scrambling down it and running towards the horses, followed by a huge yellow dog. It was a boy, whose tunic was decorated with Crusader crosses on the front and the back. Before he had taken ten steps, Tewfik had unslung the bow from his shoulder and fitted an arrow to the string. He was pulling it back, ready to fire, when Salim shouted, 'No! Stop! I know him!'

'Who is it? What is this?' the doctor called out testily.

'It's the Frankish baron's son, the squire Adam, who helped me rescue my family,' Salim called back.

He slid off his horse. Tewfik had reluctantly lowered his bow, but was ready to raise it again at any moment. Salim limped forward, warily eyeing the dog.

'Faithful! Get back here!' Adam called out.

Faithful's hackles were raised and there was a growl in his throat, but he dropped back obediently to Adam's heels.

'Please,' Adam said to Salim, 'I've been waiting here since yesterday. I've been watching for you. You're the only person who can help me.'

The memory of the pikes and swords slashing down on the helpless prisoners of Acre surged into Salim's mind. He glared at Adam, hot with anger.

'I not help you. Go away. Franks murderers.'

He turned back, ready to mount his horse again.

'Please!' Adam said again. 'Listen to me! I didn't know they were going to kill the prisoners. I – I was sick when I saw it. And I helped you and your family.'

Dr Musa, impatient to get on, called out, 'Hurry up, Salim. What does the boy want?'

'I don't know. I don't care, either,' Salim said furiously.

'Ask him what he wants! Quickly!'

'What you wanting?' Salim asked Adam unwillingly.

'The little girl, Tibby, you remember her?' Adam said, licking his dry lips. He'd had nothing to eat or drink since he'd run to the embankment to take up his watching position the day before, and his throat was cracking with thirst. 'Her ma, Jenny, she was killed when the siege tower burned. I'm in charge of Tibby now. She's disappeared! Sold to slavers, Dr John says. He thinks they've taken her to Jerusalem.'

'Dr John? What's he saying about Dr John'? interrupted Dr Musa, who had recognized the name in the incomprehensible stream of Frankish.

'A child's been stolen and sold to slavers. He wants to get her back. Dr John says they'll have gone to Jerusalem,' Salim said grudgingly.

'A child? What child? How old is she?'

'I don't know, *sidi* Musa. A baby. Her mother was killed. She was this boy's sister.'

Adam stepped forwards, sensing that the doctor might be more sympathetic than Salim. He put a hand on the neck of the doctor's horse and looked up at him.

'Please,' he said. 'Please.'

'What's he saying?' the doctor asked Salim.

'*Min fadlak,*' Salim translated unwillingly. 'He says please.'

'So this boy,' Dr Musa said, with careful disbelief, 'wants me to take him, a Frank, to Jerusalem, to find some unidentified slavers and get a strange child back?'

'I suppose so.' Salim shrugged. 'I'll tell him to go away, *sidi* Musa. He's crazy, and anyway, it might be a trick. Look what the Franks did to our prisoners. You can't trust any of them.'

'Oh Lord, why do you send such trials to torment a poor old man?' cried the doctor. 'Open your bag, Salim, quickly. Fetch out a decent Damascus tunic and a skullcap. At least his hair's dark. He could pass for a Kurd if he doesn't open his mouth. Tell him to keep it shut if we meet anyone on the road. He's to pretend to be deaf and dumb, do you hear? Deaf and dumb!'

'What about the dog?' Salim was scowling at Faithful. 'He's vicious.'

'Good to have a dog,' Tewfik said unexpectedly. 'Warns off attackers. There's plenty robbers between here and Jerusalem.'

'So the dog stays!' Dr Musa raised his hands in a gesture of helpless resignation. 'Ask him, Salim, does he have any other livestock about his person? Scorpions in his pockets? Snakes wrapped round his waist? No? Then tell him to change his clothes at once, and for heaven's sake let's go on.'

Adam had spent the last twenty-four hours in a fever of impatience and anxiety. He'd realized at once that his only hope of recovering Tibby was to ask for help from the boy Salim. The first great difficulty would be to find him. Since the massacre of the Saracen prisoners, there could be no more civilized contact between the two armies. The Saracens would want to take revenge on any Crusaders they met.

He'd decided to return to the old site of the Fortis camp, up near the boundary of the former Crusader camp, deserted since the army had moved inside the city of Acre itself. He would hide out there, hoping that Salim would appear at the vantage point where Adam had sometimes seen him during the siege. He hoped too that Faithful would find him there, at the place he'd known so well.

He'd slipped away from Acre without telling Sir Ivo what he intended to do. He'd have been flatly forbidden from undertaking anything so risky and impossible, he knew.

He'd found a good look-out place on the embankment and had lain there all the previous afternoon, straining his eyes as darkness fell to try and pick out the boy's shape or the sound of his voice among the turbulent comings and goings in the Saracen camp. He only allowed his eyes to shut when the moon had risen to its full height and everything was quiet for the night. Just before dawn, he'd felt a wet nose push against his face.

'Faithful!' he said, sitting up to hug him.

The dog's return comforted him. Whatever happened next, he wouldn't be quite alone.

The Saracen's dawn call to prayer woke him and he raised

his head with a start, afraid that he'd missed his chance of seeing the boy already.

This is stupid, he kept telling himself. *There's thousands of Saracens up there. It's like looking for a grain of barley in a sack of wheat.*

The rising sun was in his eyes, and by nine o'clock it was already uncomfortably hot.

But I did see the boy up there often, he thought stubbornly. *He might come again today. He must!*

He didn't want to think about what he'd do if and when he found Salim. There wasn't much chance, he knew, that he'd agree to help him. And even if he did, Adam had no idea where or how far away Jerusalem was, or how he might get there. He'd think about all that only when – if – he found the boy.

It was so difficult staring into the rising sun all the time that Adam nearly missed Salim. He'd been watching a pair of lizards chasing each other across the beaten-down earth. He looked up just in time before the doctor's little procession disappeared round an angle of the earthwork, recognizing them only by the medicine chest and the familiar rump of the old black mule.

He felt almost dizzy with relief when they'd let him approach, and astonished when he'd understood that they were actually on their way to Jerusalem themselves and would allow him to go with them. He put on the strange tunic and skullcap they'd given him, and from that moment on everything felt unreal, as if he'd entered a dream. He'd done what he had to do. Now things were out of his control.

Unanswerable questions nagged at him. What if Tibby hadn't been sold to the slavers after all, but was still with Jacques? What if the slavers had taken her somewhere else, and not to Jerusalem? And how could he be sure that he could trust the boy and the doctor? They had every reason to hate him, after all.

Somehow, none of that mattered now. The strange dream wrapped him round. He felt as if unseen feet were guiding his and that all he had to do was follow.

The Blessed Virgin herself must be with me, he thought, with a shiver half of fear, half of joy.

Two hours later the doctor pulled his horse up under the shade of a large old fig tree to rest during the greatest heat of the day. Light-headed with hunger and thirst, Adam felt his exalted state had intensified, and the landscape all around, shimmering in the heat, seemed to him filled with dancing spirits, willing him on his way. The spreading branches of the fig tree hung over a cistern of clear cool water, and it was only when Adam had sunk down on his knees and drunk from his cupped hands that the mists began to clear from his mind.

Faithful had been padding along quietly beside him. He lapped greedily at the water then flopped down a little way away, the rumble of a quiet growl emerging whenever Salim, the doctor or Tewfik threatened to come too close.

'Here, Faithful,' Adam commanded, clicking his fingers. 'Friends.'

He led the dog to Salim first. Salim backed away, alarmed.

'Don't let him see you're scared,' said Adam. 'He's got to get to know you. Let him sniff your hand.'

Nervously, Salim stretched out his fingers.

'Friend,' Adam said sternly again.

Faithful's tail began to wag. He gave Salim's hand a lick and whined. Salim dared to pat him quickly on the head, then went to the cistern and carefully washed his hand while Adam introduced Faithful to Tewfik and the doctor.

'Now lie down,' he said, pointing to the place Faithful had chosen before. 'Stay.'

Faithful obeyed. Salim, who had passed the last two hours

feeding his resentment of Adam with angry memories of the murders at Acre, couldn't help a smile of grudging respect.

'That's a well-trained dog,' the doctor remarked. 'Unclean animals, dogs, but they have their uses. Now, Salim. Unpack the provisions. When we've eaten we'll ask this young man how he intends to proceed.'

The food, which Adam accepted gratefully, was strange to him. The bread wasn't bad, though it was flatter and more chewy than the bread he was used to, and the cheese was all right, though it was rather salty. But the round black oily things with hard stones in them were disgustingly bitter. Only politeness stopped him spitting them out.

'Olive,' Salim said, noticing his face. 'Frank doesn't like olive, but olive very good.'

'Now get him to tell us,' Dr Musa commanded Salim, 'all about this child. Why is he looking for her? Who is she? How does he propose to rescue her?'

Haltingly, Adam began to explain, as Salim translated sentence by sentence. Even to his own ears, his story sounded thin and foolish. He talked more than he intended about Jennet, and how he'd known her all his life, and treated her as his sister, and how she'd died when the siege tower had caught fire.

'You don't have brothers or sisters of your own?' Salim asked, interested in spite of himself.

Adam shook his head.

'No – well, yes. There's Lord Robert and his sisters, I suppose. But they're not my real family. They don't want anything to do with me.'

'What about your uncles and aunts?'

'I haven't got any.'

'He hasn't got any relatives,' Salim told the doctor wonderingly. He couldn't imagine what that could be like.

Everyone he knew had families, endless, complicated networks of people who belonged together.

'Then this little girl,' the doctor said at last, scaring Adam with the ferocity of his expression as his huge brows came together in a frown of concentration, 'is the only person in the world he counts as his relative?'

Salim translated the question. Adam thought for a moment. He supposed it was true.

'Yes,' he said.

'So what are we going to do with him?' exploded Dr Musa, lifting his hands in despair. 'The boy clearly has no money. He can't buy the child back. Steal her, then? Risky. Slavers are not known for their kindness of heart or their gentleness.'

'And we don't even know if they're heading for Jerusalem,' Salim chipped in.

Tewfik, who had been sitting politely a little way away, coughed to attract attention.

'It's likely that they have,' he said, in his deep, guttural voice. 'There's a big market for slaves in Jerusalem. Prices are good there.'

Adam looked anxiously from one face to another, trying to gauge their mood. The talk in Arabic went on for what seemed like a long time, as the whole topic was thoroughly thrashed out. At last, Salim turned back to him.

'We can take you to Jerusalem with us. Four days' journey from here, or five maybe. All the time, you keep mouth shut, pretend to be boy from Acre, like me. The doctor, he will ask in the city about slave market. Then if we find her, to get her back is your job.'

'Four or five days?' Adam was surprised that Jerusalem was so far. 'But what if they get there faster and sell her straight away?'

Salim couldn't help feeling sympathetic to Adam's obvious

anxiety. In spite of himself, this strange quest was intriguing him.

'Maybe they arrive quicker than us, but slave market not every day. They keep her some times before they sell.'

By the end of the second day, Adam felt as if he'd been travelling with the doctor for weeks. At first he'd been too preoccupied with his dogged intention to save Tibby, and his sense of desperate urgency, to look at the landscape around him. At night, when he closed his eyes to sleep, he'd seen only the pale stony path he'd been staring at all day, and had little more than a hazy impression of the rocky, dry, steep hillside along which the doctor's little procession wound at such an infuriatingly slow pace. He did stare at the occasional camels that passed, and shuddered once at a huge snake sunning itself on a rock, but he was soon used to the endless terraces of olive trees, and he took the passing peasants on their donkeys for granted after the first couple of encounters, when his heart had beaten fast with the fear of being discovered.

It had never been hard for him to stay silent. He'd always found it much harder to talk. Salim had taught him to reply *Alaykum a-salaam* if anyone greeted him with the words *Salaam alaykum*, and he'd learned to mumble the strange sound quite convincingly. Even at night, when they stopped in a small inn or trading post, no one took much notice of him, and Salim was always beside him to deflect unwelcome interest.

Salim and the doctor intrigued him more and more. He'd quickly discovered that behind the doctor's facade of severity was a heart of the softest kindness. The Crusaders' first impulse, he knew, had been to kill any Jews they could find, in revenge, so they claimed, for the killing of Christ. He'd never really thought about it. But now that he knew the doctor – a man of such skill and compassion, who was so

347

comically rumpled and untidy, and yet who commanded such respect from everyone they passed along the way – he was filled with shame.

The path they were travelling on was usually so narrow that they had to go in single file, the doctor and Salim riding ahead, and Tewfik and Adam following with Suweida. Sometimes, though, on the broader floor of a valley, the path widened out, and when it did, Adam would run up to walk alongside Salim's horse. He worried less about Tibby when he could talk to someone. It helped the time to pass more quickly.

'The doctor's a Jew, isn't he?' Adam asked diffidently on the third morning of the journey.

'Yes.' Salim ducked to avoid a branch overhanging the path. The question didn't seem to interest him.

'But you – you're a – a Muslim,' Adam persisted. Salim looked down at him, surprised that he needed to ask. 'You don't mind then, working for a Jew?'

Salim frowned. He couldn't understand the question.

'Dr Musa, he is a great doctor,' he said at last. 'I learn from him too much.' He thought for a moment, sensing that there was something else behind Adam's question. 'A very good man. Like my own uncle or my grandfather.'

'But the Jews, I thought they were wicked,' Adam blurted out. 'They killed Jesus. Only of course, you don't know Jesus, being an infid— I mean, a – a . . .'

'Of course I know the Prophet Jesus!' Salim said, affronted. 'Jesus a very great prophet. Only the Prophet Mohammed, peace be upon him, is greater than Jesus.'

Adam had only ever heard the Prophet Mohammed described as anti-Christ, a fiend and the son of the devil, and he surreptitiously crossed himself. He didn't know how to answer.

'You don't hate Jesus, then?' he said, floundering.

'No! I tell you! He a great prophet!'

'But the doctor, he does. Hate Jesus, I mean.'

Salim laughed.

'Why Dr Musa he hate the Prophet Jesus? Jesus was a Jew, like him. He call Jesus rabbi. Teacher.'

The path narrowed at this point and Adam was forced to drop behind. Salim, riding on ahead, tried to think things over. He couldn't make Adam out. He asked such stupid questions, and he had such strange faith in the dust he wanted to collect in Jerusalem, which he actually believed would save his mother from hell! Then too he was ignorant of the most basic good manners, and never even washed his hands before he ate.

But there was something impressive about the Frankish boy. It was amazingly brave to set out to rescue the little girl from the slavers when he didn't know the country and couldn't speak a word of the language. She wasn't even his daughter or his sister.

If I'd been all alone in the world, without any family at all, I'd have crumpled up completely, he thought.

Then there was his astonishing skill with dogs. Salim never ceased to marvel at the almost human communication between Adam and Faithful. The dog seemed to understand Adam's every word and gesture, and obeyed him at once. Even the village dogs, who barked hysterically at the approach of strangers, calmed down at a word from Adam.

A few paces behind the horses, Adam was also deep in thought. His world of certainties was crumbling alarmingly. The people he'd been told to hate and despise, the Jews and Muslims – infidels, Christ-killers, persecutors of the Virgin – were treating him with the utmost kindess, sharing their food with him, paying for his lodging, putting themselves at risk for him, and all this after the cruel and unjust treatment they'd received from the Crusaders.

I never realized that Saracens were ordinary people, he

thought, *just farmers and merchants. They're like the people at home in Ashton, in a way.*

He'd been deeply impressed to discover that Salim could read and write. He'd been surprised too to see both him and the doctor pray. He'd watched Tewfik and Salim rise and fall on their prayer mats, and the doctor rocking back and forth, his prayer shawl draped over his head.

Wicked idolatry, Father Jerome would have called their prayers. Perhaps it was, but there had been no smell of sulphur, no fumes from the fires of hell, as he might have expected. There had been only a kind of quietness and peace.

They came to the last staging post before Jerusalem, up in the cool hills, on the fourth night of their journey. The sun was setting, and far over to their right the water of the Mediterranean Sea shone like a sheet of gold.

Adam had woken that morning in the grip of a nightmare. He'd been running after Tibby, who was tied to the back of a monstrous, dragon-like creature with wings and a lashing tail. She'd turned into Jennet, who had held her arms out to him and screamed in terror. He'd tried to run, but his legs had been weighted down, and he hadn't been able to lift them properly. With a superhuman effort, he'd nearly reached her, when Jennet had disappeared and Tibby had taken her place. Just as he was about to put out his hand and touch her, the creature had launched itself into the air and flown away, far out of reach. He'd woken shouting and sweating.

It was the devil I saw, taking Jenny to hell, he thought with a shudder. *Even if I get the dust from Jerusalem, I can't put it on her grave.*

The fate of Jennet's soul was another burden on his mind. It added to his sense of impatience. He'd been nagging at Salim all day.

'Are we nearly there?' he'd kept saying. 'How far is Jerusalem from here?'

When the doctor turned his horse, with a sigh of relief, into the courtyard of the khan, and the khan servants hurried up to greet him and help him dismount, Adam could have cried with frustration. This place, a staging post for travellers, was a large square courtyard surrounded by arched alcoves set against the walls. It was in the middle of nowhere. There was no sign that a city was within miles.

'But I thought we'd be at Jerusalem tonight! You said it was only a few miles away – just over the next hill!' he protested to Salim.

'Fifteen miles. Is too late tonight. The gates of Jerusalem shut now. We stay here tonight. You hungry, no? Nice food here, Dr Musa say. We have good supper, then we play knucklebones game again.'

Two men trotted past, bowing under the huge bales of cotton they were carrying on their shoulders. Salim gave Adam a warning nudge and led his horse off to the water trough.

Salim was surprised by how much he was looking forward to the evening. He would never have imagined, a week ago, that he could feel so friendly towards a Crusader, a sworn enemy, one of the army who had driven his family out of their home and nearly murdered Ali. But he couldn't help liking the Frankish boy. There was a dogged loneliness about him, an untouchable quality, that stirred Salim's sympathy. He'd sensed that Adam, like him, had never had many friends of his own age. Playing a simple game of knucklebones with another boy was, to Adam, as much a novelty as it was to Salim himself.

After those first strange questions about Muslims and Jews, Adam hadn't brought up the subject again.

I changed his mind for him, Salim thought proudly. *I taught him something.*

Although the smells of cooking were wafting enticingly out of the khan's kitchens, Salim knew that it would be a while before they could hope to eat. Dr Musa was well known here, and people were already coming up hopefully with symptoms to offer and requests for treatment. Sighing, Salim obeyed his master's beckon and went to sit beside him on the mat spread out in the alcove where they would sleep that night. He saw Adam settle himself inconspicuously in a quiet corner with Tewfik, who had begged some scraps for Faithful from the kitchen.

It was almost dark by now. A torch had been lit in the kitchen, and dancing shadows fluttered out through the door on to the white stone arches that surmounted the alcoves. Under them, men were sitting on mats, talking quietly and clicking their worry beads. Adam, peering round, thought how different this place was from the travellers' taverns he'd seen in England and France. There, ale and wine had flowed freely, and men and women together had drunk and shouted and brawled in a fug of stale air rich with the smell of unwashed bodies.

Half of him liked this restrained, orderly, clean world, but at the same time he missed the cheerful rowdiness of home.

The doctor seemed to have finished his consultations at last, and servants were bringing bowls of food to his alcove.

'*Ta'al*,' said Tewfik, nudging Adam. 'Come.'

They were crossing the courtyard when the watchman swung open the heavy double gates to admit a big group of late arrivals. Two men in the gowns and turbans of prosperous merchants rode in first on stocky little horses, followed by four others on donkeys. The wrists of these men were tied together, and their legs were bound under the donkeys' bellies. Behind them came a couple of pack camels, a woman carrying something heavy in her arms and two other men, who wore the simple short tunics of labourers and carried heavy cudgels.

Adam's heart leaped in his chest and he caught hold of Tewfik's arm.

'It's them!' he whispered hoarsely. 'Those two men. It's them!'

Tewfik shot him a warning glance, then walked up to the turbaned merchants and began to converse pleasantly with them. Salim, seeing what was going on, stood up and limped across to Adam.

'It's them!' Adam repeated. 'That woman, look, she's carrying a child, see? It's Tibby! It's got to be!'

'Shh,' Salim said. 'Stay here. I listen.'

He went casually up to join Tewfik.

'From Acre, did you say?' Tewfik was saying. 'A long walk!' He raised his chin questioningly towards the bound men. 'How much do you expect to get for them? Where are they from?'

'Two are Franks, curses be upon them,' one of the merchants answered. 'They're for the galleys. The Africans too, maybe.'

Tewfik let his gaze wander towards the woman, then looked down quickly, trying to indicate curiosity without bad manners, in case she was a wife or relative and so ought to be respectfully ignored.

'My sister,' the merchant said shortly. He turned away to speak to the owner of the khan who had hurried up to greet him.

Tewfik and Salim walked back to Adam who was biting his lip in an agony of impatience. Faithful had sensed his excitement and was standing tensed, his hackles raised, ready to break into a bout of hysterical barking. Adam bent to calm him, holding his collar in a restraining hand.

'Are you sure it's them, Adam?' Salim asked him. 'It could be. They said they've come from Acre.'

'I'm nearly sure. I only saw them from a long way off,' said Adam, trying to breathe normally. He'd imagined that the two traders he'd seen with Jacques would be alone with Tibby. The sight of such a big group, especially the two tough-looking men with cudgels, had come as a shock.

'Maybe it's them, maybe not,' answered Tewfik. 'A child would have woken up by now being carted about like that. You can't see in this light. It could be a rug, or a sack of nuts, or anything.'

The traders had been allocated two alcoves on the far side of the khan from where Dr Musa was already peacefully eating his dinner. In the last glimmers of light from the darkening sky, the woman could just be seen. She was laying her bundle down on the ground.

'Oh!' groaned Adam. 'That can't be Tibby. She'd be wide awake and squawking. They've sold her already. We've come too late!'

'No, no. Maybe is all right,' said Salim hopefully. 'Maybe it is a child. If she cry in the night, we know for sure. My little sister, she always cry in the night, but when she sleep in the day, you cannot wake her if you try.'

'What are you doing over there?' the doctor called across to them. 'Are you planning to sleep tonight without eating? Is that it?'

Dr Musa listened gravely as Salim, between mouthfuls, told him their suspicion. Then he shook his head.

'How could a child remain so quiet?' He paused, frowning. 'Unless of course it has been drugged. That, certainly, is a possibility. Syrup of poppies, perhaps. In any case, there's nothing to be done. Even if there is a child, we can't tell that it's the right one until we see it in the morning.' He gave a gigantic yawn. 'My old bones are calling me to sleep. Unpack my prayer shawl, Salim. At the very least, I must give thanks tonight that we have come safely so near to the end of our journey.'

He stood up and shook out his gown. The khan had settled down now for the night. The only sounds were the chewing of the camels working on their cud, the snores of a pair of muleteers in an alcove nearby, the last clatter of pots from the kitchen and, from the hillside above, the sharp yap of a jackal, which set the khan dogs outside the doors barking furiously.

Faithful, who was lying at the bottom of the steps leading up to the alcove, had ignored the fuss of the dogs outside, but something else was exciting him. He sat up and cocked an ear, then suddenly let out a deep bark of his own.

'Keep the dog quiet,' Dr Musa said sternly. 'Do you want to disturb everyone?'

But Adam was watching Faithful. He was on all fours now, his hackles raised, his nose stretched out, alert, straining towards the alcove on the far side of the khan. As he did so, there came the unmistakable wail of a child, and a little voice, slurred and confused, cried out in English, 'Ma! Want Mama!'

'It's her! That's Tibby!'

Adam was on his feet too. Without thinking, he was about to rush across the courtyard and snatch Tibby up. But Dr Musa put a restraining hand on his shoulder and said something to Salim.

'He says come, sit,' Salim said. 'First we make plan. Now.'

A moment later, the four of them were sitting close together as far back in the alcove as possible, their heads bent forwards.

'The first thing,' Dr Musa said, 'is to establish if this child really is the one we're looking for.'

Salim translated.

'She is!' said Adam. 'I heard her voice. I know it. And she was speaking English!'

'Then it's simple.' The doctor yawned. 'Tomorrow morning I'll approach these fellows and simply buy the child from them.'

'He'll buy her,' Salim told Adam.

Tewfik was talking now.

'They won't sell to you, *ya-hakim*. I heard them talking when they were unloading their camels. They've sold her to a buyer already.'

'Ah, what a tangle this is! Why did I ever consent to such a mad adventure!'

The doctor threw his hands up, knocking his turban sideways.

'If we can only get Adam and the child out of here tonight,' Tewfik went on, 'and hide them somewhere nearby, I could meet them in the morning with the horses and take the two of them back to Acre. As your honour knows, I was supposed to escort you all the way to Jerusalem, but it's only one more day's journey. If you could manage it with the mule, on your own . . .'

'Of course! You think I've never walked before?' the doctor said irritably. 'But it's too dangerous. These are ruffians. Did you see them? They'd pursue you, and beat you up, or worse. And if they took you to the authorities you'd be branded as a thief.'

'But you'd tell the merchants that you were sending Tewfik out to search for Adam,' Salim interrupted in an excited whisper. 'You'd tell them you were sure they were making for Jerusalem. They'd chase after them, but really Adam and Tewfik would be riding the other way back to Acre.'

'A criminal mind, I see,' the doctor remarked acidly, 'and in one who looks so innocent! But there's one great flaw in this master plan of yours. How do you propose to smuggle a large boy and a small child out of this place? There's only one entrance, which is heavily barred and bolted with the watchman sleeping right beside it.'

'What are they saying? What's going on?' Adam said, tugging at Salim's sleeve.

Salim explained.

Adam drew in his breath. He'd been planning on his own while the others had been talking.

'I could get out across the roof,' he said. 'There're stairs up to it. I saw them earlier. And you could let me down on the other side with the rope you use to tie the chest on to the mule.'

'But Tibby,' objected Salim. 'You cannot climb down and hold her at the same time.'

'I'll tie her on to my back, like the—' Adam stopped. He'd been about to say 'infidel women'. 'Like a woman,' he finished.

Salim translated rapidly to the doctor and Tewfik.

'Ridiculous!' snorted the doctor. 'It's far too dangerous.'

But Tewfik's teeth showed white in a grin. He was clearly enjoying this adventure.

'Slavers took my brother,' he said. 'Ten years chained to an oar in the galleys. He's crippled now. That's why I volunteered to come with you. It'll be a real pleasure to pull a trick on crooks like them.'

The moon was rising now. It lit the courtyard in a ghostly light. Nothing was stirring. The watchman by the gate had wrapped himself in his cloak and was lying as still as a sack. Even the camels had stopped chewing. A slight breeze had sprung up, stirring the wisps of hay by the horses.

The four had fallen silent, all of them thinking furiously.

'The baby's fast asleep again,' Salim whispered at last. 'She'd be making a noise if she wasn't. I could go over there, and if anyone sees me I could pretend I was walking in my sleep. People expect me to do strange things because I'm –

because of my leg. You could tell them, *sidi* Musa, that I'm not right in the head.'

'I'd be telling the truth, as a matter of fact,' growled the doctor.

'You know how little children sleep so deeply. If Allah wills, she'll stay asleep and not make a noise till I bring her back here to Adam. She knows him. He can keep her quiet.'

'You expect me to lend my good name to this outrageous nonsense?' grumbled the doctor. 'Because if you do, then I suggest you make a start at once, while the cloud I see approaching the moon is covering it.'

Swiftly, Salim relayed this to Adam.

'I'm to go now?' Adam was unexpectedly dismayed. It was one thing to plan how he'd snatch Tibby and go back to Acre on his own, but quite another to leave this little group, which felt almost like a family. He'd come to trust Salim and the doctor absolutely. He felt bereft at the thought of parting from them. He tried to see the doctor's face, but the shadow was too deep and he couldn't read his expression.

'How do you say "thank you"?' he whispered to Salim.

'*Shukran.*'

Adam reached forwards and caught hold of the doctor's hand.

'*Shukran,*' he said fervently. '*Shukran. Shukran!*'

He wasn't used to showing his feelings and shrank back again, embarrassed.

The doctor's hands were on his shoulders. He was talking rapidly in Arabic.

'He says sorry you never reach Jerusalem,' translated Salim. 'But he says, don't matter. Never to worry about your mama. No need for the dust. Nothing good in that. But God, he is good. She not go to hell.'

The doctor was still speaking.

'Tell the boy this,' he said. 'It's from the word of God, from the Bible we share. *Though I walk through the valley of the shadow of death, I will fear no evil, for thou art with me.*'

Salim's forehead wrinkled as he tried to turn this into English.

'From your Bible,' he said. 'Word of God. Doctor say, when you walk into death, like into a valley, into a shadow, there is not to be afraid. God with you then.'

'God was with his mother too, at the moment of her death,' the doctor went on, his voice calm with certainty.

'He with your mama too, when she die,' said Salim.

'Go on. Now.' The doctor was pushing at Salim, who stepped down noiselessly into the courtyard. The cloud was over the moon and it was so dark that the watchers in the alcove could see almost nothing. Silent as a shadow, Tewfik had slipped away too. Adam, straining into the darkness, saw only a patch of slightly denser blackness moving near the horses.

He's fetching the rope, he thought with a shiver. *It's really going to happen.*

He felt his way down the pair of steps. Faithful, lying at the bottom of them, stirred and thumped his tail sleepily.

'Quiet,' breathed Adam. 'Be quiet.'

And then, suddenly, Salim was in front of him with Tibby in his arms. She was lying dead asleep against his shoulder, her pale golden hair glowing dimly in the darkness. Faithful sat up and whined, then let out a bark of welcome, which sounded so loud that Adam and Salim froze, expecting the whole khan to wake and come running.

'*Quiet!*' hissed Adam furiously. 'Down! Lie down!'

With a whine, Faithful subsided.

Adam felt the doctor's hand on his arm. He was giving him something – a long wide piece of cloth. Now Salim was laying Tibby against his back and the cloth was being wound round them both, securing her firmly in place.

'What is it?' he whispered to Salim.

'The doctor's turban!' answered Salim, a choke of laughter in his voice.

Salim was feeling wildly excited and triumphant. Picking up Tibby had been easier than he'd expected. He'd been quite prepared to act the fool, like a boy who didn't know what he was doing, but it hadn't been necessary. Tibby had been lying on her back near the woman, on the outer edge of the alcove, her arms flung out in the abandonment of sleep. She'd mumbled something and given a little cry when Salim had picked her up. Salim had soothed Tibby with strokes on her back, and she'd been still again at once.

The worst part had been carrying her back across the courtyard. He hadn't been able to see where he was going and was terrified of stumbling and dropping the little girl.

Tewfik was back now with the rope.

'The stairs are in the corner,' he whispered, leading the way.

Adam turned to the doctor for a last goodbye.

'You're good,' he whispered, knowing the doctor couldn't understand, but needing to say it anyway. 'I won't let anyone tell me different. I'm sorry for what we did in Acre. I didn't understand when I took the cross.' The others were waiting impatiently. '*Shukran*,' he said again.

As he crept stealthily after them towards the stairs, Faithful arched his back, stretched out his forelegs, opened his mouth in a gigantic yawn, then shook himself and followed.

I don't know how I'm going to get you out of here, Adam thought. *You'll have to work it out for yourself.*

It was unlucky that the moon came out again just as Tewfik, Salim and Adam were halfway up the steep stair leading to the flat roof. Silhouetted against the white stone, they knew they were horribly visible. They stopped instinctively and shrank against the wall, then forced themselves on.

The khan was built on a hillside, and it was easy to see from the roof that the wall was higher towards the front than the back. Peering over the side, Tewfik led the way along the top, looking for the best place to lower the rope. He stopped so suddenly that the others nearly bumped into him.

'Here,' he whispered.

He tied the rope round a stone jutting up from the corner of the wall, laid one end round his waist and dropped the other end over the side. It was impossible to see if it reached the ground.

It'll just have to, Adam thought, with a lurch of his heart.

He caught hold of the rope and was about to lower himself down when Salim said, 'Wait. You meet Tewfik tomorrow, but where?'

Tewfik was scanning the hillside above. In the moonlight, half a mile away, was a small white dome surmounting a square building.

'He meet you there. You hide till he come,' whispered Salim. 'Is tomb of saint. Very quiet place.'

It was hard climbing down the rope. Although it seemed to be securely fastened round the corner stone, and Tewfik was bracing it too, Adam was afraid he would fall. To his relief, the rope was only a metre short of the ground. He nearly missed his footing as he landed, and dislodged a stone which went rolling noisily down the hillside.

At once, a fearful noise broke out. The khan dogs, who had been sleeping outside the main gate, burst into a cacophony of hysterical barking. They came racing round the corner of the building, heading straight for him. He picked up a stone and stood with his back to the wall, protecting Tibby and braced to fight them off. Above him, Faithful was answering the dogs with a furious tirade of his own.

On the top of the wall, Salim stood, rigid with horror.

Beside him, Faithful was running up and down, out of control, desperate to get at the dogs below and fight.

A voice called out from the courtyard.

'*Meen?* Who is it? What's happening?'

The watchman had woken up and was making for the steps. Tewfik landed a brutal kick on Faithful's rump. His bark changed to a shocked yelp as he went flying over the edge of the wall. Tewfik had time only to drop the rope before the watchman had stumbled sleepily to the top of the steps.

'What's happening?' he said again.

'Nothing, *ya-bawwab*,' Salim said soothingly, his mind racing for an excuse. 'We – we thought we heard something up here. We were afraid there was a thief. There's nothing. A jackal disturbed the dogs, that's all. I think they've killed it.'

'Killed a jackal? They've never done that before. Let me see.'

The watchman approached the edge of the wall and was about to look right down on to Adam's head. Tewfik and Salim stood by the corner stone to hide the rope, praying that he wouldn't see it.

'What's a dead jackal, more or less?' Tewfik said sternly, barring the watchman's way. 'You should keep those dogs tied up. I never heard a noise like it. I shall have a word with the owner in the morning.'

The watchman responded immediately to the authority in his voice and retreated from the edge of the wall.

'I'm sorry, sir,' he said, leading the way down the steps again. 'It's the owner's fault, after all. Again and again I've asked him for decent rope to tie them with. They chew through it every time.'

'Well, that's enough now.' Tewfik pretended to yawn. 'Let's get some sleep at last.'

*

Adam, standing just below, had watched in astonishment as Faithful came flying through the air. He was afraid the dog would be hurt, but Faithful leaped up as soon as he'd landed and launched himself at the khan dogs. Daunted by his size and ferocity, they began to back away, their barks turning shrill with fear.

Adam waited until the noise above had died away, then, with Faithful at his heels, he set off as fast as he could across the rough hillside towards the white dome in the distance, praying that Tibby, who had been so miraculously quiet all this while, would sleep on until they were out of earshot.

Salim lay awake, watching as the moon slowly set behind the far wall of the khan, then stared up at the stars, bright diamonds wheeling slowly across the black velvet sky.

He was thinking, as he had so often done before, about Adam, and the strangeness of his life. He was trying to imagine the place – England – that he came from. Endless cold, and mists, and rain, people said. And the English were dirty, wild and violent. He couldn't picture it at all. Adam had tried to describe Fortis to him, and the valley where he'd been born. He'd said he would live in his own manor when he went home.

A property of his own! At his age! Salim thought wonderingly. *And yet he's all alone. He'll be there alone.*

His thoughts moved on, in a natural sequence, to his own family.

They'll be safe in Damascus now. Thank God, they're not in Jerusalem. If Malek Richard attacks, it'll be even worse than Acre. At least we won't stay there, if that happens. The Sultan will want sidi *Musa with him again. We'll be back with the army.*

He shuddered at the thought of the Crusader army, which even now might have left Acre and be crawling towards Jerusalem, the columns of men and horses eating up the miles, killing and raiding all the way, like a vast hungry animal devouring everything in its path.

He must have fallen asleep at last because he woke with a jerk at the sound of shouting and running feet.

'What?' he said stupidly, starting up. 'What?'

The doctor was still snoring, genuinely asleep, but Tewfik, lying further away, opened one eye, caught Salim's and shut it again, feigning sleep.

The events of last night came crowding back.

Now we're for it, Salim thought, his stomach contracting nervously. *Now we've got to fool them.*

He swung his legs over the edge of the alcove. The traders were standing in a knot round the khan owner, shouting angrily, and the owner, in his turn, was pointing accusingly at the watchman, who was waving his arms about, trying to make himself heard. Near them, the four slaves sat in a dejected huddle, taking no interest in what was going on.

'There was a noise, masters,' the watchman was babbling. 'The dogs were going mad. I went to look. Up there!' He pointed to the roof. 'It was a jackal. The dogs had killed it. I saw it with my own eyes. Ask that man, and the boy. They were up there too. They saw it too.'

He pointed towards Salim. All eyes turned to the doctor's alcove. Salim bent over Dr Musa and touched his hand.

'*Sidi* Musa, wake up! They're coming!'

By the time the angry crowd had reached them, Dr Musa had sat up and was draping his cloak round his shoulders in an effort to look dignified.

'My turban!' he was saying crossly to Salim. 'Where's my turban? I laid it down here last night. What have you done with it?'

The khan owner was the first to reach him. He was clearly upset.

'I'm sorry for the disturbance, sir. These people have lost a child. A slave of theirs. Your boy and your man – excuse me for asking – did they see anything during the night?'

'You were up there on the wall!' the watchman broke in, desperate to excuse himself. 'It was a jackal, wasn't it? The dogs were going mad!'

'I heard nothing,' the doctor said. 'I composed myself to sleep, and I slept. As for the dogs, the wretched cur belonging to the boy who was here barked a couple of times, I believe. Why I ever permitted him to attach himself to us – but he pleaded so hard! We met up with him on the road only yesterday. On his way to join his master in Jerusalem, so he told us.' He bowed courteously to the slave merchants. 'A man in your line of business, I believe.'

The slave merchants looked at each other.

'It must have been Abu Hussein's boy!' one of them said furiously. 'The dirty villain! If he's stolen that child I'll kill him with my own hands.'

'My dear sir, how could anyone have stolen anything from this very well-guarded khan?' the doctor asked peaceably. 'If I'm not mistaken, the gates are still shut. There's no other way in or out, is there?' He turned to the watchman. 'You haven't opened up for anyone today? I thought not. Then the boy must still be inside somewhere. In the kitchen, perhaps, begging for scraps for that monstrous hound. The child too, no doubt, playing in some corner. Now, Salim, my turban! What have you done with it? Produce it at once!'

A shout from above made everyone look up. One of the traders' men had run up on to the roof.

'There's a rope here!' he called down. 'Someone's climbed down this way!'

Instantly, everyone but Salim and the doctor made for the stairs.

'Go with them, Salim,' the doctor said quietly. 'It's your

turn now. God forgive me for the untruths I've uttered today. May the rescue of that poor child justify them.'

As Salim reached the others he heard one say, 'Yes, that's what must have happened. Abu Hussein – that son of a dog! – he must have got wind of the child and sent the boy to tail us. The little thief took his chance, got in with the doctor and stole her from under our very noses! Here you—' he said, turning suddenly on Salim. 'The boy who was with you. What was his name?'

'I'm not sure.' Salim turned innocently to Tewfik. 'Was it Adnan? Akram? Adam? Something like that. He was very quiet. Hardly spoke two words to us. I think he was a Kurd.'

'A Kurd! I thought he had a furtive look to him.'

'What are we waiting for?' said one of the merchants, who had puffed up the steps last after the others. 'Saddle the horses! Never mind loading up the camels. Two of us must go after him as quickly as we can. The rest will follow with the other merchandise. Which way? On the Jerusalem road, of course! Where else can the boy be going?'

Adam had made his way quite easily to the tomb on the hill. It stood alone above the terraces of olive trees, and as far as he could see there were no other buildings nearby. Carefully he unwound the doctor's turban and eased Tibby off his back. She sighed and whimpered in her sleep, but still didn't wake. He laid her down on a patch of smooth ground, folded the turban and tucked it round her to protect her from the cool night breeze.

He sat against the tomb's wall and looked out across the moonlit valley below. He could see the khan in the distance. He laid his hand on Faithful's head, taking comfort from it.

'We did it,' he said out loud. 'We got her back.'

But he was oppressed, too, by the thought of Tibby. He'd wanted desperately to save her, mainly for Jennet's sake, but now that he had her he realized how little he knew about children. What would he find for her to eat? How could he stop her from wandering off? What if she called out loud in English when they were close to other people? Worst of all, how could he hide her mop of blonde curls, which would attract attention everywhere?

Tewfik'll know what to do, he thought, gratitude to the doctor welling up again. *Sending him back with me, that was the grandest thing. If I could do something for him I would, but I won't ever see him again, I suppose. Nor Salim either.*

He wished he'd said goodbye to Salim properly. He'd turned out to be a true friend after all, even if he was a cursed Saracen.

His mind veered off on another tack. What was it the doctor had said? He tried to remember.

The dust was no good. That was it. *It didn't work to get you into Paradise.*

He'd wondered about it lately, in his heart of hearts. And what was that about death being like a valley in the shadow? If it was in the Bible it must be true. 'Not to be afraid,' Salim had translated, 'because God is with you when you go into it.'

But that's when God judges you, he thought with a shiver. *That's when you get sent to hell.*

He imagined his mother standing in front of God, the great eyes under the white eyebrows seeing into her soul, the deep voice questioning. And beside Him the Virgin in her blue robe, her face soft with compassion.

She'll see that Ma was good all the way through, he thought. *Anyway, that sin, with Lord Guy, was a long time ago and she paid for it all her life.*

He felt as if a burden had rolled off his back.

Not to be afraid of death, the doctor had said. *Not to fear for Ma any more.*

He'd have masses said for her soul when he was home

again, for her and for Jenny too, just in case, but all was well with them both. He could feel it in his bones.

King Richard, Sir Ivo, Lord Robert and all the rest of them would be marching now towards Jerusalem. There would be another siege, more battles, perhaps another massacre.

I won't ever see Jerusalem, he thought, *but it doesn't matter now. I'm going to take Tibby home.*

His eyes were closing of their own accord. He stood up and took a last look round, checking that all was safe, then lay down.

'You'll see off anyone who comes, Faithful,' he murmured, and he fell asleep.

The sun was already high before Tewfik appeared on the hillside below. Adam had been watching anxiously since dawn, trying to keep Tibby quiet without knowing how to go about it. She'd woken at last, and though floppy from the effects of the drug she had clearly been given, she was crying for something to drink. He stood up and hugged himself with relief when he saw the two horses leave the khan and pick their way up the hillside towards him. Someone else was riding the second horse. Screwing up his eyes, he recognized Salim and grinned delightedly. He'd be able to say goodbye after all.

Salim cantered ahead of Tewfik, reining the horse in with the expertise that Ismail had taught him.

'What happened?' Adam asked eagerly. 'Did they suspect you?'

'So funny!' Salim laughed. 'The doctor, he is very good at stories. He tell them you are servant of other slave men in Jerusalem. You steal Tibby for them. They are so angry! They send their men at once to Jerusalem to follow you. Then they go away themselves, but slowly. Only now they have gone. Sorry you wait for us so long.' He swung himself down off the horse and gave Adam a packet of bread and cheese loosely wrapped in cloth. 'The doctor, he send you this, for you and her.'

He squatted down to tickle Tibby, who responded at once with delighted laughter. Then he took a flask out from inside his tunic and held it to her lips. She drank greedily. Adam felt envious. Salim seemed to know just what to do with her. He was used to children.

'I wish you were coming back with us,' he said. 'It'll be funny, just Tewfik and me.'

'I miss you too, Adam,' Salim said. 'Sad to say goodbye.'

He stood up and put out his hand. Adam took it in his. This was the end, then, of their strange friendship. He knew that they would never meet again.

'*Shukran*,' he said. He pointed at Tibby. 'She'd say it too if she could. I'll tell her all about you when she's old enough to understand. About what you've done for her. I wish I could do something for you and the doctor.'

Salim shook his head.

'Not to think like that. You help my family out of Acre. They are safe because of you.'

The memory of the massacre fell between them like a shadow.

'Come on,' said Tewfik. 'Let him go, Salim. We have a long way to go today.'

Salim helped Adam tie Tibby on to his back again.

'Thank the doctor for his turban,' he said. 'I bet he looks funny without it.'

They both laughed, and once they'd started they couldn't stop, their deeper feelings hidden.

Salim cupped his hands for Adam's foot to help him mount. It was strange feeling the child on his back, but she settled down quickly, chewing on the piece of bread that Salim had given her.

He watched as the horses picked their way along the hillside.

They would avoid the main track to Acre, he knew. Tewfik would find other, quieter routes where they would meet few travellers. A few minutes later, they were out of sight.

With both of them mounted, and no slow mule to hold them back, the return journey to Acre was faster than Adam would have believed possible. Tewfik had led the way, riding fast along small tracks up in the hills, stopping only to eat and sleep. Tibby had fretted sometimes, and twice she had screamed with such red-faced rage that Adam had been afraid that a scorpion had stung her. They had stopped and he had unwrapped her, staring at her helplessly. But Tewfik, who had children of his own, had laughed, and coaxed her back into a good humour. Most of the time, though, she'd slept against Adam's back, soothed by the jolting rhythm of the horse.

The hills just inland were alive with Saracen troops, and several times they'd been challenged. Adam had waited quietly, his heart in his mouth, while Tewfik had made some kind of explanation, wondering, for the hundredth time, why this man was doing so much to help him. They'd met King Richard's forces at sundown on the third day. Hugging the coastline and keeping to the flat plain, the Franks had progressed only a few miles south from Acre and were now camped round the port of Haifa.

They could smell the Crusader army before they saw it. The evening breeze wafted towards them the hot familiar stench of human filth, the same foul miasma that had hung over the camp outside Acre. They halted on a low outcrop from which they could look down on the walls of Haifa and the vast mass of men and horses that covered the plain around it. Tewfik nodded at Adam and turned his horse, and Adam, understanding his gesture, dismounted and lifted his hand to shake Tewfik's.

'*Shukran*,' he said, putting his heart into the word. 'I'll never forget you.'

Tewfik took the reins of Adam's horse and waved a hand in a matter-of-fact farewell. A moment later he was trotting back towards the nearest Saracen position, half a mile away.

Adam narrowed his eyes against the glare of the setting sun to read the forest of banners fluttering above the Crusader camp. To his relief, the black hammer of Martel was easy to pick out. It was a mile or so away. It would be dark by the time he reached it, but that was no bad thing. He'd get close enough to call out and make himself understood before a nervous archer could put an arrow through him.

Faithful bounded ahead of him, barking joyously, as Adam entered at last the ring of familiar faces round the Fortis cooking fires. His palms were clammy with nervousness. Sir Ivo would be very angry, he knew. He didn't know what kind of punishment was reserved for squires who ran away, but if Lord Robert had a say in it, it would be cruel.

'Well, look who's here!' One of the squires had seen him. 'We rather hoped we'd seen the last of *you*.'

The boy's sneering laugh attracted others. Adam hardly noticed him. He unwound the doctor's turban, freeing Tibby, who, tired and hungry, stood and bawled, her fists bunched into her eyes. There was an answering cry from behind the nearest tent and Joan flew forwards, her gown, ragged with age and wear, billowing out behind her.

'Tibby! My little chick!' She scooped Tibby up in her arms. 'No need for that now. Old Joanie's here.' She smiled delightedly at Adam over Tibby's head. 'How ever did you get her back? I was feared I'd never see you again.'

'Later, Joan. I'll tell you later. Get her something to drink. She's thirsty. And food. She hasn't eaten much all day.'

'Come with me, lovey,' Joan crooned in Tibby's ear, and

Tibby's cries died away as she was carried off towards the wagons.

'Where have you been?' one of the friendlier squires asked. 'You're in trouble, Adam. Squires don't simply run off and abandon their knights. Or didn't you know? A whipping's the least you can expect. Lord Robert's absolutely furious.'

Adam licked his dry lips.

'It was the little girl. Slavers took her. I've been nearly all the way to Jerusalem to get her back.'

Mouths gaped open.

'What? You've been *where*? Who are you trying to fool?'

'The Saracen doctor helped me. I travelled with him.' A small glow warmed Adam as he thought of his adventure. He didn't care that none of them seemed to believe him. These fools would never have dared go so far or do so much, for all their clever swordplay and horsemanship.

'The Saracen doctor? But he's a *Jew*,' one of them was saying.

'What is this?' Father Jerome's tall, black-clad figure stalked into the firelight.

'It's Adam Fitz Guy, Father. He claims to have been to Jerusalem. With the Jew doctor,' eager voices told him.

Father Jerome's hawk-like eyes swept round the group.

'Get back to your duties. You –' he pointed to the nearest squire – 'fetch the sergeant. This boy is under arrest.'

'Sir Ivo,' Adam managed to say, 'where is he? Can I see him?'

Father Jerome was already turning away.

'Your knight has been badly wounded. You have forfeited the right to serve him, or indeed to speak to him ever again.'

Adam barely shut his eyes that night. Two men-at-arms had dragged him away to a dismal corner of the camp where other prisoners, chained together, were lying on the ground. Most were sunk in silence, but one, on whom the marks of recent torture could be seen even in the dim light of the newly risen moon, was raving dementedly.

He tried to think, but his mind was numbed with the shock of being a shackled prisoner. If only he could speak to Sir Ivo! If only he could explain! But if Sir Ivo really was injured, perhaps even at death's door, there would be no one to listen to him. Lord Robert would relish this opportunity to put him away, perhaps forever. He'd be lucky to get away with his life.

He lay on his back, watching as the moon sank, brightening the stars, which in their turn faded as dawn approached. A kick in the ribs roused him.

'Get up. Get moving,' a rough voice said.

Adam struggled to his feet. His shackles were removed, and with a man on each side of him he was marched ignominiously through the camp, stared at by the yawning, slowly stirring men.

Most of the Crusader army had camped overnight in the open air, and only a few nobles and senior churchmen had bothered to unpack their tents. Lord Robert, keen to uphold his dignity, had had his father's pavilion painstakingly erected. Adam's heart sank as he saw the black hammer fluttering from its crest.

The guards halted outside. A squire, looking out, called back inside, 'He's here, my lord.'

A moment later, Lord Robert himself appeared. He had dressed hastily and his belt was tangled in his tunic. Adam read greedy triumph in his face, and felt his fists clench nervously.

'Desertion,' Lord Robert said, his high-pitched voice squeaky with satisfaction. 'Running away. An insult to your knight and to me. I shall send you to the galleys. Ten years chained to an oar will teach you.' A squire came in and tried to catch his eye. 'What? What is it? I said I didn't want to be disturbed.'

'Father Jerome's here,' the squire said.

'Tell him I'm occupied. I'll be out in a minute.'

But Father Jerome had already marched in.

'Have you heard his statement?' he demanded, bending a thunderous frown on Adam. 'What has he to say?'

'There's no need. There's no time,' Lord Robert said, irritated. 'His actions have condemned him.'

'I *will* tell you,' Adam said with the boldness of desperation. 'Anyway, it concerns you.'

Lord Robert's eyes shifted sideways.

'I told you, there's no time. The heralds will be calling the departure any time now.'

'Let him speak,' said Father Jerome.

Adam tried to gather his thoughts together.

'It was the pedlar, Jacques. And Tibby,' he began, but his voice cracked with thirst. He stopped, coughing.

'Water!' Father Jerome called out. 'Quickly!'

A beaker was poured out for Adam. He drank it in one gulp. The cool liquid cleared his head. He began to talk, the words tumbling over each other in his haste to tell it all. Outside could be heard the shouted commands of sergeants, the clatter of breakfast pots and the snorting of horses as the camp prepared for the arduous day's march ahead.

Lord Robert flushed at the mention of Tibby, then he turned his head and stared out of the tent.

'This doctor, it's the same man who attended Lord Guy?' Father Jerome asked, as Adam described how he'd lain in wait for Dr Musa.

'Yes.'

'The Jew?'

'Yes, Father.'

Adam faltered at the distaste he read in Father Jerome's

face, but he plunged recklessly on. He thought he saw the priest's eyes widen as he described the snatching of Tibby, and the escape over the wall of the khan, but otherwise Father Jerome listened without expression. Lord Robert didn't move at all.

'If I hadn't rescued Tibby,' Adam finished defiantly, 'she'd have been sold to a Saracen and brought up an – an infidel.'

Father Jerome nodded, and Adam saw that this had hit its mark.

'That is true, and your motives, I have to admit, were pure,' Father Jerome said at last. 'Your story even has much to commend it. But you have been consorting with a Jew and with the cursed Turks. For whatever reason, good or bad, this is a sin, and you must do penance. Fifty paternosters . . .'

Lord Robert spun round, his eyes blazing.

'A few prayers? Is that all? For the crime of desertion? Do you want to encourage every other squire to run off on a jaunt of his own whenever his fancy takes him?'

Father Jerome stared steadily at him. After a moment, Lord Robert dropped his eyes.

'You are forgetting, perhaps,' Father Jerome said coldly, 'that the immortal soul of a child was at stake here. A child to whom, I believe, some special duty is owed. You are right, however, and there is a greater punishment in store for you, Adam. You must give up the glory of serving Christ in this blessed crusade. Sir Ivo, as you were told last night, has been injured.'

'What's happened to him, Father Jerome? Will he live?'

'That is in the hands of Our Lord. The Saracens in their wickedness attacked on our first day out of Acre. Sir Ivo was struck from his horse and his leg was crushed. Several bones have been broken and it's doubtful that he will ever walk – still less ride – again. He is at present in the grip of a serious fever. He's to be removed today to the coast and put on board the next ship that sails for France. Lord Robert, will, I'm sure, agree that you should accompany him and see him safely home. You'll take the child, of course, and the woman who cares for her.' He paused, and drew a deep breath, as if gathering up the threads of a sermon. 'Your punishment, Adam, is a severe one. You will never enter Jerusalem. You will never stand before the Holy Sepulchre and know that your sins have been washed clean. You will never enter into the special place in Paradise reserved for the mighty ones of the Lord.'

Lord Robert had stood by, fuming, and seemed about to burst into passionate speech, but Father Jerome's raised hand silenced him.

'Oh, go away, Adam,' Lord Robert said at last. 'Just get out of here.'

Ten minutes later, Adam was kneeling by the litter on which Sir Ivo lay, among dozens of other wounded men in a crude open-air hospital. The knight's face was thin and pale with pain. Beads of sweat stood out on his waxy forehead. He stared at Adam, but his eyes quickly wandered away without showing any sign of recognition.

'I'm sorry,' Adam whispered. 'Please, Sir Ivo. I should have been here to help you.'

Dr John came hurrying up.

'Adam! Thank God you're here. You foolish boy! I suppose you ran off after that child.'

'Yes. And I brought her back,' Adam said, standing up. 'Sir Ivo looks bad, Dr John. Father Jerome says he's to go home and I'm to go with him.'

Dr John smiled.

'I'm very relieved to hear it. He'll need the most particular care. Stay with him here. We'll be on the move in a moment. The ship's waiting for you at the beach.'

'I have to fetch Tibby,' Adam said. 'I'm taking her home.'

He set off at a flying pace towards the wagons, where he knew that Joan would be with Tibby.

It was a long moment before Joan grasped the meaning of Adam's news.

'What? We're leaving? Now? Going home? Tell me I ain't dreaming, Master Adam!'

'You're not, Joan. Be quick though. Fetch anything that's yours and bring Tibby down to the beach.'

'You mean it? Oh, blessed Mary and St Hunna! Thank you, thank you! I'll just need to say goodbye to Susan, and Wat, and—'

'Don't take long, Joanie. Come at once if you don't want to be left behind.'

He left her and bounded back to the open-air infirmary. News had spread that the wounded were to be taken off in a ship, and a number of people, both Fortis men and those from other contingents, had come to say goodbye. One after another the remaining few knights of Fortis, then several squires and men-at-arms, came to touch Sir Ivo's hand and wish him God speed. He turned glazed eyes on them and made no sign that he had heard.

Adam hung back.

No one will want to say goodbye to me, he thought. *Anyway, I'm in disgrace.*

But to his surprise several of the squires came up to him and clapped him affectionately on the shoulder.

'Sorry you're going,' they said. 'Safe journey.' And one muttered, so that the others couldn't hear, 'I wish I was going home with you. I've had enough of this.'

Roger Stepesoft rushed up just as Sir Ivo's litter was being carefully lifted on to two pairs of strong shoulders.

'When you get back to Ashton,' he said breathlessly, 'seek out my mother, will you? My girl's with her, or should be. Tell her – tell them I'm well. Better tell 'em about Treue too. They'll let his people know.' He turned away briefly, then covered up by punching a hand into the air. 'Fortis and Martel!' he shouted. 'The Holy Sepulchre!'

He ran off to join the other men-at-arms.

The sea was crowded with ships which had been sailing close in to the shore since the fall of Acre. As there was no jetty, the wounded, crying out with the pain of being moved, were being carried out to the hospital ship on the backs of soldiers.

It was clear that it would half an hour or more before everyone could be safely stowed on board. Adam, who had walked beside Sir Ivo's litter to the beach, waited impatiently. He was still unable to believe in the incredible turn his life had taken. He watched as Joan came hurrying down with Tibby perched on her hip, and smiled as she began at once to quarrel with the man who was to carry her to the ship.

'Not like that!' she shouted, as he heaved her up over his shoulder. 'Mind the child. Keep her dry, or you'll hear me curse you!'

The two of them were safe on board at last. Adam, still ashore, looked round, trying to imprint on his mind his last view of the Holy Land, and saw, some way off, a familiar figure. Jacques had appeared further along the beach. He was standing among a crowd of those with bandaged arms, heads and chests but who were still able to walk. He was holding up a twig, and as Adam sprang towards him with a cry of rage, Jacques's silky voice became clearer and clearer.

'A sovereign remedy!' he was saying. 'As you all know, my suffering dear ones, our cruel enemy – our *devilish* enemy, has crushed your limbs, and cracked open your bones, and stuck you full of arrows. But why suffer the torments of pain, the fear of infection and the agony of corrupted blood when the answer lies so close at hand – in *my* hand! Do you see this?

A simple twig, I hear you say, such that any fool could pluck from a tree, but I tell you, my brothers, this . . .'

Adam had pushed through to the front of the crowd. Jacques saw him and faltered, his face turning pale under its grime.

'Don't listen to him!' Adam was scarlet with rage. 'This man's a cheat and a crook! I saw with my own eyes how he filled little bottles with common dirt from beside a stream in England and sold it as the dust of Jerusalem. That twig's no more special than my thumb.'

Jacques had recovered his composure.

'Gentlemen!' he cried. 'Wounded heroes! This fine young man, the scion of a noble house – a bastard of that house admittedly – is out of his mind. A sad story. A head injury. Hit by a rock at the fall of Acre. And since then, his wits—'

'He sold a Christian child to the slavers of the Saracens!' roared Adam. 'Watch out! He's trying to escape!'

Jacques had at last lost his nerve. Taking a few steps backwards, he turned and hared off down the beach, his long legs kicking up spurts of sand. Rage gave Adam speed, and he flew after him. Jacques looked round, saw that Adam was nearly on him, then bent down and scooped up a handful of sand, flinging it into Adam's face. Adam faltered, pawing at his sand-filled eyes. Then he lunged forwards and caught the hem of Jacques's cloak as the pedlar sprinted off again. The cloak fell off Jacques's shoulders into Adam's hands. With a howl, Jacques spun round and tried to snatch it from him.

'Give it to me,' he spat. 'Give it or I'll kill you!'

But other people were running up now. Jacques, seeing a tide of angry men rolling up the beach towards him, gave a yell of rage and turned and ran again, disappearing a few seconds later round a curve of the beach.

Adam stood still only for a moment to watch him go before

he rushed back to Sir Ivo. Not for anything would he be accused of desertion again.

He'll bring his own destruction, he thought. *God will punish him.*

As he reached Sir Ivo's litter, he heard his name being called. A messenger was pushing through the crowd of people on the beach, waving a document in his hand. Adam's heart lurched. Had Lord Robert changed his mind? Was he to be hauled back to the army to face a hideous punishment? But there was no point in staying silent. Other people were pointing him out.

'Here!' he called out. 'I'm Adam Fitz Guy.'

The messenger came up to him and put the roll of parchment in his hands.

'You're a tricky one,' he said crossly. 'I've been calling and calling you for the past many minutes.'

'What's this?' Adam said, staring at the document. It was sealed with the hammer of Martel, that much he could see, but the letters that danced across it were a meaningless jumble of marks to him.

'Your bond of freedom,' the messenger said impatiently. 'Your title to the place – what was it? Br – Bro—'

'Brockwood.'

'That's it. You're to take it to your lady when you get home.'

'To Lady Ysabel?'

'How should I know what her name is? Her seneschal will deal with it. The seal's here, look. Mind it isn't broken.'

Adam found he was still holding Jacques's cloak. He put it down on the sand as he tucked the document securely inside his tunic. It felt almost hot against his skin.

My freedom, he thought. *It's my freedom. My future.*

He bent to pick up Jacques's cloak. It was heavier than he had expected. Running his hands over it, he felt bumps and hardnesses in the lining. He ripped a section open. Inside was the gleam of gold.

So that's where he kept it, the money he cheated and lied for, Adam thought, almost bursting out into laughter. Quickly, he folded the cloak over, covering the tear to hide the coins from curious eyes. *I'll keep all for Tibby. He owes it to her, after what he's done.*

He tied the cloak round his waist, disliking the feel and smell of it, but still choking with laughter at the thought of the fury that Jacques must now be feeling.

That's it. Justice. There is some justice after all.

Those who could be taken piggyback by single bearers had boarded the ship now and only the more seriously hurt, the men on litters, waited to be carried through the water. It was Sir Ivo's turn at last.

'Here, let me,' Adam said, pushing aside one of the bearers.

He lifted the end of litter and stepped into the sea, shuddering as he felt the water suck at his feet, but taking a deep breath he marched on, deeper and deeper, till the little waves were lapping against his chest. Holding Sir Ivo high up, above his shoulders, he reached the ship at last, and other hands leaned down to pull them both on board.

In the courtyard of Dr Musa's house in Jerusalem, three elderly men sat in the cool shade of a vine which had been trained over a trellis. A woman's voice was calling an order to a maid from an inner room. A tray of beans was laid out to dry in the sun, and Suweida the mule stood half asleep in a stall in one corner, on the roof of which a flock of white doves cooed and strutted.

'You can't go back to the army, brother!' one of the old men was saying. 'At your age? It would kill you!'

'Jacob's right. Think of your health,' the second chimed in.

'And Leah. You've no idea how she suffers when you're away from home.'

Dr Musa stretched out an arm and laid it contentedly along the carpet-covered bolster against which he was leaning.

'There's no need to persuade me. I've decided. My days of campaigning are over. I refuse to live in a tent, patch up hot-headed young men, eat army food and run about the countryside any longer. I shall stay quietly here at home, resume my old habits, see a few patients and study Torah, which, at my time of life, is surely the will of God.' He paused. 'But I'm bound to say that this wretched war is likely to drag on. Malek Richard is certain to besiege Jerusalem, and if he takes it—'

'If that looks likely, I'll pack up my family and move to Baghdad, or even down to Basra,' interrupted his brother. 'I won't stay here to be slaughtered like an animal. You'd be a fool too if you stayed, Musa.'

Dr Musa sighed.

'I won't, of course, if it comes to that, but I don't believe it will. Saladin may have lost Acre, but the man's a marvel. I've watched him closely these past two years. I've seen him pick himself up from a deep depression, ride out at the head of his army, inspire them with his oratory, then go back to his tent and coax his allies into fighting on when the odds seem all against them, while all the time he's half cramped over with the constant pains he suffers in his stomach. I tell you, if any-one can save Jerusalem, it's our Sultan, peace be upon him.'

The other two muttered in agreement.

Salim, who had been sitting nearby, idly playing with one of Leah's kittens, yawned and looked up at the sky to assess the time. The hours had dragged wearily by since he and the doctor had reached Jerusalem two weeks ago. Their arrival had caused something of a sensation. Leah, the doctor's kind but fussy wife, had become almost ill with the joy of seeing her husband after so long an absence. There had been visits from the great men of Jerusalem, the governor, and the commander of the garrison, and every member of the Jewish community had called to pay their respects.

Salim, released from his duties, had spent hours exploring Jerusalem. On the very first day he had found his way to the vast stone platform that dominated the city. As he'd walked up the stone steps, he'd felt a strange expansion in his chest, as if his very heart was swelling. The Prophet himself had stood here. His feet had trodden on these stones. Allah had blessed this place.

Above him rose the dazzling golden Dome of the Rock, and beyond it the stone portals of the great Aqsa mosque. Salim had given his shoes to the guardian by the arch and walked across the huge courtyard. The smooth white stones were warm under his feet. There had been tears in his eyes.

This is the heart of it, he'd thought. *This is the place of Islam. The barbarians will never take it from us again. Never, never again.*

It was a long time since he'd felt inspired by such holy certainty, and been warmed by the desire for jihad. What was it the preacher in Acre had said, two long years ago?

The greater struggle. That was it. *The true jihad. The inner fight against man's lower nature. Against cowardice and selfishness.*

Workmen were still busy repairing the facades of the mosque. The Crusaders, during their century-long occupation of Jerusalem, had turned the Dome into a church and used the mosque as a grain store. Crosses and blasphemous images of the Prophet Jesus and his mother had been erected everywhere. The jangle of bells had replaced the calm, reflective call to prayer. Gallons of rose-water had been needed to purify the place.

They're on their way to take it again, Salim had thought with a rush of anger. *They want to snatch it all back from us and trample on it again. What's their holy sepulchre compared to this? I wouldn't care if it was pulled down. It's what they deserve.*

The kitten fastened its sharp little teeth on his finger, bringing Salim suddenly back to the present in the doctor's courtyard.

What am I doing here? he thought impatiently. *I should be out there with the army. How can* sidi *Musa bear to stay here, doing nothing all the time, when those murderers are coming nearer every day?*

He was about to jump up, to interrupt the old men and ask if there was an errand to run or a visit to make – anything to get him away – when he heard the clatter of hooves and loud voices in the street outside. Someone knocked on the door. He limped across and opened it.

Six bay horses, magnificently caparisoned, were jostling nervously in the narrow street. Their riders, resplendent in scarlet brigandines, were dismounting.

'Ismail!' gasped Salim. 'What are you doing here?'

Ismail took off his pointed helmet and tucked it under one arm, shaking out his long dark hair.

'*Kayf halak*, little brother? How are you? What are we doing here? We've come for you, of course. The Sultan, may Allah bless him, is suffering from his stomach. He can't live without the doctor, he says. You're to come back with us.'

Salim's heart kicked with joy at the thought of being out on campaign again, but his smile faded.

'He won't come. He keeps saying he's too old and tired. It's true too, Ismail. He looks bad. He needs to rest. Come and see him.'

One man stayed outside to hold the horses but the others, politely taking off their shoes by the door, followed Salim and Ismail into the courtyard. The doctor looked up, and his face fell in almost comical dismay when he saw them.

'Rascal!' he cried, struggling to sit up and push his turban straight at the same time. 'Villain! I know what you want. You've come to disturb an old man, no more and no less. I won't do it, I tell you. The answer's no!'

Ismail grinned.

'*Salaam alaykum*, doctor. I hope you're well.'

'Peace be to you too,' sighed the doctor. 'No, I'm very ill. I'm old and tired. My feet hurt. My bones ache. My digestion needs calm and the cooking of my wife.'

Dr Musa's two guests rose to their feet.

'We'll leave you, Musa,' Jacob said. He wagged a finger in his brother's face. 'Now mind you don't weaken. Send the Sultan your abject apologies. Tell him what you like, but don't go. Why don't you send the boy in your place? He can't idle his time away here forever. How does the verse go? *The way of the lazy is strewn with thorns but the path of the industrious is a broad highway.*'

Pleased with himself, he nodded his way to the door. Dr Musa was looking at Salim, a startled expression on his face. Ismail sat down under the vine beside the doctor, while the other Mamluks stayed at a courteous distance.

'*Ustadh*,' he began. 'The Sultan's stomach is tormenting him. All his old symptoms have returned. And every day Malek Richard – may Allah deprive him of life! – marches closer and closer to Jerusalem.' He laid a wheedling hand on Dr Musa's sleeve. 'How can Saladin fight the barbarians with his stomach on fire like a brazier? Richard is a lion in cunning and strength. There's no other Frank like him. We can't beat him without Saladin, and he needs you. Come back with us, doctor. You're a great man. I owe my life to you. Come back with us.'

Dr Musa's eyes were still resting on Salim, who was standing beside Ismail, his face flushed with excitement.

'The Sultan's old symptoms have returned, you say?' he said at last. 'There's no new trouble?'

'No! It's his stomach again. You should see how he suffers! I haven't been close to him myself, naturally, but his servants talk about it all the time.'

'And there's nothing new? No weakness in the limbs, no flux, no vomiting?'

'No no! The old trouble, that you were so clever in treating.'

'Solomon is still with him?' Dr Musa persisted.

'The apothecary? Yes. But he doesn't know the correct way of combining all the herbs. It was Salim who always did that. Salim did it perfectly, the Sultan's servants said.'

The doctor slapped his hands triumphantly down on his knees.

'Precisely, my dear boy! It's Salim you need! I shall send him back with you. He can take the medicine chest and my poor old mule. He knows to perfection the dosage Saladin requires. Day after day he made it up for him. Salim, you're to go back, do you here? No more lazing around in the fleshpots of Jerusalem! Don't tell me you haven't longed to be on the road again. You think I'm blind, is that it? You think I haven't noticed how you yawn, and tick off the hours?'

Salim was staring at him, aghast.

'I'm to go without you? To attend on *Saladin*? How can I? I don't know anything! Who'd take any notice of me?'

'Modesty!' cried the doctor. 'A great virtue. But in this case, misplaced. You'll work with Solomon, my boy. Ismail, find a lodging with your men tonight. I'll need the rest of the day to instruct Salim properly. Come back tomorrow morning. He'll be ready then, I promise you. Leah! Ink! Parchment! Everything must be written down! The exact symptoms, precise prescriptions! All eventualities must be covered!'

Salim woke early the next morning, roused by the voice of the muezzin calling the faithful to prayer from the minaret nearby. He got up, rolled up his sleeping mat, struggled into his tunic and slipped out of the doctor's house, following the shadowy figures of other worshippers making their way to the mosque.

Dr Musa and Leah were waiting for him when he came back. Leah, who had got up while it was still dark, had prepared a lavish farewell breakfast. She made Salim sit down and pressed on him boiled eggs, bowls of curd, bread, honey and cakes crusted with crushed thyme. He did his best, though he was too excited to feel hungry.

'Enough!' said the doctor at last, as Leah tried to press a third egg on Salim. 'Do you want him to explode?'

Salim laughed and stood up. Now that the moment had come to leave Dr Musa, he felt a rush of love for the old man, and sadness at saying goodbye.

'*Sidi* Musa,' he began. 'I—'

'Wait!' The doctor held up a commanding hand. 'Leah, the – the things!'

'Things? What things?' she said. 'Why do you never explain what you mean?'

He was waggling his eyebrows expressively towards the open door behind her. She understood, laughed and darted away. A moment later she was back with a fresh gown laid across her arms, a light goat-hair cloak and a long strip of white material that could only be a turban.

The doctor smiled delightedly at the expression on Salim's face.

'Well? What are you waiting for. Dress!' he commanded.

'But a – a turban?' stammered Salim.

'You think you can run around in a skullcap like a child forever?' scoffed the doctor. 'You want every lowly person – every *ignoramus* – to think that the trained assistant of the great Dr Musa is nothing but a boy? How old are you?'

'Sixteen next month, *sidi* Musa.'

'Sixteen! The age of a man! Put them on, Salim. Let's see you. Put them on.'

Half an hour later, Salim was trotting fast down the steep road that led from Jerusalem, his escort of Mamluk cavalry surrounding him and Suweida, the medicine chest strapped to her back, running gamely behind. His stomach was churning with excitement and apprehension. What would the Sultan say when no Dr Musa came to him, but only his boy? What would he do if Saladin's sickness grew worse, and the old remedies no longer worked?

The turban, neatly tied by Leah, felt odd and heavy on his head. It had already had its effect. Ismail, arriving as the last end was being tucked into place, had opened his eyes when he saw Salim dressed finely in the clothes of an adult.

'Are you ready, brother?' he said.

He didn't call me 'little', Salim thought, straightening his back. *Everything's different now. It's up to me. I've just got to do my best.*

Dr Musa had accompanied the little troop to the gate of the city, and had stood there, his thumbs tucked into his belt, his eyes red and moist, as Salim had ridden away. Behind his small, untidy figure rose the great golden Dome of the Rock and the Aqsa mosque. Salim turned once to look at them before the cavalcade swept on over a hill and down the far side, and Jerusalem was lost to view.

EPILOGUE

A year passed, and the great crusade of Richard the Lionheart was all but over. Struggling through the heat, his men suffering from disease, hunger and thirst, and harassed all the way by Saladin's troops, Richard never reached Jerusalem. The Franks turned back before they had even seen the Holy City, and in the autumn of 1192 they sailed for home.

Saladin did not have long to relish his victory. He died two years later, but famed for his chivalry, his name lived on, celebrated even by his enemies.

And what of Adam and Salim?

Skip forward ten more years, and Adam is the master of Brockwood. He manages his manor and its demesne well, with Tom Bate, Jennet's father, as his right-hand man. He has married Margaret, the miller's daughter, and there are three sons already chasing old Faithful's puppies about and teasing Tibby, who, nearly twelve years old and very pretty, has all her mother's warmth and liveliness and none of her father's cold arrogance. Lord Robert himself keeps his distance from Brockwood. He spends much of his time away from Fortis, trying to ease himself into favour at court and increase his power and wealth. So far, he hasn't had much success.

Sir Ivo is a frequent visitor to Brockwood. His fighting days are over but his faith burns as bright and sharp as ever. He and Adam reminisce, sometimes, about their days on Crusade, but when Sir Ivo talks of the glory of the cause and the wickedness of the infidel, Adam turns away and lapses into a long and thoughtful silence. He doesn't want to think of the battles, the thrill of the charge, the clash of sword on shield and the slaying of the enemy. He remembers the kindness of a Jewish doctor and the friendship of a Muslim boy. He wonders if they're still alive, and hopes with all his heart that they are.

Adam will never find out that Dr Musa died quietly, five years after Saladin saved Jerusalem from the Frankish invaders. He was reading in the courtyard of his home one afternoon, gave a little cry which no one heard, and when Leah came to bring him tea an hour later, she found that he had gone.

The news travelled swiftly to Damascus where Salim wept when he heard it. Years of study in Baghdad have completed his medical training and he is now a respected doctor. His father's fortunes never recovered from the loss of Acre, and Ali, restless and moody, has not settled to the business. Salim looks after his family now. He loves living in the big house he has bought in Damascus. He loves Leila, his wife, and likes to spoil his two little daughters. He's busy all the time with patients who flock to him with their ailments.

But sometimes, when Salim hears news of the wider world outside, especially when Ismail, now captain of his own Mamluk troop, sends him greetings, he sends his groom to saddle the magnificent Mamluk-trained horse he keeps in his stable and rides out on the plains around Damascus, happy to be on his own.

What happened to Adam? *he wonders.* Did he ever find his way home again with the child? What can it be like for him, in those cold forests of the north? And does he ever think of me?

This book could not have been written without the encouragement and expert knowledge of Carole Hillenbrand, Professor of Islamic History at Edinburgh University.

I am also indebted to Talya Baker for her advice on Jewish lore, to Marion Kerr who translated the Latin, and, as ever, to David McDowall for his wide knowledge of both European and Middle Eastern history.

The Fastest Boy in the World

Elizabeth Laird

In my dreams I'm always running.
My feet fly over the ground and I'm sure
that if I could just go a little bit faster
I'd take off and fly like an eagle.